TALES OF ENSHIN
THE RELUCTANT SAMURAI

TALES
of
ENSHIN
THE RELUCTANT SAMURAI
Stories of Old Japan
BOOK 2

▼

By
Roald Knutsen

R

RENAISSANCE BOOKS

TALES OF ENSHIN, THE RELUCTANT SAMURAI
STORIES OF OLD JAPAN:
Book 2
by Roald Knutsen

First published 2012 by
RENNAISANCE BOOKS
PO Box 219
Folkestone
Kent CT20 2WP

Renaissance Books is an imprint of Global Books Ltd

ISBN 978-898823-03-2

British Library Cataloguing in Publication Data

A CIP catalogue entry for this book is available
from the British Library

Set in Bembo11 on 11.5 by Dataworks, Chennai, India
Printed the EU by Scandinavian Book

For Pat and Susan

&

Except for you
Whom could I ever love?

Sōgi (1421–1502)

CONTENTS

PREFACE

▼

According to one of the oldest *Iai-jutsu*, or 'Drawing-Sword',
traditions, the founder was a warrior who amongst his
contemporaries stood out as possessing an unusual and rare
character. In his mature years he made it his custom to wander
the highways and byways of the war-torn sixteenth century Japan
riding on the back of a water-buffalo. His reason for this was that
it enabled him to converse with the people he met, high or low,
and on equal terms since, if they wanted to talk then this must
be conducted at the same slow pace as his ox. His understanding
of *heihō* (tactics and strategy) was of the highest order making his
custom all the more remarkable in a period when many samurai
were often haughty and their seniors arrogant to the point of hardly
deigning to address the lower ranks in person and treating women
– even samurai women – as of 'no-account'; the only exceptions
were chiefly their concubines.

The central character in this short collection of stories is a former
samurai of the Torii clan, once Deputy Constables of part of the
mountainous Kōzuke province, who was increasingly unhappy with
the violence and self-seeking of that period and became a shaven
monk, taking the name Enshin. After a period studying medicine in
a Shingon monastery he travelled the provinces in order to minister to the poor and needy. In the course of his travels he rescues a

badly neglected black ox, who he names Kuroi-san, and is joined, at length, by a former Torii servant, Toshiaki.

These tales are not in any way history but merely intended to provide an amusing 'window' into life as it might have been in the disturbed *sengoku* period of the later decades of the Muromachi era. They are the creation of a swordsman who has devoted most of his life to these classical warrior traditions but are nothing more than an idle imagining of these times now past . . .

Roald Knutsen
Autumn 2011

1

KUROI-SAN, THE GENTLE BLACK OX

▼

When a young man, scarce out of his teens, the second son of Torii Munemori had served in the armies of the Uesugi and seen much action in the wars conducted by that mettlesome family. He had witnessed brave acts, examples of selfless loyalty and great bravery; but in mountainous Kōzuke he had also experienced the other side of that coin and realized that his life lay in retiring from the duties of the warrior in order to help the needy and pray for the repose of men's souls. Accordingly, he bowed low before his father and fearlessly requested permission to shave his head and enter monastic life. Realizing that his son earnestly desired to follow this course, Munemori would not stand in his way and suggested that he place himself in the confines of the Hōrai-ji in distant Mikawa, a monastery whose abbot was a cousin.

For ten long years the young man underwent daunting spiritual and physical austerities before the Lord Abbot sent him to a remote mountain temple high amongst the peaks of Shinano where he cleansed himself of the last vestiges of pride through long periods reciting both the Lotus and Heart Sutras. Two more years passed but still he could sense that his spirit remained unquiet and Torii Enshin, for that was the name he had now taken, came to the conclusion that he must undertake travel through the provinces and so purge his soul of false ideas borne of his warrior lineage.

────────□────────

He found that the country had greatly changed from that which he remembered from twelve years before; a land that now was riven by the nightmare yoke of war, where warriors daily galloped to battle, where fires consumed both the guilty and the innocent in the horrors of Hell, where no one could feel secure and not even cloistered nuns were safe from violence and foul rape ...Terror came suddenly under many guises and there was, in several regions other than the most remote, an almost total breakdown of law and order. Only here and there were strong feudal lords able or interested in the protection of the poor; most others were concerned with watching their neighbours and their vassals like hawks, jealous and suspicious of their every move, constantly conniving with others to treacherously gain an advantage, however slight, that would increase their lands at the expense of those who once exercised just government by the natural right of their high patrimony.

────────□────────

Enshin was an unusual monk in all respects. He was firstly skilled in the arts of healing, advanced even for his day. Even considering his long period of seclusion and his warrior background, he had the unusual gift of being able to talk to all classes without anyone sensing patronage. Quite early in his travels he realized that even by walking he simply was not able to meet enough people. It was a paradox, perhaps, but the misery he encountered everywhere meant that many poor people, including clouds of shaven monks, were on the move, trying to eke out a living by their wits. So, in western Mimasaka, after he had long remained in one village beset by sickness and starvation, curing many ill people and labouring hard to help them find food, he was at length asked what payment he desired but refused everything from these poor peasants. When pressed, he pointed to a pitifully thin ox standing dejectedly beneath a spreading maple tree.

'Although oxen are valuable, I will accept that animal in recompense,' he said.

'Oh, that's easy,' replied the headman, the owner of the largest farm in the village, including its only watermill, a man famous for his stinginess in most matters, 'the ox belonged to old Seibei and he died a while ago.'

'He had no relatives?'

'They all went west to the mountains, too.'

'Why has no one taken the beast as his own?'

'Because Seibei swore when he died that he had placed a spell on all he owned . . . and that amounted to very little . . . no one hereabouts cares to test his words and they think the ox may be possessed by a fox spirit! Please take the animal if you wish, honoured monk; if it is indeed possessed you alone might cure it.'

Thus it was that Enshin came by the ox. At first he was sorry for the poor beast; it, too, was suffering from starvation and its bones stood out starkly beneath its lacklustre hide. However, it was a gentle animal and gradually Enshin's patient kindness, unchanging for man or beast, encouraged it to eat and grow stronger while the odd pair lived at the upper end of a remote gulley in the mountains, a valley that ended in a gushing waterfall.

———— ⊟ ————

By the time that the warm reds and russet browns of autumn shaded the mountainsides to a blaze of glorious colour, Enshin's ox had become sleek, though by no means fat. The sores that had covered parts of its neglected hide had healed completely and the black hair regrown, even if it was a trifle patchy to the expert eye. The priest felt that his companion was ready to carry him onwards, he knew not where; perhaps their steps would take them towards Enshin's old home?

The young monk's worldly goods were the clothes that covered his ascetic frame, a wooden bowl, a small wallet that he carried slung around his shoulders that sometimes contained a rice cake or a handful of millet but more often than not nothing at all, and a short oaken staff about a man's height in length. This staff was not even finished off with the usual priest's iron rings, so poor was he. His ox possessed just a thick hempen blanket that served to cushion his master's buttocks as he sat sideways with dangling feet and to cover his friend at night when the two lay down to sleep.

Somehow, despite the almost universal unrest, the monk and his bovine companion never seemed to go really hungry; the simple peasants they encountered seemingly willing to give them something to maintain the devout healer's sustenance.

In the following year, in the midst of the rice planting at the beginning of the sixth month, Enshin and his sleek black ox passed through Obama in Wakasa, intending to make their slow way round the northern end of Lake Biwa and travel on into Mino and Owari. But at that time the Asai clan were embroiled in a war with the cadet branch of the Takeda family and the whole border between

Wakasa and Echizen was in a ferment. Not that the political struggles interested Enshin as there were plenty of calls on his excellent skills in medicine to take up his days, but the discomfort and danger of having so many armed bands hurrying through the little towns and villages made the poor farmers dreadfully afraid.

The priest was standing amidst the mire of the farmyard where he had sheltered for a few weeks. It was pouring with warm summer rain.

'Come, good Kuroi-san; time we were on our way!'

The ox licked its black muzzle and stared at the steam rising from the turfed roof of the small gateway.

'People think it odd, you talking to your animal like that, priest-sama,' laughed the farmer's wife.

'Never mind, honoured mother! My ox and I have been to many places together and, besides, you never know who's soul now inhabits his humble body. But I do realize one thing, he was a kind and gentle person in his previous life.'

'Does the ox answer you?'

'Of course,' smiled Enshin.

'He does?'

'You have seen him do so!'

'Oi, oi, Enshin-sama,' smirked the farmer who was named Gunbei, 'you had best travel through the hills to Imazu and find a boatman who will ferry you across Biwa-ko. Unless, of course, you want to take a look at the Mountain Gate first?'

He referred to the Holy Pagodas on Hiei-zan, naturally, but that meant a long detour and crossing the southern part of Omi where fighting was endemic and dangerous, even for a man of peace and tranquillity.

'Hiei-zan? No, I think I shall take your advice and go to Imazu. Maybe one day, the Buddha willing, I shall see the Holy Pagodas. Tell me, Gunbei-san, how far is it to the lake?'

'Fifteen or twenty miles; just a couple of days' walk, sir.'

'Not for Kuroi-san and I . . . more like four days!'

They all laughed.

'Oka-san, can we spare some rice cakes?' Gunbei called out to his wife.

Enshin protested.

'Rice cakes? Gunbei-san, no . . . no! You have only millet or buckwheat! Rice I cannot accept!'

'Honoured priest, we may eat poorly because of the tax gatherers, but we would far rather give the best to you than to them!'

'This is a sacrifice that may earn you merit; who can tell?'

Gunbei twisted his lined face into a smile.

'Merit is to be hoped for if my next life is not to be as bad as this one,' he remarked with a deep-felt sadness.

Lifting his hand encouragingly, Enshin settled his wallet comfortably and pulled a small sack of yellow *takuan* radishes more centrally on the ox's back. He tugged affectionately at Kuroi-san's flapping left ear.

'Off we go, old friend,' he said, and the ox climbed to its feet and moved slowly on their way, swaying from side to side as it ambled along. Enshin sat straight-backed settling a wide brimmed straw hat and cape to ward off the worst of the downpour. He pulled out a deep-voiced bamboo flute from his breast and gently began to play.

Just outside the gateway, sheltering under a spreading tree, squatted a sodden and dejected figure.

———— ☐ ————

'Master . . ! Master . . ! May I be permitted to talk to you?'

The man had run forwards and fallen to his knees in the muddy roadway, bowing his head into the flood.

Enshin stopped blowing on his flute and regarded the bespattered figure in some surprise. It was a very long while since anyone had offered him this sort of respect.

'Please get up . . . I am no exalted being!'

'My lord . . .' The man started to say as he came to his knees, his hat in his hands, eyes cast down.

'I am nobody's lord, just a poor mendicant monk.'

'Lord, I am sorry . . . I . . .'

The fellow came to his feet, soaked through and muddied from head to foot. He held his broad straw hat by his side but caught hold of the ox's rein. Gunbei, who had watched the whole incident, rushed forwards, his bandy legs thrashing through the mud.

'Is everything alright, Enshin-sama? If this coarse fellow is annoying you, sir, I'll drive him away!'

He made a fierce face which made the monk laugh.

'No, no, good Gunbei; there's no problem! In any case how could a little man like you even think about dealing with this fine big fellow?'

The heavy rain had washed much of the mud from the man's face and closely looking at him as he stood so humbly stroking Kuroi-san's head, Enshin's memory was stirred. It was just like a scene from years before when his father's servants approached to make a request . . . Suddenly he remembered who this man was!

'Why, you're Toshiaki . . ! By all that's wonderful . . !'

Enshin slid down from the rump of his faithful ox.

'Toshi the carpenter! How is your wife . . . and your respected mother?'

'My lord, they have both passed away ...'

'Oh, please don't call me "lord"; I am just a humble monk as I told you ... now tell me your news. I'm sorry to learn about your loss but they may have gone to a better life. Let us hope that it is so.'

'You'll be alright, sir?' The farmer was clearly mystified and not a little nonplussed.

'Yes, Master Gunbei; this man is an old friend and I'm glad to see him. Have no fear.'

Reassured, the farmer bowed deeply and scuttled back to the shelter of his gateway.

'Come, Toshi-san; I think you've been waiting for me quite a time ... now I wonder why you happen to turn up here in this remote place ... that is an interesting question to be sure? Something has brought you here, I suppose, but first please tell me how you found us both, my ox and I?'

———————□———————

The carpenter had left the Torii domain three-and-a-half years before when war had swept Kōzuke and threatened the very survival of the clan. He had determined that only Lord Munemori's second son would have the authority to set matters aright and so, without anyone's knowledge and soon after his wife had been brutally killed, he had left on his difficult search. (*What happened to the Torii fortunes is chronicled elsewhere and may someday see the light of day ...*) His search was fruitless until only three or four days ago and he had almost given up all hope of ever finding his former lord's son when, by a stroke of astonishing good fortune, he had been forced by the rains to seek shelter in Obama's one remaining temple, the other one and the shrine having been recently burnt to the ground by drunken ashigaru.

The old priest, almost in his dotage, was reluctant to accept anyone beneath the ruinous eaves but had relented when he heard Toshiaki's sad story.

'It's a strange world we live in, carpenter,' he had said, 'but here in this village we have suffered from much sickness until, one day, we were found by a wandering monk from Hōrai-ji ... Isn't that where you said your priest came from?'

'Hōrai monastery? Yes, that's where I told you.'

The old fellow was very deaf and just smiled vacantly. He remained silent for so long that Toshi thought that he had fogotten what he was going to say.

'Well, master; what about this monk, hey?'

'Monk .. ?'

'The monk from Mikawa!' Toshi thought he had better shout.

'Alright, alright . . . no need to bawl,' the priest mumbled, testily. 'Anyway, he's not the one you're seeking as he's come from Mimasaka . . . A long time . . .'

'Mimasaka?'

The old codger leant over and cleared his throat into a pot brim-full of phlegm.

'No, he came from Mikawa . . . That's what I told you . . .'

Toshi realized that he wouldn't get much sense out of this old bonze but he decided he had better go and look at this monk just as he had already sought out hundreds of others before.

'Where will I find this man, grandfather?' he asked.

'Grandfather? In my day youngsters like you would have been thrashed for being disrespectful about their betters . . . ah, well! Times are a-changing! Ehhgh! He's down the road at Old Gunbei's farm. They've had the sickness and the monk made them better, I heard.'

'And how do I find the right farm, old man?'

'You just look for the black ox. If you find the one you have found the other!'

Cackling to himself and coughing, the ancient creaked to his feet and slowly made his way to his tiny sleeping quarters leaving Toshiaki to lie down on the hard boards where he was.

———— ☐ ————

Imazu stank of fish and nightsoil. It was difficult for Enshin to decide which was the most offensive. On the one side lapped the waters of the great lake and a huddle of fishing boats bobbed and swayed at their moorings and more were drawn up onto the shore; on the other side, just beyond the narrow cluster of delapidated houses, were the rice fields that stretched across the little coastal plain to the tree-covered mountain slopes just to the west. In every flooded field toiled the straw-caped farmers and their families, all bent double as they went about the back-breaking task of planting individually each rice plant from the small bundles that lay neatly in the water covered mud. With every squelching step of their bare feet they stirred up the raw smell of human and animal manure that they daily threw into the flooded fields.

The little town, a pretentious description for such a miserable place, was full of every type of person, especially poor samurai and footsoldiers, all 'wave-men' turned loose after many a lost war; all hopeful of finding fresh employment on one side of the dangerous border or the other. None of them were particularly fussy; none of them could afford to be, either, or most would have starved long before. A few probably lived by robbery and theft, but in this throng were also many who had been caught up in these upheavals and lost everything, not once, but several times, and who had seen their closest kin savaged and murdered by the riff-raff who claimed to be soldiers on the strength of wearing some parts of tattered harness but were indistinguishable from mad bandits. In such hard times as these almost anywhere was better than the place where you knew suffering was rife. Inevitably the refugees were attracted to the great city of Miyakō to the south or the imagined paradise in Kaga under the protection of the Hongan-ji priests who had so recently wrested power away from their feudal lords.

It was for one such near-destitute group, the pitiful Kiichi family, that Enshin managed to agree a bargain with an elderly fisherman to ferry them, Toshi, himself, and Kuroi-san, across the upper part of the lake to Nagahama on the Omi shore. This was not a regular ferry, mind you; just one of the larger unwashed fishing boats that often plied these rich waters. Sturdy enough, no doubt, to brave the billowing waves and occasional stormy winds: strong enough, too, for the owner to agree for the black ox to travel in its broad waist.

As Enshin and his companions made their leisurely way towards the broken-down jetties on the waterfront, he saw that the pebbly beach was thronged by poor folk and armed ronin gathered there, doubtless, hoping to find someone who would carry them south or east to the distant blue shores.

A small boy dodged through the crowd towards the priest.

'Reverend sir,' he called out shrilly, catching sight of the monk.

Enshin looked around for who was shouting.

'What is it, young man?'

The lad was only about ten, he supposed.

'Oji-sama says to hurry . . .'

'Why is that?'

' 'Cos a whole lot of people are demanding to come on board.'

'In that case, Kiichi-san, we must do as our young master says.'

It was the stooped man who stood at Kuroi-san's head he addressed. Behind him, at the ox's rump, stood huddled Kiichi's younger wife and their daughter, both gazing timorously around at the throng.

'Whatever you say, Honourable Monk,' agreed Kiichi.

They pressed on with the boy in the lead although there was no hurrying Kuroi-san's ambling pace, and finally came to the shore where the boat was moored.

'We are here, grandfather!'

'None too soon!' said the fisherman, testily. 'For what you're going to give me, I must need my head seeing to. Others would give me more!'

'But you are taking us, nonetheless?'

'I said I would, didn't I?'

The fisherman grumbled away under his breath but already his grandson and Toshi were encouraging Kuroi-san up the thick doubled planks laid over the low sides and with remarkably little difficulty the huge black animal settled down in the middle of the boat and placidly munched at some dried grass that the lad had snatched from a covered heap next to one of the nearest paddies. Enshin helped Kiichi and his family aboard not failing to notice that Kiichi's wife was heavily pregnant under her close-clutched bundles. Toshi and he went and squatted down beside their cloven-hoofed companion and while the fatigued carpenter put his head down and was instantly asleep, the monk began to tell his rosary beads. The docile ox gazed mournfully at the shouting throng before finally resting his bearded chin gently on the priest's shoulder as if he was listening to the holy sutra.

'Hey, you; boatman!' A rough voice hailed them from the jetty. 'We three want to cross to Omi!'

'I have no space left, sirs,' apologized Oji-san.

'No room? We can see plenty of room!'

Enshin looked up from his prayers and saw three rōnin staring at them from the quayside.

The fisherman said: 'The boat will be dangerously low in the water, sirs; I cannot take any more.'

The biggest of the three, a man with a wolfish look about him, sneered.

'You've made room for that stinking animal so you can make room for us!'

His two friends kept set faces.

'But, sir . . .'

'You're not thinking of arguing with us, you filthy fish-gutter! Either we come aboard or we'll sink your stinking boat with our yari butts!'

'Calm yourself, master,' said Enshin, sensing that matters might rapidly get out of hand if they went any further. 'Oji-sama, surely if Kuroi-san and I moved a little forward the balance would be better and these gentlemen can more easily come with us? Wouldn't that be a reasonable solution?'

'Make up your mind, fisherman; we'll not wait long!'

Realizing his danger, the old man reluctantly agreed but the three rōnin had already hitched up their greased striped *hakama* and were stepping over the low gunnels, They settled themselves in the stern, the leader perching on the edge of the little transome deck where the owner plied his oar. His fellows were not very appealing, either, thought Enshin. The first had only one eye that looked malevolently out from a terribly smallpox-cratered face. All his clothes were worn out and ragged, particularly around his collar and the hems of his hakama. His companion was worse, if anything. Because of the hot damp day, he had removed his *kimono* and wore a sleeveless *haori* of uncertain colour. This exposed a long livid scar that ran all the way down his left arm from the shoulder to the thick muscles of his forearm; the wound was not that old and the lower end was still inflamed and weeping. Both men wore their hair untidily tied back with grubby strips of cotton. Only their leader was more carefully dressed, though even his clothing had seen far better days, but Enshin couldn't help but note that all three had swords whose handles were well-worn from a great deal of use. In each case, the silken cord bindings were in good condition, unfrayed and taut. They were katana that had often been out of their scabbards . . .

The lad had cast off the moorings and was just pulling the stern one aboard and coiling it down. The flat-bottomed fishing boat slipped slowly away from the shouting crowd as the old man worked at the sculling oar. Their movement brought out the stale smell of green weeded rocks from under the rotting wooden supports of the jetty. Gradually there came the steady 'slop' . . . 'slop' . . . 'slop' of the wavelets under the jutting flat prow.

'Careful, boy! You're wetting me!' snarled the man sitting on the decking.

The lad glanced down and saw that the wet rope was dripping water everywhere.

'I'm sorry, master . . . I . . . er . . . I didn't realize . . .'

'Wipe it up!' ordered the ronin.

The lad hastily glanced about and grabbed up a torn piece of sacking. He fell to his knees and began to mop hastily but without warning received a hard back-hand blow across the side of his head.

'That'll teach you to be more respectful to your superiors!'

The cuff nearly pitched him over the side. The boat rocked showing just how low they were in the water.

'He meant no harm, sir samurai,' said Enshin mildly.

'And he won't do it again! Now you shut up, priest! Speak if you are spoken to!'

Not a word was said for a long while as the shore gradually receded and the boatman threaded his way past a number of moored craft to the open waters of the lake.

'Honoured priest,' called down the sweating old fisherman as he pulled at his oar. 'Please deign to use your hand to measure how far we are above the surface amidships.'

Enshin smiled and leant over to look at the blue-grey water. He put his hand out, fingers splayed.

'We have about a handspan, Oji-sama,' he called.

One of the rōnin spat into the lake and a trail of spittle fell across Enshin's wrist.

'That'll be alright provided there is no wind,' muttered the grand-father, but he was plainly worried and kept a close watch on the surface and the skies.

Soon they rounded the southern tip of the promontary, some-times called Omi-no-mori, where the mountains dipped straight into the lake, and they stood out in the direction of a distant island that lay close to the centre of their course at this northern end. All was flat calm and placid under the gradually lightening skies.

One of the rōnin, the one with the pocked face, yawned aloud.

'Is this boat full of corpses?' he shouted out, with a peal of sar-donic laughter. 'No one says a word!'

'They are afraid of your good looks, Tomoe,' remarked the leader. 'I've seen 'em look sideways at you.'

'My looks?'

Somehow the remark had touched the man on a raw nerve. Probably the leader knew that it would do so Tomoe just sat there and glowered around hand over the side, his left hand fingering the hilt and iron guard of his short sword. Nothing was said for some minutes.

Eventually, the third man grunted and stretched out his cramped legs, kicking Kuroi-san in the back.

'Get out of the way, you damned cow! You take up far too much space!'

But the ox ignored him.

'You hardly expect the wretched beast to understand you, Yotsu-san, or do you?' hissed the chief. 'He only listens to the monk!'

Yotsu twisted himself round and curled up the side of his mouth.

'You know, Ishikawa, the bloody farmers don't like Tomoe's face and this animal is too damned big! It was unlucky that we took this craft!'

The rain had stopped long before but in its place a faint mist began to rise across the warm waters of the lake; both the northern mountains and the shore they had left behind became indistinct and finally vanished . . . Still the fisherman pulled and pushed at his single oar, inured to that laborious task, and the craft went slowly on its way across the glassy waters.

Slap, slap . . . slop, slop . . .

Up in the bows, Kiichi's lined face had relaxed in sleep as he dozed with his head partly against the thwart and partly cushioned by his wife. She sat very still with the girl cradled against her breast. The only movement came from the fisherman's rhythmic heaving at the oar against the creaking thole strap. His grandson, after that heavy blow, huddled as far away as he could from the gaunt rōnin, hardly daring to ease his cramped limbs.

———— 🁢 ————

Only Enshin and Kuroi-san were at their ease; the one lost in thought contemplating the strange way in which the placid lake merged with the pale skies, a slightly pinkish mist rubbing out the land as though it were an illusion; the other quietly chewing on the sweet grass, content to be beside his master.

Somehow there was a growing aura of foreboding hanging over the small craft as it continued to nose out into the seemingly endless waters. The further the old man sculled, the closer came the rising wraiths until all that was left was the smooth water and the ringing white mists; not even a patch of blue above. Not a sound was to be heard but the interminable slap of the wavelets under the flat prow . . .

———— 🁢 ————

'Do you have any idea where we are, fish-gutter!' rasped out Ishikawa. 'In this mist we might be going round and round in circles!'

'I have fished these waters for more than fifty years, master . . .'

'So you can't get lost, eh?' sneered the rōnin.

'We will reach the Omi shore in about three hours, master.'

'As long as that! Pah!'

Yotsu stood up and stretched his limbs.

'He has no more idea than any of us where we are,' he shouted. 'He's just spinning a yarn and that's the truth!'

'Please . . . please take care, sir; the boat is rocking too much . . .'

The fisherman was worried.

'Too many people. Eh? Is that what you're saying? Perhaps we had better put that right!'

Yotsu snatched up his yari that lay with the other two along the righthand gunnel. He glared about him.

The priest still sat telling his rosary beads. The black bull gazed round at the rōnin with large mild eyes. Kiichi lay silent in the bows, but he and his family looked with terror-filled eyes at the three warriors.

The old man was about to say something but before he could do so Yotsu snarled out an imprecation, stepped his left foot up onto the transome, and stabbed the triangular sectioned blade at the boy who cowered right up into his grandfather's bare legs. The keen point stopped a hair's breadth from the child's side. Terrified, the boy stuck out his arm, fingers spread, as if he could ward off the dreadful menace, but the rōnin screeched with cruel laughter, encouraged by the other two. They all thought it a huge joke.

Enshin said: 'Masters, sometimes these strange mists beguile and cloud the mind. If you harm the child and he dies, the good oarsman may, in the keen grip of sadness, cast himself into the waters to accompany his grandson from this Middle World . . . Where would we be then?'

'The priest spoke! You heard him . . .' The smallpoxed face of Tomoe, puffed like the skin of a toad, twisted malevolently. 'Damned monk! Ishikawa told you to shut your mouth . . ! Do you want the spear?'

'Calm yourself, lord samurai,' said Enshin, softly. 'My words are for your good as well as the rest of us.'

'Keep your damned advice, you stupid windbag!' spat Tomoe.

Yotsu looked as though he might well turn his yari but Ishikawa interposed: 'No, wait!' He saw a chance to mock the priest. 'Perhaps he is a learned man and can quote us something on which we can meditate?'

'Meditate?' snorted Tomoe. 'Oh, I see what you mean!'

Yotsu just scowled.

'Well, monk . . ? Can you?' snapped Tomoe.

'You think that we are lost in these mists, sir? Possibly we are, but in the "*Hagoromo*" the two fishermen say: "*Early mist close-clasped to the swell of the sea; in the plains of the sky a dim, loitering moon.*" Even if we have now by chance lost our way, the moon will soon rise after the sun has set and the mists will clear. We are not far from land.'

Ishikawa pulled a long face at Enshin's words for he realized that they were the truth.

It was Yotsu who was unpredictable.

'To hell with you all,' he snorted derisively. 'The boat must be lightened, the old man said so! So it shall be! If the runt dies and Oji-san follows him, who will care a single jot?'

His yari punched forward and twisted violently. With a shrill scream the boy toppled back over the stern, but Yotsu didn't stop there; the blood-streaked blade raked upwards into the old fellow's groin and the rōnin thrust it deep into the thin stomach so that the poor fisherman was impaled, his muscles in agonizing spasm. Jerking the blade back, Yotsu left his victim doubled over to pitch out of sight with a splash.

Kiichi's wife began to sob uncontrollably.

'Be quiet, bitch!' shouted Tomoe.

Yotsu turned round with his yari across his shoulders.

'It that woman wants to scream, let her . . . Maybe she will have better reason in a moment!'

He roughly threw the spear down and stepped past the ox.

'What are you going to do?' called Ishikawa.

'Enjoy myself . . . and you . . .' Yotsu thrust his disfigured face directly at Enshin, 'you, bloody priest, you keep your mouth shut or you'll join the other two back there!' He hooked his thumb behind him.

Tomoe stood up and holding onto the wale, moved forwards after his crony, a crooked leer spreading across his puffy face.

The priest muttered a prayer and continued to caress Kuroi-san's muzzle.

'You would like me to control the situation, wouldn't you?' Ishikawa shrugged his shoulders. 'You are thinking that Yotsu and Tomoe-san will stop if I tell them?'

From the bows came a low moan as Kiichi realized what was about to happen. His face muscles were working but there was nothing that he could possibly do. The very helplessness of their situation urged him to overcome his downtrodden servility in some desperate attempt to resist . . . but what was there when faced with two merciless armed men in that confined space? His eyes rolled and the spittle ran from the corners of his open mouth . . .

Yotsu shot out his scarred arm and grabbed the girl from her mother.

'This one's for you, Tomoe; I know how you like boys but as I have just killed the only one you'll have to make do with this!' He grinned maliciously. 'I'll have the woman . . . first.'

The priest thought that possibly the rōnin had not realized that Kiichi's wife was so close to her time.

□

The girl, a thin emaciated child of about eleven summers, was too shocked to scream. She opened her mouth but no sound came forth. Tomoe pitched her roughly face down into the bottom of the boat where some water slopped about beneath a wooden grating amongst debris of rope ends and stinking bits of fish. In falling she struck her head hard against one of the fishing line stanchions and the blood began to flow darkly from a nasty cut above her hairline.

But Tomoe had no pity and took out his katana and dirk, never once taking his eyes off the girl's buttocks, and he began to undo the ties of his filthy hakama.

Yotsu was preparing in the same manner and it was this slight delay that seemed to give Kiichi his chance for one desperate act of bravery. The rōnin had kicked off his trousers in a heap beside him and had reached forward with both hands to tear the thread-bare kimono away from the woman's body. She tried to clutch her clothing to her but he was far too strong and his iron fingers ripped the kimono open, almost lifting her to her feet. The boat pitched violently and some water splashed over the side. It was then that Kiichi saw the short-bladed gutting knife lying almost at his foot . . . As Yotsu held on to the gunnel with his right hand and forced his left one against the poor woman's knee so that she would open her legs, so Kiichi grabbed the knife hilt and flung himself onto his wife's attacker in a howling frenzy . . .

The rōnin had come through too many wars not to reach his mature years almost intact. His left hand snaked up and grasped the poor man's thin arm and twisted hard. The thrusting blade stabbed instead into his daughter's shoulder as she lay just behind, but in falling, Kiichi's head was caught by Yotsu's other hand and violently snapped the wrong way. Everyone in that fishing craft heard the sound of his neck breaking . . .

'Shit! What possessed him to do that?' exclaimed Yotsu. He gripped the limp corpse by the sash and cartwheeled it over the side with a splash. Sucking in his breath, he spat out a stream of saliva before turning once more to the woman who was now sobbing with fear . . . For the first time he saw her distended belly, all blotched and bruised from the kicking infant in her womb . . .

———□———

The one-eyed Tomoe hauled up the bleeding girl and doubled her over the side, her long matted hair falling into the calm waters alongside close to the floating corpse of her father. Four thin threads of blood slowly streamed away, curling and convoluting with the motion of the rocking boat. He dragged up her patched brown kimono; her skin gleamed like pale coral in the diffused evening light. She was weeping quietly.

'Sit still, monk,' warned Ishikawa in a hard voice, 'this is none of your business.'

Enshin simply sat as if meditating, neither looking at the infamous pair in the bows or at the saturnine features of the leader, but he was totally aware of everything that had occurred so quickly in the

past few minutes and the preparations that Tomoe and Yotsu were
making before raping the girl and her mother. Not only was he
aware of the past and the present fleeting seconds, but his inner mind
saw into the future and he knew exactly what he must do.

'Ishikawa-san,' he said in his soft deep voice, 'for more than
half my life, even counting when I was an infant and child, I have
followed the Path of the Lord Buddha.' There was something in
his tone that made the other two pause and turn their heads. 'Fate
decides everything and our actions surely affect our soul's progress
towards Enlightenment . . .'

'I told you before, priest, shut up . . !' growled Ishikawa.

' . . . your actions in this humble craft remind me of the famous
lines:

> How shall I act when
> Cruel death takes the place of life?
> Bold strokes sever both cords
> The drawn sword brightly shining
> Against the evening skies.'

'If you will not be silent, I'll cut the tongue from your head!'
Now there was a real menace in the rōnin's venomous words.

'Think on what I have said, O masterless man!'

In disbelief at the temerity of this shaven priest, Tomoe had caught
up his katana; forgotten now the soft buttocks of the young girl who
he was about to defile for ever. A sort of animal growl welled up
from deep in his chest.

Yotsu had half-listened to all this while he gazed slightly bemused
at the swollen child-filled stomach of the woman lying defenceless
before him.

'By the gods, cut the bloody priest's throat and quick about it,' he
shouted angrily. 'He'll go on preaching even while we have our fun!
Kill him, Ishikawa!'

He turned round and stabbed his left hand towards Ishikawa.
'Come on,' he bawled, 'do it now! I can't get at him because of this
damned cow!'

'Do you take your orders from hirelings, rōnin?' asked the priest.
His words had exactly the expected effect.

With a shout of anger Ishikawa went to draw his sword but
remembered that he was holding the scabbard in his right hand and
must shift it across. At that moment Kiichi's pregnant wife caught up
the fish knife and thrust the blade up into the momentarily inatten-
tive Yotsu's groin right through his bared testicles and into one of his
femoral arteries . . . The scruffy rōnin's eyes opened very wide and

in disbelief he jerked his body away and stared in amazement at the thick red blood spurting from his groin . . . then the pain came . . .

Ishikawa roared and his sword leapt upwards ready to strike down at the priest's bare head and neck . . . but Enshin's staff was between his hairy legs and sharply struck at the nerve behind the rōnin's taut left knee. Unbalanced, he half-fell to regain his hold in the bobbing craft and this time the tip of the staff jabbed upwards, smashing into the base of his nose . . . The whole roseate sky seemed to explode into a thousand brilliant points of light and darkness instantly followed as the back of his head cracked against the thole-post of the steering oar . . .

Standing just beyond the docile ox, Tomoe's smallpoxed face suffused with blood. He, at least, was ready and his sword would not fail to despatch this pestilential priest to Hell!

'Die, monk!' he yelled, stepping forward over the bull's folded forelegs.

'Watch out!' shrieked Yotsu, from what was about to be his death agony.

Toshiaki whispered something to the ox and Kuroi-san threw up his great head and his curved right horn with its sharp point pierced Tomoe's belly, tearing through his gut. The ox shook his head again and the screaming samurai fell back like a straw doll across his intended victim's brown legs. In a moment he was spattered in Yotsu's blood.

The woman didn't hesitate but stabbed with the stumpy needle-pointed knife into his staring eyes . . . again and again . . . Yotsu rolled over his comrade and was soon dead, too, beneath that sharp rain of blows.

'It is enough, woman! They'll not have their way ever again!'

She looked up at Enshin as though she had not heard his words.

'It's all over,' he repeated, gently.

———— ▱ ————

The western skies flared orange and red for a long while, soon shading to a brilliant crimson; as night began to close in the mists thinned. Distant mountains loomed and the waning moon rose, a reminder of Enshin's earlier prediction.

At Nagahama, the rōnin, Ishikawa Takakage, was handed over to the magistrate and summarily sentenced to die by crucifixion as a common criminal. The following morning when he was dead, his head was cut off and exposed together with those of his two murderous accomplices, on the special benches known as *gokumon*, the four bloody executioners' yari, used to piece his sides at the final moment, racked behind the grisly exhibits. A terse account of their crimes of murder and attempted rape was brushed on a notice board nearby.

Enshin, riding on his faithful ox and accompanied by Kiichi's widow and daughter, travelled slowly onwards and eventually reached the Mikawa Hōrai-ji where the unfortunate woman was brought to bed and delivered of a still-born boy. Through the priest's intercession she was straightaway employed as a wet nurse by the Naganuma family in nearby Nagashino. Through this, she and her daughter found sanctuary and peace for many years afterwards. The Naganuma family eventually became faithful followers of Lord Tokugawa Ieyasu.

The holy priest, Torii Enshin Mitsumune, continued his wanderings in the company of the faithful carpenter, Toshiaki, in search of the Truth and some stories survive about this but, unfortunately, the chronicles are silent on his ultimate demise. Some swordsmen believe a tradition handed down for many years that, in the fullness of time, both he and his black ox passed from this world and their bodies were thought to be buried in a remote temple near to Aizu in the mountainous north, but we cannot be certain about this.

This tale of long ago is as Enami-no-Saemon wrote:

> *The Fiend's violence is requited,*
> *The fisher's boat is changed*
> *To the Ship of Buddha's vow*
> *The rescue of the Lotus Law.*

2

AN UNFORTUNATE INCIDENT

▼

Long before he reached the straggling little border town of Kashiwara, a number of well-meaning people of low estate had informed the monk, Enshin, as he made his leisurely way along the muddy highway perched on the sleek rump of his faithful black ox, Kuroi-san, that the border barriers beyond the town had been closed, The way into Hitachi province was blocked by the vicissitudes of war; not that this disturbed Enshin's spirit one little bit, but he politely enquired of his latest informant, a man who led an emaciated pony grievously overloaded with woven materials, where he might find inexpensive lodgings.

'Nay, good priest, you cannot be expected to pay for some rat infested shed. There would be no merit earned by anyone mean enough to begrudge a holy man a space to lay his head. Go to my friend Heibei; he keeps the teahouse next to my humble shop. Your fine ox may share my nag's fodder for a few days and you shall not have to worry. Do you say proper medicinal spells, honoured priest? In that case, maybe you can cure my servant girl who keeps passing out with what she describes as the vapours . . .'

'What do you think, Kuroi-san? Shall we stay with this good man a while?'

His remark earned him a curious look from the wool merchant.
'Does he answer you, master?'
'Often, though usually when we are alone after a long day.'
'Well I never!'
Enshin smiled to himself since this was almost the first break
from the vociferous outpourings of speech to which he had hardly
replied more than five or six words in the whole time. He hadn't
even found out the name of his new friend as yet. When finally
they made their way along the muddy main thoroughfare of the
tawdry little town and, after settling his friend, the ox, he was
taken next door and welcomed by a beaming Master Heibei, the
owner of the little teahouse. At once, he was seated at a low table
just inside the room that was open to its verandah fronting the
street, a place ideally suited to watching life pass by whilst telling
his rosary beads.
'Talks a lot, sir priest, doesn't he?' grinned Heibei, a jolly looking
man who seemed to be permanently bobbing down into a bow.
'Your friend? A voluble man, indeed, and a successful one, no
doubt? Do you know, despite his many and varied words, he didn't
tell me his name!'
'Magobei-san! He is successful at that, master, but this war might
beggar us all.'
'Wars come and go, Heibei-san; just be patient and say your
prayers for protection. I think you are a kind man, too, for offering
a poor monk hospitality.'
Heibei touched the side of his nose and winked.
'You can't hide real quality, if you knows what I mean,' the tea
master said, conspiratorily, 'if you don't mind me saying so?'
'Is it that obvious, Master Heibei, even after all these years?' Enshin
half-smiled to himself and nodded his head. 'But you wouldn't
breathe a word . . . no? I've been a poor monk for a long time and
am no longer a warrior either in body or spirit.'
'Quite so, master; quite so! A bowl of good tea with some ō-soba
and vegetables for sustenance?' He winked and turned towards the
kitchen where his wife and a couple of girls, probably his daughters,
peered from behind the hanging curtain. 'Ō-soba for our guest,
oka-san!' he shouted, unnecessarily.
'At once, husband,' his wife shrilled.
Enshin settled himself more comfortably in his corner of the open
front, permitting himself a chuckle as the thought passed through
his mind how many shopkeepers similarly loudly repeated orders to
their wives whenever they fancied he was more than a simple wandering monk . . . Such behaviour must be repeated countless times
throughout the length and breadth of the country, he supposed, if it

happened to him perhaps once or twice each week! Still, it was an engaging custom and demonstrated that common courtesy wasn't yet dead despite the terrible wars . . . Contemplating the busy scene in the main street outside, he turned over in his mind the general impression that there was an ever-present feeling of incipient menace that maybe didn't exist in the past. Was it because there were many more armed ashigaru and swaggering low-ranking samurai thronging the muddy sidewalks? Was it the fact that these generally ignorant wave-men felt empowered by the fact that they could bear arms with impunity, or was that thought the product of his own more cultured upbringing, a natural, though misplaced, sense of his superior breeding, scarcely compatible with his humble calling? As he appreciatively sipped Heibei's infusion of tea, almost unprompted there slipped into his mind the opening words spoken by the priest in the play 'Kumasaka' written a century ago in what may have been better times:

> These weary feet
> That found the World
> Too sad to walk in, whither,
> Oh wither, shall wandering
> Lead them?

Zenchika Ujinobu-sama had brushed those lines and they marvellously encapsulated Enshin's own search . . .

It was a little after noontide; the heavy rain during the previous night had cleared to the east at dawn leaving the street a morass of patchy mud and litter through which most of the passers-by must trudge. Many wore high-platformed wooden geta but some of the poorer went about in sodden straw waraji or, in many cases, even barefoot. War throughout the Kantō provinces had forced up the prices of even the most basic of foodstuffs, particulary for rice, now hoarded by the local lords in order to maintain their military strength, though dried fish seemed plentiful enough. Only the ubiquitous takuan was still cheap and many a peasant farmer or ragged soldier seemed to have at least two or three of these yellow radishes dangling from the back of his sash making a somewhat absurd sight, for all the world like so many tails!

As Enshin quietly observed the scene, a ranking samurai wearing black-laced armour as he haughtily sat on his horse, was led along in the middle of an escort of more than twenty spearmen, scarcely deigning to look to either side, let alone at the supplicants amongst the rōnin in the crowd who had swallowed their pride and entreated for employment, hunger or plain destitution emboldening their pleading. The warrior rode on, the throng sometimes brutally forced aside by the yari-mochi; this was not yet their time.

'Tell me, Heibei-san; is that samurai a local man?'

'Who? Shōni Tameyemon?' The teahouse owner vigorously rubbed his hands on a small cotton towel dangling at his waist. 'He's one of Lord Satake's hatamoto, sir priest, and . . .' lowering his voice, Heibei whispered '. . . a man who thinks above his station!'

'Many do these days.'

'True, sir; that is very true!'

A little later, two peasants stumbled past with bent shoulders under the weight of huge loads, followed by a wandering mendicant wearing a large round woven basket over his head and playing on a deep-throated *shakuhachi* flute. Somewhat oddly, he carried a long katana thrust through his obi and Enshin noted, as the fellow passed just by Heibei's verandah, that the hilt bindings of this sword were well-worn from use. Three saturnine-looking rōnin were seated, deep in conversation, on the steps of a potter's shop just opposite the teahouse and the priest saw that the men were drinking heavily from a large gourd which they passed between them. From their boisterous behaviour the gourd clearly contained strong liquor. An unusual splash of colour in that drab scene was provided by the arrival of two kimono-clad young girls escorted by an older duenna and a rather decrepit looking old retainer which indicated their rank. At the other end of the street, just within Enshin's line of vision, a couple or three samurai swaggered into view, probably the worse for ō-sake, freely sending passers-by reeling out of their way and singing snatches of some folksong or other in raucous voices.

'Best watch out, sir,' warned Heibei, craning his neck round the side post, 'those gentlemen might herald trouble.'

'Let us pray that it's not so,' murmured Enshin, but he, too, could feel danger in the air.

The sun went behind a large black cloud and drops of rain began to fall just as the girls and their escort stopped outside the teahouse. At once Heibei darted out onto the verandah and, with many bows, invited them to step inside and take shelter from what promised to be a heavy shower, perhaps to taste his delicious tea? The duenna gave him a frosty look and unfolded two oiled umbrellas, one of which she handed to the younger girl whilst she, herself, put up the second over the head of the elder. She bowed her head slightly when she saw Enshin but otherwise ignored the humble Heibei.

A burst of discordant laughter came from the samurai as they pushed past a labour carrying a wooden frame who wasn't able to get out of their way in that narrow street.

The peasant staggered back a couple of paces and fell to his knees, bowing his head low into the filth, but as he did so, a rotten cord holding his only bundle of faggots suddenly parted and the branches tumbled into the street at the feet of the rōnin opposite. One branch just snagged the sleeve of one of them who was about to drink, slopping some wine out over his haori and kimono.

'Ugh . . ! What's this?' he exclaimed, jumping to his feet.

'It wasn't the woodcutter's fault,' swore one of his companions, 'he was pushed against you!'

The samurai, who carried a yari, sneered. 'Are you blaming me?' he demanded. 'Apologize at once, fellow!' He smirked at his companions.

'Why should I? It is you who should apologize!'

The hard-bitten looking young rōnin curled his lip, looking the drunken young man up and down.

'Say it, boy, or I'll cut your arrogance down to its proper size!'

Just then the two girls and their escort tried to pass on the nearer side of the thoroughfare. The young warrior had levelled his yari and the butt end thumped back into the younger girl causing her to yelp and drop her parasol. The diversion was enough to afford the rōnin his chance. He drew his sword in a flash and severed the haft of the spear just below its handstop. At the same moment the ladies' superannuated attendant tried to place himself in front of his charges but the angry samurai whirled his broken spearshaft and dealt the old fellow a nasty blow at the base of his jaw, bowling him over into the slime.

The other two samurai drew out their swords and faced the rōnin then slowly backed towards the teahouse, straight into the distraut women. With a coarse laugh, one of them seized the nearest girl and dragged her in front of him as a shield. The furthest rōnin stepped down from his verandah step and circled to his right, warily watching the belligerent samurai. As he circled, he passed in front of the basket-wearing flautist.

'Let that girl go, sir!' demanded the second rōnin. 'To shelter behind women is no way for a warrior!'

'Come and take her, then!'

The samurai thrust her out to arms' length. At that instant a sword-blade flashed and the circling rōnin pitched forward, cloven from hip to shoulder by the flute player. The second and younger girl moved slightly . . . Enshin was instantly aware of what she would do . . . The middle samurai raised his sword above his head and uttered a terrible shout, at once dashing forward to attack; a dirk appeared in her delicate hand and with a deft thrust, she deeply cut the throat of the man grasping her elder sister. His grip relaxed as he sank to the ground but the girl slipped in the mud and fell into the path of the other samurai's missed cut which badly wounded her shoulder and arm. Sobbing, she collapsed in a heap, her duenna desperately trying to shelter her from the fight that immediately ensued.

The younger girl, standing alone, bravely held her dagger up as some sort of defence and backed towards the teahouse steps. Despite their inebriated state, the two remaining samurai soon cut down the rōnin then turned to chase after the girl, well aware that it was she who had knifed their companion. One of them, passing the crouching elder girl and her nurse, viciously slashed backwards, as casually as a lad might cut at a thistle head with a stick, killing the old woman outright.

'Heibei-san, you must excuse me a moment,' apologized Enshin, rising to his feet. 'Take this lady to your wife – without delay!'

He stepped onto the verandah boards, his stave seemingly supporting his weight.

'Sirs,' he said in a firm voice, 'matters have surely gone far enough, don't you think?'

The monk's sudden appearance came as a surprise, causing them to pause. The girl, seeing her chance, slipped into the teahouse. Recovering, the two samurai made to follow but Enshin barred the way with a smooth sidestep.

'I have just observed that this has gone too far.'

'Get out of our way, you insolent priest!'

'And should I not do so; what then?'

'Then we will kill you and send your soul to Hell!'

Enshin smiled gently.

'That may not prove so easy.'

Out of the corner of his eye he noticed that the basket-wearing swordsman had moved across to his side of the street and was now just at the left-hand side of the planked apron some two or three yards to the left of the warriors. 'Please, sir; do not take any part in this,' Enshin added, mildly.

'Why not, monk; you seem about to do so?'

The leading samurai uttered an oath and cut at Enshin but his eyes bulged incredulously as his sword flew from his hands and buried its tip deep in the mud far down the corpse-strewn street. A second later Enshin's staff caught him under his arm and spun him into the path of his friend. Like lightning, the monk stepped in and took the second man's sword from his apparently nerveless fingers. The flautist, basket now abandoned, nimbly leapt up behind him but

Enshin, grasping his two captives with one hand, pointed the blade straight at him.

'I recommended that you didn't take part, but now that you have done so all must be resolved by the Buddha's Law.'

'Fool!'

'Advance one more pace and you will see the futility of action contrary to that Law!'

The flautist laughed, slowly raising his sword to his right shoulder. Enshin, holding his blade unwaveringly at a level with his attacker's eyes suddenly ducked down his body beneath the captive pair and, with effortless ease, spun them round to his left where they sprawled down in a heap. With a sudden leap, he cut to the front, whirled the sword behind his right hip and swept the blade round at knee level, cutting the head from the shoulders of one of the samurai who was trying to draw out his dirk ... In stepped the flautist, cutting hard at Enshin's shoulder, but the blow was met and slipped leaving his side exposed to a heavy jabbing blow from the monk's reversed sword. The attacker fell heavily, quite winded. It was the work of a moment for Enshin to secure him with a length of cord that he drew out from his robe.

'Heibei-san!'

'Master?'

'Hurry to Magobei-san and request that he summon the magistrate and some armed men!'

'At once, lord!'

Enshin turned and bowed to the girl who stood at the back of the teahouse with Heibei's wife standing respectfully behind her.

'I regret what has occurred, my lady.'

She drew herself up, her face impassive.

'Sir Priest, I am deeply grateful for your intervention. I am certain my father will feel the same way.'

'My lady, may I know the name of your parent?'

'He serves Satake-dono.'

Heibei's wife wrote the shape of a character with her finger on her other palm and Enshin, a sharp observer, said: 'Ah, of course! Your honoured father is Shōni-dono.' He bowed once again.

'You know him, honoured priest?' the girl said, just a trifle surprised.

Enshin inclined his head slightly.

'He must be more circumspect in these troubled times.'

'I think it may be possible after this.'

'It is a sad day, my lady, but I will pray for the souls of those who have travelled on.'

'Even for those who committed this crime?'

'It was their fate, decreed by the Lord Buddha.'

He turned to Heibei who had come bustling back. 'Please go with your wife and see if something can be done for the wounded lady, please.'

Mrs Heibei had already summoned her daughters and waved her husband aside to keep shop, but the girl was sinking fast and the duenna already dead.

A few minutes later, Shōni Tameyemon hurried up with many retainers. He ostentatiously ordered the crowd cleared and took charge. When, eventually, he got round to expressing his thanks to the monk, Enshin could not be found although both Heibei and his friend, knew very well where he was. As they weren't asked, they didn't feel it necessary to say.

———————□———————

Torii Enshin had retreated to Magobei's stable where he sat quietly on the clean straw with his friend, the glossy-coated black ox. After intoning prayers for the souls of the dead, innocent or guilty alike, he gently stroked Kuroi's soft muzzle and ears. The animal lay beside him listening gravely to the whispered account of the incident. The monk concluded by quoting to his faithful companion the words of Yama, the King of Hell, in the play 'Ukai'.

'Kuroi-san, I remember these lines by Master Enami-no-Sōemon and I'm sure you will recall them, I've recited them often enough:

> Hell is not far away:
> All that your eyes
> Look on in the world;
> It is the Fiend's house.'

Kuroi-san lowered his muzzle to his friend's lap, his great eyes infinitely sad at the cruelty and folly of mankind.

3

THE OIKAKE-ISHI

▼

Before Torii Mitsumune became a shaven monk at the age of twenty-four, later taking the name Enshin, he had seen much hard service doing his duty for his overlord, Uesugi Akisada. The sixth year of Eishō[1] saw a very hard winter with exceptionally heavy snows in the mountains of Echigo on the further side of the Three-Province Pass and conditions were hardly any better in the Torii lands around Kusatsu that lay on the south-western sides of the high peaks of the Mikuni range. The previous summer's harvest had not been good and with the very hard winter many peasants faced real hardships and even actual starvation.

Almost from the year Mitsumune came of age and took his adult name, he had experienced warfare. His father's lands, lying across the main routes through the mountains between the Uesugi and Nagao strongholds in Echigo to the north-west and the rich Kantō plains to the east, had been the route taken by many contending armies. The Nagao and their overlords, the Uesugi, although powerful, lacked sufficient strength to wrest the Kantō from its lords and along

---

[1] 1509/10

the Kantō end of the Tokaidō highway, a formidable powerbase was being developed by the Shin-Hōjō lords under the able leadership of Hōjō Sōun. The result was a whole series of campaigns in one direction or another that were, in some ways, best described as glorified raiding by either side or by the lesser lords hungry to take advantage of the instability to increase their own domains.

A little east of the miserable town of Yuzawa lay the yashiki of Shimizu, sometimes called the Nagao Iga yashiki. In those days, for now it is destroyed and its once proud walls fallen and covered by rank shiba grass, it was commanded by a warrior named Abe Uemon-no-jō and it was to this lord that Torii Mitsumune was despatched in the depths of that winter with a secret message from Nagao Tamekage to his cousin. Mitsumune was selected for this task partly because of his youth and toughness in those winter mountains and partly the fact that the Torii held a key position commanding the few routes across the difficult passes.

Torii Mitsumune needed to be strong for the winter snows in Echigo were proverbial, unlike lands to the east and the south-west where three or four inches was considered heavy, here the snowfalls built up to ten or fifteen feet with ease. It was such a winter once described by the old poet:

> All traces of the valley
> Are buried in deep snows;
> Only the very tips of the trees
> Mark the mountain roads
> In winter's iron grip.

It was the terrible conditions that the young samurai encountered that winter when nature and warfare combined to reduce all but the powerful to abject despair that finally decided Torii Mitsumune to become a priest so that he would be able, in a small measure, to help relieve those poor souls for whom life in this Middle World was every bit as bad as torment in Hell. Many years later circumstances gave him the time to recollect his experiences and preserve them in the Torii family archives.

————— ☐ —————

The young warrior and his single attendant had set out from one of the barrier forts a few miles west of Yuzawa in bright sunshine, passing through the ramshackle town that was bursting with ashigaru and samurai of every description about noon, but an hour later, with heavy clouds gathering behind them over the coast, they were forced in the end to shelter in a small Shugendō temple from the violent blizzard that had blown up as the afternoon light failed.

It was fortunate that several Torii servants who had accompanied the detachment of retainers at present serving with the Uesugi armies, were at the barrier fort when the young man prepared to leave with his orders. One of these lackeys, a broad-shouldered carpenter named Toshiaki, promoted for the present to a *yari-mochi*,[2] had come forward with a straw matted bundle that he tied to their packhorse.

'You may have need for these, master,' he had said; 'you never can tell with the weather this side of the mountains.'

'What is in there, fellow?' asked Mitsumune's aide.

'Just some straw leggings and the like, master.'

'Who ordered you to do this?' demanded the samurai.

'No one, sir; it was just my idea.'

Mitsumune looked up from checking the saddle straps of his own horse.

'Don't be too hard on him, Gunbei-san; this man . . .?'

'Toshiaki, master.'

'. . . Toshiaki! I remember now. . . and his family have served the Torii for many generations. I thank you, Master Toshiaki, although from the look of this sunshine we won't have need of them.'

The yari-mochi bowed.

'I have also checked your food, sir . . .'

Gunbei had already mounted up. Now he turned his animal's head and couldn't help growling: 'I suppose you decided to add extra rice, too?'

The ashigaru bowed his head again.

'Pah!'

'If this man is right, we may have cause to thank him for his foresight, Gunbei-san,' observed Mitsumune.

'He is presumptuous, my lord!'

'We shall see . . . Time to leave!'

Despite being born into a very old and proud bushi family, exposed daily to the warrior's manners and customs, there seemed to Mitsumune, even in his youth, that in these disturbed times where warfare had become common across the provinces, there had been a shift in attitude amongst the samurai. There was an increasing arrogance, a lack of compassion for those who served them and without whom the warrior would have been seriously weakened. After all, without the hard work of the farmers, the strength of any

---

[2] A spear-bearer for his master.

domain would be far less; their whole society depended upon what the villagers grew and therefore on the peasants' welfare. Men like Gunbei simply didn't understand and, perhaps, never would.

———□———

'I give thanks for finding this temple,' observed Mitsumune, eying the powdery flakes of snow that were already settling across their tracks. 'We must find proper shelter for these horses, Gunbei-san.'

The retainer grunted, possibly thinking that his master and he should eat first, but he caught hold of the reins and followed the bushi to the rear of the building where cover might be found. Luckily, there was a small byre that might also have doubled as shelter for yamabushi groups or peasant pilgrims entering the mountains in more settled times, but from the look of the place that had been a long time ago. Fortunately, Toshiaki had also thought of packing some forage and coarse oats for the animals and Gunbei was amazed when his master started to remove his own saddle and lift down the pack pony's load. Perforce, he had to assist.

By the time they closed up the stabling as best they could by hanging a few threadbare mats to keep out the worst of the wind and snow, then picked their way to the doors of the temple, the snowstorm had closed in on them.

'Perhaps you were a little hasty to criticize that yari-mochi, Gunbei-san,' said Mitsumune, throwing down the mat-covered pack that Toshiaki said contained straw clothing. 'Looking at that snow out there, we may well need this.'

The interior of the temple was cold and dark, but at least it kept the elements at bay. Gunbei fumbled in his wallet to find his flint and steel so that they could have some light both to see and fire to cook and after a few strikes managed to get a spark to ignite his twist of dry tinder and they soon had a flame. In no time, they could look about the shadows of that austere hall. There, looming at the back, stood a figure that was unmistakably Fudō-Myō-ō and beside him another carved statue of that gaunt ascetic founder of the Shugendō, En-no-Gyōja, but as Mitsumune held up a flaming brand he realized that they were not alone. From somewhere around the *jodan* he thought he heard a low noise and, changing the torch to his left hand, drew out his *tachi* as a precaution . . . Hearing the noise again, this time clearly a muttered groan, he advanced onto the platform and peered about behind the statues. At once, his nostrils were assailed by a foul stench and he began to realize the cause.

Huddled down against the back wall lay a jumble of bodies, only one of whom showed any sign of life at all. The two samurai found

a couple of lanterns and lit them in preference to the naked flame of
the tinder torch, and turned to examine who or what lay concealed
in the shadowy depths.

Six people lay close together clad in filthy rags; they were all dead.
There were two men, three women and a child. A seventh man,
barely alive, was the one who had groaned and lay a little apart from
the others. With the stronger light of the lanterns fixed safely to their
holders, Mitsumune saw the unmistakable signs of an assault: there
were several broken arrows lodged in the walls and next to the jōdan
platform an ominous stain darkened the bare floorboards and spattered the adjacent wall to a height of three or four feet. Someone
or more than one, had been beheaded there, without the shadow of
a doubt.

'Pass me the water gourd, Gunbei-san, if you please. Let's see if
anything can be done for this man.' He wetted the poor fellow's
cracked lips and eventually managed to pass a few drops into his
mouth. 'Here, give me a hand to lift him out. There's nothing can
be done for the rest.' He could see that they had passed from this life
several days before but that the cold weather had slowed down corruption although it had done little to stifle the stench of the bloody
running flux.

The two warriors laid the sick man below the image of Fudō
Myō-ō, for all the world like an offering to the deity, and Mitsumune tried to get him to take a few more drops of water. With a
piece of dampened cloth he carefully eased away the thick crust that
sealed the man's eyes, shaking his head the while as he realized that
the fellow was on the very brink of death.

At last his ministrations were rewarded as the peasant made a
louder groan and feebly tried to lift a thin hand to his face, though
without success. One of his eyes, less sealed with the yellowish dried
mucus, opened a little, and the unfortunate man gazed upwards for
a few seconds before finding Mitsumune's face. His breath rasped in
his throat but he managed to whisper his gratitude.

'How long have you been here?' asked the Torii warrior.

All he got in reply was a series of scratchings on the boards, so he posed
the question again. This time he counted eight scraping movements.

'Eight days?'

'Uh-hhh . . .'

'Without food or water?'

'Uhhh . . .'

'Were the others your family?'

'Arhhh . . . yesss . . .!'

Mitsumune could see that these people were already far gone
with starvation before the last eight days.

'Did soldiers come here?'

The peasant summoned up enough strength to confirm this.

'Were they the Nagao?'

'No.'

'The Uesugi?'

The dying man took a little more water but was suddenly retching and sick. Gunbei turned away in disgust.

'Was someone killed in this hall?'

The man's chest heaved and his single eye opened wider. 'Yes, lord; the soldiers forced us . . . my family . . . back there then dragged in . . .'

'Prisoners?'

'Three of them, master; two men and a . . . a lady.'

He had managed to raise his head but now it fell back to the floor and Mitsumune thought he had died, but gradually he saw the rise and fall of the man's chest. Patiently, he sat there wiping the man's brow with his cooling cloth.

'Have you any idea who the prisoners were?'

The dying man managed to nod his head.

'One was lord Tamekage's brother, master . . . I'm certain sure . . .'

'You've seen him before, eh?'

'All my rice was collected by his bailiff, master . . . We were behind . . . two years and lord Tamenaga came with his men a month ago and burnt . . . burnt everything! They . . .'

'Drink a little more water!'

The bony fingers tried to grip his mailed *kote* sleeve.

'We had no rice left . . . only some millet . . . They burnt it all . . . and crucified the village elders, sir . . .'

Torii Mitsumune said nothing but he could picture the scene . . . and the despair of the peasants who knew full well that this was the beginning of winter and that they would all die slowly of starvation.

'They raised them on crosses, lord . . .' the man's voice was hardly more than a whisper now, 'but they didn't run spears through them . . . just left them to . . . to die in the cold . . . then they herded the women and children into our only barn . . . and . . .'

A great tear welled from his one open eye and his face puckered as if in pain, but the warrior knew that it was the pain at the memory . . .

'They set fire to that barn, didn't they?'

The peasant couldn't reply, only imperceptibly nod his head.

'I will pray for their souls, I promise.'

'Before they left, the soldiers speared all the others . . . They were about to kill us when more men rode up with their prisoners . . .

They brought us here . . .' The man opened his eye wide and turned his head towards Mitsumune. 'You are not like them, my lord,' he whispered. 'You are from the Torii-ke, aren't you . . . different . . . Pray for us, sir . . . pray for . . .'

His head fell to one side and his last breath rustled out from his lips. Mitsumune sat there for some minutes before he shook his head sadly and came to his feet.

Gunbei had found the stone floor where the yamabushi priests prepared their food and was busy breaking up a wooden screen to make a small cooking fire. Already he had hung a small cauldron on the iron hooks above the beginnings of this fire, having filled it with fresh snow. Turning over in his mind what he had learnt from the dying peasant, Mitsumune stood at the door and peered out into the raging snow storm. If this continued they would be unable to move for a few days and he, at least, was grateful for the yari-mochi's foresight.

It was difficult to know what was going on in these domains, the various minor lords seemed to change sides so often. Here was a mystery. The question that was in his mind was why should the Uesugi execute lord Nagao Tamenaga, one of their own? Tamenaga was the brother of Tamekage, the head of the Nagao-ke, the man who had rebelled and killed Uesugi Fusayoshi three years before. That was the time when the Torii had been coerced into joining the faction of Uesugi Akisada perhaps better known by his Buddhist name, Kajun . . . But peace had been restored in the face of a threat from Hōjō Sōun and, so far as everyone was concerned, the two powerful families of the Uesugi and the Nagao were reunited. Was this killing the culmination of a long nurtured vendetta? And now, held up by this storm, he was bearing a message to Nagao Tameshige in the Iga yashiki . . . The more he thought about it, the more Mitsumune sensed danger. There was a stench not of the bloody flux suffered by those starving peasants but of further rebellion! It might well be that he had been selected to carry this sealed message, now secured beneath his waist sash, to give Abe Uemon-no-jō the impression that the Torii, themselves, supported the insurgents; this might lead the commander of the important border yashiki to think that the whole border was about to rise in arms against the Uesugi-ke. Or, conversely, maybe the Torii were to be sacrificed and their lands seized by the Uesugi to strengthen their own hand against the Nagao . . ?

Early the next morning when the daylight was sufficiently strong, Mitsumune opened the creaking shōji and struggled round through the snow drifts that had built up under the wide *roka*[3] eaves to see to their horses himself, leaving his retainer to prepare their breakfast. He judged that at least another foot or two of snow had fallen during the night and that the strong winds from the north-west had piled up the snow against the northern end of the prayer hall almost to the thatched roof. The steep pitched roof, itself, bore a thick mantle that might threaten the outer posts that in this province were placed at intervals along the outer side of the verandahs to support the frequently tremendous weight of snow.

Their three horses seemed to be fine and there was plenty of hay piled up at the end of the byres, though Mitsumune did wonder in passing why the yamabushi who frequented this place needed the fodder. It was possible, of course, that this small temple, little more than the prayer hall so far as he could see, served as a staging point for pack horses used to carry supplies further north into the Dewa Sanzan around Haguro. Anyway, he was grateful that their animals would not suffer serious hardship if they were forced to remain here for some time.

It began to snow heavily once again whilst the two samurai slowly ate their breakfast of rice and takuan radish and Mitsumune observed: 'We may have to shovel some of the weight from the roof, Gunbei-san, if this goes on.'

His follower frowned as he looked across at the broken-shuttered window aperture, the black upright bars thickly crusted with blown snow from the previous night's storm. Quite a drift lay on the floorboards beneath. He merely grunted.

Mitsumune didn't know this man, Gunbei, at all. He wasn't one of the lower class samurai that served at Kusatsu or any of the surrounding yashiki, so far as he could recall. A little later, he casually asked where his family lived.

'Uhh! We have a three fields farm near to Komochi village, master.'

'Komochi-mura? A long time ago that belonged to the Yūki-ke ... Yuki Naritomo, wasn't it, who lost those lands to the Uesugi?'

'That is correct, master. The Uesugi lord then gave the village to the Torii-ke ... as a reward for their part in that war. We have served your family ever since.'

Mitsumune thought that either Gunbei was naturally taciturn or he harboured some sort of grudge for the change in his ancestral lord's fortunes. If he remembered correctly, the Ashikaga had later restored much of the former domain to the Yūki forty or fifty years before, but the ground had been repeatedly fought over by

---

[3] *roka*: a passageway.

many clans since then, particularly the Kantō Yamana-ke and the Ogigayatsu Uesugi from Sagami province.

Their repast finished, Torii Mitsumune sat a little apart and began to clean his longsword blade and pay attention to the hilt bindings.

'How long did your family serve the Yūki-ke, Gunbei-san?' he asked, casually.

'My grandfather was the third generation, my lord.'

'And before that?'

'Before that my ancestors were village headmen.'

Mitsumune put down his sword carefully having just replaced it in the newly tightened hilt, stretching back to ease his shoulders.

'It is a good thing to own one's land. *Gōshi-samurai* are often the most faithful, you know,' he observed.

'With just ten *koku* a year?' grunted Gunbei.

'But you have your farm and pay no tithes.'

This man definitely had a chip on his shoulder, thought Mitsumune.

———— 🔲 ————

On the following day, despite the wintry conditions, the corpses of the peasants were beginning to decay and smell quite noticeably but to bury them was out of the question; nevertheless they would have to be removed.

'See if you can find a couple of *kosuke*, Gunbei-san,' requested the warrior.

'Kosuke? What's that, master?'

Seeing his follower's mystification, Mitsumune laughed.

'Of course, you don't know our local word for a snow shovel! There's bound to be some under the eaves. That's where they are usually racked ready for winter use.'

Kosuke were duly discovered and they set to digging a rough snow tunnel directly out to where they supposed lay the centre of the open compound. That was where Mitsumune proposed they stored the corpses so that they could be dealt with after the spring thaw. All morning they cut out lumps of the packed snow and piled it where the deep drifts blocked the northern end of the verandah. Satisfied they had gone far enough, they then carried the blotched bodies of those starved wretches out to the end of their tunnel and finally sealed them in by collapsing the roof and packing the snow tight. All that was left to bother the samurai was the sight of the bloodstains marking where Uesugi Tamenaga and his two fellow prisoners had been murdered. The stains were a constant reminder of the deception and duplicity of war.

———— 🔲 ————

Ten days had passed since their arrival and at last a slight thaw had set in which sent a large avalanche of packed snow sliding down from the main roof, much to Mitsumune's relief since it meant that no one must risk climbing up and cutting the thick accumulation away. The weather improved to the point where they could actually see out over the drifts; the light flooding into the prayer hall made it a 'shining Buddha world', as the saying goes. It was just possible that they could move on towards the Nagao Iga yashiki if the thaw continued. After all, it was now the fourth month and better weather couldn't be far away.

During these tedious hours and days, Mitsumune had daily spent long periods of time in prayer and meditation before the statue of Fudō Myō-ō as had been his custom whilst near the Kusatsu temple. Such austerities came naturally to him and he was certain that they sharpened his awareness in the military arts. Between these periods of contemplation, he employed his heavy rosewood *bokutō* to keep his mind and body alert, honed ready for any eventuality. Each night he slept on the jōdan at a place where he had discovered two floorboards that had slightly twisted on their joist seating so that under the pressure of an unwary step they gave a slight creak. He was sufficiently suspicious of Gunbei's loyalty to ensure that he slept lightly after the manner of many kenshi. He must find sleep, of course, but he needed his inner-awareness, his *zanshin-no-ri*.

'You see, Gunbei-san, that yari-mochi was prudent in his fore-cast! We certainly did need the extra food and also the contents of this pack,' he remarked, opening up the coarse sacking with the point of his dirk. There, neatly packed by the former-carpenter, lay a number of items that were of the greatest use on the western side of the mountains of this province. The retainer, increasingly morose, merely glanced across but said not a word. If they returned safely, Mitsumune resolved that he would not employ the fellow again. If he had said more than fifty words the whole of the time they were immured here he would have been surprised!

'If we find the weather promising tomorrow morning, we shall attempt to reach the Iga yashiki but I think the snows will be too deep to take the horses, so the journey will have to be on foot. The fort cannot be more than four or five miles from here and we have already passed the highest point. Toshiaki-san has provided us with small snowshoes, which is just as well, particulary if it freezes hard in the night.'

As he had hoped, the morning dawned frosty and clear. Where the snows had melted, especially over the trackways, and although it lay a foot or two deep, it was frozen hard and often the slopes were almost sheets of ice. After turning the three horses loose in their stable, free to eat the stacked hay which was enough to last them at least two more weeks, Torii Mitsumune and his follower had donned the straw cloaks and tied on their snowshoes and *happaki* leggings and started on their way. At once, Mitsumune realized the worth of these wide shoes made from a curiously shaped frame of bamboo just under a *shaku*, about a foot, wide and secured firmly with twisted cord to their *yukigutsu*, or straw snow footcovers. These wide shoes not only prevented them sinking into the snow drifts but also stopped them sliding on the icy areas. By noon they could see ahead and below them the course of the Nobori river, not wide since it has only just risen from its source in the nearby mountain, but winding like a black thread along the narrow valley until it suddenly disappeared under the great overhanging Oikake Rock.

Keen-eyed, Mitsumune thought he saw a distant glint as if a sparkle of light from a polished yari blade, but he could detect not the slightest sign of movement in the frozen landscape.

'Gunbei-san, did you see anything ahead?' he asked.

'Nothing, master.'

'It may have been close to the Oikake Rock down there . . . I'm probably wrong and it was the sunlight reflecting from one of those famous icicles that drip down from the overhang!'

The lower they came, the more difficult the way through the snow. It was a true saying in these parts that 'it took a strong man to travel more than five miles on a winter's day'. Beside the track at this point stood two typical Echigo farmhouses, one where the roof had partly collapsed under the tremendous weight of snow, but the other standing like a hummock rimmed with black, its shuttered windows and walls clear under the *hisashi* of the roof. Of course, hisashi is the local word for *tanashita*, the eaves, more familiar to those who live on the eastern side of the mountains.

'We shall take a short rest here and eat something from our store,' said Mitsumune, turning his steps towards the first house, gingerly probing the deeper drifts as he left the firmly packed pathway. 'Oi, there! Anyone within?' he called out, but there was no reply. 'Look inside, Gunbei-san, if you please!'

The taciturn man did as he was bid and forced his way under the overhang, first knocking aside three long icicles that threatened to break off and impale the unwary. The Torii warrior watched him pull back the outer shoji then heard his exclamation.

'None here, master, only corpses!'

When Mitsumune reached the doorway and looked inside he understood what Gunbei meant.

The smell that greeted him was of corruption, as great a contrast to the purity of the mountain air as it was possible to get. There were at least ten bodies lying inside and who could tell how many more concealed in the rooms beyond. These poor emaciated people, clearly peasants, had not died of starvation, though; that was very clear. They had been savagely butchered by spear thrusts or arrows .. . and now, with the thaw, came the horrors of decomposition ...

Gasping for fresh air, they both beat a hasty retreat out into the snow and without a further word trudged on towards the looming rock, all thoughts of eating driven far from their minds. It was strange, of course, that the real violence of war should have come to this remote border area and yet no word of any fighting had reached the Torii-ke relatively close by. The fact that these unfortunates and those they had found starved to death at the mountain temple had died some time before, though probably within the last four weeks, preserved by the bitter cold, seemed to point conclusively to a sudden insurrection ... Now Torii Mitsumune began to wish he knew the contents of the package he had been ordered to carry to Abe Uemon-no-jo, but, whatever the contents, if he tampered with the seals it would be more than his life was worth ...

———— 🔲 ————

The old track that led towards the Iga yashiki skirting the turbulent stream took them high above the valley floor and passed under this mighty overhanging cliff, a great boulder famed amongst many redoubtable rocks in Echigo province. Travellers who know about such things say that the Oikake Rock, shaped somewhat like an open fan, is some one-hundred-and-twenty-five feet wide and over a hundred feet in height. The track, passable in those days, narrows beneath the overhang that covers the river below like a roof, so large that it would allow fifty people to easily seat themselves there and still all be sheltered. As the afternoon sunlight lit up the face of the rock, the light struck through the huge icicles that hung down from the lip of the overhang, some almost the full height of that stupendous rock. The melt water that gave birth to these ice spears coursed down at the mercy of capricious winds giving rise to strange and fanciful shapes but the magical fascination of the sight nearly cost Mitsumune his life.

It was fortunate that the trackway following the cliffs just before reaching this rock was practically free of snow and for convenience, the warriors had removed their wide snowshoes though not their straw-woven over-covers. The former were rather tiring to wear over a long period of time and their removal brought some real feelings of relief. There was one advantage of their tramp through the thawing snows and that shortly became manifest as they rounded the last tight bend that would bring them beneath the huge rock.

Facing Mitsumune and blocking the path stood two armoured men!

'You carry a letter, Torii Mitsumune!' shouted out one. 'Hand it over to us now!'

The young man's mind registered many things at that moment and a calmness settled on his spirit; he judged instinctively that these strange samurai stood about twelve feet distant, well over two sword lengths; he knew at once that the man on the inside was older than his companion and more senior in rank and therefore in experience, but that he had left his yari leaning against the rock wall; he realized, too, that the chief danger to him, personally, was Gunbei who hadn't stopped at the first sign of attackers but had moved up close behind him and even now his left thumb was pressing his swordblade loose in his scabbard . . .

'You are mistaken, sirs,' said Mitsumune. 'What makes you think that either I or my companion carry anything of importance. You see, we do not even have our armour. Hardly what you might expect, is it?'

The older man stepped slightly to his right . . .

'Gunbei-san,' said Mitsumune, 'step up beside me, please . . .'

His keen hearing heard the slow slide of his follower's sword being withdrawn . . . an almost imperceptible rasp of the steel blade on the inside of the copper collar that strengthened the mouth of the man's *saya* and, at the same moment a drawing-in of Gunbei's breath . . . In that instant, Mitsumune tossed down his staff to his right where it clattered to the rocky trackway, his left hand drew out his long dirk twisting his left hip, and he stabbed backwards into Gunbei's belly . . . With that unexpected action he had gained a split second advantage of surprise; his longsword flashed out as he leapt in a whirl of speed to cut the armoured man to his right front precisely through the base of his neck, his blade finding with unerring accuracy the finger-breadth gap between the man's neck guard and his *sode*. His victim had not even reached the ground before he turned to deal with the younger man who had recovered enough to raise his sword in preparation to attack. Without a pause, the Torii warrior closed the distance and received the cut on his blade so that the two swords locked together with their *tsuba* entangled.

'Who sent you, assassin?'

The samurai glared at him.

Mitsumune without warning jerked up his hands, slightly spinning the man's balance to his left, and, dropping to a crouch, disengaged his tachi and sliced behind the fellow's right knee . . . The man staggered and fell with a howl of anguish but the swordsman had already twisted round and delivered a strong single-handed cut up under an attack from the stabbed Gunbei, his blade supported by his left hand, finishing him off by cutting back through his left hip so that his treacherous follower fell dying across the hamstrung samurai . . .

'Great Fudō Myō-ō, I am grateful for your assistance,' he murmured as he stepped away from the bodies, his senses sharpened against the danger of further attack, but he was alone.

Sheathing his slung sword, first carefully wiping the streaks of Gunbei's blood from the trenchant blade, he retrieved his dagger and picked up his staff. Time now to find out who these men were and who they served. His treacherous companion was choking out his last breaths but Mitsumune grasped him by the collar of his damp snow vest and pulled him aside. No possible danger would come from him! The older of the strange samurai lay in a widening pool of blood, his head nearly severed. He had died immediately the sword had struck . . . Only the second of the attackers remained a danger, lying on the stony platform, his face contorted with the pain from his slashed hamstrings but still armed. With a deft flick, Mitsumune sent the fellow's sword skating away over the edge to the foaming river below. He placed the end of his stave hard against the man's throat and snatched away his dagger, tossing it after the long sword.

'I have need to know who sent you on this errand?' he asked mildly enough, but hardly expected a reply. 'Well, patience is said to be a good thing. I can wait, I expect!'

He turned the other armoured man's corpse onto his back then bent down and lifted up his left shoulder guard. As expected, there beneath it was a small pocket in the lining where many samurai kept a piece of paper and writing materials, even the odd silver or gold piece, whilst in the field. He felt inside carefully and drew out the dead man's small seal. Breathing on the surface, he pressed it to the corpse's wrist and read the characters.

'So, he was named Iida Naotaka, was he? As you and he bear the same *mon* on your armour, I take it that you serve the Uesugi-ke. Am I correct?'

The wounded samurai still didn't reply which made Mitsumune force him over onto his face and quickly tie back his wrists using the man's own armour cord and secured the longer free end in a slipknot around his prisoner's throat. This being done he sat him up, ignoring the man's groans from the pain of his injured leg.

There were about two hours more of daylight, thought the Torii swordsman; not really enough time for him to walk the rest of the way to the yashiki and looking at the gathering clouds threatening more snow, no possibility of other travellers on this road. He decided that he should find some rocky shelter to spend the night but he would leave the wounded man where he was. Maybe he would talk in the morning . . . if he didn't freeze to death.

———————□———————

He was incorrect in his judgement about further snow but that hardly mattered as he lay reasonably comfortably beside a small watchfire he had managed to build next to the niche he had found near to the further exit from the great overhanging rock. The dead Gunbei's straw snow vest had kept his legs warm and now, as he sat in the cold dawn light eating a rice cake, he felt strengthened and refreshed. Kicking out the fire and making sure that the embers fell into the snow below, Mitsumune strolled slowly over to his wounded prisoner.

'What is your name, fellow?'

The young man looked much the worse for wear after his painful night on the cold roadway.

'My name is Takeo, master . . .'

He could hardly speak through his chattering teeth.

'So, who sent you here?'

'We were sent by one of the Uesugi hatamoto, master . . . Iida-san knew who it was. There is a faction who . . . who . . .'

He faltered.

'Who?' prompted Mitsumune.

'They wanted to force Abe Uemon-sama to change sides . . .'

'Change to whom? Do you know that?'

'Some of the Uesugi are struggling amongst themselves, master . . .' Takeo, if that was his correct name, coughed and gasped for breath as the cord tightened round his throat. 'Lord Kajun is expected here . . . your message was intended to give Lord Uemon-no-jō doubts . . .'

So there was an intrigue; if Uesugi Kajun was supported by a general commander like Abe Uemon, then many would join to fight against the Nagao; if he didn't join then Kajun would lose and the long-standing rebellion would falter . . . Who would win? Difficult to say, but probably the Nagao. And if they won, what real difference would that make? After all, the Nagao-ke were closely related to the Uesugi and had been since the Wars of the Gempei three-hundred-and-fifty years ago . . .

Mitsumune reached a decision. He must go to the Iga yashiki come what may. What should he do with the two corpses and his prisoner, that was the question? The former were easily disposed of by pitching their stiffened carcases over the cliff into the snow bound river below. The wounded man would have to go with him but could only walk with the aid of crutches which the resourceful Mitsumune fashioned out of Gunbei's and his staves. First, he tied one of Gunbei's snow shoes to the samurai's foot then brought him to his good leg.

'Get walking, Takeo-san, and be thankful that you are still alive!'

Shouldering the remainder of the food and taking up Iida Naotaka's yari that he had discarded before the fight, the pair began the slow and, for one, painful struggle the last two miles to the shelter of the yashiki fortress. Torii Mitsumune wondered what fate had in store for him there?

———□———

It was in the middle of the afternoon, in the brilliant late-winter sunshine that gave the Echigo landscape an delicate sublime beauty, that a small party of ashigaru under the direction of a young samurai met the two as they came within sight of the outer yagura tower. Within half-an-hour they were brought before the commander, General Abe Uemon-no-jō.

The general, fully equipped in a black lacquered armour, sat on a folding stool to the rear of the entrance jōdan flanked by two of his officers. Mitsumune and Takeo stood before him, the latter a sorry sight by now.

'So, who are you?' demanded the warrior. 'Men who come through such conditions are either mad or have important business!'

'I am Torii Mitsumune, second son of Torii Munemori, my lord,' said the kenshi, bowing respectfully. 'This man is named Takeo and he is my prisoner!'

'Hmm! That may seem the case to you, Torii-san, but you may both be *my* prisoners, might you not?'

Mitsumune bowed again.

'Quite possibly, my lord, but first I am commanded to give you a sealed message. This was the reason for my difficult journey to this fort. May I take the letter out from its place of concealment?'

It was a prudent request since any movement might have resulted in injury or death at the hands of the general's bodyguard. Receiving assent, he felt inside his inner kimono and withdrew the folded letter still bearing its intact seal, handing it carefully to one of the senior retainers who, in turn, passed it to his master.

'Place mats for Torii-dono and his – er – prisoner. Not too close to each other!'

Uemon-no-jō broke the seal and took out the folded paper inside. He read the contents slowly then looked over the letter at Mitsumune.

'You know what is written here, Torii-dono?' he barked.

'I think I can guess, my lord.'

'Should I do what I am asked, eh?'

'That will be your decision, my lord, but perhaps you should know other factors before you come to your conclusion.'

Uemon-no-jō threw back his head and laughed deeply.

'I know your father, Torii Mitsumune, and I respect his fame as a warrior!' He glanced across at one of the retainers. 'Dress that man's wounds and conduct Torii-dono to my apartments where he may bathe and change into clean clothing! He is to be treated as an honoured guest, you understand!'

———□———

Later that evening, Torii Mitsumune sat with General Uemon-no-jō and two of his hatamoto enjoying some fine tea. The general never drank ō-sake or any other strong liquor, fully understanding the danger of such refreshments at a time when even a momentary inattention could be fatal.

'You know, Torii-dono, that to despatch you as a messenger was a shrewd move. Do you think that my enemies, if they are such, thought that I would act on the instruction to have you killed for your imputed sedition? Or would they feel that I would regard you as a double agent? I wonder? What do you think?'

' "All warfare is based on deception", my lord. Perhaps they thought that if I was killed by you, my father would be warned of the Torii-ke's fate if he didn't join the rebel side. On the other hand, if he kept out of the intrigue within the Uesugi-han, he might prove a strong supporter of your kinsmen.'

Uemon-no-jō pointed at his Councillors with his folded fan.

'We all thought that it would come to something like this, didn't we?'

The two Councillors nodded their heads in agreement.

'Do you think that Uesugi Kajun is behind this intrigue, Torii-dono? We have been cut off here by the deep snows for two months and have no fresh news.'

'All I can say is that Lord Tamenaga was present when the peasants were killed or condemned to starvation when their food stocks were destroyed. It seems that the intention was to cut you off and so force you to the wrong decision.'

'Hmm! I wonder why you were met by those two samurai by the Oikake Rock, and why your retainer was a traitor?'

Mitsumune smiled wryly.

'That was a further deception, my lord; a double bluff!'

They ate the meal served so elegantly in silence, but later Uemon-no-jō asked Mitsumune if he thought his father would join the Nagao side should his kinsmen decide to take power and put an end to the feuding?

'For what my opinion is worth, my lord, I think my father would always take the honourable course. You know that we, too, are related to the Nagao-ke through a marriage contracted just after the end of the Nanbokuchō.'

———□———

Spring came in the late-April of that year and it was reported that a decisive battle took place near to Izumozaki between the Nagao armies and the adherents of Uesugi Akisada, known to many by his Buddhist name, Kajun. The latter was defeated and fled to the Yukōji temple, according to some sources, where he committed *seppuku*. The Nagao-ke under the leadership of Nagao Tamekage, took over the Uesugi lands but wars, uprisings and disturbances continued throughout the Kantō provinces until the middle of the following century. Unity was only achieved eventually when his son, Nagao Terutora, formally adopted the Uesugi name and became the redoubtable Uesugi Kenshin.

All this was far distant in the future when the young Torii kenshi, Mitsumune, finally returned to his home, more determined than ever to request permission from his father to enter a Buddhist monastery and take the tonsure. He daily prayed through that spring for the poor innocent souls of those who had so cruelly lost their lives through starvation and the harshness of war. The memory of his snowbound winter journey prompted him to write a poem that is preserved to this day:

> If one could only show
> Those who long for the spring,
> Promise in the melting snows;
> Green shoots and blossoms
> In the mountain village.

4

RETRIBUTION

▼

Torii Mitsumune had long before renounced the warrior's way of life and taken the tonsure after a period of preparation at his uncle's monastery on Hōraiji-san in Mikawa province. He took the Buddhist name Enshin, and wandered the highways and byways of many provinces devoting his life to ministering to the poor and needy, sometimes spending weeks and even months in the poor farming communities beset by the vicissitudes of life in these troubled times. Eventually, he received word from his home that he should return, a message that finally reached him through the diligent searching of a former servant of the Torii-ke, a carpenter named Toshiaki. From this moment Toshiaki insisted on accompanying Enshin and never regarded him other than his master, a man of high warrior rank, which indeed he was.

Now Enshin was once given a water-buffalo in recompense for curing a whole village of some deadly malady and this ox, named Kuroi-san (which means, broadly speaking, 'Mr Black') had also become Enshin's companion and confidant, carrying his master on his slow travels at a pace that allowed the priest to converse at everyone's ease with people of all estates, high or low, since a poor priest seated upon the back of an ox could hardly present a threat.

Everything the three wanderers experienced was noted down by Enshin and the notes placed in his somewhat battered wallet. He was a man who had just one vice, an insatiable thirst for knowledge.

It was in this first year of the Tembun era that Enshin had resolved to visit the great mountains of Kumano for no other reason, perhaps, than a certain curiosity aroused by his delving into the Torii-ke annals and the story he had once heard of a Torii ancestor, the lady Terute-hime, who had trodden those paths some hundred-and-thirty years before. It was a long and sometimes difficult road that the three followed and, sometimes, time hung heavily on their hands when they were forced to remain for several days in some poor hamlet or other. On one of these occasions Toshiaki, who had idly been tossing some flat pebbles across the placid Kumano river, turned to his master and asked if he would like to hear an odd thing he had heard whilst searching for Enshin five years before. It was high summer and the rainy season was finished. Even amongst these soaring heights the heat was oppressive but, as the long evening drew on, it was very pleasant by these waters.

'Certainly I would like to hear your story, Toshiaki-san, provided you cast no more of those stones so that I can begin to charm a fish or two onto my hook for our supper. What do you say, Kuroi-san; you would like to hear it, too?'

The ox settled himself onto the grassy turf as he placidly raised his ponderous head in evident assent.

———— ☐ ————

'I think I was somewhere in Bizen ... the northern part ... because I was intending to try and find a priest I had heard of who lived near Daisen ... yes, that's right. One day, while I had been a couple or four days doing some repairs at a shrine, for which I was paid with food and shelter, I took an early morning walk down by the river that passed by the hamlet ... not quite as wide as this one, of course, though deep ... when I came on an old man hurrying along towards the village and in some sort of a nervous state, too. On his back he had a crude frame to which were tied a number of trimmed brushwood branches; they were not very well-secured since some of them fell out as he stumbled towards me. Some distance behind him trotted a largish dog and as I watched, the man shouted out at the animal to go away and leave him, but the dog took no notice at all.

'Quite evidently he was beside himself because of something he had seen or done but not because of the dog, since he used the animal's name as he threw stones to deter him. Soon the fellow reached me.

' "What's the matter with you, grandfather?" said I, picking up the last of his sticks to tumble down and handing it to him. "You're in a bit of a hurry, and you're losing all your wood, you know?"

' "It's my dog . . ." he puffed, chest heaving, "he's . . . he's . . ."

' "He's what?"

' "He's . . ."

'At that moment, the dog bounded up and dropped something at his master's feet. The old woodcutter jumped back, his face a mask of horror . . . missed his footing and began to slide on his face down towards the river, He'd have fallen in, master, if I hadn't grabbed his arm and managed to haul him up. It was then I looked at what the dog had dropped and saw it was a human hand!'

Enshin had been listening to his companion's story whilst he cast his fishing line as far out as he could towards where he had just seen some ripples indicating that a fish had come up to take an insect, but now he glanced across at Toshiaki.

'A hand?'

'That's right, master; it was a hairy hand that I saw at once had been severed just above the wrist. A right hand.'

' "Where did your dog find that?" I asked.

' "We were round that bend, master, down where the ferryman takes people across the river, an' I had just tied another stick to my rack 'ere when I chucked a stone into the river, it bein' shallow jus' there . . . In 'e went with a great splash while I looked about for to see old Jubei, the ferryman, 'cos we go back a long way, but 'e weren't to be seen . . . nor 'is boat, neither."

'The old fellow paused and wiped his runny nose with the back of his hand. "Just then," he continued, "that dog comes out and shakes 'imself all over me legs . . . and I sees 'e 'as *that* in his jaws! I just took to me heels and ran!" '

'So, what did you do?' Enshin enquired.

'I told the old fool to keep his mouth shut while I went back along the riverbank to take a look. Oh, and I asked him his name which he said was Hanzō. The hand, whilst wet, looked very fresh to me when I turned it over with my staff.'

'Was leaving him there well advised, Toshiaki-san?'

'Perhaps not, master, but I needed to find the ferryman as I wanted to cross that river on my way to Daisen. Anyway, along I went and found the place where the old man had dropped some of his wood and the dog had come out of the water. It was easy to recognize because of the trampled grass . . . and a few drops of blood. There was nothing else to be seen so I walked on to where the track took me through a copse overhanging the river. Just beyond there I saw the ferryboat, its line caught up in a fallen branch. Luckily it had snagged or it would have drifted on to where the river plunged through some rapids.'

Enshin held up his hand.

'Hold on a moment, my friend; I believe we are in luck . . .'

Sure enough, a large fish had taken Enshin's worm bait but looked like breaking away after quite a spirited fight when Toshiaki waded in and grabbed it, triumphantly carrying it ashore.

'We shall eat well to-night, master!'

'I'm intrigued by your story. Carry on with it while we see if we can catch another to feed us tomorrow.'

'Where did I get to . . ? Oh, yes! Well, I managed to get hold of the painter by hoicking it up with a forked stick, but found no fer-ryman, only a longsword lying in the bottom.'

'A longsword? A katana?'

'Aye, and its *saya*, oddly enough; not inside it, mind you.'

'The sword was lying loose, eh? That's odd? Were there any signs of a fight?'

'None, master; that's just it. Anyway, I managed to get into the ferry and poled it back upstream to its mooring place where I tied it up securely. Then I thought I would look at the sword.'

'And?'

'I could see at once that it was a good one but as I'm only a hum-ble carpenter, how am I to know how to appraise a blade?'

Enshin smiled to himself. He knew full well that Toshiaki was a fine craftsman with wood and had made several excellent white-wood *saya* and *tsuka* for one or two of the senior *hatamoto* back in Kusatsu. When he made such beautiful mounts he had every oppor-tunity of studying valuable blades. And didn't he often work for the Norishige family, the Torii clan swordsmith back in Kōzuke?

'I take it you looked at the blade . . . and its mounts. Come on, Toshiaki-san, I've known you long enough to know that you are trying to fool me . . . We grew up as lads together; I know you too well!'

'You've got another bite, master . . .'

'Let the fish tire itself out! Now, the truth!'

Toshiaki untied his wide straw jingasa and wiped his brow on his hand-towel, smiling broadly. He bowed to the priest.

'I didn't look at the sword until I got back to the village, and having first taken off its tsuba and cleaning away some mottled himo threads, bluish-brown they were, I wrapped the blade in some clothing so that no one would know I had it. Back at the shrine I went to my quarters and hid the sword under a loose floorboard then went to the only drinking house there was and called for some ō-sake. The old woodcutter, Hanzō, sat in one corner and it was clear from everyone else's behaviour that he hadn't said a word. Anyway, after a while I got up and went over to him, taking a sake jar with me.

' "Got over your shock, eh?" I asked, but I knew at once he was still too upset or afraid to talk. In fact, I realized that it was the latter. He remained rather taciturn and eventually muttered something to the effect that he couldn't say anything about whatever it was, or more. He was afraid for his sick wife. Anyway, he tailed off and abruptly left the tavern.

'The next day, I casually asked my priest at the shrine if the ferry I'd heard about was still working or was the river low enough to ford at some place when I felt it was time to leave. He told me that it was all over the village that Jubei, the ferryman, hadn't been seen though his boat was moored where it should be. Three samurai had been held up on the further bank but had given up hailing for the wretch and cast about until they were lucky enough to find the shallows below the falls downstream. Not very pleased, they were, at the delay. It was evening before I finished that day's work up in the roof of the *haiden*, the light too gloomy to look at any blade, so off I went again down to that tavern . . .'

'That fish will be done nicely, master, I reckons . . .'

So it was and very tasty, too, in the velvety mountain air. Enshin thought that he must be careful not to be lulled into liking this life of wandering!

'I sat in the same alcove, at peace with the whole world if it wasn't for the memory of that lonely forearm and hand. There was something that slightly nagged in the back of my mind, master, but for the life of me I couldn't place it . . ?

'The three samurai that the priest had spoken of sat behind the partition near to where I was and I could hear just about everything they said even though they weren't talking loud . . . On the contrary, if I leant back, which I did, I could make out their whispering . . .'

Toshiaki paused to pick out a couple of bones from his back teeth. He looked at his master in a conspiratorial way, clearly savouring the suspense.

'Well . . ?'

'I gathered that they had been following someone they didn't name, who had something of theirs . . .'

'The sword, perhaps?' prompted Enshin.

'Didn't say, master, but they did mention going to the nearby yashiki that defended the path I had come along from the Makabe domain. I had no problem at the barrier alongside since I carried a passport from Kōzuke. I did gather, though, that all three were rōnin and from their accents I guessed they came from Higo or even Satsuma.'

'A long way from Kyūshū, wasn't it? Remote, too!'

'You could say that, master. This place was in the far depths of the country, alright. Could be described as "*inaka*", "in the sticks"! There was one thing, though, that made me prick up my ears . . . One of the three, at least, was an instructor in kenjutsu, and the others seemed to treat him with some deference.

'At that point, old Hanzō came in, seemingly in a better frame of mind, and came over to join me after some banter with two of his cronies watching a group of gamblers . . . dice game, master, and not for me!

'After a jar or two of the rice wine, I leant across to whisper in Hanzō's ear: "What did you do with that . . . er . . . relic?" The sweat started out on his brow but he managed to reply that he had tied a stone to it and dropped it in a pool where the river never dried out in summer. It wouldn't be found, he reckoned. His hand was shaking as he lifted the next dish of ō-sake . . . A little later, the three samurai got up to go and the moment old Hanzō caught a glimpse of them, his face turned ashen, even in that bad light I could see his fear, and he had to stoop down in case he was seen.

'As I was going to leave, I asked the old fellow if he wanted to give me a hand up at the shrine on the morrow; it would earn him a few coppers if he did, and he agreed.

'The next morning, having squared it with the gūji, I had Hanzo helping me pull up some of the lighter scantling I needed to repair the corner supports of the roof. No one came to the shrine in the early mornings, not that I'd noticed, so I asks him why those sam'rai had upset him so? Perhaps he felt he could talk better at the shrine with only the gods to hear, and in any case, I knew about the "hand"; it was "our" secret, so to say. He told me that he had been cutting wood a week before on a mountain about three miles further downstream but had stopped chopping about noon in order to prepare a number of bundles ready for carrying back to his house. Stock-in-trade . . . He had sat down to eat a rice ball and have a drink when he saw two samurai down on the river bank not five yards away from where he lay behind a pile of boulders. He was hidden by the underbrush so they hadn't seen him. Prudently, he kept very still . . . The two were clearly arguing and eventually Hanzō understood their quarrel was over the relative merits of their sword traditions. Like many of these . . . er . . . gentlemen, they eventually came to blows, or, in this case, tested their arguments with their wooden swords. Hummph, 'tis common enough a sight so old Hanzo knew what he was seeing, alright.

'It was all over in a few seconds, such fights usually are, and one of the two sat on the ground nursing a split head; Hanzo could see the blood flowing down. The other man stood over him demanding to know if "the sword was up at the yashiki"? When the defeated man made some reply, he was struck again on the shoulder, the victor yelling angrily that he needed to know.

'In the end, this rōnin . . . "he was the one I saw at the tavern", says Hanzō, kicked his opponent to his feet and tells him to get back to the yashiki and tell the swordmaster there that "the man who did this demands a match". The rōnin goes off one way and the beaten sam'rai goes upstream. Well, Hanzō waited some minutes before following on, and sees this bleeding sam'rai stop at the ferry and talk with Jubei. He wasn't close enough to hear what was said but Jubei poles off across the river and the sam'rai goes on after rinsing off some of the dried blood in the river.

'After Hanzō had gone, happy with his pay, I went to my room and took out the sword. After cleaning it carefully, I looked closely at the blade and realized at once that it was of high quality. It was a good long tachi, strongly curved, and certainly not a sword to be found lying out of its saya in the bottom of a common ferry punt!'

'Did the blade bear a signature, Toshiaki-san?' asked Enshin.

'You know I can't read those sort of characters, master . . . so I copied them down carefully to show to the old gūji, who I judged I could trust.'

'Could you?'

'I'll come to that later, master. First, I examined the *tsuba* and the other mounts and saw that they, too, were of high quality The tsuba, in particular, was really interesting; the sort you'd like, master. Plain iron guard was finished off with almost crude hammer marks but giving a beautiful surface and pierced with a bold wild boar . . .'

Enshin came to his feet and kicked some of the sand onto their little fire.

'Time we went back to the inn, Kuroi-san. Doubtless you are ready for some hay?' He looked across at the carpenter. 'The tsuba had an *inoshishi*, did it? Unusual, that? One would expect it to belong to a swordsman, one who follows the old paths! It was a good one, as tsuba go, my friend?'

'It complemented the blade. The fittings were plain but the little *menuki* tightening the hilt binding each showed a pair of charging boars, an' I reckoned that was notable, master. They went well with the tsuba.'

'Did you show the signature characters to the priest?' asked Enshin as they started back towards the inn.

'Oh, yes. He seemed a bit surprised but didn't make any comment when I said it was from something I had seen on my travels way back in Nara. The characters read: "*Bishu Osafune-no-ju Kagemitsu*", master.'

Enshin turned this information over in his mind for a while.

'What did you do then?'

'I chipped out a slot in a wide split piece of old bamboo trunk and put the blade inside, packed so it wouldn't rattle about, then bound up the shaped handle so that the bamboo looked like a heavy practice sword, the tsuba I sewed to the underneath of the saddle cantle where it would never be found except during a really thorough search. The rest still lie hidden up in the roof of that shrine.'

'I never thought you so cunning!' laughed Enshin.

'Prudence, master; simply being careful!'

They both grinned but it was certainly true that such precautions often meant the difference between life and death. After they reached the little inn and Kuroi-san was comfortably bedded in the corner of the stable, Toshiaki continued with his story.

'The next day I dressed in my cleanest kimono and *sashinuki-bakama*, my only good things, of course, master, and took the road to the yashiki. At the gateway I told the two guards that I was a master-carpenter and sought work repairing sword scabbards and the like. Well, I wasn't going to get very far without a proper introduction but it so happened that a senior retainer was just inside and pricked his ears up at what I had said. In short, I was ordered inside and taken through the outer courtyard and along beneath the plastered inner palisades to an inner back gateway leading to the practice yard. There, I was told to wait, so I sat myself down on a side step, straw hat in hand, and watched the sword practice.

'It hadn't been going on for more than an hour when I was summoned to the verandah of an adjoining building and bowed low before another senior samurai, this time wearing *kamishiho* as befitted his rank. While I remained bowing, my eyes to the ground before my hands, he asked who I had served and several other questions before pronouncing himself satisfied to an associate. A lackey was summoned and I was ordered to sit up and look at a fine *shirazaya* placed on a low plain table before me. I noticed at once a split in the side of the scabbard and pointed it out when asked.

' "Can you repair that?" the senior officer demanded.

' "May I pick up the shirazaya, master?" I asked.

'The samurai nodded and I found to my surprise that it contained only a wooden blade, not a steel one. A label lightly secured to the saya was brushed with the same characters as the blade I had concealed! There was no doubt about it. My surprise must have shown but was interpreted as being caused by the absence of the live blade for which the shirazaya was made.

' "You must work with the *hinoki* wood blade! Start straight away! You are employed!" I was told.

' "It is usual, master, to be permitted to do such precise joinery with the real sword to hand."

' "It is not possible!!"

'Having made this statement, the senior retainer rose to his feet and left, leaving me bowing low once again.

'I was shown to a place where I could work, clearly where a predecessor had exercised similar skills, and this small open workshop overlooked the practice yard, too.

'When I was working the following morning, for I realized I would have to remake the entire scabbard and began by selecting a suitable piece of wood from the many lengths stored on racks at the side, practice had already commenced in the yard and the air was filled with the familiar sound of hardwood on hardwood as the bokken were blocked or countered. Finding what I wanted, I sat down on the round mat and began measuring up when I saw out of the corner of my eye that the senior of the three rōnin had been brought to the yard.'

Enshin nodded his head.

'I wondered when he would come into the story again?'

'At length, he appeared to have been invited to have a bout with one of the students and stood up after first removing his outer coat and his *katana*. He tied back his sleeves with what seemed to be a braid *tasuke* and hefted his bokuto. In my humble judgement, master, he looked very strong; and so he proved, despatching in short order three of the fortress's swordsmen with about as many blows. At length, after some hesitancy, one of the senior *deshi* was called forward but fared little better; well, he lasted about five cuts before he was pitched almost bodily into the edge of my platform, his right fore arm broken by a severe strike above the wrist.

'Just then there came a shout and the proceedings were halted and the injured man helped away. Moments later, I was summoned by a footsoldier to attend on my master. Not knowing who I served, I followed and motioned to sit on the verandah of one of the inner buildings. Sitting in the open was old Hanzō and in front of him lay a corpse that had clearly been fished out of the river.

' "Hanzō! Is this the ferryman, Jubei?" demanded the senior retainer.

'Poor Hanzō was almost speechless with fear. He could hardly squeak out: "*Hai!*" as he bowed into the dust.

' "Did you kill him?"

' "I couldn't do such a thing, sir!"

' "He was hit behind his skull before he went into the water . . . You did it, didn't you?"

' "Master, I swear to you, I couldn't . . . Jubei was my brother-in-law, sir; I . . . I couldn't do such a terrible thing, sir . . ."

'An ashigaru sitting as guard just behind the unfortunate wood-cutter fetched him a great blow with the lower end of his spear that completely winded the decrepit old fellow who now gasped for air like some great fish out of water.

' "Did you steal the sword?" said his interrogator.

' "What sword, master? I . . . I heard that a sword was missing but I haven't seen one . . ."

' "Answer properly, filth!" hissed the guard, again striking the old man.

' "Honoured master, I know nothing more . . . The missing sword, why, 'tis common knowledge in the village . . ."

' "He knows nothing!" said the senior retainer. "Send him away!"

'One of the yashiki samurai sat forwards, bowing low.

' "Sir, the visiting kenshi requests a match with Omura-sensei."

' "He does, does he? Permission refused . . ! No, wait! I've changed my mind! We shall hold the match in one hour's time. What is this man's name and what clan?"

' "He announced he is named Harada, master, Harada Saburō, and is a rōnin."

' "Did he claim to belong to a sword tradition?"

' "He said he practised the Kage-no-ryū, sir."

' "Is that so?"

' "You are dismissed . . . One hour's time!"

' "Master!" '

----□----

'A number of retainers were permitted to watch the match and a line of them commandeered my work platform as a viewing point. Just out of sight, in the shade of the practice hall roof, I understood the lord of that yashiki, Hata Mimasaka-no-suke, who was the brother of the clan lord, himself, came to observe.'

'Excuse me breaking in on your story, Toshiaki-san, but didn't you practise in the Kusatsu heihō-jō? Do I not remember correctly?'

'Just a bit, master . . .'

'For twelve or more years, just like me! Just a little bit, eh?'

'Shall I continue, master?'

Enshin nodded slightly.

'This Harada Saburō came into view swinging a heavy bokken all about him then the yashiki master-at-arms, Ōe Jiroemon I was told, appeared at the further end of the yard. They took up their positions some twenty feet apart, I suppose, and bowed towards the hidden

Hata Mimasaka-no-suke, then to each other. Both knelt down on
one knee, their swords lying straight out ahead of them, and tied
back their deep kimono sleeves. They bowed again, one hand to the
ground, fingers extended, then came to their feet, sword in hand.
Before the drum beat out the order to begin, Harada Saburō held
up his right hand and in a loud voice demanded the right that live
blades should be used rather than the lesser wooden ones.
     ' "The outcome will be just as clear, Harada-sama; live or wooden
blade! In this yashiki all matches are held with wooden blades!"
     ' "It is not for the warrior to fight with toy swords!" pressed the
rōnin.
     ' "Toy swords, as you put it, or not; it is the law of this clan!"
     'Harada bowed slightly and shrugged. I could sense that the watch-
ing samurai were not enamoured of his rather arrogant attitude, but
I suppose it's not for me to make any comment . . .'
     Enshin smiled. He knew Toshiaki for a shrewd man who would
not approve of such boorishness, either.
     'The moment Ōe Jiroemon took his first posture, a rather wide
right in-no-kamae, and Harada took a one-handed open low position, I judged they would be evenly matched . . . huh! I was right
at that! The Hata swordsman was wily and moved with care to his
left while Harada-sama watched him like a hawk. It was the former
who attacked first, beating down with his bokuto three times one-
handed to strike the hard ground before whirling the sword round
in a great cutting arc at knee height, which almost caught Harada
unawares. He jumped back to avoid the cut and struck back . . .
The oak swords clashed together, Harada's a two-handed cut whilst
Ōe's blade was horizontal protecting his forehead, grasped by one
hand with his left palm supporting the blade . . . and keeping the
pressure on it so that it would be difficult for Harada to disengage.
For a moment they held this locked position then, amazingly, Ōe
Jiroemon tossed up the other's blade and whirled his sword down
and across his opponent's belly to the right . . . but Harada was
ready and arched his hips back and his shoulders forwards so that
the reaping blade didn't touch . . . But it was very, very close, I can
tell you, master; just a whisker away . . . Harada struck downwards
hard; so forcefully, in fact, that he also hit the ground, which was an
error since his opponent was able to strike at his forearm. Harada
was like lightning since the cut missed when he snatched his hand
away. They both drew back for a moment, then rushed in like lions
cutting at the other's head. The heavy bokken clashed and I think
everyone thought one had struck home but the drum beat and the
senior samurai, whose name I didn't know yet, announced that the
match was over and was a draw. That was a fair decision since both

men had a smear of blood on their foreheads and it was clear that both thought they had been cut in that fierce attack.'

'It was what is termed "*ai-uchi*", eh?' said Enshin.

'It was a very close call, master.' agreed Toshiaki. 'The rōnin, Harada-san, was not a happy man at that decision, but he didn't say anything at the time, even receiving praise from the appreciative Ōe Jiroemon. He was invited to remain but declined and was escorted from the yashiki.

'Nothing more was said about the dead Jubei or the stolen sword, which made me wonder why I had been called to observe Hanzo's questioning. Anyway, as evening drew on, I also made my way back to the shrine. It went through my mind that I might be suspected of complicity as I was a relative stranger and that sooner or later some-one would mention that I knew Hanzō and had enquired about the ferry. That would be enough to arrest me for questioning and one thing would lead to another . . . So, later that evening, following my usual custom I walked down to the tavern taking with me the sword fittings and the hidden blade in the bamboo suburi-bokutō. Going round to the stables I found the rōnins' horses in their byre and hid everything under some hay piled up in the corner. Then I went round to the front and called for ō-sake. Of course, everyone knew I had found a new job which made me rather popular and the wine flowed freely. I took care of that, but not too much to be obvious.

'Just before I thought it time to leave, the swordsman, Harada, came in and demanded wine. His two confederates joined him and that attracted two of the serving girls. The swordsman saw me and called out to bring me over. When I sat down, he asked if I thought he had won the match. At his words a silence fell as everyone waited for my reply. I had to be careful, of course, so I said that while I knew very little about the *bugei*, his attack and defence seemed the more subtle . . . which I could only offer as making him my favourite had I been a gambling man. That seemed to satisfy him and he sent me away with another jar of ō-sake which I contrived to knock over when I sat down out of their sight.'

The moon was rising and Enshin yawned. 'Can you finish your story in the morning, Toshiaki-san; it's late and the mountain air is strong.'

———□———

The following morning, their innkeeper announced that he had heard that the way south had been re-opened. It was an earth tremor that had blocked the road with boulders somewhere just south of Totsukawa. A couple of samurai had told the village headman that

they had just come through from there . . . Enshin paid for their
keep but it was only a fraction of what a traveller might expect since
he had spent a lot of the time curing anyone who needed his skills.
As his black ox ambled slowly down the dusty track that sometimes
veered onto the shingle banks of the Shinano river, the priest sat
on Kuroi-san's haunches holding up a paper umbrella to shade him
from the strong morning sun. Toshiaki walked alongside wearing his
wide flattened straw hat, his legs naked since this was going to be
a scorcher of a day, without any doubt. Because of the heat, Enshin
had devised a straw hat for Kuroi-san, secured to his noble head
just like any jingasa, but with hanging fringes to deter troublesome
horse-flies.

'So, you had reached the point where you were in the tavern on
the evening after the match. It is getting interesting, Toshiaki-san, so
please continue.'

'Indeed, master; now things began to happen . . . we were all sitting there, some gambling at the dice . . . there didn't seem to be
any criminal element running this . . . some making merry with the
one or two women who always frequent such places, the three rōnin
weren't throwing their weight around, and the rest of us talked about
everything that farmers and odd-job men always do . . . when we
heard horses galloping down the street and the *shoji* were abruptly
thrown back by two samurai from the yashiki backed by three or
four *yari-mochi*.

'One of the samurai . . . they were all wearing armour, by the
way . . . glared around him then shouted out that the immediate
border *seki* had been closed and that everyone was to get out into
the street! To reinforce his words the yari-mochi levelled their spears
and began to freely use the butts in the manner that footsoldiers do
when they are given the slightest authority.

'Only the three rōnin remained inside when the rest of us unceremoniously fell out into the street, one or two considerably the worse
for drink. I noticed that one of the two samurai remained inside.
At this point, the street widened and in this space crowded the whole
of the villagers, or so I thought; the scene lit by flaring torches held
up by the footsoldiers.

' "Our lord has lost a treasure!" bawled a man in full armour sitting astride a war-horse. He waved his riding cane. "Every house
will be searched; every person here will be considered guilty until
this treasure is recovered! The borders are closed!" He turned in the
saddle and shouted for the search to begin.

'Well, master, I could see quite well that these soldiers had already
set about their task with relish to judge by numbers of weeping
womenfolk from the yashiki side of the village. On all sides we could

hear the sounds of breaking partitions, falling shoji, floorboards being prized up; in short, the brutal ashigaru at his favourite pastime . . .

'One of the drunken peasants staggered about waving a sake jar then was violently ill against the mounted man's horse flanks.

' "Idiot! Look what you are about!"

'The man looked up, swaying unsteadily; "You're lookin' . . . for that there sword, ain't yer?" His face was vacuous and vomit mixed with spittle glistened all down his front. "Jus' you ask that there gūji up o' th' shrine . . . jus' ask 'im . . ."

'One of the ashigaru swung his spear butt round and fetched the drunk a crushing blow to the side of his head, felling him under the trampling hooves.

' "*Baka!*", bellowed the samurai, lashing the soldier viciously about his head and shoulders. "Arrest this man at once!"

' "Open up, there! Open up! Clear a space!"

'I could see in the light of the torches a small group of spearmen dragging something or someone through the terrified crowd. They flung down their captive and, of course, it was the unfortunate woodcutter, Hanzō, who was bleeding heavily from two deep cuts to his head. His hands were bound in front of him, too.

'The leader of the samurai who had entered the tavern walked over and kicked the wretched man hard.

' "You know more than you claim, wretch! Out with it now or it will be the worse for you!"

'Hanzō groaned and tried to shake the flow of blood from his right eye.

' "I don't know anything about the sword, master; nothin' at all . . .!"

' "We think you do!"

'The samurai pointed to one of the ashigaru and the soldier began beating poor Hanzō with a billet of wood until the old fellow curled in a whimpering huddle on the ground.

' "Tell us! Was it the gūji? He's been named . . . Was he your accomplice?"

'Just then the priest was dragged down into the torchlight and I thought at once that it would be my turn next once he told the samurai about the characters he had read for me . . . "Time for a diversion," I says to myself, and what better than the tactic of raising fire . . . So I melted back through the crowd into the deep shadow of the side alley that ran beside the tavern, and in no time set a discarded torch that had nearly burnt out to the straw thatch of the adjoining house. The thatch was tinder dry and flared up at once, the flames hungrily running along the underpart and taking hold . . . By that time I was well away to the further side and rejoined the crowd.'

Enshin merely grunted but said nothing.

'I was now the other side from where the fire was taking hold and just as some of the soldiers were about to lay into the priest some-one saw the first flames and bellowed out the alarm ... "FIRE!" ... "FIRE" ... and panic took hold ...

'In the mêlée that ensued, and as I said it was a relatively con-stricted street, it was quite easy to evade the Hata soldiers but first I took the risk of grabbing the old man and hauling him to the side of the nearest house where I cut him free and rushed him across the narrow rice paddy at the rear. Dogs were barking, the samurai roaring, the villagers crying out in desperation and fear ... perfect cover to make our escape round and down to the river bank. I sat old Hanzō down knowing that in his state he wasn't likely to wan-der off, and went back at a run to see if I could find the gūji if he hadn't been dragged off ... Well, I was in luck, he was standing, quite bemused and wringing his hands, gazing at the conflagration that had now caught hold of the tavern and, in the breeze, sparks threat-ened the roof of a third building on the opposite side of the street. By now, also, the horses of the several samurai and those of the three rōnin were screaming out in fear and the swirling smoke added to the chaos ... Fire, master, is a great weapon when used well ...'

'Now, I wonder where a mere carpenter learnt that?' Enshin observed, dryly.

'Er, master, it was you, yourself, who gave me this teaching, long ago ...'

'The bad old days, eh?'

'It depends on one's viewpoint, master.'

'You rescued the gūji, then?'

'Yes, I had no problem with that part at all. It took only a short while to find Hanzō and between the priest and myself we took him past the ferry place and up a mountain track to where he had a crude shelter built partly into a sort of cave; he wasn't so far gone as all that though he had taken nasty blows for someone so old.

' "Look," I said to the priest, "the Hata will be looking for both of you over this sword business but not for me. I suggest that you both stay hidden in here for a few days and I'll bring you food. Keep in here and you'll be safe. Either this matter will resolve itself and be forgotten or I'll get you across the border."

'The gūji agreed while Hanzō merely groaned. I dressed his head as best I could then slipped down to the river to fill a gourd with water. I could see the flames from the village lighting up the further mountainside. After giving them the water gourd, I ran back to the the fires and joined the crowd. One thing I was glad to see was that the stables behind the gutted tavern had escaped which meant, of course, that the sword was alright.

'The following morning, I shouldered a bag with a couple more of my tools, and walked down through the smoking ruins . . . four houses had been lost besides the tavern . . . and presented myself to the guards on the yashiki gateway.

' "Back to work, eh?" grinned one. "That was exciting last night, wasn't it?"

The other guard spat over into the deep dry ditch. "Captain Mototada was like a bear with a sore head when he came back . . . Lost 'is suspects, 'e did!"

' "Here, careful and keep your voice down . . . Idiot! He'll 'ave the hide off your back if he hears you speak familiar like that!"

' "Was true, wasn't it?"

' "Aye, true enough, but 'e flogged that stupid fool, Toto, fer 'itting old Hanzō with 'is yari butt."

' "They were looking for a sword, I heard," said I. "Did they find it?"

'The first guard looked at me and shook his head. "You go on in, carpenter, and keep yer mouth shut. They'll all be on edge this morning, I'd say."

'At the guardhouse a lackey escorted me to my work platform and I got down to shaping the block of *hinoki* wood that I had sawn down the day before. Even here there was the occasional smell of woodsmoke from the burnt out houses up the road. The day was cloudy and it threatened to rain, the clouds hanging thick between the mountains so that no ridges could be seen. The young samurai being exercised in the yard got on with going through their forms, cowed, I suspect, by the grim face of their instructor, a hard-looking man with the remarkably brawny forearms of many swordsmen who have come up the hard way . . .'

Enshin smiled slightly at that observation by Toshiaki, looking at his own thickened wrists. Practice was often brutally hard under the Torii bugeisha, he recalled! The carpenter continued . . .

'It was while I watched these youngsters put through their paces, when it struck me that the severed forearm that Hanzō's dog had retrieved from the river was that of a swordsman. Not only that, but it had belonged to a man who hadn't done hard manual work before; the fingers were smooth and there were no *mame* when I had poked open the palm . . . It was the arm of a samurai, no doubt!

'Although I was seen, no one bothered me all day, but as I was sweeping up and putting my work aside before leaving, a servant girl brought me a cloth which she said contained some vegetables and rice balls, the gift of the under-steward. I trudged back to the shrine to clean up. No bathhouse for me that night, I ate a rice ball, then wandered down to the village, or what was left of it, with some food in a wallet tied across my back. Peasants being what they are, some enterprising storekeeper had rented out his shop front to the tavern keeper . . . knowing the sort, he was probably an uncle or cousin or something . . . and the place was half-full just as before. Every single conversation was about the lost sword and the fact that the old dod-derer, Hanzō, and the gūji were missing . . . Run off through fear, though no one thought either had the slightest bit more knowledge about the affair than any of them. It was all a complete mystery so far as these downtrodden villagers were concerned.

'A couple of new faces were amongst the gamblers and anyone with half-an-eye could see that they were foot soldiers sent along from the yashiki in old grubby clothing to keep their eyes and ears open as spies.

' "Border's still closed, then, Magobei?" called out someone to a decrepit bent farmer who lived somewhere down that way.

' "Oh, aye; barrier's closed off!" he agreed.

' "No one's seen the ferryman, 'ave they?"

' "Not one hide or hair, you old fool. If we 'ad, we'd 'ave told you like ev'ryone else . . . We'd all 'ave 'eard!"

' "He was found, I 'eared," I piped up.

'Everyone looked at me in surprise but just then as I was on my second jar of o-sake, master, when two of those rōnin came noisily in but without the one named Harada. It was clear that one of them had been drinking heavily, too; anyway they sat just near me deep in some conversation that I couldn't quite catch. The one worse for drink sud-denly jumped up and hissed loud enough for me to hear that he thought "Saburō" was about to cheat them and . . . but his companion pulled him down and handed him a full cup before he could say more. By "Saburō" I supposed he meant Harada, their leader . . .

'Soon, I went outside to piss in the ditch, then carefully went round to the old tavern's stables where the three kept their horses. Only two were there, the other gone. I checked under the straw that the sword was still there then went back to wait and see where the two rōnin would go. When they came out, the one was so drunk that he had almost to be carried back to the nearby house where they were staying.'

Toshiaki sighed and scratched the side of his nostrils.

'To cut a long story short, master, I had an idea that this swordsman, Harada Saburō, had something to do with the lost ferryman, Jubei, and the missing sword, but I couldn't for the life of me think what. Making sure that I wasn't seen, I crept off down to the river and within the hour delivered the food to my hidden pair, glad to find Hanzō recovered. Next morning I was back at the yashiki at my work.

'About noon, out comes the sensei, Ōe Jiroemon, and walks across to me. No one else was there, you understand.

' "What do you think of that wooden blade, Master Joiner?" he says, sitting himself down on the edge of the stoop and carefully picking it up from the padded stand I had fashioned on the first day.

' "It is a fine piece of work, master," I replied.

' "It is a fine sword that it represents! Do you know who the original was made by?"

' "There is a label on the saya, master, but I cannot read the *kanji*. From the shape of the wooden replica you are holding, sir, I would guess that the sword was made by a Bizen master . . ."

'Ōe-sensei looked closely at the "blade" and along its curve. "Hmmm!" he said, evidently preoccupied with something. He watched me carefully chiselling along the lines I had delicately scribed on the inside face of one of the billets then put the "blade" back on its stand. "I can see by your wrists that carpentry produces forearms that closely resemble those of bugeisha. Do you think that is true, Master Joiner?"

' "It could be, master, but that is beyond my knowledge . . ."

' "But you know about swords, don't you?"

' "Very little, sensei; only what I have seen during my work for my former masters."

' "That was in Kōzuke-no-kuni, wasn't it?"

' "True, sensei . . ."

' "The Torii-ke were your employers?"

'I wondered where all this was leading as he asked me a whole lot more. Finally, he said: "The Torii-ke were trained in the Oda-ryū, were they not?"

'Perhaps I showed a tiny bit of surprise, I don't know, but he got up at this point, gave me a slight bow . . . totally unexpected since I was a mere lowly minion . . . and went off back to his dōjō.'

'There was nothing more?' Enshin asked. 'It was unusual that he should ask about my family but, then, he could have travelled the provinces earlier in his career.'

Toshiaki brushed a persistant fly aside. 'Shall we rest, master? I'm sure that Kuroi-san would appreciate some fresh grass and you the shade.'

They settled down at a wayside stall, served a refreshing cool drink by an old crone; the ox contentedly grazing beside the tall bamboo grove.

'The sun was sinking when I left the yashiki and returned to the shrine. I had just checked my horse and given it some fresh hay when I became aware that I was watched. At the further side of the open compound stood a man carrying two poles.

' "Master Joiner," called out a familiar voice, "I think it is time we practised, don't you?"'

'It was Ōe Jiroemon-sensei?' asked Enshin.

Toshiaki nodded.

'I crossed the yard and bowed low. He handed me one of the yari.

' "This place is too public for a practice; we'll go down along the riverbank!" '

———— ⊟ ————

'Did you cross blades?'

'Oh, yes, master; we certainly did! And very interesting it was, too . . . We walked down to the village, it looked exactly as if it had been fought over, and on through the three paddies to the river, then turned downstream to the bend where Jubei should have plied his ferry. All that way, Ōe-sama said not one syllable . . . just strode along with his yari under his arm whilst I stumbled in his wake. Suddenly, he stopped and turned; reaching inside his kimono he produced two pieces of cloth, tossing one to me. After that he threw over a short length of soft leather.

' "Tie on the *tanpō*, Master Joiner; I want to see something of the Oda-ryū!"

'I protested that I was but a novice and wasn't of any real skill but he simply ignored me and secured the leather wrapping over the short yari blade and then the white cloth, folded as an additional pad, making the weapon relatively safe.

'This done, he stood up straight and bowed gravely to me, exactly as if I had some rank, master. Just think of it, a kenshi bowing out of respect for someone lacking a surname! I bowed back, naturally, and came to the usual right position, as I recalled from my youth! He came to the left posture which, of course, meant that our spears were levelled mirror-image, as it were. I vaguely remembered that I should probe so first I feinted a high thrust and followed this with a low one; both met with a slight "brushing aside" motion . . . then he struck sideways at my lead-ing leg, probably to catch my balance as it shifted, but I struck back . . . *jibari*, is that not? Again we circled before he changed his posture by raising his rear hand and lowering the point with the leading one . . . Instantly he thrust upwards, but I dropped to kneeling . . . well, almost, as my left knee only feathered the ground . . . and I struck his spear upwards and thrust at his side, and missed. He was very fast and to this day I don't know how I didn't catch his side . . .

'Just as we were circling again, my yari under my left arm, a voice shouted out: "Ōe-sama, now we have the best chance of a return match!"

'The *kenshi* stepped back a pace and, lowering his blade, bowed deeply to me, saying: "Master Toshiaki, this encounter has been a pleasure. Now, if you will excuse me, I must attend to some unfinished business. I am sorry but I know you will understand."

'About fifteen yards away stood the rōnin and all three had their sleeves tied back with their tasuke.

'I shook my head. "Three against one displays unsatisfactory odds, sensei. Permit me to fight on your side!"

'Ōe-sama smiled briefly "Unbind the *tanpō*, good Master Joiner, and thank you; I accept your offer!" He called out: "I take it that the match will be with live blades, Harada-san?"

' "It was not permitted the other day, Ōe-sama; today the match is on my terms, don't you think?"

' "You will allow this carpenter to fight alongside me, sir?"

' "If he is so tired of life, of course! I know him, anyway; he's one of those trash who guzzle rice-wine all night in the village. You're welcome to his support!"

'By this time the shadows were getting deeper and I realized that what light there was would soon fade to twilight gloom. The coming combat promised to be short . . . and rather dangerous. The rōnin drew out their swords and fanned out on either side of Harada with the intention, so far as I judged, to divide our intention. On my side the danger threatened from the youngest warrior who slowly moved up the slope to his right until he reached a point about ten yards separate from Harada; then, quite suddenly, he yelled out his *kiai* and ran up two or three more steps before hurling himself like a lion towards me, his sword braced back to his right shoulder as he attacked . . . The intensity of his shout and violent onrush was intended to create fear, but he failed to allow for the unexpected . . . His rope sandal cord snapped, the sole turned under his foot and, just as he was about to slash down at my spear, he stumbled. I stepped to my left and hit him on the side of his head with my shaft ferrule causing him to pitch down the slope into the path of his companions . . . The danger was not so much him but his sword as he had tried to make that cut . . . The katana flew towards Harada who reacted unimaginably fast. With a single movement he deflected that blade and darted half-a-step out of the falling samurai's way, cutting one-handed across his hip. "*Baka!*" he spat out. There was no time to think, though; the chance was in their favour and Harada seized it . . . cutting, one-handed, at Ōe-sensei, forcing him back a pace, then striking at me two-handed and taking the blade from my yari . . . He yelled ferociously and cut at me again but I warded the blade and thrust back with the iron *ishizuki*, lightly striking his left hip, I think, but he recovered and cut back again . . . see, master, I carry the mark of his blade to this day . . .'

Toshiaki pulled aside his brown kimono to reveal a four inch scar running across the top of his right leg. He had been very lucky indeed thought Enshin.

'What happened then?'

'I felt the sting but thrust upwards again with a couple of sharp jabs. I think the rōnin was slightly off balance on the rough slope . . . Out of the corner of my eye I glimpsed Ōe-sama cut down the third of our attackers, left and right *kesa* he used, then turn and shout at Harada to face him.

'Now there was a slight pause . . . I moved back a pace or two and felt the warm blood running down my thigh, but I kept the butt end of my yari pointing at the swordsman, realizing how fast he could move. Ōe-sama was positioned a little down the hill slope, now an indistinct figure in the gathering gloom; his opponent had lowered his sword out to his right side . . .

' "You know what I have come here for," Harada said, rather to my surprise.

'The Hata-ke swordmaster grunted, saying: "Let's get on with what we are about, Harada-san; other reasons are of no importance!"

'Out of the corner of my eye I became aware of a slight movent in the thicket below the bamboo grove that masked the secret track that led up to where Hanzō and the priest were supposed to be concealed, but Harada Saburō had begun to move in to his attack . . . his sword showing as a thin strip of white against the dark background of the river. He still held it low and out to his right while Ōe-sama had come to the spear posture known as the "reversed-high-mist-yari" . . . At first, in the gathering darkness, I could detect no movement by either protagonist but I sensed they were slowly circling from Harada's delicate crossing of his leading foot, toes feeling the grassy ground for a safe place to put his weight . . . A minute passed, nay, two . . . without warning the master's right spearhand came down and the yari blade punched forwards catching Harada's gathered sleeve just below his right shoulder. I hadn't realized that they had come within range even . . . The blade snagged the cotton just at the moment that the challenger swept up his blade at Ōe-sama's left armpit . . . the cut never reached its target . . . Harada grunted and came back to *in-no-kamae* at his right shoulder, his whole body gathering for a decisive attack, when the yari shaft reversed and Ōe-sensei brought the ishizuki up beneath his opponent's jaw. The swordsman fell backwards down the river bank and into the water with a splash . . .'

' "Hanzō! Assist Master Toshiaki to pull that man from the river," called out Ōe Jiroemon.

' "Master!" the old fellow replied and I could see that the two had indeed come down and witnessed the end of the fight. The woodsman's head was bandaged by the priest but he seemed sprightly enough. Together, one grasping each leg, we managed to drag Harada Saburō from the water and, as a precaution, I pulled his short sword out from his *obi* then sat down and tied a hachimaki round my cut leg to staunch the steady bleeding. Fortunately the wound wasn't deep and soon healed. In the meantime, the kenshi had examined each of the other two rōnin in turn and found them to be dead. He came over and looked down at Harada who lay unconscious.

'"Take his *sageo* cord, Toshiaki-san, and secure his hands . . . Questions need to be asked, I think, *before* we send to the yashiki!"

'Harada's jaw was badly dislocated, but the priest, a merciful man like you, master, jerked it back into place whilst the rōnin was still out cold . . . That would have been painful later, I reckon . . ?'

'It certainly would have been,' agreed Enshin.

'We waited until Harada came round and started to groan . . . he had lost a tooth or two, as you might expect, but he was extremely lucky that he wasn't dead, at least at that time! An hour later we were back at the shrine and the gūji cleaned me up and stitched the sword cut.'

———————□———————

' "Hanzō! I would like to hear what you can tell us about this affair. Please speak freely!"

'The seamed face of the woodcutter showed his confusion and probable fear. He was unused to talking in front of such an important samurai as the kenshi and his memories of his recent treatment only worsened his state of mind.

' "Let me ask him, sensei," I volunteered, "after all, I was with him when his dog fetched back the hand . . ."

' "Hand? Whose hand?"

'I described what had happened, adding that I thought the owner had been a swordsman of long experience in the bugei judging by the thickening of the wrist, and also that it couldn't have been the hand of the ferryman, Jubei, as I had seen his drowned corpse at the yashiki.

' "Can you describe the hand in detail? I take it that you looked closely?"

' "Only that the wrist was quite thick, as I said, master, although
. . ."
' "Although what?" asked Ōe Jiroemon.
' "The owner had once been wounded at the outer base of his
thumb, master; I could see an old scar there. It was sort of jagged
though I didn't look closely."
'The swordsman pursed his lips but didn't comment.
'Then I took Hanzō here back to the village after I had found
Jubei's ferry just downstream snagged up in some overhanging
bushes. That's right, isn't it, old fellow?'
'Hanzō nodded in agreement.
' "But it isn't all the story, is it, woodcutter? Come on, have no
fear that we shall bring more trouble on your head . . . I think you
had been on the far side of the river and crossed back with Jubei.
Am I correct?"
'The old man's shoulders sagged but he looked relieved as if a
weight had lifted from his back.
' "It's true, sir, I had been on that further bank. I had been up
on the mountain some time and was gathering up my last wood
bundle when I saw Jubei bring across a sam'rai from the castle.
I knows 'im because I see'd 'im ridin' though the village with 'is
men on occasion. Even at a distance I could see who it was quite
well . . . Jubei poled off back again an' I saw 'im go off for a drink
in the tavern . . . 'e always did about noontide! Jus' after that I 'eard
shoutin' and being curious I took a look . . . I wish I hadn't, masters,
'cos fightin' ain't for me . . . Afrighted, I was, and I don't care who
knows it . . ."
' "What happened?" asked the swordsman.
' "This here sam'rai was carrying a fine looking bundle but he
ain't gone more than a hundred paces past me, downstream, you
know, when he was waylaid by three or four men and 'e 'ad to draw
his sword an' defend 'imself, which 'e did and some! He killed three
of the bandits . . . I knows they were bandits 'cos I looked at their
cor'ses later, masters . . . but one of 'em had pinched the bundle and
made off towards the falls. The sam'rai, 'aving killed the first lot,
hitched up 'is 'akama an' was off after 'im. They must 'ave 'ad a fight
by the falls and while the bandit was nowhere to be seen, the sam'rai
was wounded. He had untied 'is bundle an' used it to wrap round
his right 'and. I didn't know rightly what to do then but 'e saw me
and ordered me to 'elp 'im back to the ferry boat . . . But 'e collapsed
an' died just up where that track 'as to climb round the big rocks . . .
I thought I would be blamed for somethin' or other, so I 'id is body
under some stones an' carried on back to my brushwood . . . I meant
no 'arm, master; I really didn't!"

'Poor Hanzō wished the floor would swallow him up when he had finished his account, he grovelled so low!

'Ōe-sama pulled at his chin.

' "What did he have in his bundle, Hanzō, eh?"

' "It were a sword, master, but I weren't int'rested in that because when I had dragged 'im into the rocks, I grabbed up the bundle an' the sword an' ran . . . For some reason or other, I ain't got enough cord for me bundle of wood so I used the cord from the sword to do the job . . . I went back to old Jubei's landin' stage an' waited. Along comes the old bugger . . . sorry, master . . . the ferryman, an' poles over, cursin' me 'cos 'e knows I ain't goin' to pay 'im nothin'. I gets in and off he goes. 'E sees the bundle an' the sword and says: 'What 'ave you found, hey? That there brocade bag went over with a high an' mighty sam'rai lord, 'e says, so 'ow did you get 'old of it?' "

' "Well I told 'im of the fight an' 'ow I – er – came by both things. 'E says 'e didn't believe a word I says, so I unrolled the bag . . . Oh, great Fudō save me, out tumbled that blood-soaked hand . . . Jubei took one look an' fell backwards into the river . . . an' 'e couldn't swim a stroke . . . while I threw both the hand an' the bag over the side after 'im, then hauled off me *hanten* an' cleaned up the blood! I grabbed the sword an' nigh on fell over meself, the sword slid out so I dropped everything an' poled best I could for the shore where my dog was waitin', all sloppy tailed an' all. I took to my heels an' ran an' that's when I met you, master .. . I swear it's what 'appened, masters . . ."

'Ōe Jiroemon considered Hanzō's story for a while. It sounded like the truth, of course, and I don't think that dodderer had the wit to lie, not at his age.

' "Hmmm! And you, Toshiaki-san, you with secret skills with the spear and, I would guess, with the sword; you found Jubei's boat . . . and the sword, eh?"

'I bowed low to him.

' "The ferryman tells the truth, in your opinion, eh?"

' "Yes, master," I replied. "I knew something of what had happened when I saw a few threads of that sword's *himo* later back here. Also, Hanzō had used the himo to tie on some of his wood. He was clever enough to get rid of it later, though!"

'The gūji had been silent up to this point. Now he coughed behind his hand and said: "Master Toshiaki came to me with a piece of paper wanting me to read a sword signature, which I did. I knew at once that this probably came from the stolen sword because how else could he have it? I . . . I wasn't sure what to say or do, Ōe-sama, so I bided my time."

' "That means you have the sword, Toshiaki-san, doesn't it?"

' "By good fortune, sensei, the sword is relatively safe, but may I ask how it came to be lost in the first place?"

' "How do you think it happened? You tell me."

' "I wasn't sure in the first few days, but it all became clearer when I was given that wooden 'blade' to use as my model for the shirazaya and told I couldn't have the original blade to hand. I worked making saya for Master Masashige and his son, Master Norishige, the family who were employed by my master's family, the Torii-ke, and as soon as I examined that wooden 'blade' I knew from its shape and the fine quality of its workmanship, that it was a replica of a important *Bishu* swordblade. It is something that cannot be hidden from craftsmen who have been trained since a very young age. I didn't need the good priest here to read those characters, really; he confirmed to me that the sword I had found in Jubei's boat was indeed the work of the elder Osafune Kagemitsu; not the younger Kagemitsu, mind you. I could tell that by the faint patterning in the polished surface. Just how such a fine blade was found by me in the bottom of an abandoned ferryboat defeated me . . ."

' "Until you linked it to the severed hand?"

' "Until then, sensei." I smiled

' "The sword has to be returned, Toshiaki-san; you realize that?"

' "I wouldn't dare think about keeping something so valuable, master."

' "Good! Now this is what you must do . . ." '

'Just after dawn the following morning, two of Ōe Jiroemon's senior *deshi*, hard-bitten samurai, both, presented themselves at the shrine bringing two sets of kimono and plain hakama so that Hanzō and I could be properly dressed. The priest had put on his best robes and special lacquered eboshi. He had also provided a plain long bag for the sword, now fully remounted by myself. At about the Hour of the Dragon, mid-morning, our small procession arrived at the gates of the Hata yashiki where we were met by the swordmaster and ten of his students, all wearing body armour. We were at once escorted through to the audience room abutting the inner apartments.

'On the jōdan, wearing his full armour, sat a very important personage who I took to be Hata-dono, himself. He had greying hair, white eyebrows and bushy moustaches . . . the very image of Lord Hachiman, the god of War! To his right and left sat the four principal retainers . . . Poor old Hanzō just managed to keep a hold on himself. I think if it had gone on much more than a few minutes he would have disgraced himself on the spot!

'Ōe-sama bowed low and was ordered to give his formal account, which he did. At the end, Lord Hata pointed his fan at the bugei master and asked the identity of the thief.

' "With respect, my lord, first you need to know why it was stolen!"

' "Very well; why?"

' "Because, my lord, it is a great heirloom of your family and whoever possesses it has the right to rule the domain. 'Possession is nine-tenths of the law', as the saying goes. Your enemies knew this and the sword was stolen and taken to be given to a man named Harada Saburō, a master of *kenjutsu* from the Noda-ke, your cousins, my lord. The sword did not reach this man, Harada, but was recovered!"

' "Recovered? It is safe?"

' "It is here, my lord. Please permit Master-Joiner Toshiaki, of the Torii-ke, to return it to you!"

'While I moved forward and as best I could, placed the Kagemitsu sword before Lord Hata, I could see the four senior retainers frowning one to another.

' "Who, then, took the sword, Ōe-sama?"

' "Ōmura Iyetada-dono! It was his hand and forearm that was lost in the river when Jubei, the ferryman, was drowned!"

' "The hand was recognized by its scar, my lord. There is no doubt who it belonged to."

' "Ōmura-dono! Arrest his family at once! Examine his officers!"

'Clearly, Hata-dono was angry, very angry, but the kenshi hadn't finished.

' "My lord, this was a secret intrigue that I have been aware of for some weeks. Ōmura's family knew nothing! I know this through my own agents. Only Captain Mototada was in the plot!"

' "Mototada? Bring him bound to me this instant!"

' "He is bound in the dōjō, my lord, and so is the leader of the three rōnin who were to take the sword to Noda Kagehiro! He was the one plotting your overthrow!" '

———— ☐ ————

'Hanzō was rewarded generously by the Hata lord and I think still lives out his last days in comfort; the shrine gūji, too, master. I refused an offer to become a Hata retainer because of my quest but did accept some small funds so that I wouldn't starve on my journey.'

'I wondered how you got by, Toshiaki-san?' smiled Enshin. 'That was a truly entertaining story, but tell me, when did you study the Oda-ryū, eh?'

The carpenter coughed slightly behind his hand.

'I stretched the truth just a little, master, but you will remember how we swung bokken together when we were children? I must have learnt something then . . . and it came in rather useful on that river bank, didn't it?'

'You know, Toshiaki-san, I have a suspicion that you may have somewhat deeper knowledge than that. You might say one thing through a natural sense of modesty but I'm not sure that you could fool a master like Ōe Jiroemon. Well, perhaps I shall find out the truth one day.'

5

THE EVENING DRUM

▽

Sad were the days when the nightmare of the Ōnin War came to be regarded as only the prelude to the descent of the provinces into Hell. While few could remember back to the days of the Ōnin conflict, for most of those who were old enough, they only knew that the Hosokawa and Yamana houses had fought for supremacy in distant Miyakō and they had little thought that so soon afterwards ruin, death and destruction would become the order of the day. For most of their descendants the daily task of mere survival was enough to occupy their bodies and minds; only the few were able to maintain chronicles and pray for a better future. The established lords worried and schemed to preserve their ancient domains; in many cases, their vassals, sensing their master's decline, formed combines amongst themselves to usurp control at the expense of their ancestral rulers; many in the lower warrior ranks and even amongst the lowly ashigaru, saw the main chance to clamber up to positions of authority; whilst on the land the pressures on the farmers frequently became intolerable and desperate in the extreme.

To some, this description of conditions in those days may paint too bleak a picture; others may think it hardly enough. Who can really say? The young mendicant priest, Torii Enshin, recalled later in his life when he had the time and chance to write of his early experiences, how he once stood in the company of a hard-bitten yamabushi up on the hills at Idzumi quite close to Sayama, staring out across the pleasant prospect to the north of the whole province of Kawachi. It was one of those serene warm spring days where the crystal clear air gave one the feeling that one could see fifty or a hundred miles with the greatest ease.

'Tell me what you observe, my young friend,' asked the yamabushi.

With the warmth of the morning sun on his back, Enshin took in a deep breath of the pure air.

'While I was brought up in high mountains of the north, I find this landscape harmonious and uplifting. It is a pleasure to be able to stand here and take it in.'

'Yes,' replied the yamabushi, 'I agree for it is all of those things to me as well, but is there anything else you sense in your being?'

'Well, sensei, I feel a regret that our provinces are so disturbed despite their great beauty, if that is what you mean?'

'I was born close to here, and grew up on these very hills. See, far to the north behind the blue mountain ridges lies Miyakō; over there, just beyond those hills marking the border between Kawachi and Yamato are the beautiful temples of Nara; and down there to the south lies Yoshino and Koya-san . . . Sublime, isn't it?'

'Tell me, my friend, what it is I should be seeing?'

'Kawachi is a scant twenty miles wide . . . you can see it clearly from here . . . and a mere seventy miles in length, two days leisurely ride on a horse, I'm told . . . But can you imagine it a little over forty years ago when the farmers down there rose up in arms against their landowners, their priestly masters; and, in their turn, the samurai joined in on their own account? Some warrior groups fought on the farmers' side, others joined the priest-armies, and other warrior-landowners fought them both!'

'Sounds like a common occurrence, my friend.'

'Yes, it is now, but here the three-sided war continued in that valley, just twenty miles wide, remember, at its extreme, for ten long years. The Ashikaga bakufu, just two days ride away, did nothing to stop the fighting . . . absolutely nothing! In that apparently idyllic vale, soft and sweet to our eyes, there are still peasants dragging out their lives without an arm or a leg or their sight . . . Ten whole years of bloody war . . . .'

Enshin, understanding the depths of his companion's feelings, didn't reply, but he could see the tears of anguish that freely coursed down that ascetic man's seamed cheeks. It was an incident that impressed itself deep into his memory.

A year or two later, not a little disturbed by the sights that he had witnessed resulting from the aftermath of a violent conflict in Harima

near to Ako, he had wandered north from the Sanyō–dō highway and
followed the Chigusa river upstream. He had a vague idea of finding a path through the mountains alongside Ushiro-yama either into
Inaba or Mimasaka province, it really was of no significance which.
In that year, the harvests had failed for the second time in succession,
and already sickness and famine tightened their iron grip across the
region; wherever he wandered there was work for him to do.

———————— ☐ ————————

For five months, Enshin settled himself in the tiny Enkō–ji temple
which he had found lying derelict at the end of a meandering path
through some barren rice-fields near the mountain-girt hamlet of
Kobara. After finding the temple, Enshin had sought out the village
headman, only to pray over his departing soul as the poor man sank to
oblivion. After ministering as best he could, he was able to relieve the
diseases suffered by the villagers, and was gladly allowed to occupy the
Enkō–ji, and even given some help to repair the leaking thatch.
     Between his voluntary duties in trying to free the poor farmers
of their afflictions and tilling the dead priest's little rice paddy for
the coming spring planting, for Enshin found it difficult to accept
more than the barest subsistence food offered to him by his grateful
patients when he knew they, themselves, had next to nothing, his
own body weakened and he became quite thin and emaciated. In
the hamlet there lived the widow of the miller and it was she, realizing the true value of this wandering priest with his skills of healing,
who daily tramped out to the Enkō–ji to nurse him back to health.
     Her husband's watermill was in dire need of repair, its waterwheel
rotten and several of the wooden blades missing. Even if these were
replaced, Enshin, who passed the mill every day to and from his
abode, could see that the drive shaft was fractured and wouldn't
allow the wheel to turn under the pressure of water from the race;
not that it mattered, there was nothing to grind . . . All that could
be said was that the ruin provided Mistress Ei-ko with a roof over
her head. With the widow's kindly help in keeping the humble temple clean and relieving him of some, at least, of the harder chores,
Enshin regained his strength and zest to help others. He now had
some extra spare time and with the approach of spring confidently
expected to replenish his store of herbs and useful roots from which
he could prepare his simples.
     That winter had been relatively mild but in the third month it had
turned very cold with thick frosts and sudden heavy snows across
all these western mountains. Kobara was even cut off for nearly
ten days, reminding the young priest of the snows in Echigo and

Kōzuke. Looking out from the verandah of the temple across the glistening wastes down the valley, he was struck forcibly by the wonderful beauty of nature, and just how magical the mountains became whenever the winter sun broke through. He imagined that the lazy days of summer would bring an equal tranquillity to this quiet backwater. But, alas, nothing in this life is permanent . . .

———— ☐ ————

Travellers passing through the valleys from Chizu to Ohara the previous autumn, just after he had arrived, had told of problems for the Ashimori clan at Koge. It was thought that the Ashimori heir had been killed or, at any rate, had suddenly died, but that was all they knew. Then, just before the snow storms closed the mountain roads, Enshin was told, quite casually, by some wandering yamabushi, that hostilities had broken out between the Awakawa and the Gamo-ke, both families being vassals of the Ashimori. Vaguely, the Gamo-ke held lands along the Wakasa-gawa just the other side of Ushiro-yama, and the Awakura defended the border crossings slightly west at Chizu. Even if Enshin had wished to depart for Inaba, he wouldn't have been able to do so while the barriers were closed.

The fighting appeared to have worsened as the thaw set in, though possibly it may have seemed that way as the passes cleared. The barriers were fast closed and heavily guarded but refugees managed the crossing with the help of guides who knew the secret mountain paths well. A number of those fleeing the fighting were peasants forced out by the rampaging soldiery but others were wounded samurai chiefly from the Awakura-ke, who had suffered a crushing defeat at Mochigase but had managed, despite pursuit, to get back to the Chizu stockade. When they reached what they thought was safety, they found that the castle commander had changed sides to the Gamo-ke lord and barred the gates, thus forcing them to seek safety over the border in Mimasaka. Unfortunately that road was denied them, too, as the Gamo general had sealed the border when he took Chizu.

Led by Awakura Yoshisuke, the survivors managed to cross the mountains in three small groups, the general's one reaching Kobara late in the afternoon during the first week of the fourth month. A day later, another traveller, this time a hunter from Nagi, excitedly told of fighting by troops of Omura Hidetada, whose lands were in Mimasaka along the Inaba border, that destroyed two bands of men who had crossed the mountains from Inaba. Omura's forces were hard on his heels, he thought.

Panic set in amongst the peasants, hemmed in as they were by the mountains. At this time of year it would be impossible to hide out in the thick forests and the valley narrowed and ended only half a mile further on from the Enkō-ji. To save bloodshed, the Awakura general gathered his ten remaining men and took them to the temple where it was inevitable that he would be captured, but it seemed that Omura Hidetada was unwilling to arrest him there and then. Perhaps he had attacked the fleeing samurai in the mistaken belief that they were infiltrators crossing into his domain in advance of the Ashimori army and now realized his mistake?

During the course of that day, about fifty more Ashimori men joined those already there and the general decided that Ei-ko's watermill could be defended by resolute men. Work was started at once and proceeded apace during that afternoon and the following morning.

All the while, Enshin sat outside on the sunny verandah on the only rather threadbare round mat to be found in the Enkō-ji, watching with interest the Ashimori preparations. With purposeful efficiency, bamboo poles were cut, sharpened, secured with horizontal lengths, and driven in lines into the bare fields beside the mill; to their front many shorter wickedly pointed lengths were randomly thrust into the soft ground with the intention of laming man or horse attempting any assault. Out on the southern flank, the ashigaru had felled as many trees as they could in the time and lashed then together to make an impenetrable barricade as a defence against encirclement, but it passed through the Torii priest's mind that much depended on the numbers the enemy brought up for any attack. On the other side of the mill rose the steep mountainside for it was here that the river had cut itself a small cliff. He supposed that Awakura Yoshisuke considered he was safe enough on the northern side provided his men held the centre and left . . . Well, that remained to be seen . . . There was little that he, Enshin, could do about the situation so he called out to the widow Ei-ko join him and enjoy the late afternoon sunshine.

'What shall we do, master, if there is a battle?'

'Oh, there'll be one, alright. I think we should simply compose ourselves to remain as calm as possible!'

She laughed into her striped sleeve.

'Remain calm? I'm not sure I can do that, sir. We might be killed, too.'

'While that is certainly true, our best defence is to appear passive, Ei-ko-san. I have some slight experience of such matters.'

'Are you sure?'

'Come, mistress, let us drink some tea and perhaps intone a prayer to the Lady Kannon? She may take pity on you and give her protection.'

'Is that what you pray, good master?'

'Not really,' he laughed. 'What will be has already been determined. We cannot change our fate.'

A slight mist rose in the late afternoon and the sun's fiery disc softened
to a red orb as it sank towards the mountains further down the valley.
As the light thickened there was a certain sharpness in the air; it was
early spring, after all. Along the fortifications set beside the mill, men
hardly moved; they were eating a small meal and waiting to find out
what their fate held in store. General Awakura came back to the little
temple and requested Enshin to chant a sutra on his behalf as he sat
before the statue of the Bosatsu silently following the priest's chanting
with his hands raised before his face, telling his rosary beads.

The general, despite his deperate situation, which must have been
without hope, displayed an absolute calmness both in his body and
his spirit that Enshin instinctively understood and admired. He was
reminded of the old warrior axiom:

> *There is one thing for the warrior,*
> *one thing only;*
> *to face death unflinchingly.*

There was nothing more to be said or done.

'Will you take tea with me, my lord?' he invited as he bowed low.

'Tea? Why not? I am grateful for the invitation.'

The widow Ei-ko bowed politely and bustled off to heat the
water while Enshin offered his guest the round mat.

'No, Master Enshin; it is your place and I am intruding in my
armour. I am content to sit just like anyone else.'

'It is a beautiful evening, my lord.'

'There are times in our lives when we appreciate such things. Tell
me, Enshin-sama; were you once a warrior?'

'Is it that obvious, my lord?'

'There are some things that cannot be disguised no matter how
hard we try.'

Enshin smiled.

'My family come from Kōzuke, sir, and you are correct.'

'You have had some experience of war?'

'More than enough, my lord.'

The general mused for a while in silence as he looked across the
three fields that separated the temple from his hastily constructed
fortifications.

'Your father is a man of rank, I think; it shows in your calm bearing in the face of the coming attack down there. The majority of men, including all the priests, would long since have vanished out of fearfulness.'

'My father commands many men, my lord.'

'Hmmm!' Awakura Yoshisuke sipped the fragrant tea. 'Please forgive my many questions, but you have studied the heihō, Enshin-sama?'

'Until I renounced the world, yes.'

'How do you assess my situation?'

'My lord, you have prepared on three sides. The work is good. But what about your rear?'

Yoshisuke smiled sadly.

'Times are changing, Enshin-sama, and I think my lord's clan will sink into oblivion very shortly. I, and my ancestors, have served the Ashimori-ke more than four-hundred years and we have received many kindnesses and gifts from them. Now the clan is divided by self-serving traitors. It is my intention to fight for my lord's honour until the end. If his enemies choose to attack from the rear, so be it. I do not intend to retreat but shall follow on my lord to serve him in the next life.'

'You are prepared for this, my lord.'

'Oh, yes. I would rather die with honour than live with dishonour.'

'Some might say that the old creed of the warrior has now changed, my lord.'

'What do you think, Enshin-sama?'

'I think, my lord, that only the words composed by Prince Otsu adequately expresses what I feel:

> *The sun lights on the western huts;*
> *Evening drums beat out the shortness of life . . .'*

Awakura Yoshisuke murmured the stanzas with him then, as Enshin fell silent and he was about to continue, they both heard on the still air the low throb of a taikō drum on the still sunset air. With a deep sigh, the general turned to his humble host and bowed low. He took a large gold piece from a pouch on his armour sleeve and placed it on the boards in front of Enshin.

'Please say prayers for the repose of our souls. They will aid us when we report to the Lord Emma-ō.'

———————— ☐ ————————

The battle, when it came, was very short and all over within the hour. The first arrows were exchanged between the Awakura men and those of Omura Hidetada just as the setting sun touched the distant ridges. It was clear from the outset that General Awakura was determined that his men would die bravely and quickly. Observing the movement of both sides' banners, Enshin, sipping more tea on the Enjo-ji verandah, saw the rapid reduction of those flags marking the Awakura; at last, in the gathering evening shades, he saw none at all.

The burning of the old mill brought a tear to widow Ei-ko's eye but it would have had to be rebuilt, in any case. Both she and Enshin admired the departed spirit of the Ashimori general, the purity of his soul stood out in stark contrast to the perfidy of those to whom the precepts of the ancient sages signified nothing.

When the villagers had returned two days after the battle and helped bury the slain, Enshin stood alone beside the grave of Awakura Yoshisuke and, with a heavy heart, completed the poem of the prince:

There are no inns on the road to the grave −
Whose is the house I go to tonight?

6

THE SWEET SMELL OF SUCCESS

∨

During the years that the young priest, Torii Enshin, trod the byways of the Western Provinces, he spent some months in the small town of Yokota in the province of Idzumo. He had been invited to reside there by the local lord, Kido Iga-no-suke, who had heard favourable reports about the priest as a healer. Enshin had arrived in the town - really, hardly larger than a village – just as the plum trees flowered in the third month and, at the insistence of Iga-no-suke Takanori, had set about treating an outbreak of a certain type of the pox that afflicted a number of his retainers and footsoldiers.

Whilst engaged in these duties, for once having at his disposal no less than three assistants who daily searched the fields and forest edges for the herbs that Enshin required, he learned that the Kido-ke were of the bloodline of the powerful family of lords of the same name who served the Mori clan in Suō province to the southwest. Iga-no-suke Takanori was one of the *kofushin-hatamoto* vassals of Shimane Idzumo-no-kami, lord of most of this province; that is to say that Iga-no-suke was a rear-vassal. Enshin quickly understood that, because of the last year's bad harvest and the outbreak of disease during the winter, the lord of the Yokota fief had fallen behind in the distribution of the rice stipends to some of his immediate supporters and they, in consequence, had only passed on a reduced amount to their lower-ranking samurai.

This had the result of causing increasing friction between some of the middle-ranking retainers and had begun to divide them into two or three factions. Such combinations could, if allowed to harden, lead to further dissent and eventually to rebellion. It had happened in so many places because these samurai, themselves, needs must borrow money in order to buy rice in from the merchants but without the security of knowing all would soon be brought back to normal by the clan treasury. Yet it seemed to the Torii priest that this province had not been cursed with the violence he had witnessed elsewhere. The peasants appeared content enough, the farmers weren't oppressed by severe tax burdens, and there were no signs here of the unrest caused by the militant religious movements in the central provinces.

The late spring that year proved unusually warm but the heat seemed to make the factions more bad-tempered and mistrustful, something that Enshin felt able to discuss with the priest, Kōken, who served the little temple that provided him with a small room in which to sleep and prepare his various medicinal compounds.

'You seem worried by something, my friend,' Kōken said one early morning as the two broke their fast, 'Can I help at all?'

'Well, I'm not really worried, just concerned that there seem to be some problems amongst Lord Iga-no-suke's followers.'

'Oh, you mean the distribution of the tax rice?'

Enshin nodded and pulled a face.

'I've seen how these things can get out of hand but it isn't my place to offer advice, is it?'

'You have a solution? A healer of illnesses and a healer of political problems, too!' laughed Kōken. 'Tell me what you think would ease the situation?'

'The important thing is to stave off any major rift, don't you think?'

'That sounds reasonable! Play for time, eh?'

'Talking is better than fighting any day, though I don't suppose many hot-headed samurai would agree, do you? I would be happy to explain my ideas to Kido-dono but I do not want to become involved as that's bound to cause resentment.'

They discussed the problem a little further then Enshin picked up his wallet and prepared to go to the samurai-yashiki to treat his remaining three patients; Kōken went off at the same time to officiate at the burial of one of the local farmers.

Late in the afternoon, a messenger came from Kido's mansion, inviting Enshin to talk to the hatamoto the following morning. Before the appointed hour, two servants of yari-mochi rank came to escort the priest as a mark of respect to the gates of the yashiki, where he was ushered to the inner council room where he found gathered two of the senior retainers, the Chief Steward and the Commander of the Yashiki Guard. Both men greeted him affably enough. Shortly afterwards, Kido Takanori-dono entered and sat down in front of a fine folding rack of arrows. Everyone present bowed very low but Kido-dono commanded them to relax.

'Enshin-sama,' the Steward began, 'I hear from Kōken-sama that you thought, perhaps, you may be able to help resolve our dilemma. Is this so?'

Enshin bowed again. 'As I understand it, my lords, there is a delicate situation.'

'That is very true!'

'If I may be able to speak freely as a humble priest . . ?'

'That is why we have invited you. Your reputation as a healer is sound; maybe you can heal our present malaise, too.'

'My lord, I need to know all the facts, not just the rumours and hearsay.'

The three bushi exchanged nods of approval and the Steward set out the situation in some detail.

After asking some questions, Enshin smiled and brushed his hand over his shaven head,

'As I see it, then, my lords, the initial fault lies with your clan paymaster in delaying the rice distribution because of circumstances over which he had no control. This has been the cause of some regrettable, even immoderate, talking between three of the officers responsible for their own groups, thus giving rise to further discontent spreading through the lower ranks.'

Kido Iga-no-suke agreed that this was the case.

'The rice distribution problem will soon be resolved, my lord?'

'Within the month.'

'That is certain?'

The Steward confirmed that it would be so.

'In such a situation many clan lords would react violently, my lord.'

Kido Iga-no-suke looked gravely at him.

'Yes, I realize that! They would regard such loose talk and the forming of factions as something to be stamped on hard.'

'But you can foresee lasting problems, my lord?'

'Yes; if I were to decide on that sort of action, there would be no knowing where the matter might end.'

'Hmmm . . .' Enshin stroked his chin, turning over in his mind a possible solution now that he had the facts. 'May I suggest, my lord, that Councillor Yoshida, here, makes an announcement apologizing for the delay in the distribution and inviting all those retainers affected to come to the yashiki so that matters can be explained . . .'

'That won't mend matters!' exclaimed Yoshida Saburō, the Steward.

'Ah, but if I may explain further, sir; it will diffuse the situation. Either the problem can be treated as one of incipient rebellion and dealt with by force, or it can be regarded as a lapse of correctness. The former course would only alienate further those with a fancied cause and be disastrous. By talking and involvement, they might come to see reason and be completely turned about.'

'And if they don't come to their senses?'

'Oh, I think they will, my lord, if you will permit me to elaborate . . .'

———— ⊟ ————

Accordingly, two days later after reassuring meetings had taken place so that it was widely known that Yoshida Saburō would explain the situation and the measures he was taking to clear the matter up, the middle-ranking officers and a number of their subordinates, all formally dressed, came to the yashiki in the expectation of enjoying a repast and wine. Because of the numbers attending, the entertainment was arranged in the main courtyard where awnings had been set up to provide shade from the hot spring sunshine. In fact, it was an exceptionally hot day and very soon everyone sitting in the broad compound, all dressed in their kamishimo over their best kimono and hakama, began to feel the heat and in consequence, developed almost to a man an excessive thirst. One of the Steward's junior officers fussed around saying that he couldn't understand what had caused the delay and urged everyone present to be calm as refreshments were to be served very shortly.

Another hour passed without either water jars or a more senior officer making an appearance and matters were beginning to take a more volatile turn when Hayashi Nobuo, the Steward's immediate subordinate, came out, almost wringing his hands and full of apologies, to tell the leaders of the three factions that his master, Yoshida-dono, was so worried and upset by the problem and the trouble that was causing, that he remained in his quarters trying to dispel the terror felt by his wife and children. In the meantime, now realizing just how many retainers had been affected by the faulty rice distribution, he felt that, out of his own pocket and not from the Clan

treasury . . . which would mean involving Kido Takamori-dono, and
that would never do from the point of view of accepted protocol . . .
he would like to invite the three senior representatives of each group
to take dinner with him. The others would at once be served drinks
and then some fine food now being prepared.

Feeling that somehow this near-abject apology had given them
a sort of victory, the respective leaders mollified their followers and
followed Hayashi Nobuo through to the outer Council Chamber
where they found their places already set with small tables each laden
with a number of elegant dishes. The cunning priest, Enshin, had
suggested that a variety of salty and pickled delicacies, such as fish
in fermented soya sauce, salted bream and mackerel, fine fried salted
whiting, pickled sliced vegetables, and some bowls of fermented
plums, all juicy and rich, should be served. In the meantime, the
lower ranking samurai waiting in the outer compound were invited
to partake of similar dishes, served to them in the comparative cool
of the verandahs that surrounded the courtyard on three sides. Wine
cups were brought out and placed by everyone but, again, there was
an inordinate delay before the wine appeared. In the meanwhile,
everyone felt the pangs of hunger and had devoured every scrap
of food with their o-hashi. At last, the great pitchers of wine were
brought in, both to the officers inside and the samurai outside, and
without more ado, the parched men drank their fill, calling for more
since the wine hardly touched their throats in their haste to quench
their great thirst.

While the senior officers were greedily refreshing themselves
in the outer Council Chamber, Hayashi Nobuo again apologized
that Yoshida Saburō-dono had been mildly afflicted by an old
indisposition but wished them all to slake their thirst on the wine
he had provided. He would surely be with them soon. Accordingly, and ignoring the fact that the wine had turned a little sour,
(its winter storage had maybe caused this), they offset the taste
by consuming all the ripe plums. It was shortly after this that
the Steward, Yoshida-dono, slipped into the room and took his
place on his raised mat. At once bowing deeply, he apologized yet
again, explaining that it was probably all his personal fault that the
distribution of rice stipends had been delayed: 'It was because of
the dreadful harvest, the failure to collect even a small part of the
rice taxes from the farmers in half their domain, the pressing, nay,
urgent, need to preserve the seed rice or there would be a further
disastrous crop this present year,' etc., etc. 'This is why at this meal
served to you in recompense for your forbearance, I was unable
to offer you any rice at all . . . even my own family have eaten
none for two weeks and it is only the generosity of our suzerain

that supplies have been obtained, to the general depletion of our clan treasury.' He went on to say that he had even contemplated committing *seppuku* for his failures in his proper duties on more than one occasion in the last week . . . but had been dissuaded by their lord . . .

The senior retainers listened to his words politely enough but were becoming more and more uncomfortable as the salty food, their great thirst, and the sour wine began to take effect in their systems. Enshin's suggestion that some finely ground convolvulus be sprinkled on some of the food had also been followed; convolvulus being a well-known laxative speeded the process until his 'victims' could hardly cover the noise of their stomach's groaning and the imminent threat of even worse effects . . . At length, the course of nature in all of them would not . . . could not . . . be denied.

'Sir,' one of the officers cried in a strangled voice, 'Sir, I must leave the room . . .'

'Why so?' exclaimed Hayashi Nobuo, apparently affronted, 'it is against all etiquette in the presence of your superiors!'

'But, sir, I must . . .' And at that the poor man, to his utter confusion and embarrassment let fly a tremendous blast.

That did it!

Four of his fellows scrambled in haste to their knees and tried to bow low to excuse themselves but the mere movement of bending forwards proved the final straw and one and all leapt to their feet and, holding the seats of their hakama, rushed for the *shoji* to find the nearest latrine . . . and regrettable as it is to mention such indelicate matters, none of them were able to get there in time. The remaining four senior samurai realized by now that the sage Steward, Yoshida Saburō-dono, had played a great trick on them all, well-knowing that all the men invited to the yashiki were the aggrieved retainers. They understood, also, that their ill-advised complaints were really not the fault of the Kido-ke and were a serious deviation from their proper duty of respect towards their lord and the clan councillors . . . and now there was no hope of getting out of the situation that they had caused and avoiding the indignity of polluting both themselves and their lord's yashiki . . !

By all the kami, it was too late by far. Precipitately, they mumbled their excuses amidst a variety of natural sounds and pungent odours, and as a body hurled themselves out of the sliding doors only to find that every one of the 'honeypot' seats throughout the yashiki was taken with numbers of their men waiting in every stage of distress . . . and it was an inescapable truth that some had not made it in time . . !

A full seven days after this incident, reports of which spread like wildfire wherever men sat down to drink ō-sake and gamble of an evening, the priest was invited to attend the yashiki and sat in informal audience with Kido Iga-no-suke Takanori-dono, Yoshida Saburō-dono, and Hayashi Nobuo-sama.

'Well, Enshin-sama, I expect you heard reports of the full story, didn't you?'

'I did, indeed, my lord!'

'I think we were successful, don't you?'

Enshin smiled.

'I think, my lord, that the Honourable Steward now has quite a formidable reputation for playing tricks!'

They all laughed.

'At least we rid ourselves of that bad ō-sake from the stores!' Hayashi Nobuo said. 'Still, it proved . . . er . . . drinkable in the end!'

'With a-vengeance, I should say!' added Yoshida-sama.

'But, tell me, my excellent priest; where did you get the idea for this . . . er . . . solution? Was it your own invention?' asked the hatamoto.

'I make no claim for originality, my lords. I have been fond of reading fine books for to do so seems to me to enable us to converse with wise men who have passed on long generations ago. Such reading is a pleasure beyond compare. In this case I simply took an incident related in the "Tales of Times now Past" that occurred in the time of Juntoku-tennō in the Chōwa period.[4] Tamemori Ason-dono used the ploy to subdue complaints from some officers of the Palace Guards.'

'It was successful then?'

Enshin permitted himself to smile again. He lightly brushed the surface of the fresh tatami where he sat.

'I see that some of the matting has been renewed, my lord?'

'Ah, yes! We received some . . . er . . . contributions from certain officers!'

'It is a pity, Enshin-sama, that you don't drink ō-sake, or we could all celebrate our bloodless victory, eh!'

---

[4] About the year, 1015.

7

THE CAT

∇

One of the characteristics of Enshin, the priestly second son of Torii Munemori, was his unusual love of animals; witness his constant companion, Kuroi-san, the sleek black water-buffalo. Less well-known, in his more youthful years, was his friendship with a cat which came towards the close of the time when he had been some years in the tutelage of his uncle's monastery built under the towering cliffs of Hōrai-ji in Mikawa.

It must be remembered that here was a young samurai of high rank, burgeoning master of the arts of warfare, many of whose ancestors had been famous warriors; yet he had followed his conscience and shaven his head. To turn completely away from one's roots is almost impossible but Enshin studied the arts of medicine, never truly believing in the efficacy of mumbled prayers and occult formulae that bordered on the arts of sorcery; instead he learned about the healing properties of plants and enquired into the truth lying behind many peasant simples for the treatment of both diseases and wounds.

To his tiny room tucked away into the remotest, most inaccessible fold of Hōrai's encircling amphitheatre of cliffs, he brought many of his collected herbs to examine, to dry, powder, soak in different liquids, and eventually catalogue their various effects, often treating himself or those of the monastery servants who came to him to relieve their ills. All this activity was calmly watched over by a large greyish-red mottled yellow-eyed cat who had, one fine Spring day, not three years before, simply entered his private retreat and taken up residence. Many people were wary of cats because of their alleged 'spirit' possession, but a few doted on them. Enshin wasn't sure in his mind if the cat should be discouraged or permitted to stay; eventually he decided it should be the latter. So here was Murasaki, so named because his mottled coat took on a dull purple in certain lights, firmly ensconced on a soft woven mat that Enshin had made for his own comfort, solemnly observing with the greatest apparent interest everything that the young priest did during his waking hours.

Murasaki exhibited several peculiar characteristics, too. The first was an extraordinary light step, a mode of progression across difficult ground where obstacles lurked, that caught Enshin's concentrated attention and began to fire his imagination. The cat also had an evident and uncanny understanding of what was being said. Murasaki 'knew' full well even if sometimes he expressed little response. A third property was the animal's lack of appreciation of music and especially Enshin's singing or chanting voice. He definitely didn't like anything faintly modulated to the tonic scales. When Enshin, kneeling, intoned the sutras, the cat would listen with wrapt attention but when he punctuated the passage a second time ... not the first, mind you ... by striking his little bronze bell, then Murasaki would get up from his round mat, stretch all his sinews and limbs, and walk over to seat himself deliberately before him, usually on his open scroll, and place one raised paw (claws never extended) on his lips. This happened not just once but many times. Eventually, Enshin was compelled to exclaim: 'Murasaki-san, you may not like my singing but I must read my scrolls. If you will permit me to read and sometimes to chant, then I shall invite you to sit here on my left shoulder. That way you will encourage me and I shall have my hands free to follow my text or to brush my characters.'

To his great surprise, the cat immediately climbed to his shoulder, turned about so that he faced forward, and from that day always took this position whenever Enshin was about his studies.

It was Murasaki's exceptional care in passing over hazards that soon deeply interested the young priest. Like all cats, this one sometimes liked to be amused by a tightly rolled fragment of cloth dragged about on a cord. He would even retrieve such a 'mouse' when thrown. He also liked to chase after thread but very soon tired of such belittling games; however it was the skill that Murasaki demonstrated dodging low floor-level flicks with a longish thin spatula of bamboo that made Enshin think.

Although he had renounced the calling of war, like many priests he retained a lively interest in the *heihō*, the philosophy of generalship particularly exemplified by the art of swordsmanship and the use of the spear. In no manner did he regard these arts as incompatible with his calling, rather did he view them as complementary since they probed the psyche of man and, by degrees, uncovered many deeply buried truths.

'It seems possible, Murasaki-san,' he said one day after a long session seeing how the attentive animal dealt with blows coming at a descending angle rather than horizontally, 'that once, in a previous life, you were a skilful warrior, an expert with the halberd?'

It was this sort of 'cutting' attack that Murasaki excelled at avoiding so if one believed in the continual process of rebirth through the cycle leading to attaining the Buddha's perfection, then assuredly in an earlier incarnation the cat had been a warrior of great skill; one who must have lived before the final decades of the Kamakura shogunate, for had that previous life been later, Enshin reasoned, then the cat might well have been able to avoid thrusts such as those delivered with the yari. Oh, he dealt with the thrust alright, employing a form of *yawara* that entailed deflecting the attack and catching it whilst rolling onto his back. That seemed difficult to apply to the *bugei* but when it came to the reaping attacks with the bamboo slip wielded like those of the naginata or nagamaki, then this feline reigned supreme.

At dawn every day throughout the year, rain, shine or snow, Enshin climbed the long series of steps that steeply led up to a cave dedicated to the All-Powerful One, Fudō Myō-ō, and subjected himself to more than thirty immersions in the icy waters of the *mizogori* cistern about halfway up the mountainside. His ascetic devotions completed, he would descend to search for fresh herbs across the slopes beneath the cliffs behind the monastery where the little Hōrai brook danced and burbled away to join the larger Tōyō river near to the Nagashino stockade. Just as the morning sun struck across the edge of the eastern cliffs, he would take up his wooden sword or his long staff to vigorously practise for a full two more hours, at length washing his almost naked sweating body beneath a little waterfall where the stream gushed out of the sheer cliff face above.

On this particular day he was joined by Murasaki who jumped part of the way across the waters and settled comfortably on top of a smooth rock midstream From this vantage point the cat observed all his movements. When he paused at one point he thought he detected a slight furrowing of the cat's brow and wondered if he had, in fact, made an error that had earned disapproval? It was possible, of course, and on reflection, perfectly likely. His memory was jogged and into his mind sprang one or two of Murasaki's evasive steps . . .

'Why not', he thought, 'why not try them to see if they could, indeed, be applied to the use of the yari or naginata?

When he returned to his room he turned over this problem in his mind and soon sketched down many little 'thumbnail' figures developing some moves that entered his brain. The conviction dawned on him that he had come across something of great interest . . . A few days later he began to polish the moves with the help of one of the servant's sons.

———□———

Regrettably, Murasaki the gifted cat, vanished from the monastery during the very severe winter of the first year of Tai-ei,[5] the same month that Enshin took leave of the abbot, his uncle, and moved into mountainous Shinano for two more years before commencing his wanderings amongst the poor oppressed folk in the provinces. The cat's legacy lived on when, in later life, Enshin began to pass on his skills to his two or three disciples. We can see in the two 'Great Tiger Scrolls' still preserved in the Torii archives, the eight 'forms' based on Murasaki's interesting technique – all examining counters against attacks by the halberd. Although Enshin never gave a name to his teaching style, he always held that intuitive inspiration was often revealed by nature at the behest of Marishi-ten. This deity's 'messengers' in transmitting her secret heihō were a number of different creatures, the best known being the secretive tengu, of course.

It is a curious story but one that the monk wrote down as now it has been told.

---

[5] 1521.

8

THE AGENT

∇

In the months after the battle, if it could really be graced by such a title, that had been briefly fought beside the ruined mill, the priest, Enshin, had prayed for peace for his troubled soul. His heart had already been heavy when he had wandered slowly westwards through the provinces witnessing the destruction that war, pestilence and famine had visited on the poor, and had sought out this seemingly forgotten backwater in Mimasaka close to the border with Inaba where he could minister to the sick and succour the needy, but even here, at the once deserted little Enkō-ji temple, the turmoil had insidiously coiled its way through the tortuous valleys and burst forth before his saddened gaze.

The brief hours that he had spent supping a delicate infusion of tea made by the miller's widow, Ei-ko, and praying with the ill-fated Ashimori general, Awakawa Yoshisuke, had deeply affected him for he truly understood the sense of bitter betrayal that this warrior had felt for the imminent downfall of the ancient house of Ashimori. Here, in the Enko-ji, nestling deep in the beautiful mountains where the borders of three provinces met, it hardly seemed possible that war had planted its bloody fist... Here, where Inaba lay just over the ridge to the north, Harima to the east, and Mimasaka finally petered out on Ushiroyama's flanks immediately behind the temple roof, Enshin had sought peace but instead gazed into the jaws of Hell . . .

———————☐———————

The priest heaved a deep sigh and shrugged aside his dark thoughts. He sat cross-legged, as was his custom, on a thick round mat, the sort that warriors always favoured as it allowed them to rest comfortably whilst easily being able to rise should an emergency suddenly threaten, his right arm resting on a small curved table, and gazed with pleasure at the tray of tea that Ei-ko-san had just placed before him.

He looked for a few moments at the homely widow, She must be about sixty years of age, he guessed.

'Why are you always so patient with me, Ei-ko-sama?'

'Master, you ask too many questions for a priest,' she replied.

'But why? I can only be trouble living here alone!'

'Someone has to see to your needs, master; but it might also be in return for your kindnesses, you know.'

He lifted his eyes from watching the widow pouring out the pale liquid and gazed out at the fields. Great skeins of rain fell from the heavens rendering the whole prospect into a series of flat washes of grey like the softened hints of successive peaks rendered by an ink painter in an agony of black despair. Just across the field he could make out the burnt timbers of the old watermill against the flank of the looming mountain behind; there was the faint outline of the little crooked bridge, a pale run of fence gave way to the merest hint of the next hill slope. . . beyond that was nothing but the falling rain and the opalescent skies . . . nothing . . .

He became aware that the old widow hadn't moved away to the temple's little kitchen as she usually did to leave him to his private thoughts. He leant forward and carefully took up the simple teacup sipping the delicious nectar. Then he replaced the cup and gave a sigh.

'Something is troubling you, Ei-ko-sama. Tell me what it is if you wish.'

'It is nothing, really, my lord.'

'Oh, come now, Oku-san; you can confide in me.'

'Well, master; I told you once that I was born and brought up in Inaba in a little village just this side of Saji and, of course, I still have family there. Well, since the fighting between the Ashimori vassals last year things in that part of Inaba haven''t been good. In fact, they have been very difficult.'

Enshin had feared that eventually the troubles that beset the eastern region in the Kinki, the Kansai, and the Kantō would eventually reach here and he had already seen the beginnings of the same process in the struggles that afflicted the Ashimori that ended with the death of Awakawa Yoshisuke.

'But you are safe here, mistress Ei-ko; you know that.'

She shook her head, her eyes downcast.

'Perhaps, master,' she sighed.

'There is something else?'

She nodded.

'I had a visitor a while ago, lord; while you were intoning the sutras.'

'So?'

'Yes; a young man from my home village, master . . .'

'Has he gone?' The priest frowned, realizing that for anyone to venture out on a mere visit in this weather was serious, but to actually try to find this remote temple on such a day must be significant. He looked at Ei-ko intently. 'You are telling me that your visitor is still here?'

'Yes, my lord . . .'

She still insisted in calling him 'dono' even though she knew that he was now just a simple priest.

'Where is he, then? Bring him here.'

Ei-ko bowed her head and went to the left side of the verandah.

'You can present yourself, Gorobei-san!' she called out.

A straw-caped figure detached itself from the meagre shelter of a tumbledown shed on the edge of the nearest paddy and, hunched down, scuttled through the downpour across the muddy forecourt. As the man fell to his knees with a splash before the platform, Enshin could make out that he was only a youth.

'You are called Gorobei?' he asked.

The young fellow scarce raised his shoulders before bowing again.

'Of course he's Gorobei! He's my sister's grandson, so he is!'

'Gorobei, raise your head and look at me. I won't bite!'

The youth looked up slowly then evidently remembered that he was wearing a curious conical straw hat which hid much of his face. He tore it off and stared open mouthed at Enshin.

'Why have you come to see your aunt?'

Gorobei glanced across at Ei-ko who was kneeling some way apart to Enshin's left. She nodded encouragingly.

'Close your mouth, boy, or you'll swallow a fox spirit . . . Tell the lord what you have told me . . . Everything you can remember.'

Enshin held up his hand.

'First come up out of the rain, lad,' he invited.

'I – I can't get any wetter, my lord; it doesn't matter to me, anyway.' He bowed low once again.

Probably he had never spoken to a former warrior before in his whole life, thought Enshin. How sad it was that so many peasants were so downtrodden and cowed.

'Nevertheless, you will come and sit at the top of the steps,' he said, pointing to a place just out of the torrential downpour. 'Please pass him a cup, Oku-san, and I will hear what you have to say.'

———☐———

The lad's story was a harrowing one of oppression by the lords who now held sway on the other side of the Inaba border. Gone was the benign rule of the Ashimori and at once the usurpers who had torn down their masters had doubled the rice tax and taken goods and chattels where the poor farmers couldn't pay. Then a month ago the Gamō lord had decided to billet some troops in the border villages, ruffians who cared not a fig for the peasants and who took delight in dishonouring any women and girls they fancied. They behaved worse than bandits, declared Gorobei, and Enshin could see the depth of his unhappiness ...

The priest sighed. 'I regret that I have seen much the same and even worse, in the eastern provinces. There is little that can be done but pray that times will improve.' He saw the despair written in the youth's drawn face, then a thought struck him. 'You said that the Gamō have put men in the border villages? Are there many of them?'

'They are like locusts, lord; eating everything!'

'But that means there are a lot of them, don't you think?'

'There weren't that number at first, master ... my lord; but just last week many more came. Rough ashigaru, they were ... they killed five men from our hamlet 'cos they were rude, so they said.'

'Disrespectful?'

'Aye, lord; they sez that they wasn't a-goin' to drink with pigs like that ... so they took 'em out to the river side an' cut off their right hands an'. . .' Gorobei swallowed and looked round across the flooded fields as if he might be overheard. 'They cut off their 'eads, too, they did. One of 'em was old Gennei ...'

'He was my sister's brother-in-law, master,' said Ei-ko with a sniff, 'and he was nigh on eighty years old!'

'I'm sorry, Master Gorobei, but can you tell me how many men you reckon are in those villages? Only a rough guess will do.'

'Well, lord, at a guess I'd say more than two thousand ... that's in seven villages in all.'

'When you crossed the border did you see any of the Omura samurai?'

Gorobei looked blank.

'Them's our local lord's men, fool,' scolded Ei-ko. 'Go on, answer my master!'

'I daresn't cross at the barriers, mas . . . lord . . . I came over the forest trails 'cos it was safer...'

'I quite understand.'

'But I did take a look . . . Odd, it were, since the Gamō weren't there an' yer local sam'rai didn't appear the slightest bit worried. But that's 'ow I saw it, an' it please my lord!'

There followed on a longish silence before Enshin decided that if there was more to be learnt then he had best bide his time patiently.

'Ei-ko-san, have we enough food to feed another hungry mouth? Master Gorobei here looks starved and he's young, at that!'

The widow snorted. 'You wouldn't have thought of packing enough food for your jouney, would you?' she grumbled. 'Typical of the young, ain't it . . . Always expect to be fed on demand . . !'

'There ain't no food to be 'ad, mother,' muttered poor Gorobei.

The heavy rain continued for another whole day and night leaving the paddies, such as they were, brim full and beating down the rank summer grass so that in many places the causeways and the flooded fields were ill-defined and walking made dangerous where an unwary step might pitch a traveller to flounder at his peril. But mere bad weather never deterred so resolute a man as Enshin. He sensed impending danger from what he had learnt from the peasant lad. There was the obvious question as to why the Gamō were sending so many men to the border and whether they intended a sudden strike southwards? Such things rested in the vaulting ambitions of some warlords, ever avaricious and acquisitive, forever scheming to extend their power at the expense of their neighbours . . . Cunning and duplicitous . . .

Just after dawn, he dressed carefully in the robes of a poor wandering mendicant, borrowed young Gorobei's ragged straw cape, took an ancient scrip to hang around his shoulders, and set out, ringed staff in hand, with the intent of crossing through the border fort that dominated the narrow way just north of Nagi mountain. The farmer lad scarce dared raise his head until this one-time warrior now masquerading as a priest had nearly vanished into the dank mists.

'You should have gone with him, boy,' said Ei-ko.

'He wouldn't let me . . . I did ask.'

'Well, get after him now. Your legs'll soon catch him up!'

The lad looked at her, mouth open. The widow thrust another scrip into his hands and grabbed him by the shoulder.

'Go on; get off with you! He's too good a man not to have a servant who knows the country!'

Gorobei splashed through the puddles and sheets of floodwater, soon catching up Enshin. Ei-ko, watching from the shelter of the temple verandah saw the two stop in apparent conversation before the priest, just a vague grey shape in the drizzling rain, turned to look back and bowed low. Then the pair were gone across the little bridge near her dead husband's ruined mill. The old widow had found a fond place in her heart for her priest and vaguely sensed that he had undertaken this journey not so much because of the threat to Lord Omura Hidetada, whose territory this was, but because he felt the need to shield the poor farmers should a war break out.

———— ☐ ————

Enshin and his follower, Gorobei, had no difficulty in passing through the strong Nagi-seki, the Omura samurai examining travellers' passes were hardly on a state of alert. They asked not one question about the lad, contenting themselves with a request that Enshin should say a prayer for them at the Chizu temple, should he call there. It took another two hours from the border to reach a branch track that Gorobei knew and find a small Shugendō temple mentioned by Enshin.

This little temple was perched high up in the upper part of a dead-end valley that in clearer weather would be seen to peter out into a precipitous gulley gauged deep in the northern flank of Nagi-yama. The priest had heard of it from a couple of wandering yama-bushi who had stumbled on the Kobara Enkō-ji not four weeks after the brief battle and assisted Enshin in ministering to some wounded peasants caught up in the aftermath; samurai not being the most particular of people when it comes to who suffers after a victory.

The temple had no name so far as Enshin could see, but boasted an inner structure wherein was housed a fearsome-looking painted statue of Zaō-gongen complete with upstanding wavy shocks of hair, raised stamping right foot, and staring eyes that glared out at the unsuspecting curious person who opened the closed doors! Of course, it was poor Gorobei who did this and the result was his huddling, quaking with fear, in the darkest corner of the Prayer Hall. About the only thing one could say about the place was that it offered dry shelter from the incessant summer deluge although the humidity meant that everything inside felt damp and their saturated clothes wouldn't dry out.

It was two days before they heard someone approach up the last steep flight of rough steps and Enshin, kneeling patiently on the outer verandah saw that it was an old yamabushi who unsteadily climbed the last uneven stones, leaning heavily on his staff.

The old fellow merely nodded in greeting then stood bareheaded before the open doors of the hall, bowing and intoning a long prayer whilst telling off his rosary before his lowered head. At last he was finished and shuffled a trifle wearily towards where Enshin sat.

'Times are changing, my son,' were his first words as, wheezing, he sat himself down on the step below the priest.

'It is in the nature of things, respected sir,' replied Enshin.

The old man's shoulders rose and fell as he regained his breath after the arduous climb. Eventually, without any warning, he said: 'How have you left the Enkō-ji, my son?'

Enshin smiled to himself as he heard Gorobei's sharp intake of breath and knew that the lad must be totally surprised at such an unexpected a question.

'It is in safe hands, master,' he answered.

'A good woman you have there . . . I've known her since she was a small child and that's more than sixty long years past!'

'I am fearful for her, father.'

'Oh, I'm well aware of that.'

A long silence ensued until at last the old yamabushi was fully composed. Despite the fact that evening was drawing in, he came to his feet and secured his strangely rolled up straw hat by its cords below his white-bearded chin. Finally he made a deep bow and murmured: 'A man without an ear will come later. Listen to what he has to say!' He turned and was gone.

Gorobei simply couldn't understand how even a yamabushi could arrive at so remote a place, meet with a fellow priest and yet not say more than sixty or so words before going off abruptly into the rising coils of mist that threatened to thicken before night fell.

'You haven't met many followers of the Shugen ways, I think. They are always an odd lot.' To himself, Enshin added: 'That's why so many swordsmen join their ranks.'

He had long since ceased to worry himself about how many yamabushi seemed to possess knowledge that only he could possibly know. It was in their nature . . . but it was no use speculating. Now, he wondered who this earless man might be and settled himself down to wait just inside the Prayer Hall.

The promise of the mountain being shrouded in mist didn't materialize as darkness fell; instead a breeze began to blow bringing a slight measure of relief from the stickiness accompanying the summer rain. With the rising wind the skies soon cleared allow-

ing the stars to shine through the increasing gaps in the clouds;
a waxing three-quarter moon gave form to the encircling forest clad
heights.

'Light two lanterns, Gorobei-san, to welcome our visitor when
he comes.'

'At once, master.'

'No need to hurry, lad, I am already here!'

Out of the shadows beside the Hall stepped an upright figure.

Enshin, quite unperturbed by the man's sudden appearance, came
to his feet and bowed courteously.

'We were expecting you, sir. Please seat yourself down after your
climb.'

'Enshin-sama, I have been here some time.'

The priest inclined his head slightly.

'About an hour, I believe, Master . . ?'

'Hattō Hidetora. Your reputation has preceeded you, Torii-sama . .
. Ah, Enshin-sama, as is your wish.'

The newcomer glanced back at the courtyard and forest, shrugging his shoulders.

'You know, there is something about places dedicated to Zaō-sama
that give me the strangest feeling.' With an involuntary gesture,
Hidetora ran the fingers of his right hand across his ear, the movement drawing Enshin's attention to the fact that fully half of it was
missing.

Seeing his glance, the stranger laughed. 'That is the penalty for
placing one's trust in the outward appearance of men. Such trust lost
me eight-thousand *koku*, my place, and my ear. Now, Enshin-dono,
I am a mere rōnin living by my wits like any other common samurai!
But then, in different circumstances, you have also put the world
behind you, eh?'

'Much the same, Hattō-sama, there's little difference.'

'Except in one respect, honoured priest!'

'And that is?'

'You spoke with Awakawa Yoshisuke-sama before he fought his
last battle, didn't you, Enshin-dono? He was a fine bushi and you
know his family held wide lands not far to the east of here since
before the Gempei Wars. Mine, too.'

'He seemed a cultured man and one who met death as a true
warrior should.'

'He faced his demise in such a way because there could be no
return to the old ways, my friend. The dog truly savages his master
and perhaps our day is gone.'

'Is that how you view it, Hattō-sama? You see that far into the
future?'

'Oh, it will take many years, Enshin-sama, but the decline of our old values fell with the Kusunoki at Shijō-nawate nearly a hundred-and-eighty years ago.'

'Interesting you should say that. My ancestors died for that cause, you know.'

Hidetora nodded his head. 'I have heard an account of what happened in Yoshino.'

They sat in silence and sipped the tea that Gorobei had miraculously found somewhere in the temple depths.

'You may wonder why I have come here to find you, Torii-sama?'

'I think I know already.'

'Hmm! Those lands you can glimpse over there in the moonlight once were ruled by the Ashimori lords. Few wars troubled these parts until . . . now the Ashimori-ke is destroyed and those who have done this deed have eyes elsewhere. Think about it, Enshin-sama; think about what they might do and where they might go! I shall leave now but request that you remain here in this temple where you will be safe. The Gamō-ke are fearful, as all conspirators always are, that someone will rise up in their turn and destroy them, so they have their spies everywhere . . . Stay here and pray. I shall return two nights from now and you shall hear things that you need to know.'

———— ⌗ ————

To pass the time, both Enshin and Gorobei set to the following day to tidy up the temple precincts. The priest was interested to find that the building was in surprisingly good condition and there were clear signs that it was often used by the yamabushi although they saw no one. Of course, the young peasant scarcely dared go near the tabernacle concealing the fierce image of Zaō-gongen but Enshin had no such qualms and spent a happy hour or two admiring the bold carving of the sculptor, but try as he might, he could not find any carved signature. Yet, from the style and the peeling paint, he had a feeling that the figure may well have been five or six-hundred years old. But the problem with this fierce mountain deity was that while he might represent a stimulus to the more esoteric of the Shugendō mystics, he had an undoubtedly depressing effect on the minds of more simple folk, particularly the superstitious like the young peasant. All the afternoon and that evening poor Gorobei became morose and clearly fearful for the future, so much so that on the second day Enshin decided that he would chant much of the Heart Sutra in order to show the simple youth that he would be protected by the powerful Guardians.

He was intoning another long formula from the holy scriptures when a sudden shouting outside heralded the arrival of a troop of ashigaru armed with spears. The leader, a junior samurai wearing full armour but without his helmet, stamped up the steps and flung open the sliding doors.

'What have we here?' he bawled and two footsoldiers ran to join him.

Terrified, Gorobei fell to his knees and grovelled as low as he could but Enshin calmly continued his measured chant while beating out the rhythm on a small drum mounted on a stand at his right side.

'What are you doing here, priest?' demanded the samurai, not caring if he interrupted Enshin's devotions.

With a last beat with the long drumstick, Enshin turned and bowed his head to a respectful level and replied, softly: 'I am praying to the Lord Buddha for his blessing on the rulers of this domain. Would you care to join me, sir?'

'Spies have been reported nearby!' shouted the lackey, for he could hardly have a greater status. The fellow turned on the footsoldiers and rasped out: 'Get on with the search! Don't just stand there gaping!' He wheeled round and appeared to notice Gorobei for the first time. 'You! Where are you from?'

The lad gulped with fear.

'I . . . I'm . . .'

'He's my servant, sir,' said Enshin, mildly. 'None too bright, I'm afraid.'

The samurai looked at the youth as though he were something unmentionable and spat on the floor, an act of foul desecration that Enshin struggled to ignore.

'Have you seen anyone around here, priest?'

'Neither I nor my servant have seen anyone for the past three days. Perhaps, sir, you have been misled?'

Three of the ragged footsoldiers ran in and under the direction of one of their seniors, an ill-favoured fellow with a badly scarred face, they set to tearing open the Zaō cabinet, splintering the doors with their yari. As the doors burst open, so the disturbance upset the statue's balance – the figure of the angry deity stood on only one leg anyway – and Zaō slowly creaked over to one side then, amidst a terrible splintering sound, toppled forwards crushing one of the ashigaru's legs under him. There was a moment's silence before the air was rent by the fellow's anguished screams.

'Where are you from, verminous priest?' bawled the officious samurai, totally ignoring the plight of the soldier.

'I have wandered the Lord Buddha's Path for many years. He has guided my steps to reach this temple and required me to pray.'

More disturbance outside made the samurai run to the doors but with an oath he soon returned, his face as black as thunder.

'We were sent to search out spies and you are all we have found! As I see it, you must be agents; who else would want to come to this broken-down place, eh? There's no one else! Seize them!'

Gorobei jerked up his head.

'Careful, lad . . . Don't give them any excuse,' warned Enshin under his breath.

They were ineptly bound and dragged out into the courtyard where they stood in the pouring rain. Even the guard, a gaunt fellow whose kimono was in tatters, stood there with the look of a dying duck and a temper that matched the sultry sombreness of that miserable evening. Then, without humanity, the ashigaru forced their pinioned captives down the steep uneven blocks of the steps, a stone stairway difficult even for those who were young and agile with the added aid of spearshafts for support, whilst behind them a crackling noise told Enshin that these brutal ashigaru had acted in their usual manner and wantonly set fire to that venerable temple. . . . leaving the maimed soldier to perish. Perhaps the deities would send even heavier rain to quench the hungry flames, but he doubted that it would be so. It was fortunate that the domineering lackey veered off the stone flight that threatened at any moment to pitch both prisoners down to destruction, and took a narrow side track into the near blackness of the forest where they soon filed out to a cleared hillside and descended the slippery path to a motley huddle of mean hovels. Through the curtains of rain the priest could just see, in the last of the evening light, the arrow-towers and timber palisades of a newly constructed fort standing on the lower shoulder of the opposite height.

———— ⊟ ————

Forced to stumble through the cloying miasma of the village at spearpoint, the two captives were taken to the last mean house and pitched into what was once home for a couple of oxen. Enshin knew this at once, despite the Stygian darkness; the overpowering scent of rotting flesh could only come from a long-dead carcase.

Both the captives, unceremoniously dumped into this stinking place, eventually managed to sit up and with great care to lean against what might have been a wooden partition.

Enshin knew from Gorobei's suppressed intake of breath that perhaps he was somehow injured but his whispered questions elicited no direct answers. Brave lad, he thought, as he composed himself to face an uncomfortable night. There was absolutely nothing either of them could do in any case; they simply had to wait for whatever might befall them the following day. Then he heard a slight movement in the stinking straw somewhere to his left. Was it rats? Was someone else lying there? He strained his ears but heard nothing for some time but at last his keen ears registered a wheezing breath and a muttered groan ...

'Who is it?' he whispered, but thought he wasn't heard and repeated the question. The last thing he wanted to do was raise the suspicions of any guard sheltering outside.

'Hrrrh! Just a poor rōnin. No one of any account,' came the hissed reply after a long pause. 'And you ..?

At once Enshin's keen memory recognized even that hardly audible whisper; their fellow captive was no less than Hattō Hidetora!

'A wandering priest, that's all ...'

'A priest, eh; hmmmph! Listen, priest; I have no name to give you ... none that is important, but I think you know that because Zaō-gongen watches over you ... Am I right?'

'Perhaps, perhaps! Zaō may by now have a very warm residence, I think ...'

Through the cracks in the rickety doorway he could see the flickering light of a flaring torch and a voice shouted out demanding to know if all was well. That there was a sentry posted under the decaying thatch there was no doubt when a sleepy voice said, amidst a stifled yawn, 'Bugger off, Ichiemon! Get back to yer boy an' leave them as 'ave a job ter do ter get on wiv it! Of course everythin's alright. Them spies is trussed up like chickens still. They can 'ardly escape, you id'jut!'

'If that swine, Saburō, 'ears yer, 'e'll 'ave your balls for 'is breakfast, 'e will!'

The sentry snorted derisively and muttered something foul.

Taking advantage of this conversation, Enshin hitched himself across to his left so that he was closer to their fellow captive.

'Are you there?' he whispered.

'Another couple of feet, priest, but take care, you are very close to the dead oxen. The slightest touch and I reckon she's ready to burst!'

'I pray not!'

Enshin felt his sleeve grasped.

'You are unbound?'

'Yes, priest; they know I cannot escape as they've cut my hamstrings!'

'I am sorry!'

'It's not your fault, young lord; as soon as I was captured some such thing would have happened, anyway. Now all I await is recognition in the morning. Someone up at that fort will know me, that's for sure.'

They heard the guard outside swear as he shifted his position but soon after he began to snore.

'Your hands are free?'

'They are.'

'Can you untie the knot between my shoulders? These soldiers have little idea how to properly restrain a man!'

It took Hidetora only a few minutes to loosen the bindings and Enshin rubbed back some feeling into his arms.

'That's better,' he murmured. 'Now for Gorobei-san . . .'

'No, wait a moment, Enshin-dono; bide a second for there may be little time.'

The former hatamoto felt for Enshin's shoulder and leant towards him in the darkness to whisper: 'Gamō-dono plans something, that much I know, but what it is isn't yet clear. If you can get out, then cross back to Mimasaka but on no account approach the Omura . . . Enshin-dono, I fear that the Gamō have deeper plans than mere annexation of parts of the Omura lands, don't you?'

'Hmmm! I agree with you.' From his previous experience as a young warrior serving the Uesugi and the Nagao lords in the Kantō, he knew that were the Gamō to successfully invade and snatch territory in northern Mimasaka then many disaffected warriors and others would flock to serve under their banners. A skilful general offered the bait of both food and booty in abundance. But what were the further aims of the Omura-ke and were they alone in this?

'Go to your servant and free him. It will soon be dawn, priest, and we must decide on a plan of action.'

'Master,' whispered Gorobei as Enshin pulled off his bonds, 'them soldiers didn't search me not no how. In the small of my back is a dirk, please take it. Could be useful, couldn't it?'

The priest smiled in the darkness.

He found the dagger and moved across to the doorway. Just as he expected and knowing farmers, over the lintel his hand found a couple of staves and, better still, a sword! With the greatest care he felt his way back to the others.

'I have a plan, my lord, which I think is worth something.'

Quickly he outlined what was in his mind.

When he had finished, Hidetora grunted. 'Nothing can save me now, my good friend, but I can at least do something to save the honour of my name. Let me have the dirk then set your scheme in motion.'

Enshin knew that the warrior was right but his heart was heavy as he passed him the dagger.

'Gorobei, stand just behind the door on the left side. Strike whoever comes in very hard at the base of their skull once they are about three feet into this stinking place. Understand?'

'Ahhh!'

'Good; then we are ready.'

A moment later the priest let out a shriek of fear and kicked with his feet against the stall timbers which, as he had expected, gave way and splintered.

'Help us!' he bawled; 'We are being attacked . . . Get off. .!'

The sentry, dazed by sleep, shouted out something unintelligible, and dragged away whatever secured the outer doors. He called out something over his shoulder and came in at a crouch with his spear levelled, peering into the dark. Gorobei's stave, swung with all the strength of his powerful arms, smashed acros the yari-mochi's neck, snapping it cleanly so that the man was dead even before his body slumped forwards. The priest caught the spear as it fell free.

'Two men coming through the rain, master,' whispered the young peasant in warning. 'One has a torch.'

'Good, we'll give them something to remember! Stand well aside, Gorobei-san!'

As they ran up, Enshin called out in a muffled voice, that he needed help with the spy, and now, as they entered, he leant across and plunged the tip of the katana into the tightened hide across the swollen belly of the long-dead ox. With an unearthly hiss the carcase burst apart under the pressure of gas, spewing a great miasma of stinking corruption directly at the doorway into the faces of the pair. In a moment both men fell under the violent blows of Gorobei's stout cudgel.

'Pssshaw!' The stench was almost unbearable.

'Are there more, my friend.'

The youth peered out into the dank half-light.

'No, my lord; no sound that I can hear. Nothing!'

Enshin caught up the torch before it set things alight. He could now see Hattō Hidetora sitting with his legs stretched out in front of him. He was holding his kimono and haori close about his front.

'We must get you to safety, my lord. There's no time to lose but I think we can do it with the cover of this rain.'

'No, Enshin-dono. My race is run but at least I shall go to my ancestors with our good name intact. Go . .! Free yourself and this brave man . . . See, I have saved you further trouble!' He opened his hands and, to his horror, the priest saw that the former hatamoto had committed seppuku. 'Take my head, Torii-dono; take it with you and bury it beside that of my friend, Awakawa Yoshisuke. Both of us will rest in the Buddha's mercy.'

The blood, held back by the pressure of his hands, poured forward and the maimed rōnin folded forward, his neck perfectly exposed . . .

———⊟———

'The houses are deserted, lord,' reported Gorobei, returning after Enshin had wrapped up the severed head and was ready to depart.

'Good! Take the torch and set fire to every hut we pass. That will delay any pursuit, I think!'

An hour later, when the skies were appreciably lightening ahead of the coming dawn, the two men carrying their precious burden and now armed with yari and katana with a spare sword secured across their shoulders, had climbed up to the smouldering temple. Miraculously, the Prayer Hall still stood and when Enshin looked inside he could just make out the statue's eyes glaring at him as it lay supine amidst the wreckage of its dias. Below and behind them the site of the huddled village was marked by a heavy pall of smoke and they could still hear the blare of horns sounding the alarm at the nearby fort, but thus far at least they were not pursued. He caught up his ringed staff, overlooked by the ashigaru, pleased to have it back.

From this point, Gorobei took his master by little-known mountain tracks that seemed to wander aimlessly about the thick forests but were never, with just one exception, within sight of any man-made structure. They paused just once at a point where, through the tops of the soaring cedars, the young man pointed out a corner of the distant Negi Barrier and Enshin knew that they were once more on Omura territory. But in the back of his mind he was turning over and over such information he had gleaned and felt uneasy regarding how it could be interpreted.

———⊟———

The following morning Enshin with due ceremony, buried the head of the hatamoto next to that of General Awakawa in a secret grave beneath the timbers of the Enkō-ji. He had reached a conclusion and was certain that it was right.

'Mistress Ei-ko, prepare enough food for all three of us to travel, will you?'

'It's already done, master!'

'Uh . . ? Oh, it doesn't matter, but thank you.' He looked at the incessant rain. Surely the wet season must come to an end soon . . . and that would be the time of the greatest danger. 'We shall need straw capes, I'll be thinking.'

'We have those, too.' She smiled as she served him his customary tea. 'And Gorobei has made three of his funny straw *waraboshi*.'

'Then I take it that you are both ready for the journey?'

'Wherever you take us we shall go.'

A little later the three set out through the warm rain taking the lesser tracks south and west towards Kasuta where they passed their second night in a small inn, the innmaster glad to find even such poor custom. The next day Enshin asked directions to Shō-ō making it clear that he intended to pray at the temple that stood nearby and they set out again, this time with only a passing shower to dampen the glorious morning. The warm sun soon heated up the wet ground and they were forced to travel the byways through dense banks of mist and beset by many biting insects.

Once at Shō-ō, they put up at another small inn on the edge of the little town, announcing that they would be staying maybe up to a week. From the moment they arrived they became aware that the place was rife with rumours about what was happening in Inaba across the border but no one seemed to have any clear idea. For two days running Enshin walked through the town to the Shō-ō-dera in order to join the four resident priests at their devotions. After his second visit he was invited to rest and take some rather bitter tea and one of the priests asked him about the Enkō-ji and his ministrations to the nearby farmers. The conversation soon turned to the Inaba border but Enshin made sure that he expressed little knowledge of the situation other than what he had heard from the farmers.

'We heard that our master, Omura-dono, had ordered his hata-moto to recruit more men. Maybe he is worried?'

The other three priests shook their heads.

'Well, if he is worried as everyone says, why hasn't he sent his men up to Nagi and Ōhara; tell me that?' said one.

The others laughed.

'Are you a strategist, then, Gen-en?'

'I only wondered; that's all!'

Enshin smiled.

'I leave military affairs to warriors, and pray for guidance from Fudō Myō-ō in everything else. The problem is that I have seen too much war in the Kantō and my travels to here. I worry that war may destroy the livelihoods of so many innocent people and leave them with nothing but a miserable future.'

The chief priest leant across the low table to pour him more ō-cha.

'Don't worry, my good friend; if something bad will happen, we'll all know soon enough!'

'Perhaps I should return to my humble Enkō-ji? What do you advise?'

'No, my son; travel on as you plan. A few days' absence will do no harm but may serve to enrich your soul.'

Two days later the rains started again, even heavier than before and the old wooden bridge over the swollen Yo-shin river collapsed and was swept away during the night though, fortunately, no one was injured or lost their life, but the result was that the two sides of the town were completely divided as there was no way of crossing that turbulent flood.

———————□———————

Three troublesome rōnin formed a noisy and sometimes aggressive presence in the inn, however, when full of ō-saki but before they became quarrelsome, their tongues wagged freely, mostly on subjects they knew little about. For some reason, they took a liking to Enshin and seemed to respect his robes and calling. One of the trio had a nasty boil behind his left knee and the priest offered to lance it to draw off the foul suppuration and release the evil spirit who had taken up residence there. Eventually the man agreed but Enshin wisely requested that he first hand over his sword and dirk to one of his companions while the cleansing proceeded. Taking out a small bamboo tube, sealed at one end but with a cunning stopper the other, he extracted a fine sliver of bamboo, sharpened so that the tip was like a needle, Enshin had Mistress Ei-ko hold the man's leg whilst his two friends grasped his forearms. In a trice the priest drove in his needle and at once applied a cloth to soak up the vile yellow pus that copiously spurted out of the angry inflamed eruption.

'Shit!' mouthed the masterless samurai, gritting his teeth. 'Ahhhh! I hoped to march and join in any fighting down south but for this ill-luck!'

'You'll not be marching anywhere for a few days until this is cleared up,' smiled the priest, raising his eyebrows.

It was Ei-ko who picked him up: 'Fighting down south, master? Why, we all thought the Inaba border was in danger! Just think of it, another war threatens . . . How awful!'

'War on the border up there, mother?' growled one of the others. 'No likelihood of that the way things are going!'

'Sorry, masters; I was surprised, that's all.'

Their patient craned his neck round as Enshin placed some foul-smelling unguent around the deep hole in his leg and bound up the wound with a clean hachimaki.

'You are a lucky man, my friend,' said Enshin. 'That boil was very bad but if it had turned morbid a demon might have carried you off!'

But the rōnin appeared only interested in his headcloth.

'Pity to use that! It's my last one! Ahhhh, that's better! Feels less sore already. What was it you were saying, Tō-san? No, we're looking to go south alright. That's where we reckon the action will be, not up on that poxy border.'

Enshin steered off the subject from that point, sending Ei-ko back with his medicine scrip up to their room, and soon took his leave despite the rōnin wanting to reward him with rice wine.

What the samurai said filled his mind. 'South? Why south? No trouble lay that way, surely?'

The next night was to be their last in Shō-ō and when he went down to the drinkers he was welcomed by the rather drunken rōnin as their saviour. After he had once more examined the boil, finding it still clean and clearly reduced, he agreed to drink some ō-cha as he had vowed never to take stronger liquor.

'We are no longer "wave-men", priest! Fortune has smiled upon us!' grinned 'Boil'.

'You mean?'

'We are now Omura samurai! Two meals a day and silver to spare for wine! It's good news, isn't it, Tō-san?'

Their somewhat dour-looking companion sneered.

'Our trade is death so what have we got to smile about, you tell me?'

'Take no notice of him! Pour out more ō-sake, Yahagi-san, will you!'

The trio had enticed across a couple of the rather colourful girls who always frequented these taverns and apart from 'Boil' the others were soon engrossed in the usual risqué horseplay that usually led to an obvious conclusion.

'Take no notice of them,' said the leader affably, though he was clearly beginning to feel the effects of the wine, 'they are rather young and have little experience of real living . . .'

'You think there will be war,' asked Enshin, innocently.

'Boil' hiccupped and squeezed up his eyes. 'Look, you're my friend despite you're a priest . . . Never had much to do with your sort before . . . What were you before you . . . er . . ?'

'Shaved my head? Oh, I was a samurai like you.'

'You knew how to look after yourself, I expect?'

'Times were troubled, my friend.'

'Can't remember anything else . . . War? Oh, yes; war's coming alright . . . Goin' to be a shock for someone, I reckon . . . Here, give me another cup. Good saké, this!'

Out of the corner of his eye Enshin saw a couple of young samurai come through the outer door. Oddly, they had a pinioned and blindfolded prisoner with them who they roughly forced to kneel by one of the roof posts. They tied the halter rope securely ordering a gaunt yari-mochi footsoldier who was with them, to stay on guard and stepped up onto the dirty straw-covered tavern floor, loudly calling for wine. Almost at once, Enshin recognized one of the newcomers as the arrogant young lackey who had taken him captive at the Zaō temple. Here was real danger if he was recognized and denounced.

He appraised the situation and at once realized that he couldn't turn his back as he needed to see what the Gamō samurai might do should he know who he was, and if he did then the ashigaru by the door would have a clear view. One or the other must identify him as their escaped victim. He decided that he would warn 'Boil' of the situation in which he found himself and hope that he might just feel obligated enough to give him his support. Nothing was lost if he didn't; he would be taken and that was that.

Before he could say anything, the serving man who brought the wine to the newcomer's bench nearly tripped over an outstretched leg which caused the samurai to look up as he held out his wine saucer. He looked full at Enshin who sat only five or six feet away but at first didn't know him, but as he took his first draught his memory came back. His eyes widened as he took a second deep draught and muttered something to his companion, heaving himself to his feet, hand clutching for his sword. Tō-san, alerted to possible danger by the sudden movement out of the corner of his eye, thrust his girl sprawling backwards, her legs all bared, and caught up his katana. The second of the newcomers, with the agility but thoughtlessness of youth, jumped to the right, his foot coming down heavily on Yahagi-san's sword, splintering the scabbard. From that point a fight become inevitable.

'You are my prisoner,' yelled out the Gamō lackey, reaching out to grab Enshin's sleeve.

'Who, in the name of the Gods, are you?' shouted 'Boil', drawing his sword. 'This is my friend and not your prisoner!'

The Gamo samurai reddened with anger.

'Get out of the way, fellow; this is none of your business.'

'It's mine, though,' growled Yahagi and he cut at the second of the newcomers but misjudged the distance. In return, he was slightly gashed across his forearm . . .

'This priest is a spy!' shouted out the lackey, trying once more to grab Enshin. 'He was spying across the border in Inaba . . .'

'Was he now? If you want him you'll have to take me first!' 'Boil' swept back his sword above his head but missed his footing against the rising Tō-san, giving the Gamō lackey just enough time to slash wildly across his belly. The blade missed 'Boil' but badly gouged Tō's shoulder. Now the fight became general, women screaming and other drinkers scrabbling to get away over the upset benches and broken sake jars.

Just six or seven seconds had elapsed, time enough for Enshin to duck backwards. He always had the capacity to remain cool and

now his mind registered that Mistress Ei-ko had entered the outer
door near the bound captive. The ashigaru, his mouth wide open,
was about to jump up onto the tavern floor but Ei-ko had somehow caught up a mattock . . . and, inexplicably, swung it round
summoning up all her strength, and buried it deep in the spearman's
back . . . He fell with a dreadful scream as though his very soul was
being ripped from his body by demons.

'Watch out, master,' she shrilled in warning and Enshin ducked
low to avoid a swinging cut from the cursing lackey. In a trice, he
caught hold of the man's left arm and effortlessly pitched him into
the path of 'Boil's' blade. The fellow was dead before he slumped to
the floor. The second newcomer fared no better receiving a nasty
thrust in his side and a deep wound to his forehead which soon
proved fatal. Enshin looked back across the chaotic scene and to his
amazement saw that the captive was none other than Gorobei and
that he stood with his arm across Ei-ko-san's shoulder . . .

———————□———————

'No employment with the Omura-han, my friend, not after what
happened yesterday!'

'Well, it was something that might have been.' 'Boil', actually
Yamanaka Toshirō, shrugged his shoulders.

The small group had left the inn early that morning just as day
was breaking and were heading south along a little frequented track
hoping to reach the Mori fortress at Aida before dusk. The skies
were clear again but they were fortunate that a thick mist hung all
day over the Yo-gawa valley. Any pursuit despatched by the Omura
would find it difficult to locate them, that is, if such a hunt had been
instituted. Only Enshin and Ei-ko-san seemed unscathed; Gorobei
had been beaten and sustained a head wound, Tō-san's shoulder had
been bandaged up, Yahagi's right arm had been cut and was now
stitched by the priest, and Toshirō's forearm cleaned up.

'You said last night that you had been a samurai, Enshin-sama?'

'I was a samurai, Yamanaka-sama; that is true.'

'Were you ever a spy as that man claimed?'

Enshin smiled.

'Before I answer that may I ask if you were ever employed by the
Omura-han?'

Toshirō drew in a deep breath through his nose and took a fresh
hold on the reins as he led along his sturdy horse.

'No, not exactly, priest. I would have been as would Tō-san and
Yahagi-san.' He laughed. 'I see what you mean . . . you might have
gone on to be a spy, a secret agent, eh?'

'Maybe . . . maybe not, who can tell?'

'Why, then, do we travel south to the Aida yashiki? Just on a whim . . . an idle wish to pray at some temple or other to atone for some paltry men's deaths? No, Enshin-sama, I believe it goes deeper than that. Am I right?'

'Last year a honourable bushi died near my temple simply because his future was not compatible with his past; this year, not two weeks past, another fine bushi cut his belly for the same reason . . . I can well understand the motives for their deaths, Yamanaka-sama, and it is for that reason and one other that I shall seek audience with Mori-dono.'

Toshirō walked on some distance before he spoke again.

'You fear that Omura-dono plans treachery, don't you? I heard an account of the death of General Awakawa Yoshisuke and how he was attacked not by the Gamō-ke but by the Omura, but who was the other man, I wonder . . ? Omura and Gamō, eh? But what is your other motive?'

'Why do you walk, Yamanaka-sama?'

'You know very well, O-priest; very well indeed!'

'When a boil is lanced, my friend, much evil pours out and in due time the pain has gone, the wound heals, and the sufferer is whole again. In a day or two you will be able to ride that horse of yours. Shortly you can again wear your armour.'

'And then, Enshin-sama?'

'And then, Yamanaka Toshirō, you will be employed by a fine clan.'

'You are certain of that?'

'As certain as I am of many things. That is the legacy of my background and all the experience I have gained since.'

And so it turned out. The self-serving duplicity of Omura Hidetada was found out and he was shortly after assassinated by an unknown hand. The Mori moved in force to secure their northern borders, building a number of strong points, one of which was commanded by the newly-engaged Yamanaka Toshirō, the warrior who presented Enshin's information. War was averted and there was peace in northern Mimasaka for another fifteen years.

It is as the sage wrote:
Delicate indeed!
Truly delicate!
In war there is no place
Where espionage
Is not used.

9

INCIDENT ON THE ITAKO BRIDGE

▽

'Toshiaki, my friend; you were going to tell me about what occurred when you had just left Kashima near the beginning of your search for me? Why don't you do so now?'

The burly follower grunted as he wiped his calloused palm across his sweat beaded crown before drying the side-pads of his straw hat.

'Master, before I do so I reckons we should go on to the shelter of that temple gateway; it looks as if it will rain hard in a minute or two, seeing at how the clouds have come down between the peaks!'

He knew very well that his master, the priest Torii Enshin, cared little for the elements; the heat of summer, rain, snow, or wind, and that his gentle black water-buffalo, known to all as Kuroi-san, or Mr Black, was the same. But he, Toshiaki, Enshin's self-appointed factotum, had to think for all three as they trudged along the highways and byways of the provinces for what seemed no better reason than his master's curious need to lighten the burden of the poor . . . and the gods only knew there were enough and to spare of those in these disturbed times.

The black-robed monk sitting sideways on a blanket padding the ox's hips, smiled and remarked to the buffalo: 'Master Toshiaki has no wish for another wetting, I think!'

'No, master; I was attempting to preserve you . . .'

Kuroi-san uttered a low gutteral grunt.

Enshin laughed.

'My friend; we know you too well! But so be it; you are quite right and it will soon pour with rain. We shall hurry to take shelter if that will please you.'

The first large drops were already splashing onto the dusty track a minute before they reached the shelter of the decaying thatched roof. There wasn't another soul, farm hovel or roadside inn in sight. The threatening mountain storm burst overhead with startling ferocity as only it could do amongst these Kumano heights, though this was only to be expected after the first stifling hot days of early summer, and their straw *kappo* ran with water.

Toshiaki carefully shook off the rain drops and, thinking that they might well be here for an hour or two at the very least, hung them up on the black timber partition that filled the gap between the central entrance and the side wicket gate. He wondered why there was a need for such a commanding structure when the broken-down ruinous condition of the temple's outer walls would keep nothing out of the precincts, nothing larger than an ancient badger or injured fox, that is. He took their food wallet that was slung across Kuroi-san's broad shoulders and set the buffalo's drinking bucket under a stream of rainwater now pouring off the thatch by the white pebble soakaway. His master gave some handfulls of hay to his bovine friend, gently stroking the animal's soft ears as he did so. Enshin was a patient man and knew that soon, in his own time, the swordsman-carpenter would start his account.

As soon as they had settled down on the heavy timber that formed the sill across the entrance boards, cedar wood that in itself showed every sign of great antiquity, Toshiaki sniffed and blew out his cheeks before letting out his breath with a sigh.

'Let's see . . . It was about fifteen years ago, master; a couple or three months after I was given permission by the Ō-karō-dono to begin my search, that my steps had taken me across the lakes to the Kashima shrine. I had some vague idea that the kami-sama there would somehow guide me, I think . . .'

He paused to take another bite at the white rice cake so kindly made for them by the farmer's wife back in the Kawakami valley a couple of days before they set out southwards.

'One moment, master, while I fetch some water for Kuroi-san. That bucket must be half-filled by now, I reckon!'

There was a long silence until Enshin remarked: 'I found Kashima a very interesting place. I think that I could happily reside there, you know . . .'

'Quite so, master, but I soon was on my way and was ferried across Kitaura one summer's morning just like this. Well, like this except I was in the Kantō, all hot and sticky with the rain coming down like arrows. Soaked through, I was, long before I found a small inn near to those small swamps that marked where the lake started before it reached the Tone river . . . I gave up at that point and thought that I had best turn my steps up to Itako rather than risk losing my way through the marshes and ending up getting drowned for my pains!'

'Very wise of you, my friend, but do go on.'

'Well, master, the rain well and truly set in and with little or no objective pressing I decided to stay in this inn overnight. Just as well, I suppose, since at that time the Tone marshes sheltered many ne'er-do-wells and criminals who made their living by robbery. It was before Hikata-dono flushed them out and killed a great many!

'At first the inn was deserted and I settled myself down out of the way in a corner. It wasn't a high-class place, I can assure you, but I put up with any slight discomfort because it kept me out of the wet. Anyway, I must have dozed off to sleep during the late afternoon and woke up in deep shadow. Looking through the gaps in the partition because the goodwife had put me in the part that probably doubled as a stable, I saw that the main room had attracted about seven or eight rough-looking fellows, four of whom were busy gambling with dice. They drank large quantities of bad rice wine and, by the mid-evening, became boistrously drunk. About this point a couple of rōnin came in and sat themselves down on a bench. They were soon joined by two of the women who are always to be found in such places and they, too, drank heavily. About the only thing I noticed about these samurai was that they very carefully placed their swords down beside them at their left sides; well, one of them did because the other wore his sword slung, *tachi* fashion.

'Everything quietened down late on and the sam'rai were snoring lustily. Before I dropped off into sleep again, making sure that I could defend myself if it became necessary, always a prudent precaution . . .'

'True enough, my friend,' murmured Enshin.

'A bit later, I was wakened by a loud shout and set my eye to the lowest gap beside me. At first I could make nothing out but then someone across the room uncovered a night lantern which gave enough light to see the glint of a swordblade just as the man carrying it stabbed down. A sudden gasp told me that someone had been pierced. At this point all hell burst out loose and the lantern went out . . . The outer door was thrust aside and out into the rain stumbled one or two figures. I could hear feet splashing off through the puddles outside.

'I lay still wondering what I should do while in the room proper some lights were brought. Sometimes it is best to do nothing and I reckon I was right since no one took any notice of my being there until dawn came and daylight made it easier to see. I gathered that what had happened was that either one of the girls had tried to rob her rōnin but had awakened him. She was then assisted by two of the gamblers and a fight ensued. The other rōnin had escaped but not before one man had been badly gashed.

'As I came out from my stall my foot scuffed against something lying in the straw and, being a cautious man, I hooked it back with my foot so that whatever it was remained hidden in the shadows by the thick wooden post. Somehow or other, I managed to be given some thin soup and ō–soba to break my fast and, due to the hubbub, found the excuse to eat back in the stall. I was joined by a couple of seedy looking peasants so I took care to sit where whatever it was I had found was firmly concealed under my feet.

'A couple of the previous night's gamblers came in an hour or so later, loudly bewailing the fact that the second rōnin had somehow disappeared and hadn't been found. I gathered that they claimed, or so they said, that they were going to capture the man and hand him over to the clan authorities at Sawara for the nasty wound he had given to their mate, but I thought their real intention was further robbery.

'The two marshmen noisily slurping their noodle soup near me listened to what was said and from time to time passed looks between them which made me suspicious. At length, when the others had left, the pair got up and pushed past me with hardly a glance, but I heard the one say to the other something that sounded very like: "That'un must 'ave got away with them g . . ."

'I didn't catch the rest because the goodwife came back at that moment and demanded payment.

'They left and I gathered up my satchel with my tools, at the same time picking up the pongee bag at my feet. Inside it was something quite heavy though fortunately relatively small, and I was able to slip it under my kimono behind my satchel which I secured, not without some puffing and blowing, across my back in the usual artisan traveller's manner.

'I thanked the woman for my lodging, carefully counting out some copper coins, and drew my straw cape close about my shoulders, bowing with my *waragasa* in hand as I left. No one took the slightest notice of me as I was clearly nearly penniless and a peasant like themselves. I set off into the misty drizzle with a slow plodding step but soon caught up with the two men who had ate next to me.

'Can I walk with you, sirs, as I'm not sure of the way to Itako?'

' "You're a stranger 'ere abouts, ain't yer?" says the smaller of the two, a stooped man with a wizened face. He scrutinized me up and down, naturally.

'His companion snorted.

' "Join us if yer wish . . . An' o'course 'e's a furriner, daft idiot. We ain't seen 'im 'ere aforetime, ain't we?"

' "Course we ain't. Stands ter reason 'e's a furriner, it does!"

' "My name's Toshiaki," I says, and added, "That was some commotion las' night, weren't it?"

' "How should we know; we weren't there!"

' "Well, no; I knows that, but you 'eard what was said this morning . . . Man got 'imself killed and another was stabbed. I gathered that 'cos I was asleep where we 'ad breakfast!"

' "Call that there breakfast . . . Shit! Swine swill, that was!"

' "Yeah, but I thought I 'eard you say a word or three about someone gettin' away with somethin' an' I was just curious, that's all."

'The bigger of the two knitted his brows and looked hard at me.

' "Wot was that, eh? Yer knows about the . . .?"

' "Shrivelled-face" twisted round as the other was talking and dug him sharply in the ribs.

' "'Ere, 'oo's the idiot now, hey? Shootin' yer mouth off, you is. That there gold's ours, so it is!"

' "Gold . . . Did I 'ear right?" I says. "But don't either 'o you take offence . . . none intended!"

'They both hauled off a space and conferred whilst I followed up behind. At length, the bigger man says: "Since yer knows, you 'ad best join us . . . but . . ."

' "Shrivelled" shouts out: "Yer gets yer throat slit if you blabs, an' that's a fact!"

' "You'll swear not ter breath a word, eh?" warns the bigger man.

'I looks at them both with my best puzzled brow.

' "I'm not sure what you are talking about," I says. "What am I supposed not to tell a soul?"

' "About the gold . . . That there sam'rai 'ad gold an' that's wot we're after. So now you knows an' yer can 'ave a share if yer comes in wiv us!"

' "What, the rōnin was carrying gold . . ? But he can't have had much because it weighs a lot, doesn't it?"

' "O, aye; it is 'eavy, at that!" grins "Shrivelled", "Yeah, you should know as you woz a stinkin' pirate afore!"

'I acted a little simple and said: "You were a kaizoku . . . on the seas? I ain't met a sea-soldier before!"

'His mate sniffed. "You ain't met a wakō, eh? Them's all mean bastards an'll cut yer throat as soon as look at yer, they will.

So don't even think a single thought o' double crossin' us, yer understands?"

'A little later, and they had calmed down a bit by then, the bigger man says: "Me name's Jun and this 'ere's Yoichi but you can call 'im 'Yo' for short . . . Everybody does. I once nearly became an ashigaru, you know, an' I knows 'ow to swing a sword proper-like . . ."

' "E's very good at that, 'e is," chips in Yo but Jun fetches a blow at his ear which had it connected would have pitched him into a pool of water next to the track.

' "So are you going to try and find this rōnin and take the . . . er . . . gold? Could be dangerous work, so it could."

' "There's three o' us now, mate. Three agin one miserable vagabond; that's more than enough, I reckon!"

' "I've seen some wandering samurai who could take on ten men and keep one arm behind their back." I tried to sound cautious. "I wouldn't like to try . . !"

' "Yeah, well them's far spaced an' this'un ain't one o' that sort. We've follered 'im for a week an' we knows!"

' "That's right," says "Shrivelled". "Ev'ry night them sam'rai gets stoned an' all they wants is a bit o' you know what. We waits our chance then one o' us'll slip a dirk betwixt 'is ribs and the gold is ours!"

' "Just like that?" I sniffed.

' "Jus' like that . . . 'E'll give up 'is treasure with 'ardly a pip . . ."

' "You're in, ain't yer?" Jun sounded suspicious.

' "Of course I'm in," I shouted. "Ain't I sworn so?" I purposely roughened my voice in order to set them at their ease.'

———— ☐ ————

'Towards the end of the afternoon it began to pour with rain just as we reached the first houses in the village of Itako. Well, it was a bit bigger than a village, I suppose . . .'

Enshin smiled.

'I once passed through there and I think I would describe it as a small garrison town. I recall that it had a strong fort just on the eastern side.'

'Correct, master, but the year before these two and I reached there part of the town had been burnt in an attack from Sawara. We could still see some of the charred timbers even though most had been rebuilt. Shall I go on?'

'Of course! You said that this man, Yoichi, had once been a kaizoku,' remarked Enshin. 'That means he must have knocked around a bit and had some idea of life?'

'I reckoned that he had only been a simple sailor, probably only a glorified oarsman, master. In all his conversation he seemed to be as thick as ox turds, saving your presence, Kuroi-san.'

They were both immediately aware that the buffalo had a sort of pained expression as he turned his head towards them.

'Master Kuroi, I apologize deeply,' smiled Toshiaki.

Enshin nodded his head sagely. 'I'm sure you are forgiven, my friend . . . But, to continue with what I was saying: this Jun or his companion must have realized that if robbery was intended at the inn, then it was carried out by the others, or some of them, *before* these two arrived?'

'That's what I reasoned, master, but they carried on as though the thought hadn't entered their heads. Anyway, as we came to one of the first inns at Itako, I saw settled on the verandah of the nearest tumble-down ryōkan three of the gamblers. They had got there before us! And can you guess who was with them, eh?'

'The rōnin?'

Toshiaki shook his head ruefully.

'You're right, master! It was the one with the tachi who'd escaped. "Now what?" I thought. "That was unexpected!" Had any more of the ruffians already hidden themselves somewhere?

'Jun and Yoichi appeared not to have noticed and continued to slop through the rain, not pausing until they were in the town, itself. I tried to warn them but they ignored me and unsteadily picked their way across a couple of slippery planks that spanned a deep drainage brook beside the road and entered the seedy-looking inn that lay a few yards from a rather handsome bridge over the first waterway. I gingerly followed expecting to be tipped into the muddy waters at every step! Once inside, I had to wait a few seconds to adjust my eyes to the deep gloom that wasn't helped by the rainstorm out of the leaden skies. At length, I sat myself down at the side of the room with a heavy post at my back. The whole place stank of dampness, horse piss, and worse; I tell you, master, it was one of the most unpleasant establishments that I have ever had the misfortune to visit.

' "Hey, you two," I says in a low voice as at last I had them seated beside me, "you must have seen that gang from the inn back there! They're a rough-looking lot, ain't they? You don't reckon there'll be trouble, do you?"

'Yoichi stared at me. "Scared are yer, carpenter?"

' "Wouldn't you be? Their being around shows that they might be suspicious of why we're here." I appeared to think for a moment, scratching my head, then caught at Yoichi's sleeve. "You don't think that they suspect us of 'avin' the – er – you know what with us, do you?"

' "You're too clever by 'alf, yer know!" remarked Jun.

' "Maybe I am and maybe I ain't!" I said, and added: "I reckon I'll dig out me sword jus' to be on the safe side."

'Jun's head spun round at that. "Got a sword 'ave yer?"

'I shrugged my shoulders. "Who hasn't these days, eh? Anyone who travels would be stupid not to be armed at least with some sort o' blade. You're wearing one, ain't you?"

'But I fiddled about in my tool wallet and finally extricated my poor old Bizen *tachi* blade that I kept wrapped up in oiled paper tied to my straight bokutō – the one that I still have here that most people would think is a walking stick – and undid the scabbard. By the time I had found the *tsuba* and other fittings they had completely lost interest and already sunk two or three saucers of bad wine. They were further distracted by the arrival through the open shōji of the rain-soaked rōnin who threw off his cape and noisily made his way to the far side of the room.

'He must have recognized me from the previous night though I had kept well out of the way, as he slightly inclined his head. I could see that he was appraising my two companions so perhaps he wasn't interested in me? I continued to carefully put the fittings on my blade, turning slightly away from the room as I did so and finally thoroughly wetted the bamboo peg with my tongue before gently knocking it firmly into place.'

The priest slowly nodded his head in approval. The wetting of the tiny pin was an important detail before a fight. He wiped a couple of rice grains from his threadbare black habit and held his hands out under a steady stream of rainwater falling just beyond the platform.

'So, what happened then?'

'The rōnin had soon been served with rice wine, taking no further notice of us; in fact he sat sideways on to my line of sight and seemed to eye the younger serving wench with more than a passing interest. I failed to see why because she was as skinny as they make them, her face was pinched and her kimono filthy. The only thought that kept coming back into my mind was that someone had to suspect something . . . Were there three sides to all this . . ? Or were they all in cahoots with each other . . ?

'Outside the rain had changed into a violent storm with a strong wind and thunder and lightning. One could be forgiven for thinking that the Tonegawa would overflow its broken-down banks and we'd all be drowned.

'We hadn't been guzzling the sour ō-sake for more than a few minutes when one of last night's ruffians sidled in and looked about him through the gloom. An older woman, who could have been nothing else than a prostitute, grabbed his arm and led him across to where the samurai lounged with his wine and I couldn't fail to hear him asked if his mates were coming, too. The hag poured out some drink but he roughly shoved her aside.

'The pair fell into low conversation and the newcomer finally grabbed the wine jar and emptied it down his gullet, then called for another and a third. I leant my head against the upright and made a show of dozing but kept my eyes on both my companions and the other pair. Then, surprisingly, the samurai caught hold of the gaunt maid's neck and pulled her head down near his. At first I thought he was propositioning her as she was giggling. The other woman produced a folding fan and began to wiggle her hips in what might once have passed as a dance. This set some of the peasants to clapping but all I could really see was the glint of the sweat that ran down between her half-exposed sagging breasts ...

'I must have closed my eyes for a moment because when I opened them once again the skinny wench was kneeling beside Jun, pouring out more ō-sake and whispering something close to his ear. Almost at once, he came to his feet and sidled between the clapping drinkers to squat down in front of the rōnin, their heads coming close together. It was at this point I think I understood what was up, master.'

Enshin sighed. 'I thought as much, but since you are here and clearly in one piece, I guess you survived!'

The storm continued unabated but they were grateful to shelter in the dry under the gateway roof. Toshiaki sighed as he gazed at the sheeting summer rain, clearly remembering his difficulties at Itako.

'Well, master, at length I stirred and stretched out my legs. "By Dōsōjin,[6] that's bad wine; it's gone straight through me an' I need to take a leak!" Yoichi hardly glanced at me, just waved his left hand airily in dismissal. I came to my feet muttering something about going out the back but took care to leave my toolbag beside him. After all, if I was to be killed I wouldn't need them, would I?'

'But you took your sword with you?' asked Enshin, gently caressing Kuroi's noble head.

'I slipped it under my kimono as I turned. Appearing to be in some discomfort in the lower department, I sought the back entrance and, once outside, decided to double back and see if I could locate the other two men I'd seen sitting in the first inn. Well they weren't there but as there was no one about I caught down a wide brimmed straw hat from under the outshot eaves and, keeping under cover as best I could, made my way back towards the bridge over the canal. Aye, and there, sure enough, I found not two but three of them squatted down by the end of one balustrade.

---

[6] A wayside deity of the highways, figures of who were often placed at crossroads or the entrances to villages.

'Without my straw cape and bulky tool wallet perhaps these gamblers wouldn't remember me; after all, one artisan looks much like another especially in heavy rain. I paused in an alleyway out of their sight and settled my sword carefully in my *obi*, securing the long *himo* on the left side so as to give me plenty of free movement. Pulling the front of my borrowed hat down against the heavy rain, I began to give some thought to my situation. Now it appeared that there were seven against me – not good odds! It was pressing that I thought hard and acted fast.

'I passed a couple of shuttered shops reached by narrow walkways over the brimming roadside ditch and, if anything, the rain was coming down heavier than ever, great drops splashing up from the rutted road and a fuzz of spray fringing the straw eaves. Just beside me I saw a little patch of white waterlilies and for some reason I stooped down to pick one of the delicate blooms.

'Quite irrelevantly, considering the danger of my situation, I could only remember how, as a young man at your father's yashiki, I once watched your first armour being re-laced in the *katchuya*.[7] I recalled that across the top of the breastplate you had requested that the soft leather should be in dark green printed with the lily flower in a delicate line of little white crosses each flanked by two token leaves. At once I knew what I should do. It was the cross motif, master; the *itako* emblem of the warrior . . .

'The three men were hunkered down in a knot. As I came along, bent as if against the storm, I could just make out that they were sheltering under a couple of capes . . . Perfect . . . I came opposite them and leant over the rail to look down at the rainpocked surface of the canal water for just a moment . . .

'One of the three peered out just as I slightly lifted the brim of my waragasa and I saw recognition dawn in his face . . . In an instant I crossed the narrow walkway and my blade sliced across his neck sending his head spinning into the ditch. Before his body pitched over I cut down as hard as I could at one of his companions, aiming as best I was able with a slippery wet *tsuka* moving in my hands just beside the bump of his head covered by the straw cloaks. The third man, aware that something was amiss, somehow threw himself backwards, scrabbling to draw out his sword. He threatened to strike across my leading foot as I, too, slipped in the mire. In desperation, I stabbed downwards, the point of my blade ripping his upper sword arm; the pain from that wound causing him to yell out . . .

---

[7] *Katchuya*: a name for an armourer's workshop.

'That scream well and truly let the demons out of their sack, as the saying goes, and he was only silenced by a hefty kick in his throat. Still, his arm was sliced open and he was hardly going to take any part in what was to follow.

'The ramshackle inn's sliding door crashed open and five or six heads thrust out to see what the commotion was about; at a glance I noted that two of them were the one-time pirate and Yoichi. The brief fracas at the bridgehead had scarce ended and the three men, the one lying headless and the other two nursing their wounds, were plain to see. I had hoped to reach the plank bridge across the drain because it seemed to me to the best place to make a stand but I was too late, of course.

'Out came Jun and Yoichi followed by the rough-looking gambler, all waving their swords and yelling like maddened *oni*, and behind them hurried the samurai, although he hadn't yet drawn his weapon. The main bridge! That's where I might just contain four attackers and at least I had a few yards start. I whirled round and splashed off onto the slippery boards, one of my sandal ties threatening to give way under the strain. Out of the corner of my eye I registered a movement and, just in the nick of time, slashed low with my Bizen blade taking the left forearm off the man I had just stabbed . . . His hand, still grasping his sword, flew back to the feet of the baying mob . . . and that checked them for a moment. Gaining the centre of the slightly arched bridge I stopped and waited. Here there was only room for two to attack me at a time but a lot depended on their stomach for such a fight.'

Toshiaki paused to take a breath, his face aglow with the excitement of his vivid memories. Enshin sighed and passed his hand across his shaven head.

'Still there were four to one, my friend. Not exactly the odds I would have liked to face . . . What do you think, my bovine friend?'

Kuroi-san lifted his head slightly and uttered a low, deep-throated bellow. As he turned his head towards their companion it was as though he completely understood and yet reserved his approval of the violence.

'Well, master, it was touch and go, of course. The kaizoku, Jun, came on first, bawling out in his somewhat uneven voice that he knew all along that I had the gold and that I wasn't going to get away with stealing it! Huh, that was rich, to say the least. Just as if I have pinched it from him! He faltered a second or two when he saw the determination in my face – I had tossed aside my straw hat by then – but his reaction was slightly unexpected. The bare-chested gambler was beside him at that moment and I saw Jun slip his left hand behind the man's back and shove him violently forwards at me as a sort of shield . . . I hurled myself to the right hand rail to avoid the man's flailing blade and cut upwards under his left armpit . . . This was when my *waraji* string finally parted causing me to slide awkwardly . . . Maybe that was my salvation because I remember that Jun couldn't quite get at me and his cut hit the rail a foot from my head, glancing off . . . Now, his *tsuka* must have been as wet as my own but the difference was that I had had time to wind my *hachimaki* round mine to give a better grip. I stabbed a trifle hastily into his exposed side taking no proper aim, but had the satisfaction of hearing him gasp out as if in pain . . . then I was faced by Yoichi and lost sight of Jun altogether . . . So far as I knew, I had two wounded men to my left rear and the wizened accomplice to my right . . . and the rōnin behind him!

'For some reason, there was a pause at that point. It was close to dusk and the light was fading fast. There came a sudden flash of blinding lightning followed by a tremendous peal of thunder that must have been right overhead . . . I once again pitched my body to the left rail – this was only a footbridge and not four foot wide – a move that probably confused my assailants. Jun was definitely not dead as he had managed to twist round and was cutting like a madman to where I had just been, but Yoichi had me in his sights and was raising his sword and yelling out some imprecation when, and I hardly comprehended it, a sword point burst from the front of his chest, cutting off his shout. He fell at my feet in a fountain of blood . . . My sword struck Jun across the small of his back, sinking deep into his hips, and that was that! I had only the samurai to face and turned ready, my chest heaving and my loosened hair plastered down by the rain.

'However, instead of a vengeful swordsman, I saw that the samurai had stood back a pace or two and was calmly wiping his blade clean. I glanced round but saw no threats from those wounded who still lived and leant my arm on the wet railing trying to calm myself.

' "That gets rid of some rather unpleasant characters, master carpenter," the rōnin observed. "Now that it's all over, perhaps we can talk somewhere in the dry?"

'I slowly nodded my head, not certain what to think. He appeared to bear no malice and his tone, matter of fact as it was, might even have been friendly. But still in the back of my mind was the suspicion that there may have been others in the conspiracy . . .

'I bowed slightly but said: "What about these?" pointing to the dying Jun and to where the last of the gamblers writhed on the wet planking, his hand desperately trying to clutch at his pierced side.

' "Kill them if you have to . . . That one will have expired in a short while . . ." he said in a flat tone, "I reckon your cut severed his back!"

'With care, I backed away a little then stabbed down through the gambler's throat to finish him off. I kept a wary eye on the samurai all the while but he didn't move. Jun gave a last moaning gasp as I reached him and I saw his fingers, that had been trying to tear at the boards, relax. He was quite dead . . .

' "I mean you no harm, carpenter, and must admire your sword work. You have evidently had good masters!"

' "Is it that obvious?"

' "Shall we return to the inn and get dry or remain out here until we grow gills like the fishes in those streams?" '

———— ⊟ ————

'Despite the heavy rain, news of the fight had spread throughout the immediate neighbourhood and a little crowd of gawping onlookers, all soaked through, stood in groups staring at the six corpses. They quickly fell back as we walked back past them.

' "What about reporting this incident, sir?" I asked, but the samurai merely shrugged his shoulders and crossed the flimsy bridge to the inn.

'At the open shōji, the sliding door had been flung off its runners as the gambler, Jun and Yoichi had rushed out; the skinny girl and her older companion were struggling to put it back.

' "Here, we'll give you a hand," offered the samurai. Without another thought I took one side and he the other and it was back, mud-spattered but intact. The girl stood in awe, wet to the skin until she was pulled under the eaves by the prostitute who whispered something into her ear.

'We sat on the step to the main room, a little distance apart, and wiped our feet and legs. There was no one to be seen in the inn.

' "We need dry clothes, woman!" called out the rōnin, and the older woman vanished somewhere at the back of the room. The skinny waif was at our side with some warmed ō-sake.

' "Why did you help me, sir?" I asked, looking curiously at the samurai as I drank from the saucer.

' "It seemed to me that you might die a cur's death, Master . . ?"

' "Toshiaki, sir."

' "You are not a samurai, I realize that much, Toshiaki-san, but you have served warriors, have you not?"

' "My family have served for many generations, master, but I follow my father's profession. I am content."

'He nodded his head as he wiped his steaming torso on a clean cloth brought by the thin girl. I did the same but taking care to sit on the cloth-covered package. Just then, the older woman came back with some folded garments and we began to dress, still carefully separated and with our swords close at hand.

' "Clear off!" suddenly bawled out the samurai and some of the more venturous townsmen who had begun to peer through the slatted window ran pell mell away, two or three skidding into the brimming ditch.

'Our wet clothes were gathered up to be dried and we settled ourselves down on opposite sides of one of the tables, wine quickly placed before us.

' "Wench! This must be better than that foul apology you served earlier!"

' "Oh, it is, master!" she cried. "We keep it only for them samurai from the yashiki . . ."

'The poor girl was nearly in tears. Outside night had already fallen and the thunderstorm had passed away over the lakes. It still rained heavily.

' "Bring lights, girl . . . and clean yourself up!"

'The other woman reappeared soon after and lit three open lanterns also setting a large candle holder beside our table. She, too, had changed into a clean plain kimono.

' "Would you like me to serve you more ō-sake, masters?" she said through her blackened teeth.

' "No, clear off but send in the girl to sit over there if we need her!"

'Where was this all leading, I wondered? I took the bull by the horns. "You know that I have the gold?"

' "Of course," he replied. "I knew that almost as soon as you left the inn and met with those two wretches. You have it safe, I trust?"

'There was no point in trying to conceal my find further so I drew it out from my kimono, still as I had found it.

' "Open it up, Master Toshiaki. By the way, how did you know it was gold, eh?"

' "I think it was Jun who let the word slip."

' "Well, my friend, we are more or less alone so you can safely take a look."

'I untied the knotted damp cloth and there, before me, lay a heap of gold *koban*, their ovals glistening in the lanternlight. I had never before seen such an amount. At one end of the topmost I glimpsed an impressed *mon* but took care not to expose it to the samurai. From the weight of the package I would guess the gold amounted to two kin.[8]

' "Surprised, eh?"

' "You are assuring me, master, that the gold belongs to you?"

'The samurai snorted ruefully.

' "Of course I am, but if you are that suspicious, you wouldn't believe me, would you?"

' "I don't disbelieve you, master, but to set my mind at rest you must excuse me for asking this but did you look at the gold when it was in your possession?"

' "Ah, I understand! You are like most workmen, cautious when it comes to silver and gold! Well, I fully understand that and once again assure you on my word as a samurai, that this gold was being taken by my friend and myself back to our lord. You see, it belongs to my clan and was stolen away in a discreditable attack on one of our forts just after some taxes had been converted to specie. Now, does that satisfy you, Master Carpenter?"

'I grinned at him, hoping to look a bit simple. "You won't mind if I keep hold of the – er – bundle and come with you, master? Now that your friend is dead it would not be safe to travel alone, would it? To which domain are we heading, sir?"

' "Come with me by all means, Master Toshiaki, and keep hold of the . . ." He hesitated and glanced across at the skinny girl but she had turned away to bring more heated wine and clearly wasn't listening. He didn't answer me about the domain.'

———— ⌗ ————

'Thinking about the rōnin's claim about the gold, I became more and more convinced that it had been stolen and that of all the clans in the Kantō, the last one he had in mind was the Kashima-ke. I also knew that over the past ten years or so the Kashima family had suffered from much dissention and division within the fief. In such a troubled period it was very easy for the clan to be deprived by one means or another of their treasure. If he had known that the gold was marked with the clan *mon* and said so, then maybe that would have been different . . .

'About the Hour of the Tiger which was around a hour before dawn, I crept out of my sleeping place taking the utmost care not to make a noise, and sought the skinny girl's sleeping place, guessing it

---

[8] About two pounds weight.

would be out in the hay shed beside the stable. I was right and came on her sleeping body almost at once.

' "Shusssh!" says I, clamping my hand across her mouth lest she be awakened with a cry. "Don't fear! I am the carpenter . . . not that sam'rai!"

'When I was sure that she was calm, I took my hand away. She just lay there with her eyes wide in the faint light from the stars, the storm having cleared away by then.

' "Master . . ?" she whimpered. She probably thought that I had come to force myself on her slight body.

'I lay close at her side but didn't touch her, explaining that the men who had been killed the evening before were a gang of cut-throats and that I suspected the rōnin of being a member, even the leader, at that. I had to get away and quickly so I needed her help. She hardly breathed but I could feel her shaking. At length she whispered that her brother had a marsh punt and he might help. "Excellent!" I replied, and added that the samurai might very well kill her, too, because she must have seen the treasure that I was carrying . . .

'That did it, master; she quickly led me out the back and along two or three darkened alleys to her brother's shack. He was a fisherman, no doubt, as the place stank of fish . . . ugh! Within a few minutes I was taken down to one of the canals and sat with the girl in the bottom of the narrow punt while her brother, who hadn't said a word all along, poled the flimsy craft out into the main channel.

'Now, master, you know that I'm no fool; well, at least I don't think so! As we nosed out from the creek I idly watched the stars and became aware that we were turning west rather than what I would have expected should have been to the east. Odd, thought I to myself, but sat quietly enough, though I have to admit I made sure that my sword was close to hand!

'The first streaks of dawn were in the east when I saw the shape of that ill-omened humped bridge looming up. I could just make out the figure of an armed man standing by the nearer rail and thought that perhaps the local lord had placed a guard there after the discovery of the bodies, or that it was the rōnin, himself . . . The girl's brother must have read my thoughts because he leaned down to whisper: "Lie down there and cover yourselves with that matting. We have to go this way to reach the branch canal that will bring us to Kitaura . . ." Slowly and methodically he poled past the darkened inn and under the bridge, just as he probably did every day when he went out to fish . . . Covered as we were by the smelly matting, I couldn't see if that rōnin was up and about. It might have been the warmth of that summer dawn or my racing thoughts but I felt myself breaking out into a sticky sweat . . .'

———————□———————

'At last we reached the little port on the beach overlooked by the Kashima-ke yashiki and put up in an inn as the hour was very late. The following morning all three of us presented ourselves at the entrance *yagura* and a message was sent in to the guard commander. The upshot was that the steward was so taken with our honesty in returning the stolen gold that he rewarded the brother and sister with some silver. I refused any gift but insisted, respectfully, that my share should go to the girl for her bravery. I advised them to remain in the Kashima domain for some days before venturing back to Itako, just for their own safety, but I straightway crossed over to Shimosa and passed through Kazusa into Awa before seeking a boat across Sagami Bay to Izu.

'And that is my tale, master . . . At least it has passed a wet afternoon and now the sun has come out!'

'You never encountered that rōnin again, Toshiaki-san?' asked the monk.

His faithful follower scratched his stubbly chin and sniffed, thinking deeply before he answered.

'Maybe I did and maybe I didn't, master . . . If I can remember back that far I'd best save the memories for another rainy day, eh?'

Enshin sat quietly for some time, but at last he rose and stretched his arms up beside his faithful buffalo. As he tied his broad-brimmed hat beneath his chin, a smile puckering the corners of his lips, he remarked: 'You must be favoured by the gods, my friend. I hope you gave thanks when the opportunity arose? Perhaps it is as the poet says:

The summer rain:
How sweet is the warmth
That touches my heart.
Cranes rise from the reedy shore
As I seek my lord.'

10

THE PRAYER HALL

▼

During the turbulent Kyōroku and Tembun periods[9] when many lords contended on the field of battle against their neighbours, the wild mountainous region that lay east of the Shinano river on the borders of three provinces, Shinano, Echigo and Kōzuke, temporarily became a refuge for a gang of brigands. Despite their small numbers, these ill-favoured men, mostly runaway peasants who had joined up with a handful of defeated and cast-off samurai, managed to terrify the poor farmers who eked out a meagre living in the several valleys that divided the heights on the western side of Shirane-san.

This was in the years when Takeda Nobutora ruled Kai and part of Shinano and the Nagao-ke, descendants of Taira Yoshibumi, controlled Echigo; fifteen or so years before the titanic struggles between the lords Takeda Shingen and Uesugi Kenshin began. But this account, written down for posterity by Torii Enshin in his later years, has little to do with such powerful lords, being more concerned with the trials, hopes, and fears of the poor folk who often survive on the very margins of life.

---

[9] Kyōroku: 1528 – 1532; Tembun: 1532 – 1555.

This particular bandit gang thrived by occasionally raiding the little settlements dotted about these valleys over a wide area and robbing travellers who risked the roads east of the Chikuma-gawa. In some years they didn't appear, in others, they harried the folk, burning, raping and murdering at will. The local lords had their own problems and so pinpricks such as these minor depredations hardly affected them at all. Whatever their losses, the villagers were forced to give their tithes and taxes when demanded and if they starved in consequence, were there any who cared?

———— ◻ ————

One spring day in the first year of Tembun this gang, for want of nothing better to do and irrationally destructive as such marauders often are, came on the small shrine that then stood on a northern spur of Shirane-san and for no reason at all, brutally killed the poor priest and set fire to the main buildings. Convinced that they would be unopposed, the gang leader commandeered the adjacent Prayer Hall of the neighbouring unfinished Shingon temple, and there set up his base for the coming year. The conflagration, or rather the pall of smoke that hung about the forested mountainside, was seen with considerable disquiet by the peasants along the valley below and they knew full well what it signified. They were filled with consternation on two main counts; the first was that this shrine had been where the mountain deity, Taketsu-numi-no-mikoto, had presided over their welfare since time immemorial and, secondly, it was almost the start of the rice planting season when the god was invited down to take on the rôle of their field spirit, thereby ensuring a good autumn harvest. With this catastrophe, their hopes that they would have food enough for the next winter and be able to pay their taxes dwindled; ruin and starvation became a very real possibility staring them in the face.

The village elders from the two settlements hastily met, once the garbled facts were known through the hysterical reports from two woodcutters who had witnessed the attack, and they despaired in the face of their hopeless situation. At length, a young farmer named Magobei whose family had held land here since it was given as a reward for an ancestor's faithful service to Ashikaga Takauji two-hundred years before, volunteered to set out with two stalwart servants to see for himself what damage had been done and find the actual whereabouts of the bandits. It was Magobei's great-great-grandfather who had begun the building of the Buddhist temple within the precinct of the shrine but a disastrous fire through lightning strike forty years before had destroyed the main building leaving only the Prayer Hall.

Cautious because of the woodcutters' account of what they had witnessed, Magobei and his companions moved carefully through the thick forest until they were able to confirm that these murderous incendiaries were indeed in residence. Little remained of the once beautiful shrine but a few charred and still smoking timbers and all three could hardly refrain from shedding salt tears of regret.

They instinctively understood that they would find no redress from the petty lord who claimed suzerainty over their valleys and they must, perforce, think hard on what could be done whilst they sat about their campfire set in a secret gulley overnight. At length Magobei shook his head.

'We know that Ōnuma-dono will refuse to help and in any case it might be too dangerous even to petition him, but I heard from that yamabushi who came through our valley a month or so ago when the snows had begun to melt, that just over the border in Kōzuke lies the Torii domain . . .'

'They won't be of any use, either!' grunted one of his men, 'It ain't their land!'

'I know that, Hachibei; I know that only too well, but the yama-bushi also told me about one of the Torii who was once a monk at Hōrai-ji . . .'

The other servant, a wiry woodsman who was only known as 'Matsu', sniffed.

"'E's an odd one by all accounts, 'e is!'

'How do yer know that, Matsu, eh?'

'I knows these things, Hachibei-san. My father and brother often took special wood we found to his follower 'ose name is Toshiaki. 'E's a master carpenter an' always wanting *hinoki*. Me father knew this an' felled a lot of good *hinoki* to season proper-like.'

'What's this got to do with the monk, then?' demanded Hachibei.

'That's just the point if only you'ld listen . . . This 'ere monk is a good friend of us peasants, despite 'is bein' of a sam'rai family . . .'

'An high rankin' one, at that, my friends,' interposed Magobei. 'The Torii comes from old stock. They were bushi even before the days of the Gempei War.'

The two servants looked at their master in some amazement but both had heard that the farmer's ancestors had once borne arms in battle so he must know about such things. Magobei continued: 'We'll cross the high pass into the Torii domain and ask this monk what to do.'

'What, go all the way to Kusatsu; that'll take three or four days, won't it?'

'Does it matter, eh? We've got to do something as we've only got three short weeks before we have to get on with the planting . . . We have to do something to please the *yama-no-kami*, don't we?'

'Suppose we ain't much choice in the matter!'

'Not a lot, my friends; not a lot. At least we can try though I ain't got much idea of how we can get close enough to tell of our troubles . . . sam'rai ain't ones noted for listening!'

————— ⊟ —————

Reaching the little town of Kusatsu at last, the three peasants were unsure of how to approach any of the fierce samurai who seemed to be everywhere. It was hardly a propitious time due to the threat of disturbance caused by a group of the Nagao *hatamoto* who were at loggerheads with some minor lords owing their alliegance to the Takeda-han beyond the western ridges. Such was their loss of confidence that they sought refuge in a poor backstreet hostelry whose only real luxury was the freedom to bathe in the open air if they cared to scrape away a hollow in the stony bed of the shallow Kusatsugawa. Such a bath was known as a *rōtenburo* and was extraordinary since Nature had ordained that the nearer the excavation was to the river's edge, the warmer was the resulting bath!

During the early evening of their third night at the inn, still unable to pluck up either the courage or to find any reasonable excuse to approach a ranking warrior, a number of ashigaru and servants entered the ryōkan, good-naturedly boisterous and intent on indulging in some games of chance. Because the domain was not in an actual state of war it didn't suffer from the indignities imposed on many more accessible places when the faintest rumour of impending conflict brought hordes of would-be soldiers to seek their fortune. Contending lords always required huge amounts of manpower and these hopefuls were composed of every description of riff-raff . . . While mostly low-ranking samurai patronized this inn, there were always two or three rōnin, often brought down by heavy drinking, but these caused no trouble.

On this particular evening a broad-shouldered man entered and settled himself down at a bench quite near the three peasants. Almost at once, the innkeeper's wife, a woman of strong character who kept a tight control of the clientele, came bustling over and knelt down close to this man, setting out a fresh jar of rice wine and then bowing with a certain degree of respect that was noted by Magobei. She personally poured out some of the ō-sake into a wine cup then leant forward and whispered something in a low voice. He thanked her and when she had gone, turned slightly and said, in a low voice:

'Magobei-san, I heard that you wanted to petition my master?'

The young farmer hardly expected to be approached himself rather that the other way round. He frowned slightly as he looked about.

'Master? Were you talking to me?' he questioned.

'If you are named Magobei, then indeed I was. Please come over here and sit with me.' He turned his head and called out: 'Oku-san, please bring some more wine, if you would.'

'Coming!'

The young man was now quite out of his depth; all his carefully prepared speeches fled his mind and he felt as helpless as a fish out of water, nonetheless he obeyed and knelt on the floor, bowing his head low.

'Sit up, my friend! Sit up at the bench or you'll have the whole inn curious to know your business.'

'Master . . . Master, I was . . . er . . .'

The big man smiled in a friendly manner to put the inexperienced young farmer at his ease. 'First let me introduce myself. I am named Toshiaki and I am the servant of my master, Enshin-sama, the man to whom you have something to say, I understand. That is the case, isn't it?'

Magobei nodded silently, watching the goodwife bring more wine and three extra saucers.

'Those two men are your companions?' asked Toshiaki. 'Are you going to leave them? Let them join us at once.'

———— ⯐ ————

Toshiaki listened attentively as the story was told and when the three peasants had finished, for now they were more at their ease and their tongues loosened the words simply tumbled out, he shook his head.

'So that's what this is all about, eh? You want help from my master to drive out twenty or more desperadoes who have been causing problems in another lord's lands?' He leant his head back against the stout post behind him and sighed. 'Well, don't pull so long a face, my friend; you have come to find one of the few bushi in all the provinces who would help you! Not that I want to raise your hopes too far. My master long ago turned his back on the way of the warrior and took holy orders. We can but ask his advice, though; that's the best I can promise.'

Matsu, the woodcutter, looked crestfallen and bowed his head.

'We can't go back, master, without finding someone to help . . . All our people will starve if the mountain *kami* don't come down . . . That's what will happen . . . We just have to show our god that we have done our best . . !'

The carpenter sniffed. 'Have another drink. Your name is Matsu, isn't it?

'Aye, master, that's right . . .'

'Hmm! I thought so! You know that I am indebted to your father for supplying me with some excellent pieces of *hinoki*, Matsu-san? I turn them into fine shirazaya and sword sheaths . . . many of them, at that. For that at least I will help you, but it all depends on my master's opinion. You have to realize that.'

———□———

Late in the afternoon of the following day, a kitchen lad from the yashiki came to the hostelry and found the three peasants.

'My master requests that you come with me,' the lad shrilled. He couldn't have been more than seven or eight. It struck Magobei in particular that the child was clean and well-dressed.

They hastily tied on their straw waraji and followed the lad away from the yashiki towards the forested slopes on the other side of the narrow valley. Almost at once they rounded a corner of the track and saw a long flight of rough stone steps leading up through the trees. Puffing and blowing, at last they reached the top in the wake of the boy who scarcely showed any effect from the climb, and saw the vermillion painted gateway to a Shingon temple.

Magobei shrugged his shoulders and turned to ask the child to continue but he had disappeared down a side track through the undergrowth.

'We had better go on, then,' was all he could offer.

Passing through the gateway, they found the track curving between the towering cedar trees and as they rounded the first bend they saw a shaven black-robed monk standing facing them

'Greeting, sirs,' the monk said, bowing. 'I am Enshin and I have been expecting you. Maybe I can help you solve your problem. Are you ready to leave?'

Magobei's jaw dropped.

'What, *now*, master?'

'Of course!'

———□———

Three days later the small party reached the wooded slopes above the burnt out shrine on the north-western flanks of Shirane-san. Leaving the others to prepare a meal, Enshin and Toshiaki, guided by Matsu, dropped down carefully through the trees to reconnoitre the brigands' lair which lay about a quarter of a mile away and more than a thousand feet lower. They returned just as the sun sank behind the western peaks, Enshin apparently lost in thought.

As they breakfasted early the following morning watching the long skeins of mist hanging in the valleys below, Enshin looked at Magobei. 'When you last visited that Prayer Hall, were there images of the Lord Buddha and the Bodhisattvas still in place, Magobei-san?'

The peasant farmer scratched his head, thinking hard.

'I went there about six years ago, master, but not since . . . My father said that there was a statue of Fudō-sama when he was there a few months back. It was jus' before the first snows 'e went.'

'How long have those brigands been in residence? Do any of you know?'

'About a month, my lord . . .'

'Magobei-san, please don't call me 'lord'; I am a humble priest dedicated to helping the poor and the sick.'

Toshiaki shook his head.

'You'll never get anyone to believe that, master, not with your ancestors . . .'

'At least I can try.'

'I'm sorry, my . . . master!' mumbled the young peasant. 'I – er – just forgot; I'll try not to make that mistake again.'

'There's no need to apologize; it's of no importance. Now, it is time to think out a plan of action. This is what I want you to do. In the first place I want you to go down to your village and request, if they can be afforded, a sack of good rice – not millet – and a tub of the best ō-sake. This must be the strongest that can be obtained, the sort that is offered on special occasions to the deities. Tell the elders that both the rice and wine will prove the salvation of your communities. Understood? Oh, and we shall need a spavined old pony, one with his ribs showing clear.'

Master and retainer watched as Magobei and the others descended through the gathering gloom the mountainside tracks that only Matsu knew.

'You have a good plan, master?' asked the carpenter.

The priest gave a wry smile.

'None at all, my friend; just a faint glimmer of an idea.'

'Then there's no difference to some of our other scrapes, my lord!'

They both laughed just a little.

'Now you are forgetting yourself, Toshiaki-san!'

'Not really, master, as I'm sure you know exactly what you are about.'

'Ah, if only ... Plans and strategms come easily to some people but I follow the teachings of the Sonshi and try to leave these matters unsaid. If they are simple and seen in the merest outline, our inner minds will work to find the solutions. It is a lesson that is learnt from hard-won experience in swordsmanship; but then, you know this very well, my good Toshiaki, don't you?'

His follower remained silent for a few moments then nodded his head.

'It will be dangerous, master,' he observed.

'For us? Of course it will. Nothing is accomplished in such a situation without boldness and resolute determination. If we have twenty enemies and only number two then while the odds are high they are halved relative to each of us. If we seek some outside help we can reduce those odds still more ... We shall just have to see. Now, I must ask you to excuse me as I need to perform my devotions for a short while.'

Toshiaki stirred up the fire with some fresh kindling and hung their small iron pot so that the rice would cook. He had absolute trust in his master's resourcefulness and not the slightest qualms about the ultimate result.

———— ☐ ————

Before they left, Matsu, the woodcutter's son, had described where they might meet in the neighbouring valley if Magobei was successful in persuading the village elders to agree to Enshin's request. It meant another day of waiting and that brought the *kami* welcoming festival even closer. They really had little time if Enshin was to succeed with his mysterious plan ... if such a plan actually existed.

The rendezvous was about two *ri*[10] distant from the partly-constructed temple which the gang had commandeered and the track led nowhere else. It was on the second day that Magobei and Matsu appeared leading a decrepit-looking packhorse.

'You were given everything I requested?'

'Everything, master; not without a whole lot of argument and shouting!'

Toshiaki grinned.

'That figures!' He refrained from adding that 'this typified peasants all over'!

'Magobei-san; you and Matsu are to return to your village. Reassure your elders that you have delivered everything to me and

---

[10] *Ri*: about two miles.

they can start preparations to welcome the *yama-no-kami* when the day arrives.'

The priest took Magobei aside and gave him some short instructions. He knew that the young man suspected that he intended to bribe the bandits to leave the valleys alone.

'But, master . . .'

Enshin held up his hand.

'No "buts"! Be sure to offer prayers to the fox deity and to Dōsōjin for their protection. You will see us in three days time; be certain of it.'

As the two trudged off down the track, Enshin advised Toshiaki to take apart his sword and hide it inside his cunningly made hollow staff. They were to appear to be completely unarmed; simple pilgrims, master and servant. The carpenter secured his master's medicine wallet and their cooking pot above the pony's load. He sniffed and smiled lopsidedly.

'You intend to set their mind's at rest, eh, master? What comes after, I wonder?'

'You cannot draw me out, you know,' smiled the priest. 'I still have no idea so let's just see what happens, shall we?'

———— ◻ ————

As is usual with so many of these remote holy places set amongst the soaring peaks, there was a direct, if tortuous, stone stairway that climbed steeply up through the thick forest of pine and cedar. It was clear that the broken-winded packhorse could never tackle such an ascent so they must, perforce, use the longer track as it wound its way up in a series of sharp steep pitches. With the sweat running down Toshiaki's torso in streams, for the spring afternoon was unusually close, they reached at long last a rather decayed looking torii whose vermillion paint was fast flaking away and the structure required the additional support of four strategically placed bamboo trunks. Almost at once they were challenged by a ragged armed man who had clearly been napping and hadn't been aware of their approach until they were just a few paces away.

' 'Ere, stop, you two! Who are yer an' what do yer want?'

Enshin took off his round strawhat, holding it in front of him as he bowed deeply. It was just as if they had reached one of the regular highway barriers set up to examine travellers and exact tolls.

'We are just pilgrims, master. I was told in a dream that I must pray before the Lord Defender of the Law at this temple.'

'You what?'

The priest repeated what he had just said, adding: 'I am only a humble monk, sir, and this is my servant. In my dream I was also instructed to bring a gift for your master.'

The astonished guard had hardly expected anyone to come this way at all. When all was said and done, brigands never received visitors other than fully-armed soldiers bent on destroying and killing! He looked undecided about what to do but at last it passed through his mind that he had best take this priest and his servant up to the temple.

'Oi, there!' he bawled out as the thatched roof of the Prayer Hall came in sight. 'Oi! We've two visitors!'

They emerged into the open forecourt and saw seven or eight half-naked but armed men squatting or lounging around a cooking fire over which was suspended a large steaming cauldron. No one even said a word but a couple turned their heads towards the verandah steps anticipating that someone in authority would soon appear. Enshin noted that beyond the hall no other buildings had been erected although a lot of cut timber lay stacked about.

Out from the dark interior stalked two men, both wearing half-armour and carrying long yari. The leader, who wore a fine green-laced *dō-maru*, was a stocky, powerfully-built fellow.

'What the hell are you doing here?' he shouted out in a rough voice at the sentry. 'What do you mean by leaving the gate without permission . . . You, Kichi, give this wretch a thrashing . . .'

The one named Kichi leapt up from the fireside, catching up a bamboo stave, and began to lay into the cringing sentry who made off as fast as he could but not before he had received seven or eight thwacks across his shoulders and the backs of his legs.

'And who are you?' grated the armoured man balefully.

Enshin bowed low again.

'We are pilgrims, sir,' and he repeated his story of the dream.

'What have you got there?' demanded the brigand suspiciously.

'It is a gift for your leader, kind sir!'

'A gift? For us? Well, that's a rich one for sure!'

Both the armoured men shouted with laughter and they were joined in their mocking by the rest of the ragged gang at the fireside.

'The gift was ordered by my lord, Fudō-myō-ō, himself.'

'He actually spoke to you, monk?' The bandit sounded incredulous.

'Oh, yes; master . . . He and the others often do that!'

Despite their fierce exteriors, these outlaws remained superstitious men at heart and at Enshin's statement fell to whispering amongst themselves.

Just then another rough voice shouted out from the hall.

'Saburō, what's going on out there? Your row's woken me up!'

'We've visitors, Hachirō-sama; a monk and his sidekick!'

'Visitors?' The voice betrayed astonishment. 'A monk ... kill them both!'

Saburō grinned wolfishly at the savage order. He licked his lips.

'You heard what Hachirō-sama said?'

Enshin bowed again.

'If you were to kill us, as well you can, who knows what offence will be given to the Lord Fudō?'

The brigand smirked, shrugging his shoulders and rudely spitting a stream of saliva over the balustrade.

'And what do I care, eh?'

They heard some loud mutterings from the interior and a fully armoured man came stumping out, his helmet cords dangling loose.

'These are our visitors, are they? A lousy monk! Pah!'

It looked as though he had crammed his *kabutō* on his head in a hurry as one of the wide-flared lames of the neck guard had caught up in the lacing of the side flaps causing the helmet to sit uncomfortably. In a fit of irritation he pulled the kabutō off and threw it on the floor where it dropped over the steps and bounced down to the courtyard.

'No samurai would ever have shown such contempt,' thought Toshiaki. 'This wretch was never a warrior!'

'Why the hell have you come here, you filthy monk?'

'I was instructed to do so in a dream-vision, master,' replied Enshin in his mildest voice. 'The Lord Fudō told me that I was to seek out a warrior of fame who had sought protection in the Prayer Hall of this temple and I was to carry out the necessary rites and to present him with a gift from the holy King of Light, himself. You must indeed be that famed warrior, master!'

Hachirō's cupidity was aroused and the priest's words softened his temper. Putting his head a little to one side, he said:

'You heard my order just now, didn't you? Why shouldn't I have you trussed up and roasted slowly over that fire?'

The priest smiled disarmingly.

'I do not plead for my life or for that of my servant, Toshiaki, here; but there is always some purpose hidden in dream-visions, master, and who knows what might result from any disregard? Neither of us offer any threat to your honourable self and I am but a penniless wanderer. Our steps take us aimlessly through the provinces. Who knows, perhaps we might stay with you and thus add to your strength. As for the Lord Fudō, why I'm sure you know that he is all-powerful in the world of the spirits and few would venture to offend him. Would you do so, respected lord, when Fudō, himself, may wish to strengthen you and aid you to gain your own lands?'

By now the brigand chief had calmed down as he listened to Enshin's arguments. He snorted, breathing out noisily.

'So what has this Lord of Light sent as a gift?' Hachirō demanded.

'As a token of his esteem he commanded me to bring this sack containing six tō[11] of rice . . .' said the priest, pointing to the steaming horse.

'And what's in that barrel?'

Imperturbably, Enshin continued; '. . . he also ordered that I should offer a large quantity of the finest rice wine to the deity of the shrine.'

Saburō smirked, quipping: 'That there god ain't at 'ome just now . . .'

His leader guffawed, displaying a set of discoloured and broken teeth.

'It would be an insult if the wine weren't accepted! I'll tell you what, we'll look after it in exchange for yer life. How's that, monk?'

Enshin bowed gravely.

'I am indebted to your generosity, honoured master. I can see that you completely understand that the span of my life has been determined by the Lord Buddha. This clearly is not my final day so I would like to offer prayers for you later, if you will permit me to do so? But furthermore, I can offer you something else, if you so wish.'

'Oi, oi! And what's that?'

'I have noticed in the short time that has passed since my arrival here that a small number of your retainers display various maladies. I have some skill in treating wounds and sickness and would be happy to use these to help them recover.'

Hachirō puffed out his cheeks then let the air escape loudly, then his face contorted and he farted mightily.

'Well, well! This is our lucky day,' he said, smirking at his laughing men. 'Shall we let 'em stay? What do you think, Saburō?'

'Sounds a good idea to me, master.'

'That's settled then! Oi, you; Kichi . . . Have that wine unloaded an' brought up 'ere. I want to keep my eye on it . . .' He winked at Enshin: 'Them's thievin' bastards as I expect you've guessed!'

---

[11] A tō was half-a-bushel. The sack contained three bushels or eighteen gallons of rice.

Careful to present a passive acceptance of their situation, Enshin and Toshiaki kept their wits about them. Together with the men outside in the courtyard, there numbered a total of about twelve members in the gang, though it was likely that others were out foraging or whatever. Despite destroying the neighbouring shrine, Hachirō seemed to have restrained his men from damaging the hall though the floor was covered in filth and litter. As to the structure, it appeared to be intact. It always seemed odd to be in any holy place that hadn't been completed as was the case with this building. Outside he had seen considerable piles of pre-pared timber but he would guess that a very long time ago, war or famine had dried up the sources of money and the whole project had been abandoned. Yet, oddly, a number of figures of the Bodhisattvas had been installed and stood or sat on their thrones along the length of the back wall. In the centre stood an imposing statue of the Lord of Light, represented here with a red ochred face, standing on his carved lotus throne and backed by a spec-tacular carved nimbus of cosmic flames. This statue alone would have done justice to any great temple but it was unusual to find such a fine piece in an obscure and incomplete temple such as this. The other statues conformed to the strict order of the Shin-gon or Tendai requirements and in the gloom he could make out Taishaku-ten sitting on his elephant next to the eight-armed Gundari-myō-ō; behind them, hidden from the torchlight, lurked Komoko-ten, armoured in the Chinese style and fiercely bran-dishing his trident *hōkō*, and Zōhō-ten: on Fudō's right was what appeared to be an excellently carved Dainichi-nyōrai in front of another eight-armed figure which must represent Gonzanze-myō-ō and a final figure far into the shadows at the extreme end was of Amida-nyōrai. He wondered why this splendid set of statues should have been brought here to an incomplete temple that now was quite forgotten and the home of foxes, badgers and evil-doers such as these men?

After a night spent ensconced inconspicuously in a corner, Enshin approached the bandit leader and renewed his offer of doctoring any of his sick or injured men.

'We have three such idiots!' declared Hachirō after some mut-tered discussion with his henchman, Saburō. He gave the appear-ance of caring not a fig for the scum that had attached themselves to the gang but was more concerned in seeing that neither Enshin nor Toshiaki carried any weapons. Once satisfied on that score he ignored both of them completely.

'Firstly, I must offer prayers,' announced the priest. 'Nothing can be accomplished without the proper rites.'

He seated himself before the central figure of Fudō and ostentatiously took a thick scroll out of his wallet, unrolling it slowly and beginning to intone a long invocation. Enshin was well-aware of the impression that could have on ignorant peasants. The initiated would have recognized the sonorous chant for the Heart Sutra and while at first some of the brigands present in the Hall gazed at him in surprise, soon they, like their chief, lost all interest in the newcomers. He continued to chant the sacred text for a full hour until at length the priest paused to ring a small handbell; when he continued, it was in a similar tone but the words told his follower to take a close look behind the red Fudō-myō-ō, in particular at the base of the Lotus Throne, then he slipped back into his monotonous recitation from the scroll.

Toshiaki moved stealthily to the end of the *jōdan* dias and stepped behind the sacred images and set about measuring each statue in turn, occasionally tapping the carved wooden bases. Perhaps one or two of those present were listening to Enshin because one called out: 'Keep your bloody noise down, carpenter.' This turned out to be the ragged sentry from the entrance gateway, but he appeared to hold no malice and probably thought that Toshiaki had now joined the gang.

Enshin completed his devotions and turned to set about examining a couple of rather self-conscious fellows who were clearly in poor health. He told them to follow him over to the entrance doors where there was more light, but all the time he was thinking hard about what action he might take knowing that this must be decisive and totally unexpected if it was to succeed. As he completed his ministrations for the present, his follower returned and was despatched outside to search for certain mountain herbs.

———— ◫ ————

The temptation proved too much for Hachirō to resist and that evening he had the wine cask broached. Soon the leaders of the gang and gradually the rest of the mob, tongues loosened, were hazarding at dice and consuming the potent brew with gusto. From somewhere, a second, slightly smaller, cask was produced, but there could be no doubt which drink these men preferred.

'Go on; pray for us, monk! Make sure yer 'Oly Guardian there keeps us safe!' shouted out Saburō, and that prompted much laughter which was followed by petty arguments on all sides as fortune failed to deliver to some of them. Obligingly, Enshin set out some of his paraphernalia, a plan beginning to take shape in his mind.

'To be effective, masters, and to bring down lasting protection on your heads, we need to construct a *goma* altar.'

'What's that, monk?' sneered Hachirō, at last taking some notice. 'If it ain't too difficult, you shall 'ave it!'

Enshin described what was required. He had seen the bricks used for the sacred fire ritual neatly stacked at the side of the dais and had noted that a stone paving had been included before the central figure when the hall was built. It looked as if it had never been used. With Toshiaki directing, three of the ruffians soon constructed a proper altar and some short billets of trimmed wood were brought in. Soon he had what would pass to a layman as a proper ritual bonfire all ready for kindling. To the accompaniment of his chanting smoke rose billowing to the high rafters.

'My lord Hachirō and you, Saburō-dono, please seat yourselves here before the altar.'

'Only if we can continue drinking, priest!'

The pair were almost completely sozzled.

'The Lord Fudō has no objection to you continuing to do that, but he does require your presence, masters, if my entreaties are to be effective . . .'

'Kichi! Get yer arse over 'ere, too, you lazy pig . . .' slurred Saburō, the ō-sake having gone straight to his head.

Soon, all three were sweating profusely from the heat, the heavy aromatic scent of the camphor-impregnated wood, and the strong brew. The whole company was fast becoming drunk; one or two of the gang were already on their feet stamping out a folk dance to the beat of a small drum that someone had produced. The glare of the roaring fire and the rhythmic cadences of Enshin's chanting, hid the fact that Toshiaki had slipped round behind the raised dais. He had noted during his inspection that morning that because the Prayer Hall had been constructed some hundred or more years before, and the rest of the temple not completed, the fabric here had been seriously neglected. Not a day's worth of attention had been given to stem the inevitable rot that the damp mountain air could bring; the carved wood had not been treated with oils and was now completely decayed and had reached a dangerous stage. He had looked closely at the sad condition of Fudō's carved Lotus Throne where the ravages had made the carvings friable in the extreme . . . and he now understood what his master had in mind.

With care he unbound the ties of his cunningly split bamboo staff and soon assembled his katana, just in case it should be needed. He packed the staff with his folded *hachimaki* tightly folded length-wise, and replaced the rattan ties that he kept slightly oiled and flexible for that very purpose. That staff had frequently proved its worth, particularly when so weighted!

Toshiaki could just glimpse his master through the pierced carvings of the reredos and could hear Enshin begin to chant, in his loudest voice, the words of the invocation to the fierce Fudō–myō–ō ringing out over the noise of the revelry. Both Kichi and Saburō had keeled over onto their sides and seemed to be snoring lustily in a drunken stupor. Hachirō, his face as flushed red and ugly as that of Fudō, himself, was swaying to and fro, squeezing up his eyes in a mist of strong drink. It was surely time to act, thought the carpenter. That morning he had placed a length of squared-off scantling timber that he had found amongst others abandoned long ago behind the jōdan dais, wedged beneath the standing Fudō's *renge-za*, the eight-petalled Lotus Throne. A glance at his master showed that Enshin had picked up the conchshell that they had discovered amongst the discarded ritual items, a shell that may once have belonged to the murdered Shintō priest. A long mournful blast from the horagai was the signal to begin . . .

---◻︎---

'In Emma's name, what are you about?'

It was the wine-slurred voice of Saburō who, unnoticed, had crawled behind the end of the dais to be violently sick. With dripping face he had afterwards looked up and seen Toshiaki's shadowy figure about to heave down on his improvised lever. The bandit grimaced and rubbed his hand across his eyes, trying to clear his brain, his right hand already grasping for the hilt of his sword. The carpenter didn't hesitate but leapt across, thrusting with his staff, driving the end with all his strength into the brigand's throat. The man's eyes bulged and without a sound he tumbled back into his own vomit. A second or so later, Toshiaki's sword stabbed down to make certain that the fellow wouldn't interfere again. He leapt back to his lever and strained hard to drag it down . . . the sweat standing from his brow and pouring down his broad chest. At last it moved; pieces of carving began to splinter from the back of the throne . . . Toshiaki, praying that the lever wouldn't break, gritted his teeth and heaved down in a final effort and saw the great figure of the 'Defender' begin to topple forwards, slowly at first and then with increasing speed, to pitch out into the hall towards the fierce *gōma* flames.

The great weight of the deity smashed down into the fīre, hurling the burning brands out in all directions, the great carved screen followed and instantly its bone dry wood ignited, the artful cosmic flames becoming grim reality amongst the startled gang. Hachirō, realizing his deadly danger, turned in haste to escape but was hampered by three of his drunken crew . . . all were pinned beneath the statue amongst the fiery brands . . . Total chaos ensued in the sudden enfolding darkness before the hungry tongues of flame lit the terrible scene. The whole floor of the Prayer Hall became a blazing inferno in seconds, the fierce barrier of fire blocking any means of escape.

'Master! Master . . . This way, my lord,' urged Toshiaki, and he caught at Enshin's smouldering sleeve and bundled him behind the splintered remains of the reredos, then out by the small hidden door always to be found in such a private place. Behind them, the smoke billowed thickly and the terrified but trapped survivors were coughing and retching uncontrollably. Once out, they closed the door against any who might follow and vanished up the forested slope.

Amongst the trees, Enshin quickly beat out the last of the smouldering ash and ruefully commented: 'I think that the Lord Fudō has suggested that this robe is rather too old and shabby, this is why he has filled it full of more holes. Perhaps I should replace it when we return to Kusatsu?'

His retainer merely grinned, but as he looked back at the glare of the burning temple hall he admired his master's resourcefulness.

——— 🔲 ———

When daylight came the conflagration had died away leaving a pall of thick white smoke rising up from the mountainside then spreading out horizontally along the valley to join the usual mists that made these craggy heights so beautiful to behold. They could just make out two or three forlorn figures moving about the open courtyard and these soon hurried off in a westerly direction as if anxious to get away from the tortured spirits of their fellows or the vengeance of the local peasants. The watchers could detect no other life amongst the debris.

'Shall I find a path down to the villages, master?'

Enshin shook his head.

'No, Toshiaki-san; I think we have fulfilled our rôle in this matter, don't you? Those farmers will have no more trouble from these particular bandits though they should recommend themselves to the protection of some lord. Better to pay extortionate taxes than being subject to the cruelties of brigands.'

Later that day when they rested beside a mountain stream, Enshin's follower asked his master about his plan for the defeat of the brigand gang.

'I had no plan, my friend,' smiled the monk. 'How could I when we were faced by so many evil men? No, I placed my trust in your keen eye and in the power of Fudō-dono who punishes those who defy the Lord Buddha's Sacred Law.'

What more could be said?

11

THE RED HAWKS OF THE OTO RIVER

▼

The three companions, Enshin the priest, his faithful follower Toshiaki, and the gentle black water-buffalo, Kuroi-san, gazed at the animated scene before them marvelling at the human comedy of life. After praying at the holy places in the Yoshino mountains, their wanderings steps had taken a southwards direction that, by many short stages, had brought them beyond the mysteries contained in the great Kumano Hongo shrine to experience the hot springs that famously lined parts of the narrow Kawayu valley. A few days spent here and taking to those hot waters would, Enshin believed, sooth away such vestiges of anger and worldly discontent that lay in their souls.

'One can hardly believe that in the midst of the terrible tides of war that everywhere disrupt the provinces,' observed the priest, 'so great a throng should travel the roads to come here. I am minded that we should turn away.' For no real reason he had a sudden feeling of foreboding that disturbed his spirit.

'Master, if we go a short distance upstream perhaps we won't be amongst the crowd. There are very few people to be seen this side of the river.'

The summer rains had ceased, replaced by the cloying heat of summer, yet here to their left there must have been more than a hundred men, women, and their children, thronging the many open scrapes they had excavated along the wide dry bed of the burbling Oto-gawa as it crossed the stony shallows along this section of its comparatively narrow gorge. These pilgrims, if such they were, disported themselves in the cleansing waters, apparently without a thought to the violence that lay just beyond these great mountains.

A short distance along the deserted branch track a kimono clad young woman came out from a small and slightly ramshackle ryōkan, shuffling lightly along the dusty pathway to request that they come and enjoy the hospitality her *oka-sama* would provide for such honoured guests, but Toshiaki, ever cautious when it came to parting with his master's meagre store of silver, asked her the cost of lodging. Perhaps the pretty young girl had a soft heart for she named a figure far lower than he expected, especially as Kawayo enjoyed such evident popularity.

'We shall require the most modest of quarters,' he said, 'for my master is only a wandering healer and I am not a samurai as you can see. Besides, we have Kuroi-san here to feed, though rough grazing will suffice.'

The girl smiled brightly, her fingers gently scratching the buffalo's soft nose and forehead.

'We are not a grand inn, honoured masters, and always overlooked by wealthy travellers who venture here from the towns. Besides, good sir; if your master there . . .' she indicated Enshin who was gazing up the Oto-gawa towards the verdant heights and their clear reflexions in the limpid waters, '. . . if the lord priest would deign to question my poor mother about her ailment, I am sure that she would show her gratitude . . .' The girl tailed off into an embarrassed silence, not certain if she hadn't been too forward.

Toshiaki smiled and nodded his head. He realized that she instinctively guessed his master's high birth rank even though he hadn't spoken a word as yet. He decided that he need look no further for somewhere for his master to stay and, motioning to the girl to wait a moment, walked across to where Enshin was calmly watching a couple of red hawks lazily circling against the opposite forested slopes. Briefly, he said that all was arranged, with Enshin's approval, that is, but that the girl had asked if he could find out the cause of her mother's illness.

Kuroi-san quite evidently was happy with any arrangement, calmly following the girl as she led the way to show them the stabling and small paddock nestling against the hillside. His needs attended to, they entered the hostelry and were met by the young woman's mother. At once it struck the priest that here was a very sick woman who was pale and haggard despite being no more than in her late thirties. There was no sign of anyone else living at the inn nor of any man belonging to the family other than a shuffling bent fellow, named Gunbei, who suffered from a crooked back and a distorted foot. This poor fellow never spoke but showed by his attentiveness that he worshipped the ground on which the *oka-sama* and her daughter stood.

The girl and their servant vanished for a short while before returning with a vessel full of cold buckwheat *soba* and some freshly cooked vegetables. The older woman gracefully settled herself near to Enshin's side and poured out some tea into simple cups set by her daughter.

For some time master and retainer ate in silence before Enshin carefully wiped his mouth and observed: 'Forgive me for my rudeness, respected mistress, but you are clearly not accustomed to many guests? It seems to me that in years gone by you lived a sheltered life set against a cultured background. May I enquire if this was indeed so?'

The woman put down the kettle and bowed her head.

'Is it so obvious . . . my lord?' she replied softly.

The carpenter thought that maybe the girl had said something to her mother. His master turned on his woven mat, gently telling the beads of his *nenju* rosary.

'I think, madam, that one cannot hide one's birth no matter how hard one may try. I, too, have tried for many years to become a simple wandering priest, but constantly I am reminded of my past. It is something that used to sadden me and trouble my spirit because a warrior is often feared by ordinary people and usually with good reason; yet here am I, a poor wanderer, who has been in holy orders for longer than ever I carried arms. To expiate my previous existence and for the countless iniquities of my class, I have studied and practised medicine in order to . . .'

He stopped, seeing tears hovering in the woman's eyes.

Again, she bowed low but as she was about to clear the utensils from the low table she was racked by a sudden fit of coughing and, in haste, covered her mouth with the sleeve of her kimono. In a moment, her daughter entered and knelt by her mother, her arm about her to comfort. When she had recovered her composure, the coughing fit over, the woman apologized and requested that she be excused from further attendance on her guests.

For a long while after she had withdrawn, Enshin sat in deep thought, then he turned to Toshiaki and asked him to bring his travelling wallet. Taking out his writing brush and ink stone, he carefully wrote some few words on a piece of paper. While the ink dried, he said: 'Your mother comes of a good family, doesn't she, miss . . ?'

'My name is Masa-ko, master . . .' she whispered. 'We were once part of the proud Ōyama-Yūki family . . .'

Enshin nodded his head and sighed.

'I want you to go with Toshiaki-san, here, Masa-ko-san, and seek out these simple herbs. Will you do this? You can trust my retainer and he will protect you.' Turning to the carpenter, he requested that he wear his long sword and his dirk. 'Be vigilant, my friend', he enjoined, but didn't elaborate in explanation.

The girl, who from her clear skin, must have been no older than seventeen, gladly agreed, but asked if their servant, Gunbei, could go, too.

'He knows these mountainsides, my ... master, and every plant and animal that lives there ... He will help find everything you need.'

'Then I will talk and pray with your parent awaiting your return.'

———□———

Early in the morning a couple of days later, Enshin and his retainer had left the ryōkan just as dawn was breaking ostensibly to enjoy a stroll along the northwards track. As the eastern sky lightened behind the rugged peaks and the rays of the rising sun first struck the opposite ridges, so several pairs of great hawks wheeled over the forest trees on idle wings, occasionally uttering their mewing calls as their keen eyes searched for their prey. One couple swooped down low across the placid surface of a limpid river pool and each caught up in their talons an unwary fish.

Enshin had paused, squatting down on his haunches as he observed these beautiful birds whose feathers were so beloved by warriors.

'You see, my friend,' he said in a voice little above a whisper, 'how vigilant those hawks are? I was watching them closely and saw not the slightest ripple on the river that would give away the presence of those two perch, and yet they dived down and without error snatched them out! Truly, that was a lesson for any swordsman to learn!'

'It was a beautiful sight, master,' Toshiaki replied.

His master nodded his head.

'We seem to be quite alone here. Maybe we have the chance to find a warm spring amongst the stones; what do you think, eh?'

'We can try, master,' grinned the carpenter, dropping down to the exposed bed of the river and picking up a stout branch of pine that had been left by the spring floods. It was just the right length to scrape out a shallow hole that might, if they were fortunate, soon fill with the hot waters that lay just below the valley floor. 'Those hawks will warn us of any approaching danger,' he added.

Enshin chuckled to himself, satisfied that his stalwart retainer had all along been aware of his inner feeling of a certain unease.

Not ten minutes later when Toshiaki had excavated a sizeable hole, warm water began to fill it to the level of the river; water warm enough to send a faint plume of steam up into the still fresh dawn air. As soon as the sediment settled to the bottom, the carpenter bowed and proclaimed his master's ō-furo was ready.

Stripped to his loincloth, Enshin stepped down into the simple bath and found the waters were very pleasant indeed.

'Just as well you didn't test the theory, Toshiaki-san, and dig the bath out closer to the riverside!'

He noted that the carpenter remained standing within a few feet, no further, and that his katana was worn in a manner ready for immediate use.

'Do you know anything about the Azuma-Yūki clan?' he asked, casually.

Without turning his head, Toshiaki replied that he had heard a story that the clan's yashiki had been burned some years before. They had held lands around Kanimiyama at the point where the borders of Iga, Ise, and Yamato provinces met, hadn't they? A debatable place, at best, these days, he supposed.

Enshin cupped his hands and poured several scoops of water over his head before he asked: 'Anything else?'

'I heard, too, that the Yūki had a succession problem. Weren't they vassals of the Kitabatake-ke . . ?' Toshiaki scratched his chin, thinking hard. 'That's right! I remember it was commonly said in several inns along the Ise coast that the son of the old lord died and that three of the councillors tried to break away and take the land taxes for themselves. Wasn't that at the time that the Tsu clan rebelled further up the Ise Bay?'

'You keep yourself informed,' commented the priest as he stepped out to dry himself.

'Sometimes its important to know friends from . . .'

'Exactly! Anything else?'

'Ah, I was wondering if you would press me further, master,' grinned the carpenter. 'Well, just one thing; about the time that these *hatamoto* attempted their coup, along comes a rōnin, who just happened to be passing by on his way to the Grand Shrine, I heard, and he sets up to help establish the infant son of a Yūki concubine to fill the gap. The old lord had also died by this time, though murdered seems nearer the truth, was the whisper . . !'

'And . . ?'

'And it was then that the Tsu-ke struck, setting fire to the border forts and then getting into the main yashiki . . . It was seven or eight years ago, master!'

Enshin had dressed by now.

'Why don't you take a bath, too, my friend. I will keep watch.'
A few moments later he said over his shoulder: 'You are not quite
right about the date, you know.'

'Please correct me, master . . . My memory isn't as good as it
should be; not since I set out to find you all those years ago.'

'I know it is impolite to contradict anyone but in this case we
need to be clear, I think. You left Kusatsu in your quest to find me
about the end of the sixth year of *Tai-ei*.[12] That's fourteen years ago
now, isn't it?'

'That is so; yes.'

'The Kanimiyama yashiki fell five years after you left Kusatsu.
That was when the Tsu attacked but were themselves defeated by
the Kitabatake-ke directly afterwards. Now, do you know anything
about this rōnin, by any chance, eh?'

'Only that somehow or other he wormed his way into the remaining Yūki *hatamoto's* confidence, suggesting moves that seemed alright
at the time but soon proved very unpopular.'

'Did you hear anything about where this man came from?'

Toshiaki grinned broadly.

'I know you, master,' he laughed. 'Yes! I heard that he came from
somewhere in the Kantō. He was trusted because he appeared to
have no connections with any of the parties involved in the dispu-
tations, and could offer what seemed sound advice.' The carpenter
frowned. 'He had been staying in Kuwana for some time, I think,
and then reached the Yūki domain by way of . . .'

'Tsu! Exactly!'

'You know more than I do, master.'

'Well, I will tell you something. The *oka-sama* who owns our inn
was the wife of the last Yūki lord. The girl, Masa-ko, is indeed her
daughter, her only child. They escaped the Tsu attack and the treachery of that rōnin to seek refuge here about seven years ago. This
ryōkan had once been a private lodge maintained for senior retainers who made the pilgrimage south in order to visit the Kumano
shrines, but it hadn't been officially entered in the Yūki records as it
had been part of the lady's marriage dowry.'

'Then, unless she is recognized she will be quite safe, master?'

'Possibly!' Enshin glanced back. 'Have you finished yet,
Toshiaki?'

'Almost dressed, master. Just one moment.'

---

[12] The *Tai-ei* era: 1521 – 1528, *Tai-ei* 6 was, therefore, 1526. *Tembun* 8, when
this account was set, was the year 1540.

'Those two hawks have put the thought into my mind that we should try our hand at some fishing. How about that later?'

As they sauntered back to the inn, Toshiaki had been thinking hard. 'The lady will be safe only if the rebel hatamoto who attempted the coup don't know that she escaped?'

———— ⊟ ————

Later that afternoon the two men crossed over the rickety trestle bridge that spanned the river just at the point where the shallows began and found a suitable spot to cast their lines, shaded from the heat as the sun began to sink behind the western heights. It would have been no good attempting to fish earlier but now the surface of the water was alive with insects and the fish were beginning to rise,

'We must keep an eye on those two,' smiled the priest, 'or they'll do rather better than us ... and at our expense, no doubt!'

Not a hundred feet away, perched on a low overhanging branch, were two large hawks; probably the same couple they had watched taking fish early that morning. Both magnificent birds were intently watching them.

'Master?' said the carpenter in a very low voice. 'May I ask a question?'

'About the rōnin from the Kantō?' smiled the priest.

'Why, yes!' Toshiaki wasn't surprised; he knew his master too well. 'How did you know about him?'

'I keep my eyes and ears open, too, you must remember. You would like to know if he survived the Kitabatake attack to retake their lost territory?'

'Uhh! We have a bite, master ... Look, you've a fish on your line ...'

'Watch out for that hawk, Toshiaki-san, while I try to bring him in close ...'

Enshin, like his retainer, had great skill at fishing and managed to bring a fine perch right to the shallow water at their feet. Watchful in case of being robbed, they landed the fish and soon had it safe under two flat stones. Very soon afterwards it was Toshiaki's turn and he managed to safely bring ashore yet another fish; but their luck changed when a third strongly resisting perch flopped up to the surface and was in a flash caught up in the talons of the bigger of the two hawks.

'Clever, that bird!' Enshin said, admiringly. 'He knew just when the fish would break the surface ... and when our attention would be distracted! That was true awareness!'

While the carpenter secured another hook on the broken line, he said: 'I think that rōnin may prove to be trouble, master ...'

'And why should you think that?'

'Because he will have known that the lady and her daughter escaped. It would be very easy for a man like him to find that out as everybody who came through the fighting would have had that question on their minds . . . And if she escaped then did any of the clan treasure go with her . . ? That has often happened in the past, hasn't it, master?'

'Pure speculation, my friend . . .'

'Hmm! Pardon me, master, I'm not so sure about that. I was thinking of that rōnin I encountered at Itako all those years ago. He was clever enough to steal the Kashima gold, wasn't he?'

'Eh! Another bite . . ! Am I the fortunate one to-day!' The priest's face was wreathed in smiles. 'You will not be so lucky, my feathered friend; not this time!'

———————□———————

Over the following two weeks, Enshin's herbal decoctions seemed to be having a beneficial effect on Masa-ko's mother. She looked less harassed and some colour had returned to her cheeks more than hinting that once she had been a beautiful woman. In her turn, her daughter went about her duties with a lightened step and their servant, Gunbei, relaxed slightly from his normal dog-like attention.

One slightly hazy early morning the third week after their arrival, Toshiaki requested if the servant could accompany him to pick up some small sacks of rice from a farmer's godown that lay in the adjoining valley not a mile or so away. Despite Gunbei being an outcaste, or so everyone would have thought, both his master and he had soon realized that the man had been born a samurai, though of lowly rank. He was very far from being a *himin* despite his twisted leg and loss of speech. Nothing at all had been said on the subject and both men realized that the man was totally committed to the well-being of his mistress and his dead lord's heir even though she was a woman.

Together, they trudged past the small cluster of inns alongside the river that formed the Kawayo hamlet and a little further on the steep flight of steps leading to the humble tutelary shrine perched fifty or so feet up the steep mountainside, the wheels of their small handcart crunching the gravelly track. From the forest trees above came the chatter of a troupe of monkeys and the occasional harsh voices of some crows. The roadway hugged the steep sides of the valley, sometimes with a narrow strip of vegetable field between them and the river bank, but as often as not, simply gouged out from the cliffside, in places so narrow that two such carts would be unable to pass.

Just before the valleys joined, they passed a long calm stretch of the
Oto-gawa where the waters ran deep and then came on another
band of shallows where some pilgrims had evidently scraped out
their open-air baths. At this point, which faced more or less east, the
air must have been slightly cooler and it caused a low bank of mist
to rise up from the warmer waters of the river as they passed over
the volcanic cracks below. Here, it was clear that the *rotenburō* soon
filled with very hot waters much like some of those around distant
Kusatsu. Unusually, only one early riser was down on the strand to
enjoy the luxury of a free bath.

The two noticed him first as they rounded a tree-covered spur
and a slight eddy showed them the distant figure as he stood up to
his waist in the 'bath'. A plume of steam rose lazily above the lone
bather to disappear into the lingering mist above. The man, evidently
a samurai as his swords were carefully balanced across two improvised forked twigs as though they were on a swordstand, was rinsing
his hair as they came abreast and merely paused as he glanced up.
They passed on and soon came to the small farm. Gunbei's mistress
required four small sacks of rice for her store and, as the last year's
harvest had been an excellent one in these southern mountains, the
quality was good and the price reasonable.

Where the knoll with its clump of five pine trees overhung the
river, the track on the downstream side mounted it at quite a pitch
and it took some hard work pushing and pulling to force the loaded
cart to the crest. The pair took a breather as the sun was on their
backs and the morning becoming warm.

'You know, Gunbei-san, it would be good to have a warm dip,
don't you think?'

The mute shook his head vehemently, much to Toshiaki's surprise.
He thought that his suggestion was perfectly reasonable if only they
had the time. He drew out from the little bundle he carried round
his waist two rice balls, offering one to Gunbei to refresh them
while they rested. Again, the suggestion was refused and the carpenter could see that the servant was deeply agitated.

'What's up, my friend?' he asked, hardly expecting any reply, but
Gunbei grasped his sleeveless *haori* by the lapel and urged him to
cross through the pine grove to a point where they could see the
now empty *rotenburō* scrape. He pointed down and then at Toshiaki's
katana. 'Did he mean that only the carpenter might bathe? No, that
wasn't it! What, then . . ? They had only seen the samurai . . .'

'Was it the samurai, Gunbei-san; is that what you're trying to tell
me?'

Gunbei nodded his head but the carpenter could see that the
man's expression was grim.

'There's something about this samurai, is there? Something you want to tell me?' He looked around then had an idea. Quickly, he stooped and smoothed out the dusty surface of the track.

'Here, Gunbei-san, use this twig and write down what you want to say, slowly and carefully.'

He watched as the mute scratched character after character in the dust, only wiping out what he had written when he was sure that Toshiaki understood. At last, he tossed the twig down and sat up, cross-legged, back absolutely straight despite his deformity.

'So you recognize that man as being the rōnin responsible for the Yūki downfall, eh? You have no doubt, even after the passage of time?'

Gunbei shook his head. He caught up the stick again. He wrote the character for 'sword'.

'You knew him by his sword, did you?'

What could he possibly have seen at that distance?

'The saya that I saw down there was half-bound,' wrote Gunbei. 'It was then that I remembered.'

'Half bound . . ? In what way . . ?'

Something stirred at the back of Toshiaki's mind; a vague memory from long ago, and he frowned, waiting for Gunbei to elaborate.

'He always wore a dark-green *sayamaki* sword with a matching *dō-maru* armour. He was never without it.'

'You're sure about that?'

'Yes!'

'Come on,' urged Toshiaki, 'we must get back to my master and your mistress . . . No time to waste!'

———— ⊟ ————

'There are many such green-bound *tachi*, my friends,' murmured Enshin when he had heard Gunbei's and Toshiaki's suspicions.

'Yes, master; but . . .'

'No, my friend . . .' He held up his hand to calm both men down. 'We have to be sure . . . Now, it's no use either of you two going to find out if this is indeed that rōnin, nor can *oka-sama* or Masa-ko-san go. That leaves just myself, doesn't it? Now, tell me, Toshiaki, as best you can, a description of the wanderer you encountered at Itako all that time ago. Did he have any scars or something that I may recognize . . ?' He turned to Gunbei. 'Listen carefully and if you can add anything, please brush it down here.' He pushed a piece of paper towards the servant together with his inkstone and a thin writing brush.

Toshiaki sighed when he had finished. He could see trouble loomimg, of that he was certain.

'Well, Gunbei-san; does our friend's description fit?

The mute servant nodded. He picked up the brush and wrote down something which Enshin read with ease.

'So, this man chiefly only uses his left hand, does he . . ? Hmmm . . ! From what you told me of that fight you had on the bridge at Itako, Toshiaki-san, this fellow's spent a long time training in the arts of the sword. You agree with that?

The carpenter nodded his head and Gunbei signed that he agreed.

'In that case, I must be doubly careful. Tell me, Gunbei-san, is this the first time you've seen him here along the Oto-gawa; after all, you are the one who gets around the most?'

The mute shook his head vigorously.

Enshin sat quietly and thought for a while. At length he nodded his head. 'It is possible that this rōnin is here only to take the waters, but it is equally likely that he has arrived here on a hunch through someone saying something that has put him on the trail of *oka-sama*, or more especially the Yūki treasure. What I intend to do is this. I shall leave here tomorrow morning wearing my usual priest's clothing and travelling south towards the Nachi Falls, but I intend to reappear in two days dressed as a wandering yamabushi. Understood? One yamabushi looks much like another and and this will allow me to carry my sword and a long staff. I won't come here but will take up residence at the other end of the village where I think our samurai may be living since he disappeared so quickly after you recognized him. You, Gunbei, must keep a sharp look out while you, Toshiaki, remain here . . . and don't shave. Also, dress poorly and do plenty of fishing where you, too, can watch people as they come and go.'

'What about Kuroi-san, master; he'll know you whatever disguise you wear!'

'Oh, don't worry about him, Toshiaki, my friend. I will go and talk to him. He won't give anything away! Now, I wonder if the mistress can help with my costume . . ?'

———— ◻ ————

So it was that just two days later, to the surprise of some of the villagers and certainly of their guests, a rather wild-looking Shugendō priest strode into the valley and, stopping opposite the second ryōkan at the northern end where the track from Hongu met the Oto-gawa, blew a mighty blast on his horagai that scared every bird within earshot high into the heavens. As this was barely after dawn, it brought everyone out to find what was up! The unkempt mountain yamabushi thumped the ground with his staff raising the dust and bawled out that he needed somewhere to stay and where he wouldn't be disturbed at his orisons. A dog that ran up barking furiously, fully intending to take a lump out of the man's leg, was swiftly dealt with, hoicked by the deft use of the *bonden* staff down into the river. Whilst the other curs kept up their noisy cacophony, they also took care to stay at a distance.

Sensing a certain reluctance amongst the good folk to offer shelter, the yamabushi stalked along the street blowing long undulating calls that exactly resembled those used by bushi to gather their troops in readiness to launch an attack. In those disturbed days where many armed bands broke the peace, such a call on a war conch was immediately recognized; when it was coupled by the priest's stentorian threat that he would call to his aid the deities of the storm and the flood if his request was not immediately complied with, he was met by a shrivelled servant who invited him to enter his master's establishment.

Enshin looked at the building but simply refused. 'Inauspicious,' he bellowed. He strode on a few paces then pointed imperiously at the second to last establishment. 'I will stay here!' he announced.

There, calmly drinking ō-cha, sat his quarry.

'Honoured sir, we have no room!' a querulous voice assured him.

'What! No room for a *dai-dai-sendatsu!*' Enshin exploded. 'What is this I hear . . ?'

'But, but, master . . .!'

'Find a place or I will call up a thousand devils to my bidding . . ! You understand? A thousand demons to torment you . . .!'

With that, the yamabushi took his portable altar from his back and planted himself cross-legged in the middle of the dusty track, pulled out his rosary and began to chant an incantation in an increasingly loud voice . . .

The innkeeper wrung his hands and looked imploringly about him for support but all that witnessed his plight were leaving, only a couple of curs from the dog pack still remained, curiously silent, and the nearby samurai on the verandah stoop.

'What are you gabbling about, Kuro'emon-san; there's room here for ten yamabushi and you know it!' the rōnin called out.

The innkeeper tried to signal that he didn't want this sort of guest but was suddenly thwacked across the shoulders by Enshin.

'I cannot believe that you were lying, Master Kuro'emon . . . Lying to a man such as me!. Perhaps my ears deceived me; is that possible?'

'No, no, master! No, I mean yes . . . Come in, m . . . master! Welcome . . . er . . . welcome!'

'And you have no objections, sir?' demanded the yamabushi, bowing to the samurai.

'Absolutely none!'

'Since we shall be guests of Master Kuro'emon here, permit me to introduce myself. I am named Koen-bō but prefer to have that shortened to just Koen.'

The samurai hadn't risen to his feet but bowed with reasonable formality from where he was seated.

'My name is Yakami Yoshihide.'

'Ah, is that so? You must hale from Tamba province, I would guess?'

'Why, you are correct, my friend! Well now, sit down with me . . . Kuro'emon! Bring some more refreshing tea!'

They sat and sipped the infusion for a while, looking out over this rather pleasing portion of the river valley. At length, Yakami Yoshihide asked: 'Do you know these parts?'

'Not at all,' replied Koen. 'I have come down here for the first time; my usual stamping grounds are in Kōzuke and Dewa. But I'm here now and intend to take a good look around. And you, master samurai; what is your interest, eh?'

'Are you always so direct, priest?'

Koen laughed.

'Sometimes I am the mildest of men; at others I put on an act to get my way!'

'And what way is that, yamabushi?'

'Now who is being direct?' Koen cocked his head a little as he glanced at his newfound companion. 'Well, my way is the Way of the Gods, one might say . . . I go wherever my feet guide me and in whatever direction fancy decides. There are many temples to feed one's soul but even so one has to live, doesn't one? Long ago when I first took to the yamabushi ways, I practically starved. I soon learned how to live frugally but never to ask for more than was necessary.' Enshin grunted to himself before continuing: 'With most people, a three-day visit is enough . . . After that, leave! But you are aware of this since you are, yourself, a "wave-man", are you not?'

'We seem to have some things in common, Master Koen . . . The name you have taken means "Lecturer", doesn't it? Yamabushi don't usually lecture, do they? That falls into the province of the Tendai and Shingon fraternity, eh?'

Enshin recognized that he was dealing with a sharp mind in this particular rōnin, but he laughed out loud before remarking: 'Ah, sir; I took the name "Koen-bō" not so much as meaning "lecturer" but more "one who enquires into many things" . . . People interest me; everything about them interests me, especially their more secret side . . !'

'Then, Master Koen, you'll be interested in me? Is that not so?'

'Of course . . ! And why not? After all, you are a far-travelled rōnin, that I can see from your slightly travel-worn *hakama* and *kimono*, sir, but you have also lived well. Certainly, you haven't starved nor become wolfish like so many masterless wanderers do. Therefore, honoured sir, I deduce that you have a interesting story to tell, were you to put it in so many words, of course!'

'Can you tell anything else from my appearance, master yamabushi?'

Enshin chuckled affably.

'Ah, perhaps I have already said too much? Sometimes my probing goes too far, though I'll admit that I do have an insatiable curiosity. Please do not take offence, Master Yakami!'

'Huhh! I'll not take offence, priest; but answer my question: what more do you deduce, hey?'

Enshin turned to contemplate the samurai pulling at his chin..

'I can see by your sword that you have spent many years studying tactics.' He held up an admonishing right forefinger when he saw that the other was about to say something. 'You wear a *sayamaki-tachi*; few carry such a sword unless they are expert warriors, for the inference is clear . . . And yet, sir, you are a "wave-man" and not employed . . . I ask myself the question "How can this be?" Also, your name tells me that you come from Tamba province and yet I detect a hint in your speech of a long sojourn in the Kantō region; I would even go so far as to guess at Hitachi . . . There, is that enough, master samurai?'

The samurai gave him a long look before agreeing. For a while they sat in relative silence watching a crowd of white-clad pilgrims strip and disport themselves a short distance upstream.

'Why do you wear that long sword, yamabushi?' Yakami Yoshihide said at last. 'Like mine, I can see that it has been drawn many more times than usual for one who wanders the mountain paths . . . and *that* interests *me!*'

'Ah, some of those ways have taken me to very dangerous places, sir; and not always places where snakes and evil spirits beset the paths!'

'I heard that there are many such dangerous places in Kōzuke and the north?'

'Many, indeed!'

'But to recognize my Hitachi accent would also imply, to me, that you have resided in that province for sometime, too. May I ask where?'

'I was some months in Kashima, sir, at the Tsukahara yashiki; that was after I had lived three years hard by Tsukuba-san . . . But later I was in Itako.'

'Itako, eh? And may I enquire when that was?'

'Oh, a good few years ago, as I recall. Why, is it of interest to you? Do you know Itako, too, sir?'

The rōnin grimaced. 'I passed through there once, I think . . . I think it rained the whole time. A thoroughly miserable place!'

'It was warm and beautiful with the water lilies in full bloom when I was there.' Enshin muttered a short prayer formula and shrugged his shoulders, feigning fatigue. 'I need to recite part of the Heart Sutra in fulfilment of my vows, Yakami-sama. With the sun now high, I shall indulge in the luxury of a riverside bath. Would that be to your liking before it grows dark?'

He moved himself off the round mat and bowed stiffly to the warrior, taking care not to lose sight of the other's hands as he did so.

'Yes; I think I shall join you, Master Koen. From what you have said, I agree with you that we are wanderers with much in common!'

Enshin descended to cross the exposed river bed to a point that he judged to be its widest. There he sat himself down and in a loud voice proceeded to chant in a monotone, periodically clicking his rosary beads or, at the appropriate junctures, clapping his palms together in that explosive manner that many priests affect. Nearby remained a rather large *rotenburō* that had been enthusiastically dug out over a couple of days by a group of pilgrims and he had at one time counted no less than fifteen heads in the steaming water. Finishing the ritual with a couple of short blasts on his conch, he prepared to indulge in the ō-furo. True to his word, the samurai emerged from their inn and came down onto the stones.

'Over here, Yakami-sama,' called out Enshin, now standing in only his fundoshi but not yet having placed his tachi sword on his folded clothes.

The 'wave-man' sauntered across looking completely at his ease. Before he started to undress, he sat himself down on a pile of stones left by the *kō*,[13] and gazed at the tranquil scene up and down the river. He was carrying his sayamaki-tachi in his hands, its woven himo cords neatly rolled and secured to their scabbard mounts, but

---

[13] *ko*: a group of pious pilgrims

he was careless enough to lean with his chin to the hilt when he seated himself on the rocks.

'A beautiful day, isn't it,' remarked the 'yamabushi'. He snorted through his nose and pointed at a lone fisherman casting his line out on a narrow spit of shingle a short distance upstream. 'Now, there's a contented man; one who clearly takes his pleasures seriously!' Even at that distance, he knew that it was Toshiaki depite the battered broad-brimmed straw hat he was wearing.

Yakami-san seemed somewhat preoccupied with the calm scene, merely grunting in reply. Casually placing his slung sword beside his end of the rough pool, Enshin stepped into the warm waters, feeling the exquisite stimulus of the hot spring as it reached his waist.

'Ah! That's more like it!' he breathed. 'Won't you join me, sir?'

It was clear that there was something on the samurai's mind and Enshin thought that it was his words that morning that had sunk home. The moment of danger was fast approaching, he was sure.

'Ah, yes; Koen-sama. A moment before I ready myself . . . It is my turn to surprise you with my understanding of times now past . . . Isn't that how it is stated in the *Konjaku-monogatari* . . ?'

'Why, it is indeed . . . You are well-read, sir,' smiled the priest, casually brushing the hot water from his hands. 'Please carry on with what you were about to say.'

'I am curious why you should have mentioned that your early travels took you specifically from Tsukuba-san to Kashima and then to Itako. Why, I wonder, was this?'

Enshin chuckled. 'That's easy to answer, Yakami-sama; those were the places I visited in Hitachi province. I never did fancy going up to Mitō for one thing. I heard that it is a dull place. I am a mountain man through and through. But come, sir, my direct mode of conversation has in some way offended you, I'm sure. If that is the case, I apologize . . . It is a fault that I must strive to overcome . . .'

The rōnin's expression did not change. He ignored what Enshin had said.

'And more recently, on your way here, Master Koen-bō, where did your steps take you?'

'Ah, you are indeed interested, Yakami-sama! Let me see . . . First I came through the Kawakami valley and crossed the steep tracks to pray at the Yoshino Mikumari shrine. Huh, I remember that well enough because, like your visit to Itako, it rained without pause for three whole days! Then I followed the tracks up to sacred Ōmine-san past the Kinpu shrine and that strange stone forbidding women to enter the sacred mountains!' He gave himself a couple more splashes then came to his feet in the most natural a manner that he could. '. . . You should come in, sir . . .' he urged.

Whether Toshiaki could hear their conversation for the air was perfectly still, or he had hooked a large fish, but at that instant his retainer had leapt to his feet and was floundering through the shallows with his line taut. The distraction was enough to allow Enshin to step out onto the stones close to his recumbent sword and begin to wipe himself down with a *hachimaki*.

'You were remarking on the places I visited in Hitachi before crossing to Shimosa and that my path must have been similar to yours . . . Mind you, the safest track once across the lake from Kashima is up to Itako . . . Too many brigands around those marshes and a sight too much bickering between the landowners for comfort. Why, I heard a story of one such attack that happened there years back when I was back of Kitayama . . . that was only a month or so ago. Long memories some people have since the event must have occurred as long past as the fourth year of *Tai-ei*.'[14] Enshin frowned, pausing as he drew on his checkered kimono. 'But surely, sir, you are not thinking that I knew when you were there . . . in Itako . . ?'

He secured his tachi around his waist, not bothering with his drawstring hakama and retied his small pillbox *tokin* to his shaven forehead. By now Toshiaki had triumphantly drawn in his catch and was shouting out insults at the red hawk that was skimming away across the river surface. His victim was a magnificent roach or carp, fully two *shaku* in length, maybe more.

'Itako! Of course I was there,' rasped out the rōnin in a half-strangled voice. 'I suppose, too, that you reached Yoshino by way of Tsu?'

'That is true, Yakami-sama; but then, it is very difficult not to pass through Tsu if one wishes to miss the brigand gangs that infest the Iga mountains. Mind you, I didn't linger around Kanimiyama where the area has hardly recovered since the Kitabatake armies seized control back there six or seven years ago . . .' Enshin paused, seeing Yakami Yoshihide's face suffuse with anger, and pointed at Toshiaki. 'Why, that man is indeed fortunate, but he'd better keep his eyes on that hawk or it will have his fish . .! Hey, fisherman; watch out!'

'Oh, no, you don't!' shouted out his retainer, wildly clawing at his sword in an effort to draw it out and ward off the hawk's attack. The great feathered predator screeched out and veered in its flight towards where the rōnin stood, his own sword part drawn, the hilt grasped in his left hand . . . He frowned . . . Toshiaki's wide-brimmed hat had fallen back across his shoulders and the samurai could clearly see his face. There was no more than a dozen paces between them when he remembered . . .

---

[14] 1525

'Itako . . . You have tried to trap me,' he shouted. 'Damn you both . . !'

His long tachi blade slid out from its scabbard and he leapt towards Toshiaki, yelling out that he should have killed him on the bridge for stealing the gold back all those years ago . . .

The carpenter dropped his rod and stood ready to receive the onslaught, calf deep in the limpid river water; his master was momentarily disadvantaged with the *rotenburō* between him and the rōnin. Yakami, his long sword held high at his right shoulder ready to deliver a sweeping downwards cut, plunged across the rippling stream to close the gap when the hawk wheeled in a tight arc and flew in a second time, uttering a long high-pitched mew. The distraction was enough . . . Yakami's foot slipped on a weed-covered rock just beneath the surface, the hawk's wide-stretched wing pinions brushed his sword, and he plunged, flailing, into the water . . .

Spluttering, and now literally a 'wave-man', Yakami Yoshihide tried to climb to his feet but Enshin could see an ever-widening red stain eddying out in the clear green waters of the Oto-gawa. Regaining his feet, the rōnin clutched at his side but his tachi had done its deadly work only too well; from the front of his chest appeared the point of his sword. Somehow, in his fall he had twisted and his blade had pierced him at an angle, impaling him just as he had killed that bandit, Yoichi, on the rain-soaked bridge in Itako fifteen years before.

———□———

So as not to implicate the lady *oka-sama* or her daughter in the incident, Enshin, pretending still to be the yamabushi, Koen-bō, simply gathered his things and strode off without a word into the southern heights, leaving Toshiaki, as the innocent fisherman who witnessed this samurai kill himself, to report the affair. Yakami's corpse was recovered washed up on another shingle bank quite a way downstream and the affair soon ceased to be a *cause célèbre* and wasn't even mentioned a week later when Enshin returned from Hongū. Not that he would have been noticed; priests were not really seen, they are just there . . . almost invisible in a manner of speaking . . .

———□———

'What do you think you should do now, madam?' Enshin enquired. 'The danger from that rōnin has now gone.'

'What would you advise. Honoured Priest; you have rank enough to sit in council?'

'I am poorly qualified, lady, having had little to do with such affairs since I was a young man.'

The woman sighed and glanced at her daughter who sat not saying a word.

'Our House is destroyed and the members either dead or dispersed by the four winds. The Ōyama-Yūki are no more. All that was saved was my daughter, the rightful heir, and part of the clan treasure. To whom shall we turn who won't covet that gold?'

'You could approach the Kitabatake, madam; your clan overlord is Kitabatake Harutomo, is he not? They would give you shelter and find a suitable husband for Lady Masa-ko.'

A sad look passed across the woman's face.

'No, Honoured Priest, if Harutomo-dono had wished to do something, he would have restored our House and searched diligently for a survivor. No, retaking our yashiki, or the ruins of it, enabled him to strengthen his frontier, but he found it convenient not to settle the succession dispute!'

'Then, we can reach no conclusion even if we wished to?'

'Oh, there is a solution, I am certain. Either we can remain in this valley although I know that there will be others who will seek to find us just as Yakami-san thought that we might be here since it is widely known that the gold was never found, or I can provide a good dowry for my daughter, should she wish to find a husband, and I shall go to a temple and take holy orders. That has been my inner wish for some years, to retire from this world and pray for the souls of my husband and his family.'

Enshin nodded his head in agreement.

'If this is indeed your wish, then, madam, I can only offer the advice that you should find a temple far from these three provinces. You will never be safe here.'

'Do you have anywhere in mind, sir?'

'Surely, madam, it would be presumptuous of me to suggest such a choice?'

'Not at all! Wherever you name we shall go.'

'In that case, my lady; you should travel by the main roads dressed as pilgrims returning from the Kumano shrines. No one will molest you nor question your servants. Once you have reached Tanabe, dismiss the first set of porters, reinstate Gunbei-san as a samurai, then continue by way of Miyakō to Mikawa and thence seek out the Shingon temple of Hōrai-ji. Place yourselves under the protection of my uncle who is still the abbot there. It is a place where you may find both sanctuary and peace.'

'Are you certain of this?'

The priest smiled reassuringly.

'Quite certain, my lady. I shall write a letter of introduction. You will experience no difficulties.'

Lady Yūki dabbed a tear from the corner of her eye.

'When we leave here, Masa-ko, I shall put out of my mind the whole past. Long years ago, the Princess Shikushi wrote a poem:

> *The blossoms have fallen,*
> *I stare blamkly at a world*
> *Drained of colour:*
> *From the wide empty sky*
> *The spring rains are falling.'*

———□———

'We learnt a thing or two here, Toshiaki-san, did we not?'

'Yes, we did, master; but we also lost, you know.'

'Lost? How was that?'

'That hawk watching us over there, master. He handed us the victory but in doing so he cleverly won the war!'

'You mean?'

'That big fish I caught, master; we never enjoyed it because he stole it from under both our noses!'

12

THE JINGASA

'This storm must surely blow itself out before long,' growled Toshiaki, drawing his straw raincape closer about his broad shoulders as he and his two companions sheltered as best they could out of the teeth of the howling wind.

They were quite apparently an ill-assorted trio, to say the least, for the well-built carpenter, not a samurai although he wore the two swords, squatted down beside a sleek black water–buffalo and both had positioned themselves just within the shelter's doorway in order to keep the worst of the storm from their master, a shaven priest whose only protection was his threadbare black robe. But then, everything is not always what it seems, for the priest was named Enshin and was the younger son of a high-ranking *bushi* who held a good fief in the mountain valleys near the Mikuni-toge in the northern Kantō and were vassals of the powerful Uesugi clan. Torii Mitsumune, now named Enshin, as a young man in his twenties, had elected to exchange the life of a warrior and become a priest under the tutelage of his uncle, abbot of the remote Hōrai-ji in Mikawa province; his vocation was now to wander the country using his skills in medicine to freely succour the needy and sick amongst the poor. The beautiful, if rather wet, black ox was named Kuroi-san, an intelligent animal who had been saved from starvation and certain death by Enshin several years before, and had accompanied him faithfully on his travels ever since.

Enshin half-smiled at the carpenter's muttered comment, hardly bothering to draw his damp robes closer about his shoulders.

'There's a purpose in everything, Toshiaki-san, even a storm such as this. It will cease soon, though, I agree.'

Idly, he fondled the ox's soft ear and muttered a prayer for the protection of Fudō-myō-ō as he gazed past a gap in the scrub on the cliff edge to a large fishing-boat, or it may have been a merchant-man, pitching and tossing as it laboured down the coast towards the doubtful shelter of the next headland. Even from where they were they had the taste of salt on their lips and could easily see just how large were the rolling waves as they swept up behind the vessel, lifting up the stern so far that sometimes it seemed that the sturdy craft must plunge down and vanish into a watery grave. The crew-men fought with their sweeps to hold the vessel steady, three men desperately grasping each of the long oars. A narrow strip, probably all that was left of a split bamboo sail, billowed and snapped at the foot of the swaying mast but it was clearly enough to carry the boat forward just clear of the destructive force of the seas. Without it, Enshin knew that those mariners would be lost.

'Let us pray that they weather the headland, my friends . . . It crosses my mind that it is strange for a boat to be out in such a storm. Still, it's not for me to speculate, I suppose.'

Whilst Enshin told his rosary beads, Toshiaki shook his head.

'I'm damned glad that it isn't me out there,' he said, blowing out his cheeks and wiping the rain away from his forehead with a rough hand. 'I mistrust water of any kind since it is the one thing I can't control!'

In his mind he recalled their bad crossing of Biwa-ko three or four years before, but then the lake had been mist enshrouded and oily calm. The ocean before them threatened and roared, further out it was whipped to a seething frenzy by the storm gods who railed and vented their spleen against anything and anyone who dared venture onto their domain.

Gradually the vessel receded to a distant pitching shadow, often hidden from their gaze behind the surging tide, to vanish round the low cliffs where the surf spumed and spurted so high.

'Why, look; there's the sun once again!' Enshin pointed and they glimpsed the weak orb through the haze. 'We shall have a rainbow later, I'm sure.'

All was not well and almost at the moment of safety, just as the merchantman began to nose into the calmer waters behind the blackened teeth of the outer reef, a sudden vagary of the wind spilt a strong gust round the towering shoulder of the headland and struck the vessel's stern quarter, slewing it sideways to broach-to under the crushing force of the final wave. In an instant all aboard were tumbled into the frothing sea, struggling and floundering in the surf, desperate to find solid ground beneath their feet. Only one of those unfortunate wretches was vouchsafed salvation, dragged half-drowned to safety by some brave fisherfolk who had seen the wrecking from the strand, the rest releasing their souls to continue their eternal journey.

To the rescuers' chagrin they found that they would receive no reward for their efforts for they had rescued a black-robed monk whose sole possession saved from the hungry waves was his sodden round straw jingasa. Once he had coughed up enough of the ocean to float a fleet of vessels, the survivor barely acknowledged his gratitude before demanding, imperiously it should be said, to be taken to the nearest temple. Whilst these poor folk had saved him from a watery grave, to have to feed so waspish a priest, who was clearly only marginally endowed with the arts of human sympathy and even less civility, would have been an embarassment to them all, and gladly did two of their number offer to guide him to the nearby Baikō-ji. His obligation, if only so reserved and haughty a fellow would allow it, therefore passed towards the old holy man who served the altar of this obscure and unimportant temple.

The humble Baikō-ji stood somewhat apart from the huddle of fishermen's hovels on the shoreline within a small grove of pines that sheltered the temple beneath a fold in the foothills that rose towards Nachi-san and its famous temples and shrines, not to mention the mighty waterfall where Mongaku Shōnin expiated his . . . but that is another story, is it not? Yet the four or five small buildings that surrounded the thatched Prayer Hall gave the Baikō-ji an air of faded beauty for the whole ensemble was harmonious and the temple, itself, possessed a rare carved Bōsatsu in wood, once painted and gilded, fashioned by the divinely guided hands of an unnamed master who passed on his journey towards Buddhahood five hundred years before.

It was later that afternoon that, dry and sustained by some simple fare, the rescued monk finished his orisons and sat up and took a sour appraising look at the elderly priest who was positioned a respectful distance away, supported by two young *shingyaku* novices. The ancient figure of the Buddha, his hands folded in a rare version of the *jō-in mudra* of concentration, smiled benignly at them from his lotus throne, not that our proud monk would have noticed.

'So, do only the three of you live here?' asked the monk.

'That is correct, my brother, although my wife resides in our quarters, too.'

'Is that so? And in whose domain are we?'

'This is land held since before the Gempei Wars by the Oishi family, brother. They are devout lords; generous and . . .'

'Quite so, quite so!' the monk interrupted. 'How far are we from the territory of the Manabe, eh?'

'The Manabe-ke?'

'That is what I asked. Do I have to say it twice, sirrah?'

The old priest remained impassive at this rudeness but one of the novices piped up that the Manabe domain commenced at Mihama a day's journey or more up the coast.

'Aki-san, I have requested before that you should not speak whilst your teacher converses. It is impolite towards any guest, particularly one so unexpected and exalted as Master Kōsei, here.'

The shingyaku bowed and muttered his apology but his companion, a hard-faced impassive youth, merely tightened the line of his thin lips, his eyes almost invisible behind their narrow lids.

Drawing in his breath, the priest bowed his head courteously and apologized.

'Please disregard such an error, honoured guest, but my deshi is rather young and cannot be expected to be aware of the niceties that culture demands. I was endeavouring to explain the distance to the border but you must forgive me since I have only once in my whole life crossed the Kumano-gawa at Shingu and that was when I ...'

Again, the monk cut in.

'I wish to inform Manabe-dono of my presence here!'

'. . . It was forty years ago, when I was but a lad . . .' The priest remained impassive.

'That is of no importance to me, or to anyone else! My business has that degree of urgency, though, and I would have been there now but for those incompetent fools of sailors!'

'They were all drowned, I heard,' said the priest, softly, folding his hands and muttering a short prayer. When he opened his eyes, he observed impassively: 'As the Manabe-dono resides in the adjoining province I cannot help you without first seeking approval from my lord.'

'No matter!' The monk prepared to stand up. 'I shall send a letter!'

'Pray seat yourself down,' the priest kept his voice calm with some difficulty. 'Perhaps something can be arranged in the morning. I will enquire for you in the village. Sometimes travellers with the necessary passes come through here, or we might find a pilgrim who will return in that direction.. .'

'Tchahh!'

'Calm yourself, master. Unseemly haste is rarely good for any of us.'.

'What about one of these shingyaku, eh? A priest, even a young one, can pass the barriers without hindrance. One of them will go!'

'But, my dear brother, they are simple village lads placed in my care. How would they dare to approach such a high personage or even his councillors? It would be both improper and not little dangerous, don't you think?'

'You have lived too sheltered a life here,' replied the monk; 'Surely it is time that they learned to do what they are told? Come now, I need brush, ink, and paper and without delay!'

———— 🔲 ————

'It is too late by far for your letter to leave this evening, honoured guest. As I said, I will enquire of some reliable person to carry it in the morning once this storm has abated.'

'One of those boys will take it at my command, sir!'

The priest breathed deeply and looked up.

'Whoever takes the letter will not travel in this gale! It will, as I have said, pass overnight and the messenger will leave as soon as we can hire him after dawn.'

'I am not here to bandy words. You are stubborn and in my way. You are aware that I come from a very important temple; surely that is enough to command compliance even in this . . . place?'

At last and with the greatest reluctance, the old priest was nettled so far as to abandon his natural deference. He shook his head.

'The lord Buddha enjoins humility, reverent sir; in this place he abhors so intemperate a manner. I have decided that nothing can be done to accommodate you until sunrise tomorrow and so it shall be. Let this be an end to the matter.' He clapped his hands to summon the straight-faced shingyaku.

'Yes; I am here?'

'Master Aki, be so kind and guide our guest to the room prepared by my wife. At dawn, if you please, I shall have a message to take to old Magobei, the village head, so please come here in readiness.'

Yes, master!'

Kōsei-san's face was reddened with anger but he contained himself. Outside the rain still rattled hard against the shuttered window spaces and the gale howled under the eaves. He bowed slightly in acquiescence and stalked out after the novice.

The pair hurried round the sheltering verandah and he entered the small room he had been given that lay quite close to the stable and storehouse. There he sat in thwarted ill-humour. About an hour later there came a light knocking at the shoji and someone respectfully requested admittance. It was Aki again, the lad with the shifty narrowed eyes.

As he entered, the lad peered behind him at the darkened courtyard and turned back when satisfied that he hadn't been observed.

He bowed low and without preamble said: 'Master, I couldn't help hearing what was said by my own master in the Prayer Hall.'

'Well?'

'If you don't breathe a word, I can arrange for your letter to be taken quite safely and no one the wiser.'

The monk's lip turned up in a sneer.

'Perhaps I was wrong thinking I was surrounded by bumpkins in this hole! You will take it yourself?'

'No, master; if I take it I shall be discovered. I can arrange for it to be carried by two fish dealers who you may trust. If the message is . . . er . . . sensitive, no one will suspect either of these two 'cos they often travel to the Manabe domain with some special shellfish only found on the rocks hereabouts, like.'

'You are quite certain that they can be trusted, eh?'

'They'll do, master. They won't split if they are to be rewarded, you know.'

The monk sat still for a moment or two.

'You'll want a reward, too, I don't doubt?'

The shingyaku's eyes narrowed even further and he leant forward with a conspiratorial air.

'If you want's a letter to go that bad, master, an' I can do this for you, then I'm sure that I can wait a whiles for you to see me right. True?'

The monk cocked his head a little to one side and smiled thinly.

'I can see you doing well in my temple. Maybe . . . one day shortly such a thing might be arranged . . .'

The shingyaku bowed his head.

'Now, this is the letter I want taken. There's nothing much in it and nothing to cause problems to your . . . er . . . messengers if it is looked at in passing any barrier. Wait a little and I'll write another note that I will give to your wretched master tomorrow morning for you to take, if he lets you go. If that is the case, you vanish down the coast for a day or two so that he'll think you've carried out the task, but this letter goes with your "friends". Is that clear, my lad?'

'They will be paid, won't they?'

'Oh, yes; they'll certainly be rewarded. Don't you worry about that. Manabe-dono will be generous, that is certain.' The monk pulled over his straw jingasa. 'As a token that the letter is indeed from me, tell one of your messengers to be sure to give this to Manabe-dono's steward . . . he'll know then that everything is correct.'

The shingyaku looked at the battered hat in distaste but took it, nonetheless.

'The steward knew me in Miyakō, my boy, so he'll know this jingasa with its device on the front.'

Sure enough, there was a faded red mon just discernible on the woven straw.

Everything agreed and after some more whispered conversation since walls have ears, the novice slipped out and crept round to his own miserable quarters and a little later down to the hamlet where he sought out the two fish porters he had in mind. They listened to what he had to say and agreed to undertake the journey. Fired with greed at the thought of the promised rewards which were bound to be far more than their normal trip was worth, they swallowed down their rice wine in hefty gulps, threw their straw capes about their shoulders, and ran off into the rain to find their fish cart.

At dawn, the pair were near to Shingu but, unaccountably, they veered off the main track and took a narrower one that crossed the first line of lumpy hills on the eastern side of Nachi-san, a path that would bring them down to the banks of the Kumano-gawa. It was also a byway that eventually came to the main border fortress-manor of Oishi Mizuno-no-suke, brother of the Oishi-dono, lord of this domain, and definitely not to the Manabe territory.

———— ⊟ ————

The village priest at the Baikō-ji was mistaken in his forecast that the storm would blow itself out by the break of day. It actually redoubled in force in a last paroxysm of fury that caused the two fish porters to seek shelter as best they could, already bemoaning their greed in undertaking this journey. It so happened that they chose one of those wayside booths set up by enterprising farmers' wives to sell refreshments to chance pilgrims and other wayfarers on their weary tramp to and from any of the great mystical shrines that lay scattered about these majestic mountains, but at this early hour and in such weather quite deserted. About ten paces down the same track another booth was the shelter of Enshin, his faithful ox and Toshiaki-san, but there was no contact or conversation between the porters and the travellers due to the fierce winds and intermittent rain. Only the stink of their fish cart assailed Toshiaki's nostrils but he did his best to ignore the smell, burying his face in his folded arms.

Gradually the wind abated and the early morning sun shone through the breaks in the clouds. The two porters stirred themselves, used to rising and setting about their labours with no delay, and the noise with which they did this roused Enshin to do the same.

The pair turned round their handcart and with protesting shrieks from its wet axle, trundled off up the road towards the shoulder of the hill, the others following behind at the far slower pace set by Kuroi-san.

'It looks as if we shall have a fine day, Toshiaki-san,' said Enshin, looking up at the rapidly clearing sky. 'It's pleasant to have this warm sunshine to dry away the damp.'

'You're right there, master. Those were four of the wettest and most miserable days this year, I reckon!'

The morning sun was indeed very acceptable and quickly raised their spirits.

They could still hear the protesting axle of the cart just out of sight ahead of them where the track descended the far side of the crest but quite suddenly it ceased. Half a minute later they, too, breasted the rise and, not twenty yards down the hill they saw that the porters were surrounded by three ragged ruffians and threatened by their drawn swords. To their horror, these desperadoes set about the pair and in a moment had cut them down into the rutted roadway. By now, the travellers were quite close and while one of the robbers leant down rifling the bodies his two companions stood menacingly in the path of the priest and the carpenter.

'Don't'cher come any closer,' one shouted. 'T'ain't none o' yer business!'

'Yeah! Another step an' we'll cut youse down, too!' bawled the other.

Just then, the third man stood up and said, in disgust: 'They ain't got nothin'. Jus' some stinking ol' fish an' this letter!' He waved the folded paper.

The travellers stood quite still but without fear. The only movement was made by Toshiaki as he slowly wiped one palm to dry it of any moisture that would make his hand slip on his stout staff.

The leader of the gang, the one flourishing the folded paper, spat into the roadway and peered at Enshin.

'Yer' a priest, ain't yer! Read this an' we'll let yer go!'

He thrust the letter out towards them and one of his companions sauntered across and pushed it roughly into Enshin's hand.

'Read it, you stinkin' monk!' ordered the leader, a sallow-faced skinny man who wore a filthy cloth tied about his head and secured under his chin. 'It's about the only thing they 'ad on 'em!' He spat again.

Enshin calmly examined the paper. It was a letter, alright, and despite some damp spots which smudged some characters, he saw it was addressed to the commander in charge of the Oishi yashiki ahead.

'Well,' shouted the leader, 'can yer read it or not, eh?'

'Of couse, sir,' replied Enshin, and told him what it said on the cover. 'Shall I open it?' he asked, politely.

The absurdity of the situation completely escaped the gang as they stood there with the two blood-spattered corpses lying on the ground beside the fish cart.

'Go on; get on with it!' The sallow man rounded on the others. "Ere, you two; drag these into that ditch an' shove some bracken over 'em!' Orders given, he pointed at Enshin with his blood-streaked blade. 'You 'eard me!'

'Calm yourself and I'll read it all carefully.'

Enshin broke the seal and unfolded the damp paper with care.

'That's odd,' he said as he finished reading.

'Well, is it worth anything, eh? Can us sell it?'

The priest grunted.

'That really depends. It says that this is a secret letter and that the bearers are to be rewarded.

'Is that all?'

'Not quite. It also says that "in this matter the messengers" . . .', he pointed across to where the porters lay heaped, ' "know nothing and", strangely, "should know nothing"! How odd?'

With a slight frown, he held out the paper and the bandit snatched it from his hand. In a fit of pique, the fellow glared at it balefully then screwed it up and flung it onto the track by the cart.

'Come on! That ain't worth nothin' an' we'd best be gone! Don't youse say one word or we'll find yer and cut yer throats . . . !'

Without another word all three scampered off up the hill and at the crest rejoined the track that would take them down to the coast.

'That was a strange do, master, wasn't it?'

'Odd, certainly; odd indeed!' Enshin picked up the crumpled letter, now stained at the edge with blood, and eyed it thoughtfully. 'We shall have to report what happened,' he sighed. 'What a waste of life and for absolutely nothing!'

Toshiaki snorted. He cared little for the lives of the two fish porters, more for the risk to his master and even the black water-buffalo, Kuroi-san. As he began to walk he stooped and caught up the sodden jingasa lying in the road. With a couple of holes cut in it and a judiciously placed cord it would do very well as a hat for the ox to keep off the sun.

———□———

With Kuroi-san placidly munching at some sweet fresh hay, Enshin and Toshiaki sat sipping appreciatively cups of green tea served by the innmaster where they had stopped not an hour's walk further on their road to the Oishi yashiki. The carpenter's belly had started to protest windily about its lack of food when they chanced on the wayside establishment, though he, himself, thought that if his master had one fault it was that he cared little for when he should eat.

'Is that what that letter really said, master?' Toshiaki asked.

'Do you really want to know, my curious friend?' smiled the priest.

'Master, you know me, don't you?'

'I do indeed, good Toshiaki-san, but here's a case where it might be more prudent not to know!'

The carpenter shook his head and laughed.

'I'll take a guess, then, master. I reckon you dissembled . . . Am I right?'

'Very good, Toshiaki; I can hide little from you I can see. Well, if I had told those miscreants the truth we might have had a fight on our hands, and . . .' Seeing Toshiaki about to say something he held up his hand: 'if I now deliver this letter then I fear we may deliver our own death warrants!'

'Eh? How's that?' The carpenter's jaw dropped. He was rarely surprised by this strange priest whose skill with the sword ranked alongside the best in those disturbed and troubled times. He covered his confusion by taking another sip, content to bide his time.

'Well, my friend, the letter actually reads: "The bearers are ignorant men but must not be allowed to say anything afterwards . . ."'

'Yes; it seems that they were thought to be expendable! So what does this muddied script tell us that so threatens our lives in addition to theirs? Should I not throw this paper away as those bandits did? Perhaps we should remain in ignorance, holding our tongues?'

'Good question, master, and interesting; but I reckon that you ain't one not to thirst after knowledge.'

'That straw jingasa, my friend,' said Enshin. 'Could you pass it over and let me have a look?'

Toshiaki pulled a face.

'I was going to make it into a sun hat for Kuroi-san, once it had dried out.' He handed it over, nonetheless. The black ox looked up from his breakfast and one could have sworn from the look in his eyes that he regretted his master's request.

'Sorry, my friend,' smiled Enshin. 'We'll make it up to you soon, never fear.'

Kuroi-san snorted gently and returned to his hay.

'You can see that this jingasa was once painted; vermillion,
I should say. A long time ago, too, and it's much repaired.'

Toshiaki eyed the hat with a jaundiced eye. It was a disgusting,
tattered object, but he did notice something.

'See, there, master . . . its been painted at one time with a swastika.
Turn it to the light a bit . . . There it is,' he said, pointing. 'Hey, one
of those porters was wearing a torn priest's robe, wasn't he? Might
have been his.'

'Good! Now you are getting us somewhere!'

'I am?' A thought struck him and he added: 'It could have belonged
to one of those cutthroats, though, couldn't it?'

Enshin smelt the lining.

'No, it wasn't any of them. It has the tang of saltwater about it.
I would guess that it belonged to a priest, perhaps to one of the
Shingon-shu . . .'

He began to examine the hat carefully, feeling delicately round the
edge of the lining, a slight frown furrowing his brow. With a shake
of his head, he placed it across his knees and contemplated the faint
swastika, tracing its outline with a forefinger. Suddenly, he paused.

'Ah; I have it!'

'Uh?'

'What do you make of this lump, Toshiaki-san?'

Enshin held the jingasa out with the faint black device towards
his companion. The carpenter pursed his lips as he also prodded the
tightly woven straw surface.

'I can feel something padding out beneath the swastika . . . Yes,
there is a sort of cushion the same size as that device and it follows
its shape exactly!'

'Absolutely right! The question is: what does this signify? There's
something significant about this jingasa, I'm sure; but what . . ?'

'Why don't we have a look, master. Maybe its just a pad and nothing else? Mind you, its first time I've seen such a thing.'

'Hmmm!' mused the priest, stroking his chin. 'Toshiaki-san,
amongst your many skills, how are you with needle and thread?'

The carpenter looked at his master and grinned.

'You want me to open up the lining so that you can see what's
there, then sew it back up and no one the wiser? Of course I can
do it!'

It took just a few minutes of careful teasing for Toshiaki to extract
the tightly folded pad. Whoever had placed it there so carefully that
it rested on one corner exactly behind the swastika had done so
with great skill. When Enshin examined it he saw that it was a folded
down paper sewn into the gut sack of some animal so well that the
paper wasn't even damp.

'You can sew this up again, Toshiaki-san?'

The carpenter was beginning to enjoy all this and nodded his head. On the outer side of the tight-folded paper was carefully drawn a freehand circle inside which was a three-legged crow.

'Hmm; do you know what that is?' asked Enshin, pointing.

'You know that I cannot read such things, master.'

'The circle represents the sun and the crow . . ?'

'It is the *yatagarasu*, master. We've seen it before.' Toshiaki knitted his brow, thinking hard. 'But what of the swastika sign?'

'Excellent, indeed! Still waters run deep in you, Toshiaki! Now I think we have to be very careful from this point on. This letter, if it is such, is of a very secret nature I think and I fancy it is extremely dangerous to those who possess it! Please make sure that no one comes near whilst I have a read of the contents . . . You eat up this food so kindly provided by our host.'

———— ☐ ————

A little later Enshin let out a sigh and began to carefully fold up the paper to replace it in its gut protection.

'Now then, Toshiaki . . . your best work is required.'

'Give me half-a-turn of the glass, master; that's all I shall need!'

Once all this was done, they sat back at their leisure to drink some more of the singularly fine tea offered by the innmaster and his wife and the sun was reaching its zenith when they finished, but just before they rose a young man clad in a priest's robe came abreast of the inn. He paused to rest, his chest heaving with his exertion for he had evidently been running the way they had come.

Taking in great gulps of air, the young man came and sat himself down on the lower step, some distance apart from Kuroi-san who was by now contentedly lying in the roadway, chewing the cud.

'Young sir,' called Enshin, 'why your unseemly haste, pray?'

The shingyaku turned his head and at once his eye fell on the jingasa. For a moment he appeared confused but soon managed to regain his composure.

'Ah, good master,' he said, climbing to his feet and bowing respectfully, 'I am on my way to my lord's yashiki, but . . . ' Enshin noted a slight twitch cross the novice's face, '. . . may I ask if you have seen two men on the road this morning?'

'Two men, eh? Toshiaki-san, I may have been immersed in my prayers and not noticed. Did you see anyone?'

'There were two with a barrow . . . they stank of fish, they did! Then we passed three rough looking fellows heading south. The leader had a filthy cloth tied round his head and chin, I recall . . .'

'Were these the ones you seek, my young friend?' asked Enshin.
The novice shook his head. He pointed to the jingasa.
'That hat is just like one carried by those I seek . . .'
Enshin sipped the last of his tea before he shook his head.
'I'm not sure about that, young man. That jingasa belonged to a
priest of the Shingon-shu, I think; not to a fisherman, by any means.
It must have been lost by some priest in that dreadful wind last
night!'
'Yes, but you are right; it was left at my temple by a priest who
sheltered there yesterday and . . . er . . . left in the afternoon . . . My
master sent it after him . . .'
'What temple is that, my friend? We have stopped to pray at every
temple and shrine we could find but must have missed yours in the
storm.'
'It's only small, master; the Baikō-ji is its name . . . back towards
Nachi-ura it is.'
Enshin nodded.
'Well, since it seems to be the one that belongs to the Shingon
monk you had better take it and resume your chase, eh? Your two
careless friends, if it was indeed them, must have gone before us, in
a manner of speaking.'
Toshiaki half-grinned to himself but covered up by affecting to
drink from his cup. He glanced across at his master who nodded his
head imperceptibly.
'Here, take it. When I picked it up the thing was sodden but it's
dry now, young master. It'll suit you, too. Ah, yes: by the way if you
come across them three fellows you had best steer well clear as I
reckons they were up to no good!'
'We took this rather unimportant country road because we rather
lost our way in the worst of the storm yesterday,' said Enshin. 'Can
you tell me if it leads to any temples of note?'
'Oh, yes, master; you can reach the Nachi Shrine and there's two
or three famous places in Shingu . . . You will have to go back for
those. This road goes north into the mountains and the Hongu
Shrine is about two or three days or so walk from here, either from
Shingu following the river or from Nachi along the "Old Road".'
'And your temple; the Baikō-ji, I think you said?' Enshin smiled.
'Back down on the coast, master. I already told you so.'
'Of course you did. I'm afraid my memory isn't too good these
days. On the coast, eh? That was quite a storm the past three days,
wasn't it?'
The novice plainly wanted to get on his way but Enshin kept him.
'We watched a small ship labouring in those seas. Yesterday, wasn't
it, Toshiaki-san? I don't know how so small a ship could go out in

that turmoil, that I don't!' Enshin shook his head. 'I offered a prayer to the All-Powerful Guardian to protect those in her and I hope he heard me, humble as I am.'

The shingyaku moved a little as though going to rise, but Enshin placed his hand on his arm, saying: 'You know, it's odd that we should have found your friend's jingasa. Why, if you look carefully you can see the faint outline of a painted swastika. Was your friend, the owner, an ascetic monk of the Shingon-shu by any chance? Strange that I should have prayed to Fudō-myō-ō and then Toshiaki-san here found this, isn't it?'

'I wouldn't know about that, master; he ... er ... just came out of the sea, so to speak ...'

'Out of the sea? Why, that is odd . . ! Oh, of course, you mean he landed from a ship ... perhaps it was the very ship we watched, Toshiaki-san; the very one? No, wait; out of the sea ... You mean that he was actually wrecked and had to be rescued? Why, that is exactly like my dream-vision last night! How terrible! I dreamt that something of the sort happened ... Oh, dear . . !'

'He had a disturbed night, did my master,' Toshiaki whispered behind his hand. 'He sees things others don't, lad; quite often, don't you know!'

Enshin sat there with his eyes closed, his hand still resting on the shingyaku's sleeve. He was now quite sure that there was a connection between the two murdered men, the letter, and this slit-eyed novice. He swayed a little back and forth as if in a trance before murmuring: 'I see writing ... elegant writing ... why this road, uh . . ? Why . . ?' Suddenly his eyes opened wide and he thrust his face close to the shingyaku's. 'Young man, you are on the wrong road ... You should be travelling east not towards the North Star!'

'But ...'

'No "buts"! You are in danger ... Your future is clouded ... Your very life ... ! I have seen it all clearly ...'

The shingyaku's mouth opened and closed. How could this threadbare wandering priest know anything? It wasn't possible that he knew about either of the letters or his own deceit ... Precipitately, he snatched up the jingasa and with a hasty bow, leapt off the verandah and dashed away up the rutted street.

Toshiaki frowned.

'Now I wonder why he did that, master?'

'Ah, he thought that I knew things that I don't! But now I am sure that he is on the brink of the abyss and it is of his own making!'

The Oishi yashiki was constructed in the old-fashioned mode, that is to say partly a set of rambling thatched buildings in the style of the early-Muromachi period but with the addition of a large samurai house. There were two sets of lime-washed walls, looped at intervals for defence, the one within the other, and all corners were strengthened with watchtowers. The entrance gates were further defended by imposing yagura, or arrow-towers. On three sides the fields immediately adjacent to the outer walls were evidently kept flooded and on the fourth side the ramparts were washed by a broad but shallow river, probably the Kumano-gawa or a tributary. Within bowshot lay the end of a long trestle bridge that crossed the waters to the lands of the Manabe lords, at the further end stood a smaller fort that had three or four long white banners that fluttered in the warm breeze.

When the travellers approached the drawbridge at the end of the narrow trestle causeway over the field-moat, they were briefly examined by the two outer spearmen but waved across to the main gate guard where they were about to be questioned when everyone was distracted by a sudden shouting from the other side of the heavy closed gates. Almost at once, the right-hand gate swung open and three yari-mochi appeared bundling the young shingyaku unceremoniously out to sprawl on the drawbridge timbers. He came to his feet and stood uncertainly still clutching his precious straw jingasa. One of the yari-mochi pointed across the bridge.

'Get out of here, you young rogue . . .! Information, eh? Useless idiot! Go on, clear off!'

'But, master; I belong to the Baikō-ji, not in the Manabe domain . . .'

'Get out this instant . . . That's what Captain Matsumoto ordered! The Oishi don't want you so you had better try the Manabe . . .'

The yari-mochi levelled his spear and the novice hastily backed off, his hands raised in some futile gesture to defend himself against a thrust. Throwing caution to the winds, he turned and tried to dash back up the track the way he had come. Hardly had he taken four of five steps in that direction when a bowman on the yagura raised his longbow and sent an shaft after the fleeing figure. Either it was particularly well-aimed or extremely lucky for the arrow pierced the lad's right calf right through. With a howl of pain he tried to lurch on but the result was inevitable and he was soon captured by two of the spearmen sent after him and marched back to the bridge and gateway, the galling arrow still sticking out from his leg.

'Hey, Gōrō-san!' bawled the archer above. 'You ain't goin' to send 'im off wiv my arrer, are you? Pull it out . . . and clean it on his arse!'

One of the yari-mochi waved his spear lewdly in answer and their senior nodded with a wide grin.

' 'Old 'im fast, Saburō, an' I mean tight!'

Without more ado he grasped the arrow below the fletching and gave a great yank. The shingyaku shrieked out with the sudden pain and dropped down through the arms of the ashigaru named Saburō, causing the shaft to snap but not quite into two. The yari-mochi swore and kicked the unfortunate lad hard, shouting out that the arrow was broken.

'Blast it all!' shouted out the archer. 'Waste of a bloody arrow, that! Here, bring 'im back inside and I'll cut the blade free. That's the bit I want mainly, not the rest!'

As they dragged the weeping lad under the yagura, he dropped the jingasa almost at Toshiaki's feet.

'Shall I pick it up, master?'

'Give it to one of the guards, Toshiaki-san.'

He was about to do so when two fully armoured samurai came out through the gate and politely invited the two travellers to enter and take some refreshment at the invitation of the yashiki commander. Enshin bowed courteously but without delay pointed to the jingasa now held by Toshiaki.

'I think that young miscreant dropped that, sirs,' he said, 'but we picked up this screwed up note earlier this morning, later meeting that lad, and I thought that perhaps there was some connection. Respectfully, I suggest you may like to look into the matter.'

Such was the authority in his voice that the samurai, evidently of some rank, took the jingasa and the muddied note without another thought. At once they were ushered through the gateway into the outer bailey, curious eyes looking at Kuroi-san's glossy black pelt.

'Honoured priest, your ox will be taken care of.'

Enshin smiled.

'I would be grateful if he was also treated as a special, if unusual, guest, sirs.'

From behind them another voice answered.

'It shall be as you wish, respected Enshin-sama!'

Recognizing the deep voice instantly, Enshin turned and bowed deeply.

'Well met again, Ōe Jirōemon-sama!'

'Toshiaki-san! You, too, eh. It is a long time since we last tested each other's mettle, isn't it?'

The carpenter smiled as he bowed.

'Five years, honoured teacher; five long years!'

'You remember the Kagemitsu sword?'

Toshiaki laughed.

'Osafune Kagemitsu! I'm not likely to forget that or the events that went with it, master!'

'I heard a full account from Toshiaki-san, here,' remarked Enshin, 'but tell me, Ōe-sama; you now serve the Oishi-ke?'

'That is true, Torii-sama, but the Oishi are cousins of the Suzuki-ke and close allies by the kinship. But perhaps we shall be able to talk later. First, if you would follow me I am requested to take you to my master, Mizuno Akimune Hyōgo-no-kami, who has expressed a wish to meet you.'

They followed the impeccably dressed warrior in his fine striped hakama and yoroi-hitatare over which he wore a plain jimbaori emblazoned with the Oishi mon into the shade of the inner yashiki. As Enshin had thought, it was an elegant late-Kamakura period mansion which very much reminded him of the fortified manor house in which he had spent his childhood years in Kōzuke province, that is before the wars necessitated the rebuilding of that beautiful home as a true fortress. They were greeted by Mizuno-dono in person, a singular mark of respect for so humble a priest, and found him an austere man in his late middle years who had clearly polished his character and mannerisms in the old-fashioned mode. At once, two young maids served a light meal as the yashiki master was joined by another hatamoto, one Uchijo Kagemasa. Toshiaki was seated just to his master's rear just as if Enshin held high rank, a fact not over-looked by Mizuno-dono.

With the refreshments cleared and after the general conversation petered out, Enshin was obliquely asked about his opinion of the domains through which he had recently passed and his observations since entering this territory. He soon was able to give an abbreviated account of the events that morning. Jirōemon nodded his head and described the rejection of the shingyaku and his subsequent arrest pending further enquiries. There was something odd about the lad, he suspected.

'What do you think, Enshin-sama?' asked Mizuno-dono.

'He seemed a troubled young man, sir.'

Jirōemon ran his hand across his shaven forehead.

'He claimed to have sent information to us but was rude to the guard commander, Yamana-sama!'

'Hardly surprising, given Yamana's brusque manner, eh?' smiled Kagemasa, and all three smiled.

'Umm! He probably didn't give him time to express himself clearly, that is true.'

'I thought it odd that he should claim there were two messengers, particularly as he apparently described them as "fish porters". Their stinking hides would have been enough to tell us that they were at the gates!' observed Kagemasa.

'You think the two murdered men were those fellows, Enshin-sama?'

'Quite possibly, my lord.' Enshin looked quizzically at Jirōemon. 'My retainer, here, picked up a straw jingasa dropped by your young shingyaku and I handed over the torn paper we had found earlier at the same time. Maybe if these are examined more light can be thrown on the mystery?'

'Excellent!' nodded Mizuno-dono. 'Send to have the lad brought to the garden there, Uchijo-sama, and perhaps you would care to question him between you, Ōe-sama and you, honoured Enshin? Oh, and send a party of men to arrest those three suspects, too.'

'It is hardly my place to examine the prisoner, my lord; I am, after all, only a priest.'

'Ah, but you are also a kenshi of the Oda-ryū I am told. Few things will escape either of you, I am sure.'

A few minutes later the shingyaku limped into the garden with an escort of two brawny samurai and was made to sit opposite the verandah where the five men had arranged themselves, Mizuno seated himself a little apart to one side. The jingasa was brought and placed before Ōe Jirōemon.

'What is your name, novice?' Jirōemon asked, softly. 'You may answer without fear since if you do have information, as you claim, you will be freed and even rewarded.'

It was difficult to tell just where the novice was looking, his eyes were so narrowed. Enshin thought their configuration quite remarkable.

'Speak, my boy, and you will soon return to your master's temple,' he encouraged.

'My lord, I . . . my name is Aki . . .'

'Why were you carrying this jingasa, eh? What's so important about it?'

Aki shook his head doubtfully.

'He didn't say, lord, only that it should go with the messengers . . .'

'Who didn't say? Who was it sent these messengers?'

Aki shuffled his feet and sniffed.

'My leg . . . It hurts, masters . . .'

'Answer the question, wretch,' growled one of the kneeling escorts and jabbed his sword hilt into the small of Aki's back.

'My master sent them, I think . . . lord!'

'He wrote this note, did he?'

Jirōemon held up the smoothed out bloodstained letter, then passed it to Enshin.

'Ah, he must have done, sir.'
Enshin shook his head as he reread the text.
'I don't believe he wrote this, young man,' he said. 'Few priests
would make such basic errors with their kanji . . . These are a young
man's mistakes!'
'Did you brush this letter, eh?'
The shingyaku swallowed.
'No masters . . . I was asked to go but not until dawn to-day . . . I
couldn't have written that, could I?'
'But you knew of the messengers who were well ahead of you
on the road,' said Enshin. 'In fact, they took shelter near us about
midnight, didn't they, Toshiaki-san?'
'We smelt them about then, master,' the carpenter agreed, ' because
we were just a few yards from where they took refuge.'
'Who sent them?'
'My master, sir, not me . . .'
Ōe Jirōemon stared at the discomforted lad.
'We shall find out quite easily, boy . . .'
'You brushed that note, my son, didn't you?' said Enshin, gently.
'Better speak out, you know.'
'Well, yes, I did . . . You see, my master didn't want to send
anyone . . . so I thought . . .'
'That you could earn a fee, eh?' Enshin shook his head. 'That was
dishonest of you, wasn't it?'
'What was so important that you felt you should warn us that
those "ignorant men" shouldn't be allowed to talk after they had
delivered the message?'
'I . . . er . . . I don't know about that . . .'
'But you wrote the words, didn't you?'
'I suppose so . . .'
Enshin shook his head.
'There was something here that I don't understand. What infor-
mation would be useful to Mizuno-dono and who really sent it?'
Toshiaki coughed discreetly.
'If I may venture, my lord, but perhaps the jingasa . . ?'
Ōe Jirōemon contemplated the straw hat, not failing to see the
faded swastika. He looked up at the shingyaku.
'Who does this belong to, lad!' he demanded.
'To me, my lord.'
'Are you certain?'
The shingyaku nodded but perspiration was staining his robe.
'Your temple . . . what is its name, hey?'
'The Baikō-ji, master.'
'Does it belong to the Shingon sect?'

'Er, no, master!'

'Then why do you have this device on your jingasa, boy!'

'I . . . er . . . it was given to me, lord.'

'But let me smell it, Ōe-sama,' said Enshin. He sniffed at the brim. 'There is a strong smell of sea-salt, don't you think, my friend? I'd say it had been recently in the sea.'

'Well, it was given me by . . .'

'By a priest who came out of the sea yesterday?' Enshin smiled. 'I think that whatever message was sent was from that man you mentioned at the inn back there earlier, wasn't it? He was a Shingon priest, too, wasn't he? And I think there might well be something hidden in here.'

Ōe Jirōemon felt all round the rim and the edges of the lining. It wasn't long before he, too, found the slight pad beneath the swastika mon. A few moments later he pulled out the gut-skin package and opened it.

'Hmm! What have we here?'

Now the shingyaku showed real fear; his machinations had gone horribly wrong.

'M . . . masters . . . my lords . . . I overheard that the Shingon priest wanted a message sent to the Manabe and he had been on his way there by ship but they were wrecked in our bay . . . I thought that I should serve you, my lords . . . I . . .'

'Do you know what is written here?' demanded Ōe Jirōemon. Before the frightened lad could answer, he leant across towards his lord and suggested that in the light of what they had learned the two priests at the Baikō-ji should be brought here, too. 'Now answer,' he resumed. 'Did you read this paper?'

'Oh, no, master; no, how could I know?'

'You could have sewn this message inside.'

'No, my lord; it wasn't me . . . I only made sure the porters took the jingasa with them . . . I didn't know . . ! Please, my lord . . . . masters . . . I couldn't know.'

'But what were you going to tell us that would earn you a reward?'

One of the samurai guards turned up his nose and puffed out his cheeks with a look of disgust. The novice's bowels were loosened in his fear . . .

'Answer!' shouted Kagemasa in a hard voice.

'I . . . have to take off my robe; I have another letter stitched into the collar.'

The men on the verandah could distinctly smell the shingyaku's stench.

'Take him over there and cut open the collar, Heibei-san!' ordered Kagemasa.

'Take care as we need to read whatever is hidden there.'

'Aye, master!'

While they were waiting, Ōe Jirōemon grunted and observed: 'You suspected that jingasa all through, didn't you, my friend.'

Enshin smiled and let his breath out slowly from the back of his throat.

'I suspected it from its shape. Its form is traditional to only one sect that I know, a tribe of sōhei who hide themselves in the forested slopes of Daisen in eastern Idzumo. These violent men, scarcely different from bandits, adopted the Buddhist swastika as their mon, and it is suspected that a number of unscrupulous lords make use of them as secret agents using a network of temples throughout the provinces.'

Mizuno-dono cleared his throat and slapped his thigh.

'I am doubly glad I invited you here, Torii-sama.

'There is more, my lord.'

'More? How so?'

Enshin turned the jingasa and pointed out how the swastika stood on the corner of the slightly elongated lower left arm.

'The priest who wrote that paper was of high rank otherwise the swastika would have been reversed and that arm as short as the rest!'

'So, we shall soon have taken three murderers and captured a spy, not to mention a devious young priest? At least he wanted us to have the information!'

'I'm not sure about that, my lord,' murmured Enshin.

'No, why not?'

'Let us wait until we have all the parties here; that is, if you agree, my lord?

Mizuno Hyōgo-no-kami thought for a moment. There was something about Torii Enshin that made him feel that here was a man he could trust, a rarity in those days of double-dealing and treachery.

'It is agreed,' he said, at last.

———□———

It was later the following morning when the two parties of men returned to the yashiki, the one with their three captive bandits, discovered lying dead drunk in some filthy straw behind the only tavern boasted by the fishing hamlet, and the other group a little after, separately escorting the two priests.

This time, the interrogation was conducted more formally just in front of the entrance steps to the yashiki, Mizuno and his officers including Enshin seated on folding camp stools. To add gravity to the proceedings, the two senior councillors and the Oishi lord were clad in armour. While Enshin still wore his threadbare robes, Toshiaki had been given apparel suited to a warrior retainer on the orders of Mizuno-dono, himself, in recognition of his devoted bearing towards his master.

Before the questioning commenced and any of the prisoners or either priest were brought out from the guardroom beside the inner yagura, Enshin held up the paper found in the jingasa.

'My lord, all of us have read this and found it to be only a poem.'

Mizuno snorted disdainfully.

'It seems innocuous enough!'

'Nonetheless, I will read it out again.' Enshin cleared his throat and began to recite the lines as though he were an actor declaiming in a play.

'That is all, isn't it, Enshin-sama?'

'Just that, my lord.

'Well, then; all this is a storm in a teacup. I can see no mystery.'

'Ah, my lord, but there is one and it is right before our eyes!'

Even Ōe Jirōemon looked up keenly in surprise.

Enshin smiled. 'Nothing is really ever as it appears, my lord; it is as the wise Sonshi taught: "All warfare is based on deception", and here we have an excellent example that proves his words. Uchijō-sama, if I may be so bold, would you order the bandits to be brought in?'

A group of ashigaru were summoned and quickly carried in three bamboo cages, each of which was occupied by the bound figure of a bandit, all glaring out like the wild animals they were.

'My lord, I have nothing to say about these desperate fellows other than to confirm that they had undoubtedly butchered those two poor fish porters with the intent to rob them of anything of value. They had nothing to do with anything else.'

Mizuno Hyōgo-no-kami nodded his head.

'You don't ask for mercy to be shown them, honoured priest?'

Enshin shook his head sadly. 'Only that you pass a fair sentence on them, my lord.'

'Take them down to the river bed and crucify them,' Mizuno ordered, 'but they are not to be speared through! Post a notice nearby of their crime!'

As soon as the cursing felons were removed, Uchijō Kagemasa had the two priests and the shingyaku brought in. The Baikō-ji incumbent looked a trifle bewildered although he had been treated well overnight, but had been kept out of contact with either of the other two. The strange monk kept his face completely impassive and it passed through Enshin's mind that the man was well-inured to hardship and was hardly likely to buckle under interrogation.

The miserable novice, Aki, on the other hand, showed desperate fear. The lad was a craven coward who might say anything to save his skin.

Jirōemon opened the questioning by addressing the Baikō-ji priest.

'Saichō-sama, please recount to us what you know of this affair. You may speak quite freely.'

The priest, slightly over-awed by the company, began his account, such as it was, haltingly at first but more firmly towards its conclusion. When he had finished, Enshin coughed discreetly and asked what he knew about those who believed in the *yatagarasu*, the three-legged crow, in the neighbourhood. It was clear from his answer that he was only familiar with the local folklore of the Kumano region and strange symbolic association with the three great Shinto shrines.

'You know nothing else?'

'I pray to the Lord Buddha and thrust aside superstitious nonsense about all devils, my friend,' replied Saichō gravely. 'You are a priest who does the same, too, I think.'

Enshin bowed respectfully.

'Very true, honoured friend.' He turned slightly. 'This priest is a true man, my lord. His temple rather than him should be considered worthy of some reward, should it please you. He, himself, will accept nothing I don't doubt.'

Mizuno raised his hand and a retainer politely escorted the slightly bemused holy man from the compound to a guest room where he was given refreshments. Later, he was presented with a finely painted scroll depicting the travels of Tripitaka to India in order to bring the Lotus Sutra back to China. It was a rare treasure for the Baikō-ji.

In the meantime the shingyaku, Aki, was carried forward and placed a little apart from the strange priest. By now, the novice's wounded leg was quite inflamed and swollen.

Mizuno Hyōgo-no-kami nodded to Enshin to carry out the questioning.

'Reverend Sir,' he started in a soft voice, 'I understand that you are a priest from Idzumo or Hōki. Is that not so?'

The hard-faced priest remained impassive.

'You may at least tell us your name, sir?'

Still there came no reply, just a blank stare. Enshin slightly shrugged his shoulders then shifted his gaze to the novice.

'Aki-san, tell us in your own words what was said to you by this man when he arrived at the Baikō-ji; do not omit anything, though.'

The miserable shingyaku, visibly shaking, blurted out everything he could, the words falling pell-mell from his lips. He admitted his greed and even his misplaced duplicity towards his master, the temple priest.

'Did you write that letter suggesting that your two messengers be silenced?'

'Yes, master; but I did it out of fear of him . . .'

'You were afraid of him? How so?'

'Because he said that if I failed in sending the message I, too, would suffer a terrible, painful death and . . . and . . .'

'Well?'

'I would burn in the fiery Hell!'

'And you believed him?'

'Yes, master; of course!'

Enshin shook his head in disbelief.

'No, my young and misguided friend; you didn't think any of this.' He took out of the breast of his robe a folded paper. 'You were given this letter by the priest beside you and you read it carefully before you wrote your own piece. This is the truth, isn't it.' His voice was suddenly hard.

'I . . . er . . . I'm not sure . . .'

'But you were sure enough to sew it into your collar, weren't you?'

The shingyaku's shoulders sagged and he whispered 'yes'.

Enshin held up the paper and read out the text: '*May the Lord Buddha guide you; May the Lord Fudō protect and keep you! / Water finds its proper level flowing from the heights to the plains; the moon grows larger before shrinking to nothing and begins again. Pay heed to the Sonshi. / Trust not those who come with smiles and gifts / Beware innundations.*'

'You read this then hid it and gave your hirelings – plain innocent men – your own hastily written paper. You knew very well what was intended by this false priest, didn't you? If not exactly, you shrewdly guessed at the truth!'

Enshin's face hardened as he turned back to the black-robed priest.

'You are one of that dark sect who draw strength from the superstitious mysteries you claim surround the yatagarasu. There are too many of you inhabiting the once sacred slopes of Holy Daisen . . . All those of you who desecrate this crest act as spies and couriers for ambitious lords intent on tearing down by any means rulers descending from good families. You travel the provinces appearing to be devout priests but, in all honesty, are rotten to your very souls!

'How you came to be wrecked I do not know although I suspect the casting of malicious sorcery, but wrecked you were and to your great good fortune, too. I think that but for this meddlesome young idiot your plan would have succeeded and you would never have been suspected. With great respect, my lord, here, would not have been suspicious nor would his officers. However, the three condemned felons were fools enough to murder the two fish porters at the very time that my companion and I breasted that hill top.

'And then we found and read your clever poem . . . shall I read it out again, my friend: perhaps you would care to comment, eh?'

The sōhei priest simply glared.

'The poem is hardly original,' continued Enshin, now addressing Mizuno-dono. 'It paraphrases the words spoken towards the close of Kompira Motoyasu's play, "*Ikkaku Sennin*" that I once attended at my respected father's yashiki twenty years ago. With your indulgence, my lord, I will read the poem once again . . .'

'Is it necessary, Honoured Enshin?'

'It is very necessary, my lord, as you will understand. Priest, you have written thus:

Thunder and Lightning
Filled the pools of Heaven;
Fast loosened were the floods.
The new moon waxed
The Dragon King awakens.'

'How subtle; how dangerous!' For the first time a sneer turned up the corner of the stranger's thin lips. 'So I wrote a poem to be sent to Manabe-dono. Is there a crime to be found in that? Such a poem had been promised to this lord since he visited my parent temple on Daisen-san two years ago.'

'Very possibly, my respected friend,' purred Enshin, 'but few would read it as I have done, would they?'

'Meaning?'

'Meaning . . ?' Enshin looked very serious. 'My lord, there is a message contained in this poem that is based, as I have said, on the writings of Kompira Motoyasu though it is by no means exactly his words . . .'

'So, I wasn't accurate,' interrupted the priest.

'Be quiet!' grated Kagemasa.

Enshin continued: 'Let me interpret the words, my lord . . . Firstly, we come to the "*pools of Heaven*", a reference I think to the Amegawa that joins the Kumano-gawa not a mile south of here, does it not?'

'Why, so it does!' Mizuno-done began to frown. 'Please continue, Enshin-sama.'

'Secondly, this is followed by "*Fast loosened were the floods*". Well, this word "floods" can be written meaning precisely "floods" or "*innundations*" but it can also read with a change of the kanji as

"*water torture*". Next we have "*the New Moon waxed*". What can this
mean, I wondered all through last night? Perhaps it means "*increas-
ing moonlight*", but then it is linked to "*The Dragon King awakens*".
Can you think of what that might mean, my lord?'
The yashiki commander shook his head. 'Please explain,' he
urged.
'What is the full name of Lord Manabe?'
Uchijo Kagemasa suddenly drew in his breath.
'You are right, Torii Enshin-sama! The basis of all warfare is as the
Sonshi stated! Our neighbour's full name is Manabe Ryūji Kai-no-
suke!'
'And "Ryūji" means "*Dragon*" . . . Treachery was planned by this
man, my lord, without a shadow of a doubt. The poem alerts Lord
Manabe that you may cross the Amegawa "flooding" your army
into his lands; again a play on your name, my lord, "*Mizuno*" or
"*mizuzeme*" . . .'
'Water torture or flooding! Ha, I understand!'
'Correct . . . and the "*Dragon King*" – the Manabe lord, will be
ready!'
'Have you anything to say, miserable spy, before I have you
executed?'
The captive priest continued to ignore everything that was said.
'A moment, my lord,' interposed Enshin. 'This was all a double bluff otherwise how would you decide when to attack?'
Seeing the mystification on Mizuno Hyōgo-no-kami's face, he
continued: 'It is my opinion, my lord, that this priest pursuaded
this miserable novice, Aki, that he would receive an even larger
reward from the Manabe than from you. His greed and ambition
prompted him to agree and it was for this reason he wrote his
letter to destroy his messengers! Doubtless, he looked for other
rewards, too!'

————————□————————

No decision was taken by Mizuno-dono and his councillors about
how to deal with the treacherous priest or the shingyaku but the
following morning Enshin was invited to attend the Council
Chamber and asked his opinion and advice as a heihō-sha.
'You are faced with a difficult situation, and I would advise
caution. Forearmed by this information is one thing, but to act with
haste is quite another. You must consider that what you have learnt
is deeply secret and that it may be intended as a trap. Remember, the
Sonshi said "*Uproar in the east; strike in the west*", but all that depends
on one's perspective.'

'Hmm,' mused Mizuno Hyōgo-no-kami, 'what do you mean by that?'

'What I mean, my lord, is to keep in mind the cardinal points as you would in all practice of the arts of war. No one can strike you from the south except by ships swimming on the waves, and that is very dangerous on a coast such as yours. An attack would probably come by land from either the east or the west. To the north you are protected by high and convoluted mountains and between you and any enemy in that direction are your allies and kinsmen, the Suzuki-ke. No attacker could reach you from there in weeks!

' *"Uproar in the east; strike in the west!"* My lord, the real danger is not the Manabe-ke but your neighbours beyond the Hikigawa in the Tanabe domain! This wretched priest had the intention of causing suspicion and possibly border bickering between you and the Manabe. The meddling of Aki, the novice, had this aim, too. You were intended to see that poem but just in case you didn't understand the message, the shingyaku was there to suggest matters were the other way round and the Manabe-ke were secretly preparing to make a pre-emptive strike. Trouble on this border would at once be followed by an attack from your rear. You would have been duped, my lord, for once you were embroiled in a frontier dispute here, the Oishi-ke enemies would have struck and who knows what would be the result?'

'Both letters suggest that the bearers should be eliminated, my lord,' interposed Kagemasa. 'I advise that both our prisoners be killed!'

'What do you think, Enshin-sama?'

'I can only offer my humble opinion, my lord, and that is coloured by the teachings of the Lord Buddha. Uchijo-sama has advanced a nice point. The deviousness of these two prisoners earns them condemnation but on the other hand, and just in case, their greed might be turned to your good in order to gain you time to make preparations. May I suggest that you put all the facts in front of your brother, Lord Oishi, and you immediately alert your cousins in the Suzuki-ke. Also, I would advise friendly approaches to the Manabe-ke, carefully laying out your suspicions and inviting their opinion regarding a firm alliance between your clans. In that way any plans that they may already have formulated will be foiled!'

After some discussion, Mizuno-dono agreed with everything. Just the disposal of the two prisoners was left to be decided.

'My lord, may I suggest that their duplicity is turned about? Let doctors see if the lad's leg can be saved. Meanwhile, let him observe that war-like preparations are being made by the whole garrison but make sure that these preparations cannot be seen by the Manabe men at the fort across the river. If he recovers, although his chances of the poison in his wound killing him are good and bad in equal parts, then request him to take a message west to the lord of the Tanabe domain. He will be expecting some sort of message from the Daisen priest, doubtless, but tell our young man that he must tell the truth or he will be found and murdered by your agents. If he delivers the message about war-like border preparations here he can return and be generously rewarded. As for the priest, he is too dangerous to be set free. Bind him and send him to your brother to be imprisoned for a long time, if that pleases him.

'Do these things and you will be both prepared for trouble and will have strengthened your brother's domain, but remember, it is through the reports of agents that you will remain strong!'

———□———

It turned out as Enshin had predicted. A week later, the three companions, refusing any rewards other than a sack of rice and some vegetables, continued on their leisurely way northwards to examine the secret yamabushi ways through the Kumano mountains and were well-received as they passed through the town where stood the great Kumano Hongu shrine. Whilst there were many three-legged yatagarasu reputed to be living in the region, not one threatened them and for the present their mystery remained unexplored.

13

POSSESSION

▼

Enshin and his faithful follower, Toshiaki, found themselves, one warm day during the rainy season, deep in the mountains taking shelter on the verandah of a tiny inn with little to do but contemplate the broad surface of the Kumano river. The incessant rain fell like an arrow-storm from the heavens, so heavy that the rearing mountains scarce a quarter of a mile distant faded to varied grey shapes before the most distant vanished altogether. Few souls ventured out into the storm but the monk and his follower had to smile as they watched two village women, huddled close under the doubtful shelter of a single oiled paper umbrella, splashed across the muddy street, screeching shrilly as women do. Then, as if without a care in the world, a bedraggled yamabushi strode along only to pause to offer a prayer in front of the little wayside shrine tucked between two buildings opposite. Oblivious of the downpour, he went through a long series of hand gestures as part of his orisons.

'That wanderer puts me in mind of a rather strange incident,' remarked Enshin as he sipped his tea. 'Toshiaki-san, you frequently entertain me with your anecdotes so perhaps you would like me return the courtesy, my friend?'

Toshiaki scratched his stubbly chin before replying.

'Master, please do so as I feel pretty useless today; I think this rain has got into my brain and I can't think of a thing.'

'This tea is really good, don't you agree? The goodwife said it was grown on their own bushes . . . Oh, yes; my story is quite short and will take no time at all. It concerns in part an itinerant priest no different from that one now taking shelter at last over there. . . They'll bless him for the pools of water he sheds on their floor . . ! Well, it's no real story at all, having no proper beginning and no clear end. It just happened, so to say.

'It was a few years ago when I was making my slow way through one of the western provinces, saddened by the abject want of many of those poor farmers that I came across everywhere, all suffering from a recent failure of their crops, the depredations of their lords' tax gatherers and the destruction everywhere caused by strife.

'On a day like this I sought shelter from the elements in a small mountain shrine. The place was deserted, or at least I could find no priest who served the needs of the kami. I offered my prayers and sat myself down by a half-open shōji beside the main inner doors. The evening light was thickening when a gaunt yamabushi appeared at the top of the steps and stepped under the sheltering eaves. He untied his straw cape and vigorously shook off the rain, hardly caring that I was splashed, too. Sitting down, without a word or even a nod, he took out a rice ball and some takuan for his sustenance. You might have expected that common courtesy would have demanded at least a few words, even if they were limited to the weather, but there were none. Dismissing his incivility I took out my single ball of millet, the gift of a poor peasant family three days before, and munched at it contentedly. Tomorrow would doubtless bring the lord Buddha's abundance . . .'

Toshiaki had to smile at this. He knew his master well . . . and his boundless optimism.

'Ah, Toshiaki-san, you have less faith than I do; I assure you that the very next day I ate well! But to continue: darkness had nearly fallen when some guttural shouting announced the arrival of a fully armoured samurai in the company of two followers, one of whom carried his helmet, all cursing the rain god for his copious largesse. As they mounted the steep steps I realized that they had been swallowing large draughts of rice wine so I thought to retire into the inner part of the shrine where I settled myself down in a corner behind the taikō drum, hoping that I would not be disturbed by these boisterous fellows or by the resentful kami who resided here.

Sometime later, though in the darkness I had no idea of the hour, I awoke and sat up, wide awake. I could hear the downpour outside and some faint snoring from the entrance porch . . . I also felt cold, I remember this because it was unusual for that time of the year. Sleep being out of the question at that moment I took up my rosary and began to mutter to myself part of the Heart Sutra, but I gradually became aware that somewhere, far off, a drum was being beaten very slowly. It must have been a big drum like those found in wealthy temples and shrines but, I asked myself, who would call on the kami at such an hour and with so low a beat?

' "*Ton* . . . . *ton* . . . . *ton* . . . . *ton* . . . ."

'The beat was rhythmic and at wide intervals. It sounded quite some distance away, so I thought, but the effect was to drive the sacred words from my mind and cold as I was, I thought to compose myself to lie down completely still, much against my will, to listen out for that wretched drumbeat.

' "*Ton* . . . . *ton* . . . . *tonnnn* . . . . *tonnnn* . . . ." '

'As the minutes passed – it could have been an hour or more – the muffled beat increased in tempo and appeared to be closer . . . Then it stopped! Still cold, which was a strange experience for me, as you know, I closed my eyes and tried to court sleep.

' "BANG!" '

'The heavy shōji crashed open and the figure of the senior samurai loomed against the square of grey half-light, recognizable by his bulky armour, and stood there mouthing a stream of invective and curses into the darkness. His words were unintelligible for the most part and I don't suppose he even knew that I was there. Shouting out another oath, he turned and vanished, oddly remembering to slam shut the sliding doors behind him. From that moment there was absolute oppressive silence; not a movement from him settling down or anything.

'Then the drumming started again:

' "*Ton* . . . . *tonnn* . . . . *ton* . . . . *tonnnn* . . . ."

'Now it was a different beat, intrusive, pervading, driving away sleep for no reason other than the sound was always there . . . closer, too . . . much closer, but not loud, you understand. No, it wasn't loud but rather like hearing an annoying irregular snore coming from another room. There was some alien element here that for the life of me I could not understand.

'Gradually my eyelids began to droop . . . Ha, but not for long!

'Without warning, all hell seemed to burst out beyond my sanctuary . . . shouting, screaming, fierce battle yells, the clash of weapons, the sound of heavy objects or bodies falling, then, again, total silence. All I knew was that I was shaking – and bathed in sweat. Maybe it was the first and only time in my life . . . It was like waking as a child from a nightmare . . . I had not the slightest doubt that a fight had taken place but, unarmed as I was, I knew that I was unable to defend myself and could only resort to praying to the deities and the all-powerful Marishi-ten for their protection . . .

'That damned drum started again, but more distant now . . . unceasing, insistent, irregular . . . on and on and on . . .

' "*TON . . . . TON . . . . . . TONNNN . . . . TON . . . . TONNNNNNN . . . .*" '

————□————

'It was a miserable few hours until the coming dawn began to lighten the eastern sky but I lay there patiently until the light was sufficiently strong, not out of fear for what I might find but to fully determine what action I might need to take. I slid back that heavy shōji fully expecting to view the aftermath of a bloody fight . . . but there was nothing.' No bodies of either samurai or the yamabushi; not one single hint that anyone had been there at all!

'I can see that you are completely mystified, Toshiaki-san. It was all as real as we are sitting here now. If it's any consolation to you, I am stumped for an explanation, too.'

14

THE DEITY OF THE MOUNTAIN

∇

It was a perfect late autumn day when all the world should have been at peace, a day that brought everyone from their homes to allow the warm sunshine to drive away their worries and the uncertainties of those war-torn times. If there was any fault in this weather it was to be found in the oppressive heat at the noontide for those who must, perforce, walk the dusty paths in the full glare of the sun.

For Enshin the young priest and his recently acquired black ox that paced slowly beside him, there was little such problem. Both wore wide-brimmed straw hats to give them shade; Enshin's was somewhat battered in the course of his prolonged wanderings and Kuroi-san's handed on by his former owner, a large labourer's hat with ragged holes cut for his horns. Kuroi-san, or Mr Black, was the name given by Enshin to his bovine friend.

The priest had been given the buffalo some months before as a sort of payment in kind by a parsimonious, though grateful, village elder for curing erupting boils in his family, the cunning peasant thereby thinking that in discharging his debt in this way he had the best of the bargain since the poor animal was not his property and didn't look as if it would long survive. But it did and was now beginning to regain its glossy black coat and its great strength, returning Enshin's kindness and care with simple affection and honest companionship.

'Kuroi-san, it looks as if we must find lodgings in this town, at least the weather has been kind to us. How miserable our lot would have been were it raining!'

An onlooker overhearing these words might have been forgiven in thinking that the ox completely understood what the young priest said as he rubbed his muzzle against Enshin's hand that held the soft rope halter. Both man and beast were content with their lot, the former because the liesurely pace of Kuroi-san determined that his own progress was equally slow, thus ensuring him plenty of time to observe the human condition wherever fate decided, the latter because he was undoubtedly grateful for the kindness of this singular man.

As they made their way along the hot dusty highway between the newly harvested rice fields they approached a small town marked by the increasing numbers of dwellings as the valley narrowed to pass between two sharp eminences, the left one of which was crowned with a thick grove of pines through which the priest caught glimpses of a fortified *shirō* and fluttering banners. From the balustrades of the farmhouses the goodwives had taken the opportunity of the fine weather to hang out to air all manner of bedding and newly-washed clothes. On a pleasantly light southerly breeze wafted a hint of the distant Inland Sea.

Lost in his reveries, Enshin felt Kuroi-san nudge against his right hip and, shaking his head slightly to sharpen his thoughts, he glanced around for the cause. Usually his awareness was habitual, both awaking and asleep, the result of the severe training he had received for more than sixteen years since he was a child of nine mastering the powerful mysteries of the Oda-ryū *heijutsu* and the teachings within his uncle's temple of Hōrai-ji. With a start it seemed to him that the warmth of that balmy day had suddenly been withdrawn: the pair were passing the town's grim execution field where the harsh sentences of the law were carried out. Common enough as such *kubukiri-ba* were, some more than others brought a chill clutch around the heart.

The briefest glance was enough. Here were the usual line of scaffold crosses decorated with the tattered remains of felons, both male and female, young and old, most unrecognizable after the attentions of the clouds of noisy crows and ravens. Below these ten or so frames were two long lines of crude trestles adorned with severed heads, from the hair of each fluttering a paper label brushed with the owner's name; but most horrible of all were the two low pillow mounds bearing the corpses of two men recently *sawn in half* at the hips . . . It must have been these two fresh cadavers, thickly covered with clouds of gorged flies, that had startled the gentle beast . . .

Enshin tried his best to thrust the dreadful sight from his mind but he knew within himself that the ruler of this domain must be either a cruel man or one who exercised little moderating control over his magistrate . . .Yet the few passers-by appeared normal and reasonably happy.The women chattered and gossiped as they always do and no one so much as glanced at that grim fenced space.

'I think, my black friend, that we'll look for an inn at the other end of this town,' he murmured. The ox swung his head up and down as if in agreement and they ambled on passing a sprinkle of samurai who walked in small groups, ubiquitous rōnin, sometimes half-armoured and always carrying weapons, and the town-dwellers haggling with the small merchants for their daily needs. No one paid the slightest heed to Torii Enshin and his ox, simply making way where necessary as they walked. Eventually the pair reached a place where a side track appeared to lead down towards the river and a pine grove with a large torii marked what must be the entrance to a fair sized shrine. The pair paused to look around when, at that moment a conch was blown from the hilltop yashiki with the result that the town street speedily emptied of people.

'That's odd,' thought Enshin as he led the way down the path between two narrow dry paddies and entered the sacred area marked by the red painted torii. To his pleasurable surprise quite a sizeable two storeyed gateway lay a short distance on amongst the trees, an imposing structure that must have dated from the mid-Heian period four or five centuries ago. Just beyond this gateway and to the left of the courtyard stood another old structure that was the associated Buddhist temple. First, Enshin walked across and paid his respects to the kami-sama of the shrine, then he led Kuroi-san to the front of the temple and bid him wait there whilst he went inside to offer prayers to the Lord Dainichi Nyōrai. Before mounting the four steps to the temple hall he took a woven bag from Kuroi's broad back and settled it about the ox's neck.

'There, old fellow; have some of the forage that we were given two days ago. I won't be long, my friend.'

Carefully removing his straw waraji, he stepped up to bow at the threshold and enter the Prayer Hall to commence his recital of certain sacred prayers before the statue of the Lord Buddha.When he had finished he felt that he was no longer alone and saw a very old priest kneeling to the left of the altar platform, like him telling his rosary. Enshin bowed respectfully and uttered a low greeting.

'Welcome, my son,' greeted the priest. 'I am named Ji-chin and I am the priest who serves in this sacred place . . . but before we talk please would you take some refreshing tea with me?'

'May my companion have some water, too?'

'He may drink as much as he wishes, my son.'

Some time later as they conversed over one of the most fragrant beverages that Enshin could recall, the old man asked who had guided Enshin's steps to this little out-of-the-way township within the Ōsumi domain?

'Father, the lord Buddha determines the path I follow. He tells my ox where to go and I merely follow.'

'He seems a remarkable animal, my friend; perhaps Kuroi-san is the embodiment of some fortunate soul who is near to completing the Path to Enlightenment . . . I have the feeling that he has guided you to this place, so far removed from the better known routes through these western provinces for some special purpose.'

Enshin sipped his tea in silence for a minute or two considering the old man's words. 'Is there any real difference between this town and a thousand similar places?' he asked.

'Any difference? That may depend on one's viewpoint, my son. In nearly all respects it is identical to all the others, except in one. While others are dominated by their lord's fortress, this one is, at present, the exception.'

'How do you mean, sensei? Many places that I have seen have special features, don't they?'

'Yes, of course, I agree with you.'

'Master, I wouldn't wish to appear impertinent but I would like to know this difference.'

The old man's seamed face remained deeply serious. He leant forward and murmured in little more than a whisper: 'My son, know that this is the fief of Ōsumi Kagehisa. Most people from this region would understand that this is enough to furnish you with an answer to your question.'

Enshin shook his head. 'I have been cut off from the world at large for many weeks. Please enlighten me . . .'

'From which direction did you enter this place?'

'The town? We came from the west.'

'In that case,' and here the old priest's voice softened with a tinge of sadness, 'in that case you passed by the execution ground?'

'I'm sorry to say, we did.'

'Tell me: how did you feel at that moment, my son?'

'That's a curious question, sensei. Of course the sight was doleful and it also affected Kuroi-san. He flinched against me . . . I said a prayer to aid the poor souls of those who died.' He paused before asking: 'Sensei, there may be many kubikiri-ba like this but few so depressing. Why should this be? Why so many corpses?'

'You ask questions that are difficult to answer, my son. They invite a reply but, as you are fully aware, walls have ears and temples have many hiding places that can shelter spies.'

Enshin nodded his head in agreement. 'In that case, sensei, I shall not expect an answer.' Changing the subject, he said: 'Where might Kuroi-san and I rest our heads for a few days.'

Ji-chin laughed. 'You may look no further. This temple was built with room for four priests and shingyaku, but all that are left is my poor self. You and your friend are welcome to make it your home; all that I would request is that you will help with matters of concern to the Lord Buddha.'

———— ▯ ————

Having first settled Kuroi-san in his new quarters behind the temple, Enshin returned to the main street in order to orient himself, the best place being a popular teahouse until one's face became familiar. He turned over in his mind Ji-chin's comment that this domain was ruled by Ōsumi Kagehisa and that this information alone should be sufficient to give him his answers. Difficult to understand quite possibly, impossible to interpret with certainty! Time would reveal all, he supposed.

The main street was empty, not a soul was to be seen; even a couple of stray dogs took not the slightest notice of him as they lay stretched out under a shady verandah. He paused at the junction of the shrine path and the roadway, uncertain which way to proceed. Even the shops were shuttered up and, oddly, the profusion of airing bedding and clothes had all been taken inside. Rack his memory as he might, he couldn't recall any other similar township as deserted at this hour of the afternoon. Even the birds appeared to have taken taken flight, not one sang the praises of the autumn warmth.

Quite suddenly a shōji slid open and a young girl dressed in a plain brown-striped kimono dashed down to him.

'Master . . . master, you mustn't stand there . . . It is not wise, sir . . . the lord has decreed not . . .'

Enshin gazed at her in surprise.

'It is forbidden, miss . . ?'

'Come with me, master . . . please . . .'

Her voice, though little more than a whisper, was very urgent; her fingers grasped his sleeve insistently enough for him to give way and let her lead him up the three steps to her shop. To his pleasure he saw that it was a teahouse and a tidy one at that.

Carefully sliding closed the shōji the girl stood for a moment in the half-light, one delicate hand pressed to the bosom of her kimono.

'You will be safe now, sensei . . .' she started to say when a stronger female voice called out: from the rear.

'Who is there, Yumiko? Who have you got with you, girl?'

It was the voice of an older woman, slightly querulous and apprehensive.

'It is the priest, oka-san.'

'Priest? Which priest?'

'The young one, grandmother; the one with the black buffalo . . . the one I described earlier.'

Enshin had to smile.

'Please permit me to reassure your grandmother; it would be better if she met me, wouldn't it?'

The girl, who was aged at a guess about seventeen, gave him a wan smile and he noticed that she occasionally glanced towards the front screens almost as though she fully expected something bad to burst in.

'So you are the priest with the buffalo that my grandaughter told me about?'

'I think I am the one,' he replied gently.

The old lady must have been about the same age as Ji-chin if not his senior. Her face was as deeply lined and seamed but Enshin noticed at once that she was totally blind. She beckoned him to come close to kneel beside her mat.

'Daughter, please fetch some of our best tea for our respected visitor,' her voice was slightly cracked but kindly in tone. 'Young master, please allow me to touch your face; I cannot see you but my fingers will serve as my eyes . . .'

'Do so, Oka-sama, if you so wish.'

He guided her hands to his face and felt her fingers lightly pass over every part.

'You have a strong bone structure, master, and your voice shows humility . . .' She had grasped his right wrist then his left one. 'This is a quality unusual for one who has long wielded the sword . . .'

Enshin glanced across at the girl who sat with her eyes demurely lowered, her tea tray at her right knee.

'You are perceptive, Oka-sama, although I would like to forget the second part.'

The old lady hid her face behind her fan and uttered a light laugh.

'Master, I can understand your need for such a companion as your ox. He places you as far as you could possibly be from being thought a samurai. He allows you to ask certain questions, to speak to people "of no-account", does he not?'

'Even to ladies who once enjoyed cultured living? Now, Oka-sama, you are teasing things out from me,' laughed Enshin. 'That being the case, may I ask why is all the town closed up on such a fine afternoon?'

The old lady kept her sightless eyes fixed on the opposite wall, not that she could possibly see it.

'You heard the horagai as you turned down to the shrine? I am certain that you also met with Ji-chin-sama and I can't imagine that you and he didn't talk about – well, matters here?' Her granddaughter, Yumiko, placed her hand gently on the old lady's sleeve. 'Don't worry, child; this priest is no spy from any of the sides. We are quite safe and maybe he is even our salvation.'

'Hush, grandmother, we must always be on our guard.'

'Yumiko-chan, in my heart I can feel that the salvation of our lord's clan rests with this young stranger. From touching him I am sure that he will find a way to put an end to these cruelties . . .'

———— ⊟ ————

From the highway outside Enshin heard the muffled sound of trotting horses and sensed the tension in Yumiko's posture as she listened to them fade away.

'It's another one . . .' she whispered, more to herself than to him.

He didn't comment but now realized that there was something badly wrong in this seemingly ordinary place. Shortly afterwards another undulating call on the hora floated down from the fortress above and a few moments later came the sounds of the first shutters being removed. Enshin was perplexed. He understood the words spoken but had no idea of what they really meant or the mysteries they concealed. With the slightest shrug of his shoulders, he watched Yumiko open up the closed shōji and the sunlight flooding in to reveal a pleasant neat room, a cut well above many of the seedy establishments he had visited during his wanderings. The old lady shuffled off to what was probably her usual place next to the kitchen whilst he made himself comfortable in the shade afforded by a stout wooden frame where he could observe both the street and the clientele who entered the inn. Yumiko brought him some fresh tea while he watched four half-naked *narimon* porters set down their empty palanquin beside the entrance steps and mopped their streaming brows. Their chatter brought Yumiko out to invite them to enter and quench their thirst; it took little encouragement from her for three of them to come inside while the fourth squatted down beside the narimon to watch out in case of unlikely damage. A drink would certainly be brought out to him.

After staring briefly at Enshin, all three started talking volubly once they saw he was lost in thought staring at the street.

''Eard tell another two was taken off not 'alf an hour ago!' one of them said.

'Only two? By all the gods, 'ow many can be left o' them?'

The first porter swallowed a mouthful of very hot tea, spluttered, then wiped his lips on his sleeve.

'Reckon as that's fifteen an' 'e ain't finished yet!'

'Sixteen, if yer counts that young lad two weeks back . . .'

'Fifteen or sixteen? Wot diff'rence does it make, eh?' The third porter sniffed noisily. 'That devil . . .'

'Careful, Gorō . . . yer might be 'eard!'

'Sod that! 'E's a mad dog, 'e is, an' that's the truth . . !'

The trio fell silent for a minute of two as a group of mounted samurai trotted past, their mounts kicking up a cloud of dust.

'Them's "Spearin'" Enomoto's men . . .' remarked the first man. 'I wonder what's 'e done wiv them two . . ?'

''Ow should I know, you fool! I was wiv you an' so was Gorō an' Matabei! None o' us was there!'

They all laughed sardonically.

'Eugh! We'll all find out soon enow . . . Fair stinks that end o' town, don' it?'

Another porter and a couple of ashigaru came in, also mopping their brows and sinking down on the mats beside the low tables, calling for tea. Soon the conversation became general as they clearly all knew each other. No one took the slightest notice of Enshin and he might as well have been invisible.

'Two more gone West!' Gorō remarked. 'Any idea 'oo they was?'

One of the footsoldiers, a squat badly-scarred man, scratched his chest and smothered voiding some wind with a cough.

'The lord don't care, do 'ee? Takes whatever "Spearing" sez an' allows it! "Spearing" wants 'is control, seems to me . . .'

'Of, yeah, but Makino as got the bit betwixt 'is teeth, too, ain't 'e? Reckon 'e's the one behind a lot 'o this,' chipped in Matabei. ''Ere, let's 'ave some Ō-sake, you lot!' He raised his hand to sign to Yumiko but she was already on her way, anticipating their wishes. 'The Ō-karō's behind a lot o' t'trouble, is wot I thinks!'

The first ashigaru downed a saucer of wine and pointed at Matabei and Gorō. 'You two says much more an' yer'l both end up a-dangling. 'Avin' said all that, all o' yer are right!' He sniffed. 'Good job we'se all chums, ain't it? All I've 'eard it comes down to the 'ead o' . . . the lord . . . Makes 'im mad, it does, an' then 'e lashes out in every direction!'

If Enshin had been somewhat mystified up to this point, the seriousness of the problems that beset the Ōsumi clan and the fortress town soon became all too evident. As the sun settled behind the western ridges, he left the inn and began walking the short distance to the shrine track. Just a few yards ahead of him walked two well-dressed samurai conversing together. Three other samurai emerged from a narrow side alley, evidently friends of the pair, and hailed them in a friendly manner. There was a brief exchange and the two began to walk on when, without the hint of a warning, the trio drew out their longswords and cut both down from behind. They had not the slightest chance of putting up a defence. It was all over in a flash and the only witness was Enshin, himself; the assassins simply disappeared back into the same alley and vanished. In that shocking moment Enshin half-thought that they might turn and attack him, too, but the danger passed. None of the murderous trio bore any identifying *mon* on their *haori* although he did catch a glimpse of a panel of green and white armour lacing under the plain *jimbaori* of the leader. It only showed when he raised his right arm to strike down at his victim.

He ran to see if there was anything to be done for the pair but one was clearly dead with his head half-severed from his shoulders; the other, deeply wounded by at least three cuts, still breathed.

Enshin knelt down. 'I am a Buddhist priest, master. Quick, tell me who did this thing. Speak now, sir . . .'

The dying samurai groaned as he gazed up at Enshin. Already his eyes were glazing.

'It was Ma . . . o . . .'

'Makino-dono?'

'No . . . not him . . . men sent by . . .' The man's life was ebbing fast but he rallied and opened his eyes for a moment, his remaining hand trying to clutch Enshin's sleeve. 'Not Makino but En . . .'

The effort was too much, his fingers relaxed and with a faint sight his spirit departed for the next stage of his long journey.

For a few minutes Enshin remained kneeling, his beads clicking under his nimble fingers. He looked up and was again supprised to find no gaping crown of peasant onlookers gathered at a safe distance. Only the young girl, Yumiko, stood a few feet away and even at that distance he could see tears glistening on her soft cheeks.

'I must report this crime to the Bugyō,'[15] he called out to her.

'Sensei . . . master . . . come away quickly,' she urged.

---

[15] Bugyō: the Magistrate responsible for policing.

He smiled grimly; poor frightened Yumiko was plainly afraid for him. 'I must report this incident straightaway. These men cannot be left lying here for the dogs and wild birds. Please tell me where I must go.'

'First you must clean yourself up, master; you have blood all over your robe. Come down with me to the temple where I am sure Ji-chin-sama will provide you with another robe.'

The old man took one look at his young guest and fetched a black robe and a clean bib wallet. Yumiko took the soiled habit to wash at the teahouse. When the couple returned to the high street they saw that nothing had been touched and there were still no curious bystanders.

'Go, Yumiko-san; please don't worry about me. I shall come to no hurt over this affair. Return to your grandmother but please say nothing to anyone apart from her about what has happened.'

As she hurried off out of sight in the gathering dusk, Enshin grasped his ringed staff firmly and, with the rings jangling and chanting in a low voice, climbed the steep side street to where he was told he would find the bugyō's office.

———— ⊟ ————

His account of the incident was received almost without comment by the bored samurai who eventually came out to see him. He showed little interest and that was that, so it seemed. In the deep dusk he retraced his steps to the temple where he saw to Kuroi-san's welfare before going in to Ji-chin.

'Reach no conclusions, my young friend. Follow the admonition of the master to "weigh everything before moving",' was the old man's advice.

'I think you are familiar with the "*Seven Classics*", sensei.'

Ji-chin nodded his head sagely. 'You are not the only one to change from the "yamabushi paths" to the "Ways of the Lord Buddha", Enshin-sama, my young friend. The time was, too, when I drew the "bow and arrow". Now that I have heard your account of this unfortunate incident I think it is time to turn our attentions to the needs of the body; you will have already provided fare for your ox. Am I correct?'

Enshin always thought of Kuroi-san first, whatever happened.

Sometime later, after they had eaten a frugal meal of rice and boiled vegetables, they sat and talked by the light of a single oil lantern.

'My son, you have been here just nine hours,' the old priest remarked in a very low voice just loud enough for his companion to hear. 'What are your impressions may I ask?'

Torii Enshin smiled ruefully and thought deeply before he answered.

'Sensei, my main impression is one of feeling surprise that everyone I have met and spoken to seem to have some secret they keep hidden. Somehow, this secret seems to be held in common. Am I correct in this assessment, master?'

The old man sighed.

'I cannot answer that or your unspoken questions; instead, may I suggest that you observe our town festival in three days time in which we celebrate the return to his mountain abode of the yama-no-kami.[16] This festival is not only intended to express our gratitude to the kami-sama for his benevolence with the rice harvest but also, here, to placate him for the disturbance he suffered when . . . our master . . . constructed his fortress on the sacred spot where the kami-sama lived.' Seeing Enshin about to say something, the old man raised his hand. 'No words, my son; you must sit with your new friends and observe our lords as they take their part in our festival; before that, just watch and wait. Your eyes have already been opened for many years and little will escape you, I'm certain. Remember, that only one who is delicate and subtle can come to the truth. My son, the hour is now late and I must pray as is my custom. Go to your mat and think on what I have said . . . and sleep well.'

'I will do that, master.'

'You will be up before dawn?'

'One hour before that, sensei; it has long been my custom.'

'Good! A prayer to Marishi-ten will never go amiss!'

With that parting remark, Ji-chin shuffled through to the Prayer Hall.

———————□———————

Thus it was that for the next three days Enshin spent much of his time in the small teahouse, though sometimes he took Kuroi-san for a walk along the nearby country tracks, becoming a familiar sight to the farming community. In the teahouse he passed some of the time carefully brushing part of the Heart Sutra text which he intended as a small gift to Ji-chin for his kindness. In his youth,

---

[16] Yama-no-kami: the mountain deity who descends in spring to preside over the fertility of the land and returns to the heights in the late-autumn.

his father, the Deputy-Constable of western Kōzuke, had ensured that besides studying the arts of war his son should receive a broad education and acquire an elegant writing hand. It was possible that this artistic talent came to him through the maternal line but certainly it formed an important part of Enshin's academic leanings. He also persuaded Yumiko's grandmother to permit him to examine her eyes but realized at once that she would never regain her sight. Both pupils were milky white. A Chinese monk at the Hōrai-ji had told him how some clever physicians from far beyond the Celestial Empire's western borders had been able long ago to remove the cataract by means of the delicate use of a sharp thorn and replace the pupil with the thinnest sliver of clear horn. Some patients, he averred, had recovered at least an awareness of colour and light, even of knowing that persons were nearby. It was a pity that this learned monk lacked the special skill to carry out or teach this marvel to his student.

Enjoined by Ji-chin to sit quietly and listen, Enshin did just that, listening in to snippets of conversation whilst supping many cups of the ineffable tea. Pressed as to the source of this tea leaf, Yumiko would only say that it was picked from bushes growing on the hillside just below the line of her ancestors' graves. The bushes had been planted long years ago and carefully nurtured by these forbears. Whether or not it was this same tea that loosened tongues or the unusually stout timber walls of the building, those who frequented the place were often less than normally guarded in their choice of words. Possibly the fact that the young priest seemed immersed in his writing rendered him practically invisible to the drinkers and he was even protected from intrusion by the daily regulars.

The double murder was casually mentioned by several people but what was of interest was their opinions as to the identity of the perpetrators and their motives. He quickly realized that the Ōsumi clan was divided by two factions, the one followers of the Ō-karō, Enomoto Shigeo, the other those adhering to the Makino Suenaga, another powerful councillor. The latter had charge of the Ōsumi Treasury and the former was the clan's leading general. Furthermore, he learnt that the rivalry had begun when the clan lord had fallen under the malevolent possession of some evil being. This possession manifested itself only on occasions when Ōsumi Kagehisa-dono apparently flew into violent rages, at other times remaining quite reasonable. One thing that Enshin gleaned from this idle chatter was that the lord often complained of severe headaches alleviated by potions administered by his priest-physician. Always these outbursts were preceded by dark periods of moroseness where he retired to his quarters and was not seen for days at a time. Regarding the street killings, no one seemed to know anything though, by common assent, the rival factions were blamed, the two dead men belonging to the Makino group. The fact that these killings had not brought the two groups to open hostilities meant, in Enshin's mind, that there must be another explanation.

Were the two factions strong enough to risk open confrontation and what action would Lord Ōsumi take? Then there were the ferocious executions . . . were these behind all the rest or were they just symptons of the same? He gave an involuntary sigh; all these questions crowded in, whirling in a riot inside his brain. He would just have to hope that the *matsuri* would bring the promised answers.

———□———

Early on the third morning, Enshin sat beside Kuroi-san watching him chew at the fresh fodder he had brought. He went over his thoughts with the ox, finding that by talking problems often became less dense and Kuroi-san was ever a good listener. When he was about to leave the ox came to his feet and uttered a low call. This was immediately similarly answered from some way off. Enshin looked at him quizzically; was it time for the festival to start or did he have some inner understanding? In answer to his thought as it formed in his head there came the sound of a drum beating somewhere in the town.

'I must go now, old friend, but thank you for your opinions; I will keep them in mind.'

Reaching the teahouse he sat out on the verandah taking care to be in the shade for, despite the lateness in the tenth month, this was another hot and sunny day. Here was the best vantage point to observe those taking part in the celebrations and for once Yumiko's grandmother, attired in her best kimono, knelt beside him. Her granddaughter had carefully dressed the old lady's hair so that she looked remarkably elegant.

'You shall be my eyes, honoured sir, while I shall act as your memory. Tell me what you see and I will provide the details.'

'We shall make a formidable team, Oka-sama.'

A little later she leant towards him, placing her hand lightly on his sleeve. 'Enshin-sama, I have noticed how quiet you have been whenever you come here. Now, I don't think it is because your eyes are captivated by my comely granddaughter; I think it is something else. Can you confide in so old a personage as myself?'

'Oka-sama, your words are those of an age long past. Yumiko-san has doubtless told you I have been setting down on paper some texts from the Heart Sutra; that is what has kept me so silent, as you put it.'

She laughed. 'Of course! How foolish of me to think otherwise and that you might have been memorizing small snippets of idle gossip . . !'

It was his turn to smile slightly now. 'Was the old lady really as blind as she appeared?' he asked himself. He contented himself by saying: 'Oh, madam, I do hear things, naturally, but that's life, isn't it?'

This time her seamed face crinkled as she whispered: 'You don't fool me, master priest, but we'll see by the end of this festival, I think!'

'Forgive me, Oka-sama, but what is it you think we shall understand?'

'Ah, you may not be able to cure my eyes, young master, that is beyond man's abilities. Secretly, I think you may be the bringer of better days.'

He sat silent for a while though he was certain that the old lady knew he wasn't ignoring her. At last, he said: 'Perhaps you think of me as some sort of bodhisattva, Oka-sama? Your words exactly reflect those of your priest. May I enquire without giving offence, if you are his younger sister?'

'Heh! Heh! Heh! Now you are trying to flatter me, Enshin-sama! No! I think we shall all know the truth in good time . . . Can you hear those drums beat? They will come past here very soon.'

———— ⊟ ————

As Enshin knew, along with all those who are familiar with the myriad matsuri celebrated throughout the provinces, many of these local festivities in honour of any number of *kami* varied considerably in content. According to Ji-chin-sama this festival was to honour the departing mountain deity but also had the objective of appeasing his possible anger at the invasion of his sacred home by the construction of the Ōsumi yashiki. As he understood it, this invasion of the kami's sacred abode was at odds with the beliefs of the farmers in opposition to the military aspirations of the warriors.

'First will come the *taiko*,' explained the old lady, 'they will be led by the Ō-daiko carried on a special cart and beaten by two naked men . . . Avert your eyes, granddaughter, won't you?'

The girl smiled across at Enshin.

'And don't think I don't know you are mocking me, the pair of you!'

Each drummer came as a milling dancing mass, wildly beating their instruments without thought of rhythm or tempo. They were outlandishly dressed and wore masks fashioned as oxen, On every fourth slow beat of the great drum everyone shouted out 'OI!' There must have been a hundred young men in that discordant prancing and their cacophony hung in the air long after they had passed by. Fresh shouting accompanied four groups of naked youths carrying a long pole astride which sat a man dressed in Sumō fundoshi. As the first group passed in front of the verandah Enshin saw that the pole was slotted as if it was part of a wooden torii.

He was about to ask about this when the old lady said: 'These are our champions, young priest; men who will later contest with the kami-sama for his pleasure.'

'They will fight the kami-sama?'

'Just like at some Spring Planting festivals, master, but here we have the contests twice each year.'

'The kami-sama will win?'

'Maybe, though ours is very strong. Before you ask, yes he is a son of Ōkuni-nushi-no-mikoto.'

'Then I suspect that he will be unhappy should he lose and . . .'

'That would mean a bad harvest and even starvation in punishment next year!'

'That bad? Tell me, Oka-sama, what if the sumō-tori contrived to lose, eh?'

'The people would know just as would the kami-sama. He would become angry and that would court disaster!'

The sumō-tori were followed by more drummers but this group kept up a steady rhythmic beat marching in front of an advance party of armoured samurai escorting an important personage.

'Ha, now you can see our lord, Ōsumi-dono, I think . . ?'

He was convinced that Yumiko's grandmother could see as well as he!

So this was Ōsumi Kagehisa-dono? He looked normal enough, sitting his horse upright and wearing instead of his kabutō[17] a formal black gauze eboshi. Just as they reached the teahouse the procession came to a brief stop and he noted that the ruler wore a green-laced dō-maru armour, He was preceded by four bannermen, also mounted, bearing the long white flags emblazoned with devices of a black circle containing two vertical bars, the Ōsumi clan mon.

Whatever had caused the delay must have been unexpectedly disruptive as the parade was unable to restart and a runner appeared, a slim ashigaru skirmisher in all probability, who dodged his way through the throng to his lord's stirrup and bowed low before delivering his message. Enshin had noted that as the delay prolonged

---

[17] Kabutō: helmet.

so Ōsumi-dono became more agitated but now his face darkened, the suffusion of blood at once showed up a livid scar, quite visible from where he sat; a scar running from his right cheek diagonally past his eye and across his temple to finally be hidden under the white band of his eboshi. The lord was clearly angered by whatever message he had received and without warning lashed down at the unfortunate footsoldier with his riding cane then rounded on his immediate escort whose horses, unsettled by the sudden commotion, began to rear and back away in disorder. From his vantage point slightly above that of the riders, Enshin saw Ōsumi-dono begin to sway in his saddle and finally slump forward over the pommel. He came to his feet apologizing to the old lady: 'You must excuse me, madam, but I am needed . . .' and hurried down the steps to the street.

As he did so, to the consternation of the Ōsumi bodyguard, Kagehisa began to slip sideways from his horse and lay stretched on the dusty roadway.

'Masters, I am a priest skilled in medicine,' called out Enshin. 'Permit me to attend to your lord.'

One of the hatamoto with presence of mind, dismounted: 'A priest? I don't know you! Where are you from?'

'I belong to the Mikawa Hōrai-ji, sir . . .'

'Very well, you are permitted to approach . . . Stay with him, Kikkawa-sama; watch closely!'

Enshin knelt by the unconscious warlord and felt about his neck with his left hand. He looked up at the tough looking warrior. 'Kikkawa-sama, I think it is necessary to move your master into the shade. This sun will be too strong for his condition . . .'

The gauze eboshi had fallen off as Ōsumi fell and Enshin noted that the blood vessels across the scarred temple were swollen large.

The hatamoto glared at him, more because he, too, was the focus of his peers' attention, but passed on the request. At once, three more men dismounted and the four carefully lifted their lord and carried up to the verandah where Yumiko, seeing what was intended, had brought an armful of soft mats and a neck rest.

Enshin requested her: 'Bring cold water and handtowels, if you please, Yumiko-san.'

'They are coming, master.'

———— ⊟ ————

The escort commander proved to be no less than Makino Suenaga, striking Enshin as a capable and reasonable man.

'What is your opinion of my lord's condition?' he asked the moment he joined the group gathered about the stricken man.

'My lord, your master is a very sick man. May I enquire how long he has suffered with this affliction?'

'Hmmm! His falling down? This is the first time, so far as I am aware. I would have heard, I am sure . . . His − er − wound was received in a dangerous encounter during the Eishō War[18] but, as I said, this the first time it has laid him low.'

'The wound came as a direct result of combat?'

'That is so.'

'Sir, some might suspect that your lord is possessed by a malevolent demon, but I don't think this to be the case . . .'

'You don't? What, then, is the cause?'

'It is my opinion that the sword blow struck down at this point here,' Enshin pointed to the abrupt top end of the scar, 'and injured the bone of his temple, here.' He pointed to a depressed area. 'After recovering from this injury did your master's character change at all?'

Makino Suenaga gave Enshin the briefest of shrewd looks then nodded his head. He turned and ordered the escort to withdraw to the street, ignoring the girl who was carefully wiping the afflicted man's brow with her cold damp cloth.

'Enshin-sama, this is a matter of some delicacy as I am sure you will appreciate . . .'

'Of course, my lord; of course,' murmured Enshin in reply.

'Umm, yes! My immediate question is: "Will my master live?"'

'He may do so, but he is beyond the skill of man as the damaged bone presses on his faculties. I have to ask certain questions, you understand, in order to be able to help your lord . . .'

It was important to allay any suspicions at this point.

Makino Suenaga nodded his head. 'Naturally, you must. You may consult with our priest up at the yashiki, if you wish. He is named Chen-li.'

'Thank you, sir. May I ask if your lord has had these − er − problems more frequently recently?'

'You are perceptive, priest! Yes, the answer is that he has indeed suffered more often . . . and others have noticed this, too, but you must tell me directly: will he survive?'

'He may recover, my lord, but now that he has been struck down and has not recovered consciousness despite the cold compresses, makes me fearful for the future. May I suggest that he is carefully borne to your yashiki and that you, my lord, put . . .'

---

[18] The Eishō War was fought on the northern border of Harima in the last year of the period, 1521.

'Put in place suitable precautions, eh? Wise advice, master priest. You have other skills besides medicine, I think?'

'Perhaps, sir, perhaps.'

Makino Suenaga beckoned Kikkawa and another of the escort and issued orders for a litter to be fetched. Almost coincidentally Enshin noted that Kikkawa was wearing a fine quality armour with green and blue lacing.

'Enshin-sama, please accompany us to the yashiki, won't you. I am certain that Master Chen-li will appreciate your opinions about our lord's condition.'

———————— ⊟ ————————

There was no discernible change in Ōsumi-dono's state of deep unconsciousness all that day. The hatamoto had informed the Ō-karō as soon as the cortège reached the small fortress and at once the outer gates were closed and guards mounted as if they were preparing for war. The senior retainers were summoned to attend a Council in the main chamber and the two priests were ordered to hold themselves in attendance in the adjoining room. As they heard the mumble of discussion and the occasional angry voices through the shōji, Chen-li, a staid middle-aged priest inclining towards corpulence, tried to cover up by agreeing with Enshin that unless Ōsumi-dono recovered his wits before the evening drum, he may never do so as the night hours were when the spirits were at their lowest ebb.

'Master Chen-li, I have only been here three days but something disturbs me although it doesn't concern your sick lord. May I ask you about it?'

The priest had evidently been given as his name that of an obscure Chinese monk who had flourished in the Southern Sung dynasty. Not unusual but nonetheless odd.

'Please ask, my son, and I'll help the best I can,' Chen-li replied somewhat patronizingly.

'On my first evening here, and I had only just arrived, I was unwillingly the only witness to the deaths of two ranking samurai. I was unable to report more than I saw of the incident so I was wondering if, as physician here, you could tell me anything else or who is suspected of the murders?'

Chen-li remained impassive, looking at Enshin as though he couldn't see clearly. One of his eyes was slightly clouded; perhaps cataract was endemic around here?

'I did hear of that unfortunate happening . . . Both the dead men served Makino-dono . . .' There was a certain hesitation in the priest's voice and he seemed to be chosing his words rather guardedly, thought Enshin. 'Er . . . one of them . . .' He paused yet again, appearing to wrack his memory. 'Sugamitsu-sama was in charge of those clerks working in the Chancellor's bureau . . . His companion . . . I can't recall his name . . . served, I think, in the *samurai bukiko*[19] . . . So far as I know, no one has been arrested for the . . . er . . . crime.'

So the killers remained at large. If both victims served the two leading councillors, respectively, why were they attacked and killed together? Were the two senior hatamoto involved was the question in Enshin's mind?

The Council Chamber appeared anything but tranquil. Loud insistent voices were raised to the point that Enshin seriously thought a fight was about to break out . . . Calm was eventually restored but not before Makino Suenaga's voice shouted out that someone – unnamed – might be acting against the clan's interests . . . Someone else bellowed 'Liar' before order was restored.

Both Enshin and Chen-li sat totally impassive in their adjoining room.

——— ⊟ ———

Enshin had hardly completed his nightly prayers and composed himself for sleep when he was awakened by Chen-li with the news that, as they had expected, Ōsumi Kagehisa had passed to the next world. He added that not a word was to be uttered, on Makino-dono's orders, until the 'succession' could be settled. Enshin was to remain in his quarters, only Chen-li to attend his lord if required to do so. There was a hint that this was a mild form of house arrest. Makino and Enomoto moved quickly to secure the fortress, a prudent precaution at a time when disputes and undercurrents tended to increase with dramatic speed when weaknesses appeared at the top.

Content with reading a holy scroll lent him by Chen-li, Enshin settled himself to wait for events to unfold. One of the young maids who served the lord's family, brought him some refreshing tea. Chen-li had gone to his dead lord's apartment at the time. The girl knelt beside her small lacquered tray and waited while he sipped the beverage. He looked up from the scroll with a smile as he tasted the warm drink.

'Tis is very good, miss . . ?'

'My name is Miyuki, master.'

---

[19] Samurai bukiko: the armouries.

'Then, Miyuki-san, tell me that this tea comes from . . . a certain place?'

The girl glanced over her shoulder at the closed shōji, listening intently. She edged a little closer and slipped a folded paper from the breast of her kimono.

'Master, I am Yumiko's sister . . . I cannot say more but please take this and after reading destroy it completely . . . Please, my lord, take care . . .'

She bowed deeply and left the room, composed but clearly apprehensive.

Enshin carefully unfolded the letter which was written on thin rice paper in small elegant script but not signed. A woman's hand, perhaps? It was a well-educated hand and the writer used many Chinese characters; no, this could only be brushed by a priest and that could only be Ji-chin. What was the message written in so small a script that he had to draw closer to the window screen?

> *Honoured Student, greetings.*
> *You have requested guidance in evaluating the scriptures since enlight-enment thus far eludes you. Be reassured, the Master's discourse examin-ing the strengths and weaknesses will suffice. According to the Chinese commentary on these writings you will recall the five who ventured forth whilst only three returned and where the only question was whether their reward was in this Middle Kingdom or in the Heavenly one? The story of the two woodpeckers may help, where both prepared nest holes on either side of the same tree but, being rivals, were forever flying round the bole to find out how the other was progressing. The deity of the tree became vexed. How, then, should this matter be resolved?*

Enshin read the text carefully twice over before carefully tearing the soft rice paper into thin strips and placing them in the warm teapot. He had hardly finished when Chen-li returned.

'I'm sorry but I fear, master, that this tea has stood too long. Per-mit me to call the maidservant for a fresh pot.' He clapped his hands and almost at once Miyuki appeared. 'Please bring more tea to sus-tain us,' Enshin ordered.

She bowed low and placed the utensils on her tray and slipped out while Enshin pointed out a difficult phrase in the text open in front of him, requesting Chen-li's opinion regarding the *kanji*. As the priest leant over to scan the Chinese characters, Enshin noticed a faint scent about the other's left sleeve, the merest hint of almond though perhaps he was mistaken.

Whilst the two discussed the sutra text, Enshin found it difficult to set aside the fact that Ji-chin, the two young women and their grandmother had taken a terrible risk in smuggling the letter to him. Even though it was worded to hide the real message, discovery and a clever interrogation would, at the least, engender suspicion, and that suspicion would have been enough to bring torture and a certain death to all at the kirikubi-ba. Of course, he well understood Ji-chin's allusions but now he needed time to reflect on them. Would he have this time now that Lord Ōsumi had passed away, that was the question he must address?

He knew that one of the victims served the Chancellor whilst both men were his retainers even if one was an administrator in the Samurai Bukiko. Both, to judge from the quality of their clothing, had been men of rank, probably quite senior at that . . . He recalled, too, that when the murderers appeared, for a moment it seemed that normal greetings between associates were exchanged. The attack was sudden and without warning . . . What, then, did Ji-chin mean by 'rewards being in Heaven or on Earth'? Rewards bestowed by who . . . ah, that was an important question, too . . ?

'That text certainly exercises your mind, my young friend,' grunted Chen-li. 'I had to repeat what I was saying three times just then.'

Enshin bowed deeply. 'Forgive me, sensei, but I was too deep in thought considering if some of my other interpretations were at fault . . . These words in Sanskrit can often carry different meanings and this makes them difficult to understand . . .' He sighed, adding: 'It is the doleful news that clouds my brain. I wish that I could have even a small part of your peace of mind that so clearly gives you strength.'

Chen-li permitted himself the faintest of smiles.

'Doleful indeed, my son, doleful indeed; but there are rays of light. You were asking about the sudden – er – demise of those two samurai three days or so ago. Well, I have just learnt from one of the senior guards that the bugyō has arrested three men on suspicion of the crime.'

'I shall pray for them, sensei! Did your informant say who they were, out of interest?'

'Well, I suppose as a visitor to a strange place gives you a rather different perspective on local events. The three suspects were young ostlers more than usually affected by strong wine, it seems . . . Anyway, I know no more as this will likely be the end of the matter. Like you, I will pray for their souls.'

Enshin muttered his thanks and turned again to the sutra. Other questions were filling his mind since Chen-li's words were at odds with what he actually witnessed. He talked affably, though sparingly, with the priest for nearly two more hours before a young page presented himself with a summons to attend Makino-dono. The page added that he was instructed to bring his belongings with him.

Makino Suenaga sat on a round mat placed just to one side of the jōdan dais in the Council Chamber, clearly scrupulously observing a façade of normality. If there was a power struggle, he certainly wasn't going to show it. Three capable-looking retainers sat to one side, impassive but menacing, and for just a moment Enshin felt a brief moment of doubt. However, all was set at rest when Makino-dono indicated a mat set at a comfortable distance before him.

'Be seated, honoured priest! I have called you here to thank you for your services to my lord. Do you have anything you would like to say?'

'No, my lord, other than my actions are dictated by the mercy of Amida Bosatsu. Please think nothing of it, my lord.'

Some tea was set before him, again by the maiden, Miyuki.

'You are newly arrived in this domain, I believe?'

'That is correct,' said Enshin with a bow. 'I came just three days ago.'

'An unusual stay, don't you think?'

'Unusually eventful thus far, my lord, that is true.'

'Hmm.' Makino Suenaga drew in his breath, glancing towards one of his escort. The man placed his right knuckles to the polished pinewood floor looking directly at the priest.

'Are you a rōnin?' he brusquely demanded.

'No, master, I am not. I am merely a wandering monk from . . .'

'From Hōrai-ji! We know that already . . . but you have been a warrior, haven't you?'

'That is true. I descend from a ranking family in Kōzuke; my father is lord of a fortress at Kusatsu.' There was no point in prevaricating.

'Is that so? A warrior masquerading as a priest, eh?'

Enshin bowed respectfully.

'My lords, I was a samurai with three thousand koku and my clan is still the Torii-ke. I renounced the world with the permission of my father and his councillors more than six years ago, entering the monastery where my uncle is Abbot at Mikawa Hōrai. My intention then as now is to become a healer of men's bodies and minds . . .'

Makino raised his hand.

'Enough! I have not brought you here to question you, honoured priest, but to request your assistance in a delicate matter.'

'My lord, how can I refuse your wishes?'

That brought a smile to the hatamoto's face and some suppressed mirth from his escort. The Chancellor leant forward and tapped the handle of his folded fan on the boards.

'Enshin-sama, this delicate matter concerns not only my retainers but also my lord. Two of my followers were assassinated the other day . . . you actually witnessed the incident, didn't you? At first I suspected the . . . the other side . . .'

'Other side, my lord?'

The hatamoto looked troubled. It was the same follower as before who replied. 'The clan is in danger of becoming divided between my lord, here, and the Senior General's followers.'

'Lord Enomoto Shigeo?'

'Correct! You are well-informed!'

'Not really so, masters; but I have been here three days.'

'Were not the situation so serious, Enshin-sama, we might laugh outright; but serious it is. These two retainers were senior men, as I said; one served me directly, the other had duties in the clan armouries. We wonder why they were killed and by whom? However, in the last month no less than twelve of my followers have also died, some with their immediate families. Summarily taken to the execution ground and slain! Have you heard this too in your brief time here?'

'My lord, I can understand you have a problem. I heard, for example, that the two senior retainers who died in the street may have been the victims of three drunken ashigaru. Is this really believable, after all they were men of inferior rank and skills?'

'Do you draw any conclusions, priest?' Suenaga cocked his head a little to one side.

'It may be too soon, my lord,' replied Enshin, 'however I would like to draw your attention towards the famous precept of the Sonshi.'

'And that is?'

'That "all warfare is based on deception". If I understand your meaning correctly and you wish me to make some enquiries – as an outsider, of course – I will accept but first, may I request just one condition?'

'And that is, Enshin-sama?'

'I would like to be independent and there is no hint or indication that I have your patronage. All I need is a plausible excuse for being here in this yashiki and the ability to go anywhere.'

Makino Suenaga nodded his head.

'I agree. Go back to your temple with Ji-chin-sama. You will be sent for tomorrow or the next day morning.'

'That letter was a dangerous enterprise, Ji-chin-sama!'

'It had to be done, young master; you know that.'

'Perhaps I would have reached the same path in due time and without the risk?'

'Questions, however innocently posed, would have invited suspicion. Time might not have been on your side, my friend.'

Enshin bowed slightly.

'Your words were wisely selected, master, although I must still work hard to understand their true meanings . . . Would you care to enlighten me further?' The look on the old man's face told him that he would receive no more help. 'So you want me to reach my own conclusions? Then that is what I shall do!'

'Good! Now we shall achieve a meeting of minds, my son. Let us pray that the meeting will be in accord with our hopes.'

'Has Kuroi-san been happy with his lot?' asked Enshin, changing the subject.

'He has, indeed! Several children visit him daily. He must be the best fed ox in all the provinces! You are to be congratulated, my friend, in having so refined and placid an animal such as he. Tell me, how did you come together?'

'That is a long story, sensei. One day, perhaps, you shall hear it . . .'

———— ☐ ————

The following day Enshin resumed his visits to the teahouse where he found nothing changed since the matsuri except that the regulars were full of speculation about events up at the yashiki on the hilltop. Naturally, all those connected with the clan, however lowly, were adherents of the Makino faction, if that actually existed, and this was logical, of course. He didn't hear a whisper of Ōsumi-dono's death; just how this news was bottled up was a wonder as matters of any import were the subject of rumour that spread like wildfire in a strong breeze. He listened out, also, for anything on the subject of the two barbarously executed corpses that he had seen when he entered the town with his ox. It was time he found out more, he thought, but the teahouse was plainly not the place to do this.

Accordingly, that afternoon, there being no message from the yashiki, he took his leave and, jangling staff in hand, walked back through the township towards that place of horror. A kubikiri-ba was not for the fainthearted; in such a warm spell of weather as in high summer, everyone could smell the raw scent of corruption and death from a great distance. Pity the poor souls who could only find living space within this stinking radius. Here, with the numbers of corpses measured in several tens, the stench could be overpowering.

Enshin arrived at the golgotha with a slight feeling of nausea. Despite experiencing a number of battlefields, both large and small, he felt that he would never become indifferent to places where deliberate death was inflicted. There was no doubt that many felons richly deserved their fate, but this hardening of attitude swiftly dissipated when he saw the freshly raised bodies of the three ashigaru wrongly accused and summarily sentenced for the murder of the two samurai . . . It was usual for those who were crucified to be given their quietus by the passing of a spear up through their chest but like many of the others who had suffered here in this domain this final act of mercy was withheld . . . He was unable to question these newly raised victims as all three had lost their tongues . . . cut out as a final cruelty by the executioners on orders from the Bugyō.

He shook his head as he gazed at their tortured faces where each pair of eyes implored the armed *himin*[20] to use his cold steel. Enshin intoned a prayer to the Lady Kannon before turning away to read the notice brushed on a rickety noticeboard beside the remains of the two sawn men. The hastily painted kanji read:

Pay heed! This is the fate of those who would plot against their lord.

There were no names or other details. He must ask if he wished to find out more. He looked over at the three himin who were now squatting down in the shade afforded by their crude shelter raised by the wicket gate. The presence of a priest, though infrequent, wasn't remarkable but one looked up when Enshin greeted them.

'Yeah?' the man asked.

With a slight bow, Enshin asked: 'Can you tell me if anyone left an offering for these poor souls?'

Someone whispered: ' 'E bowed, respectful like . . . First time ever . . .'

The burliest of the trio came heavily to his feet and bowed awkwardly back.

'Offerin'? No one does that 'ere, master priest.'

'Do you receive your fees, my friends?'

'Our fees?' The man snorted and looked at the others. 'All we gets is some food an' what we can find on them.' He jerked his thumb over his shoulder. 'Some of 'em gives us a bit ter make it fast at the

---

[20] *Himin*: outcastes, often employed as executioners.

end, but what we gets only jus' keeps body an' soul together, so to say!'

They all laughed scornfully and Enshin could well imagine that the Bugyō or his henchmen took their cut pretty greedily. He felt about inside his wallet and drew out three broken pieces of silver. 'Take these, my friends, and help me pray for all their spirits in case they should return as raging ghosts intent on exacting revenge.'

The three ragged outcastes were struck dumb with surprise and could hardly find the words to express their gratitude.

''Oo does yer want us t'pray for, master?'

Enshin pressed his hands together upright before his chest.

'We should entreat the Lady Kannon for mercy on those two sawn apart . . . Can you tell me their names so that these will reach her ears?'

'Wot, them two? They was a-spyin' on our master!'

Enshin fumbled inside his scrip and drew out another piece of silver, holding it up.

'Please, my friend; they have already paid their debt . . .'

'Go on, Magobei; tell 'im . . . Won't do no 'arm, will it?' Magobei's companion was eagerly eying the glinting silver.

'Yeah,' chipped in the other man, 'that there siller sez tell 'im all!'

The burly Magobei shrugged his shoulders.

'Yer won't go an' blab ter the . . . er . . ?'

'Magistrate? No, certainly not!'

'We don't rightly know their names but they was servin' "Spearin'" Enomoto, so we was told.'

'Were they condemned by him?'

'Condemned? Oh, yes; yer means did 'e send 'em 'ere? The answer is "no", priest. The Bu . . . they brung 'em down 'ere an' orders 'em ter be sawn in 'alf. No joke that, cos it 'urts real bad an . . .'

Enshin raised his hand to stop Magobei going any further with his account.

'Forgive me, my friend, but I am a healer who tries to save lives.'

'Course not, master . . . sorry . . .'

'Have you men eaten properly today?'

'Today? No, nor yesterday . . .'

'Or fer a week!'

'Then take this extra piece because you have been most helpful . . . Oh, one last thing. Did anyone come down here with the bugyō's men when they suffered?'

'You don't 'arf talk proper, master. Rather like a sam'rai, savin' yer presence,' grinned Magobei. 'Well, since it's yer 'oo asks there was one fella; 'e was an important one, at that, weren't 'e, Hiro?'

'A ranking samurai, was he?'

Magobei curled his lip into a sneer. 'Them's all 'igh rank, yer rev'rence, all 'igh and mighty; but jus' one yari thrust does fer 'em as it do fer the rest o'us . . .' Taking Enshin a little to one side, he lowered his voice. 'Yer askin' questions, master, is like they was dangerous, y'knows. Take care, master priest, but as yer're kind an' talk to us as real people not shit, we won't split . . . Yer man was a sam'rai from the fort up there an' 'e didn't belong to "Spearin'" or "Gold" Suenaga!' He began to turn away but then confided in a whisper that the man he asked about didn't have a *chonmage*[21] as if he was a lay-priest only dressed up as a samurai.

It would be folly to ask more without giving cause for suspicion so Enshin merely thanked Magobei and his companions, telling them that he would go back to the temple and say a proper mass as he intended. He bowed politely and shuffled away as priests do.

————— ⬓ —————

Could he take the word of a 'non-person', a mere beggarly *himin*, as truth, he wondered? The maze seemed denser than ever; the deaths of the two samurai he had witnessed were clouded by the wrongful execution of the three innocent ashigaru. Now there was a mist obscuring the barbarous killing of Enomoto's men, deaths ordered by who . . ? Tit for tat, maybe? Possibly both! Were Enomoto and Makino intent on picking off each other's leading retainers with trumped up excuses or none too subtle subterfuge? It certainly looked as if Ji-chin's two woodpeckers were parables for these two hatamoto, but try as he might, Enshin could see no real underlying motif. What did the old priest mean by the 'deity of their tree'? He couldn't have meant 'lord' suggesting Ōsumi-dono, or could he? When he wrote that secret missive Ji-chin couldn't have known that Ōsumi had died. Even here, that news cannot have spread that fast and, in any case, was tightly suppressed . . . no one knew . . . He must look again for a deeper explanation. As he turned over everything in his mind, Enshin resolved that as soon as he received a summons he would seek a meeting with the formidable Ō-karō, Enomoto Shigeo.

He had scarcely time to wash himself down to cleanse away the cloying stink of the kirikubi-ba when Ji-chin informed him of a letter received less than an hour before. It was the expected permission requesting him to assist Chen-li-sama where necessary amongst the garrison 'in recognition of his services in aiding Lord Ōsumi'.

---

[21] *Chonmage*: the hair dressed in a topknot.

It was warm work trudging up the steep track to the Outer Gatetower but his letter admitted him to the stout timbered guard-room in the second *yagura*. There, his paper was examined by an officious junior officer who was punctillious to an exasperating degree. Relief came when a messenger presented a note ordering that he should attend, without any delay, the exercise yard next to the armouries.

Finding this enclosed part of the sprawling yashiki presented no difficulties to a former swordsman such as Enshin, the sharp sound of hardwood striking hardwood guided him unerringly to the prac-tice yard. When he arrived he was motioned to take a place a little to the rear.

Two short lines of young samurai, scarcely adults, knelt at one side of the area and he saw at once a match of sorts was in progress. Opposite the young swordsmen, all of whom had wooden weapons, stood a powerful figure who carried a *bokutō* loosely in his right hand.

The man beckoned towards one young fellow who at once leapt to his feet with a shout, brought his practice sword to above his right shoulder and rushed to the attack, screaming out another penetrat-ing shout. It looked as if his brash assault would overwhelm his opponent but . . . *thwack* . . . and he crumpled to his knees, bokutō fallen from his hands, clutching at his left side . . . It was all over in a fraction of a second. The next youngster was more cautious but fared no better when at last he thought he saw his chance.

'War is war!' shouted out the master. 'It is cruel and bloody! Both of you would now be dead . . . needlessly wasted . . !' He pointed at two more of the youthful retainers. 'You two, consider how best to attack a strong enemy together. Think of the Sonshi . . . When the drum is beaten, attack me according to your plan! Don't hold back!'

Enshin watched closely. The two conferred together in low tones glancing across their shoulders at their nonchalant opponent who walked about totally unconcerned at the odds now against him. Enshin shook his head recalling his own experiences when he stud-ied the powerful Oda-ryū under Tsukuba's twin peaks. These two stood no chance, none at all.

The drum was struck just once, the pulsing beat fading slowly since this was a war taikō and no mere toy. Both the young men walked forward warily then divided, the one trying to outflank and distract his master by appearing the most threatening, his ally flour-ished his weapon with an accompanying yell, but the end result was the same. The master merely slipped the first attack, dropped low and cut upwards beneath the thrust, striking the lad painfully between his legs . . .

'Morihei-sama, exercise these weaklings,' the master ordered, 'and call Chen-li to attend!'

One of his assistants bowed. 'Master Chen-li is ministering to our lord. He has sent this man, a new priest from the temple!'

The swordmaster gave Enshin a bleak look.

'What is your name, priest?' he demanded harshly.

'I am named Enshin, my lord.' He bowed formally, adding in a mild voice: 'I am also of warrior stock, sir, and would ask to know to whom I speak?'

'Eh? My name? Who do you think you are?'

'If I must carry out your wishes, sir, I must do so on the correct basis.'

He could see that those standing behind the master were aghast.

The swordsman stood silent for some moments, his eyes looking Enshin up and down.

'I can see, priest, that your forearms betray the experience of weapons! They are thickened at your wrists which suggests to me either you are foolishly arrogant or you have some worthwhile knowledge! Come, we shall have a bout and then, perhaps, I shall tell you my name!'

Enshin bowed and removed his scrip. Handing it to an open-mouthed youngster who held it as though it was a live snake. He slowly tied back his sleeves as he glanced along the weapon rack. Fingering some of the spearshafts lightly he picked out one weapon at random, hefting it without any apparent interest.

'This will do, sir!'

'A yari, priest? In that case I shall face you with a naginata!'

Both men strode out to the centre of the yard.

'Priest, you do not face a tyro; you realize that, don't you?'

Enshin merely acknowledged the comment with a slight inclination of his head.

'Shall we begin, sir?'

The master's eyes narrowed. He realized that despite the recent demonstration of his skill, this opponent remained icily calm and in full control of himself. His grasp on the yari was correct and without a tremor. Slowly the master circled the priest with his halberd tucked beneath his left arm while Enshin stood still with his yari point lowered offering no threat but not the slightest hint of how he might act should an attack be launched . . . Some minutes passed slowly by and the tension was palpable amongst the silent watchers; only the master and Enshin remained unaffected.

'You are good, Enshin-sama; very good! Strong, too! You are the first man that I have faced to whom I have said those words . . .

No, it would be pointless for us to fight!' He stepped back and bowed deeply. 'You requested my name. I am called Enomoto Shigeo, sir.'

Enshin also stood back and responded.

'I was sent here in case your *deshi*[22] required attention after practice but I can see that my skills are not needed so much as yours!'

The hatamoto uttered a grim laugh. 'You are right, Enshin-sama. These young men can only learn by their mistakes, but I think you already know this, don't you? Come, sir, let us take tea together and talk a while; I am wearied of such children!'

'Don't be too hard on them, sir; they will learn all in good time and then they will be worthy of you and their clan!'

Enshin was surprised in some ways that he felt admiration for this hardbitten man. He respected his attitude and the quality of his skills; clearly he was a warrior of the old uncompromising school, the type of *bugeisha*[23] very familiar from the Torii samurai's own training.

'Why are you here, Enshin-sama? You, who have only lately arrived in this small domain?'

The hatamoto was unexpectedly direct but Enshin chose his words with care.

'Your clan has problems, sir; that I sensed almost as soon as I came to this town and saw the kirikubi-ba! The Lord Buddha has enjoined me to heal men's bodies and their souls; surely that requirement can extend to wider problems, can it not?'

The master swordsman drew in his breath. 'We need no interruptions, I think. Come with me to view the town from the chamber at the top of the main tower. We cannot be spied upon from that place!'

The yashiki was strongly constructed and boasted a single central tower built at the highest point of the hill inside carefully devised palisades. While the tower was only three stories in height, the small topmost floor was still accorded the title of the 'Tengu' chamber, partly because it was the best vantage point giving views over all approaches to the fortress and ideal for its rôle as a command post for the general commanding the defences. While Enshin recognized in Enomoto Shigeo a *bujin* with great depth of knowledge about strategy, he also recalled, because of the tengu allusion, the maxim that 'all warfare was based on deception'. Here was just such

---

[22] *Deshi*: a pupil.
[23] *Bugeisha*: a master of the Arts of War.

a situation where a man might let slip an unguarded word that could just prove fatal in the end.

Enomoto Shigeo was a forthright warrior and immediately came to the point.

'Enshin-sama, I have known you for less than an hour although I was aware of your part in attending Ōsumi-dono; yet I must ask you directly: is my enemy my fellow hatamoto? This I need to know in order to act before it is too late. Without this knowledge my lord's family and my clan are in desperate danger. I know that I am right which is why I take this serious step of asking you, a stranger, your considered opinion?'

Enshin bowed and nodded his head. 'I am no magician, sir, nor am I an agent. These are matters fraught with danger and may be impossible to answer.'

Enomoto shook his head.

'You are a strategist, honoured priest; you cannot hide that just as nothing can be hidden from you. Oh, yes, of course I have studied the "*Seven Classics*", and I can recite the "*Sonshi*" from memory . . . just like you can. Come, Enshin-sama, your opinion?'

'Very well, I will give you my thoughts but not any conclusions since I lack the knowledge to have formulated these. In this, I think you might be able to help. From what I have observed it would seem on the surface there is a factional struggle within the clan. This has so far taken the form of summary executions and assassinations that appear to be designed to drive a wedge between your followers and those of the Chancellor. Am I correct in thinking this?'

'Yes, that seems to be the case. Continue, please.'

'We should consider who is the victor in this exchange; the Chancellor's faction or your own one? Who will emerge the stronger and, more importantly, why? May I ask about your personal relationship with the Chancellor; has it been amicable, even friendly, or strained? If the latter, when did the differences first appear?'

The hatamoto leant over to gaze down at the middle bailey before answering.

'Matters have been building up for a couple of years but the secret arrests and summary executions commenced about two weks ago. I have set my people to look for who is responsible but have so far found out nothing. I believe the same can be said for Makino-sama. Whenever anything has happened there has been no warning and no one knows anything. The problem seems inpenetrable and the only results are suspicion, fear, and the attachment of blame!'

Enshin agreed. 'If what you say is correct, and I am only setting out the arguments, not attaching blame or doubting your words, then there has to be another factor that no one has considered.'

'You mean, a third party?' Enomoto gave Enshin a keen glance. 'You are suggesting a plot to weaken the clan?'

'Perhaps.'

'But a plot by who? Our lord is kin to both our families and we have served as councillors for more than three-hundred years . . .'

'And the Bugyō?'

'Kodama Iyō-no-suke? His family have served the Ōsumi faith-fully, too. No, he is a weak man in some ways but never a traitor.'

'Is there anyone else close to your lord, anyone at all?'

'There is no one, Enshin-sama.'

'In that case may I offer some advice that you may disregard as you think fit.'

The hatamoto studied Enshin's face seriously.

'You would have me call a meeting with Makino-sama, a secret meeting, yes? Seeing Enshin nod, Enomoto added: 'I agree but I would like you also to attend.'

Enshin smiled. 'Have I your permission to be accompanied by Ji-chin-sama, the temple priest?'

'You have, master; it will be just the four of us. A wise decision, sir.'

The four men met secretly the next night in Ji-chin's quarters beside the temple. Both the hatamoto had arranged for a party of trust-worthy retainers to hide themselves as guards so that no one could spy on those within. The utmost precautions were taken to prevent word getting out. When the four men were seated on their thick woven mats, Makino Suenaga asked why it was that Ji-chin was to be privy to this meeting.

'It is because he is a wise man, my lord,' replied Enshin. 'While both of you hold the interests of your clan very close to your hearts, Ji-chin sensei and I are outsiders and, in consequence, more detached.'

The two hatamoto agreed and Makino said: 'We feel that the future of the Ōsumi clan depends on what we decide here. Is that not so, Ji-chin-sama?'

The old priest bowed his head. 'My family have served the clan since Kamakura-dono was alive, my lords. Your decisions will be deeply significant.'

Enshin outlined all the facts and arguments that he was aware of concluding with pointing to the need to identify who was behind these disturbing events. Neither of the hatamoto could add anything other than to observe that their respective losses were serious. Finally,

Enshin pointed out that the three ashigaru accused and executed for carrying out the murder of the two senior retainers, had suffered *after* Lord Ōsumi's passing. The question was who ordered the executions?

'It could be the Bugyō, Kodama-sama?' suggested Makino Suenaga.

Enshin shook his head. 'I don't think so, my lord.'

'Their deaths seem to follow the same secret methods of the others,' grunted Enomoto. 'There certainly is a traitor stirring up trouble!'

Enshin bent forwards, his right hand to the floor.

'Now we approach the truth! May I ask what would happen if the Ōsumi line failed and if internal conflict broke out? Who would benefit from such a calamity?'

'Our overlord is Hōki-no-kami,' mused Makino Suenaga. 'He would decide if all else failed, would he not, Enomoto-sama?'

The general scratched his chin. 'I think Enshin-sama is thinking of what would result from open warfare. Isn't that so?'

Enshin nodded. 'That was in my mind as the first stage.'

'We are fairly evenly balanced, aren't we, Makino-dono? Huhh! It is not a question that has arisen before but ...'

'Settling any dispute by the use of arms! Preposterous!' exclaimed Makino.

'But not impossible, my lords, if this campaign of subversion continues much longer,' put in Ji-chin, 'just one more incident might be enough to spark retaliatory action by hot-headed retainers of either of you. Had you considered that? Masters, we can talk here all night and not come any closer to a solution, however I think our visitor here has a suggestion to make ... Enshin-sama ..?'

'The time of the greatest danger is at hand because with the death of your lord the secret group or persons behind these problems must make their move quickly in order to counter whatever you intend to do.' Enshin drew in his breath as he looked from Enomoto to Makino. 'My advice is that you call a full Council tomorrow afternoon. Matters will be resolved one way or another.'

The following morning Enshin and the priest went together to the old lady's teahouse to savour the delicate infusion of that special tea. The fine weather had continued now for an unprecedented ten days and, late in the season as it was, the morning was warm and sunny.

'It seems that the festival pleased the mountain kami's wrath, Ji-chin?'

'That must depend on how deep one's beliefs are seated.'

'The ancient deities are still with us, sensei, aren't they?'

Ji-chin smiled. 'You have spent a long time in the mountains, my son!'

'Well, it seems possible that the recent "passing" up there may just have settled part of the yashiro's problems.'

'A part? I suppose it is possible.'

'But you don't really think so, sensei, do you? Do you follow my reasoning? Am I feeling my way in the right direction?'

Ji-chin carefully set down his cup for it to be refilled by Yumiko. 'My son, you tended Ōsumi-dono when he fell just out there and advised he should be taken to the yashiki?'

'Correct, sensei: I examined him as carefully as I could in the circumstances.'

'What, exactly, caused his death, in your opinion?'

'That is a difficult question to answer. When I heard that he had passed from this life my first thought was that it was the direct result of his injuries in battle and then falling from his saddle; but as I wasn't called to examine him at the time of his death or afterwards, doubts began to form in my mind.'

The old lady, who had sat silently beside them, leant forwards and reached out to catch hold of Enshin's sleeve.

'Who was the "deity of the tree", Enshin-sama?' she whispered.

He looked at her, then glanced at Ji-chin, realizing in that moment that the secret letter had been composed by her although brushed by the old priest. It was she who had made those oblique allusions . . . 'The "deity of the tree", lady? That kami could only be Ōsumi-dono as head of his family! Of course, the two woodpeckers were his leading Councillors . . .'

'So, now, young man, you know everything. Act on your knowledge; act decisively as you would have done in battle!'

He knitted his brows.

'What did she mean', he thought; 'how and what do I know?'

The senior Ōsumi retainers sat formally in the Council Chamber, the two senior hatamoto taking their positions on either side of the jōdan in the centre of which was placed a thick brocade edged mat for the absent lord. A six panelled painted screen depicting a stalking tiger stood behind this mat, and just to the left side Ōsumi Kagehisa's finest armour stood, correctly mounted on its lacquered stand. His tachi was placed on the other side flanked by a page lad aged about fourteen.

'Spearing' Enomoto, the Ō-karō, sat on this side just to the right, whilst Makino Suenaga, the Chancellor, sat on the left. The senior hatamoto were ranged, five each side, in a line below; behind them at a discreet distance, were a number of the minor retainers, some of whom Enshin recognized from his earlier visits to the yashiki. All the warriors wore their body armour, the only other people present were the three priests though as a precaution Enshin had insisted that Ji-chin, like himself, should wear a light brigandine coat concealed under their robes, just in case of trouble.

Makino Suenaga made a formal statement of their lord's death and this was received without comment, clearly the news was already known to those present; also the fact that he had left no issue and there were no close kin who might be invited to continue the line. When he had finished speaking, the Ō-karō took up the current problems besetting the clan, quickly coming head-on to the suspicions of some form of intrigue that had resulted in a number of mysterious deaths, some of which appeared intentionally barbarous. At this point a number of men became vociferous but Enomoto leapt to his feet, pointing his folded fan at the discontents and ordering them to be silent and listen. His forceful character and reputation were enough to quieten the muttering.

'What is the solution? Thus far, we have been unable to find any and so Makino-dono and I have taken the unprecedented step of inviting an astute priest from Mikawa to undertake enquiries. He is named Torii Enshin and is sitting there at the lower end of this chamber. Listen to what he has to say!'

Before Enshin could even make a respectful bow, one of the Middle Councillors shouted out: 'Why do we invite outsiders? This is an Ōsumi affair and it should remain so!'

'A mere priest!' shouted out another. 'What are we, children?'

'Ōsumi-dono would have had none of this!'

At this point, one of Enomoto's followers, a huge man wearing a black leather covered armour, clambered up and stood like a mountain dominating the rest.

'My lord ordered quiet,' he roared; 'if anyone disobeys my lord's command he will answer to me and I shall not be polite! You will hear out what Enshin-sama has to say!'

Enshin rose to his feet, bowing respectfully.

'Enomoto-dono has set out the reason that I am here. I have done what I was requested to do. I shall doubtless offend some of you with my findings, but . . .' There was a fresh murmur at this but no violent outburst. Enshin bowed slightly and continued. 'Your honoured lord passed away some days ago but his death was not the result of his fall at the start of the recent festival. I will explain that in a moment . . .' He paused for a few seconds. 'However, Ōsumi–dono did suffer injury in his last battle and carried a large scar resulting from this. The blow that gave him that wound pressed down onto his brain which began to give him severe headaches from time to time, particularly at moments of excitement. These headaches were increasingly painful and blinding so that he soon became depend-ent on his physician here.' The dour priest acknowledged this with a bow. 'I have a particular skill in treating damage to the body and the head, skills I gained under the guidance of my uncle, the respected Abbot of the Hōrai–ji. I have concluded and am certain that your lord did not die as a result of his fall nor of his old injury in battle. This was not the work of a malevolent demon, either. He could only have died at the hands of someone at present unknown! That same person, or someone behind him, wished to weaken immeasur-ably the controls placed in the hands of your two chief councillors. In order to do this, two factions had to be encouraged to develop within the clan, each becoming more and more opposed to each other. The results of this intrigue would inevitably have resulted in armed conflict. There would have been blind retaliation and in the resulting strife the principle plotter would have emerged victorious, crushing any opposition.

'Unravelling these machinations was not entirely my own work and I shall not claim any credit. I was guided by two people who, from the outside, risked their lives in order to serve the interests of their sick lord and his clan. They are the ones you should praise when this is all settled.

'It is my belief that during your lord's darkest episodes he was tricked into signing execution orders carried out by the Bugyō who must, of course, act on orders that he believed came from Ōsumi–dono, himself. This may have been done through the administration of powerful potions that he became used to taking in the belief they would relieve his head, but I also believe that your lord was mur-dered by poison given in the same way.'

There was a stunned silence and Enomoto Shigeo stood, his face dark with anger, but Enshin held up his hand.

'Please allow me to finish, my lord . . .'

With his jaw muscles working, the Ō–karō drew in his breath with an audible hiss and grated: 'Please go on!'

'The execution of the three ashigaru for the supposed murder of the two retainers, killings that I, myself, witnessed, was ordered *after* your lord had passed away! However, when the two men accused of being traitors were killed so barbarously, their deaths were witnessed, too, by a strange samurai wearing armour. That man, who kept well apart from those carrying out their orders, had his head shaven . . .

If he wasn't a samurai who had taken holy orders to become a lay-priest, then who was he?'

The Ō-karō could no longer contain his anger.

'Enshin-sama's words paint a far darker picture than I had imagined! Who will he name now . . ?'

Two of his retainers also stood, closing in to the low jōdan dias, while Enshin noted that Makino Suenaga was sitting much straighter.

The latter shouted out: 'They, whoever it was, tried to divide us . . . to overthrow our lord's family . . . to usurp his place . . . to bring down the Ōsumi clan in its entirety!'

Enshin held up both hands as though trying to calm down the atmosphere. The tension was palpable . . . He knew that the crisis point was not merely approaching, it was already present. Casually, he and Ji-chin stood and walked slowly up behind the right hand councillors closer to where Enomoto's retainers were seated. No one took the slightest heed but it was a wise precaution since they were both unarmed. Suddenly he whirled round.

'Who was the agent who could go anywhere? Who was it that obtained your sick lord's signature for the executions? Who was behind everything and cunningly worked towards the overthrow of your clan?' Enshin pointed with his fan, specially carved from a piece of Chinese rosewood to resemble a large folded fan but was, in fact, an excellent defensive weapon if required.. 'You, Makino-dono, were at the centre of it all; it was you who intrigued to betray your lord! It was you who made your lord appear an unstable and cruel tyrant and it was your agent, Chen-li sitting there, who was your agent .. !'

'No!' roared Makino Suenaga, drawing out his tachi. 'You lie, priest, you . . .'

In a second the seated warriors were on their feet and swords were drawn, the clash of steel on steel and the roar of conflict filled the chamber . . . Enshin slipped swiftly behind Enomoto's retainers and caught hold of Ji-chin's sleeve as the old priest, anticipating the strife when the young priest delivered his judgement, had followed Enshin along the right hand shōji. In the first seconds of the violent mêlée that ensued, they found themselves facing the contorted face of one of Makino's retainers but the man was too close to deliver an effective cut giving Enshin the chance to strike downwards with his rosewood fan, crushing the fellow's right knuckles and grappling him backwards through the flimsy screen. Together, all three crashed to the boards in the corridor beyond. In an instant, the former Torii swordsman had plucked the retainer's own dirk from his waist and, locking the man's sword arm painfully to the floor, pricked his throat with the needle sharp point.

'Do you want to die for your master's betrayal . . ? Is that your wish?'

'But . . .'

The retainer's face was contorted as he glared up at Enshin.

'There can be no buts! Precede your treacherous master here and now or serve your proper lord and his clan!'

Ji-chin knelt up. 'Do what Enshin-sama says, my son. Death for such a cause would be shameful.'

The samurai's tensed body suddenly relaxed and his sword clattered to the floor from his bruised hand.

'I . . . I choose to serve my rightful lord . . . forgive me.'

Enshin passed the fallen sword to Ji-chin to hold as they came to their feet. The disturbance was over but the Council Chamber was a scene of carnage where three or four men lay badly wounded and several others nursed deep cuts. Both Chen-li and Makino Suenaga were being expertly trussed although the latter had received a gashed shoulder and was bleeding profusely.

Enomoto Shigeo surveyed the room and saw Enshin. 'Sensei! May I request one last duty to bind this man's wound. It wouldn't do for him to die before we have decided a suitable fate, would it?' Just two of Makino's men sat bound like their master. They were probably close kinsmen and a honourable death was their only real option; the rest, understanding their master's duplicity and deeper treachery, had thrown down their weapons or joined Enomoto's side not so much to save their own skins but in disgust at the hatamoto's betrayal of his honour.

———— ☐ ————

It was a week later, the weather having broken in the interval when a violent typhoon must have struck at the western end of the Inland Sea, that Enshin stood protected in a thick straw cape and wide straw jingasa just below the teahouse steps. Beside him, patient as ever despite the heavy rain, Kuroi-san waited as his master said his farewells.

'Do you have to leave in this storm, master?' Yumiko looked sad. 'You should shelter here until the rain passes . . .'

'I am grateful to Oka-sama and you,' he replied, 'but to remain longer in this place would be to outstay our welcome.'

'Nonetheless, honoured sensei,' she persisted, 'you cannot just leave without a proper farewell. It would be simply unheard of, my lord.'

He smiled to himself. Would he ever be allowed to forget his previous life, he wondered?

'Very well, but what about my friend, here? Does he remain in this downpour or does he take tea with us, too?'

'Not a bit of it, my . . . master. Kuroi-san shall have shelter and food, of course. Please permit our servant to lead him round to the rear.'

Enshin entered the teahouse for a final time. He was greeted by the old grandmother and guided unerringly by her to his mat, the one that he had always used. When the fragrant tea was served by Yumiko, he murmured: 'O delectable tea, so benificent to the body, the mind, and the soul', and reached across to take hold of the old lady's wrinkled hand.

'Respected Oka-sama: do you think the *yama-no-kami* will now find rest in the myriad winters he must endure?'

'Oh, I think he will, Enshin-sama,' she replied in her husky voice. 'I am quite convinced that through our entreaties he will bring blessing and plenty to the fields of the renewed Ōsumi-ke now that they have installed a new lord.'

Enshin knew that she referred to the decision to transfer power to Enomoto Shigeo until such time as the Ōsumi could find a heir in the direct blood descent. Until then Enomoto had changed his family name to Ōsumi. Everyone knew that despite his strong martial character, the domain was now in safe hands; it needed such strength since in these disturbed times weakness only invited destruction.

As the three sipped the warm nectar of those special tea bushes, the grandmother asked: 'Tell me, my lord; at what point did you know which of the woodpeckers was at fault?'

Enshin laughed and shook his head.

'All I can say, Oka-san, is that I glimpsed some armour lacing when those street murders took place . . . Need I say more?'

Although sightless, the old lady turned her head away hiding a slight smile behind her hand. She didn't pursue the subject; instead she enquired where he would go now.

'Honoured Oka-sama and Mistress Yumiko, the direction is always the Will of the Buddha who will instruct Kuroi-san . . . only that can determine my steps.'

'You will know the lines brushed by Kanze Motokiyo in his saru-gaku-no-nō, "*Atsumori*"?

> *Do not envy what is above you*
> *Nor despise what is below.*'[24]

---

[24] Kanze Motokiyo (Seami) (1375-1455). *Sarugaku-no-ō* was the old name for Noh.

'How well these words seem to be worn about your shoulders, Enshin-sama. You are the first warrior I have even known who has completely shed the sin of arrogance. When you go to rejoin your friend you will find that he carries a sack of white rice and some other useful necessities . . . No, do not thank any of us for these are an expression of gratitude that your Kuroi-san decided you should wend your steps to our humble valley.'